Nick Lake is an editorial director at HarperCollins Children's Books. He received his degree in English from Oxford University. *Blood Ninja* was inspired by his interest in the Far East, and by the fact that he is secretly a vampire ninja himself. Nick lives with his wife in Oxfordshire, protected by booby traps, poisoned darts and a fat, lazy tom cat, but why not pay him a visit on Facebook or visit his website: www.bloodninja.co.uk

D0549607

BLOOD NINJA

NICK LAKE

CORVUS

First published in the United States of America in 2009 by Simon & Schuster
Children's Publishing Division, 1230 Avenue of the Americas, New York,
New York 10020.

First published in trade paperback in Great Britain in 2010 by Corvus, an imprint
of Grove Atlantic Ltd.

This paperback edition published in Great Britain in 2010 by Corvus.

1 2 3 4 5 6 7 8 9

A CIP catalogue record for this book is available from the British Library.

ISBN: 978 1 84887 388 9

Printed in Great Britain by Clays Ltd, St Ives plc

Corvus
An imprint of Grove Atlantic Ltd
Ormond House
26-27 Boswell Street
London
WC1N 3JZ

www.corvus-books.co.uk

For the real Han(n)a(h)

世界中の言葉で「大好き」って言いたい。

T HIS WAS NOT a good place to be out at night, all alone.

Unfortunately for the young girl currently walking through the tradesmen's district, it was the middle of the night – and she was very much alone.

She walked with the slightly mincing step of a noble, and carried a delicate folded-up fan. Jewelled rings encrusted her fingers. Her soft indoor tabi slippers were unsuited to running or fighting.

The man in black was glad. Fighting he could handle. But when they ran – that was just annoying.

He glanced down at his young prey, checking to make sure that he had identified the target correctly. Yes, there it was: the distinct form of the Oda *mon* on the girl's kimono, petals within petals.

This was Lord Oda's girl.

The girl seemed blithely oblivious to the fine gold thread on her clothes, and the effect it would likely have on the residents of such an area.

This job is going to be easier than I imagined, the man in black thought.

He leaped, almost casually, to the next rooftop. He landed

without a sound and ran, his lithe body crouching low to avoid detection. The next rooftop was too far to reach in one bound, but he simply somersaulted to the ground, rolled, then jumped nimbly to grab the overhanging eave. He let himself hang there for a split second, enjoying the feel of gravity pulling at his body, then flipped onto the tiles.

A cat that had been sleeping there stood up in an exaggerated arch of irritation and was about to hiss when the ninja raised a blowpipe to his lips. The cat collapsed softly and rolled down the sloping roof. Before it could fall off the edge and hit the ground below, the ninja stretched languorously and pinned its corpse to the bark tile with a dagger.

The ninja moved from rooftop to rooftop until he was in front of the girl. He waited for the right moment, his entire body perfectly still. When the girl passed below him, he jumped, absorbing the impact of the ground with a smooth bend of the legs that turned almost instantly into a vicious kick to the girl's face.

The girl staggered back, and the ninja grinned, pressing his advantage with a flurry of kicks before reaching for his short-sword.

As the ninja's hand moved to his belt, he lowered his eyes for a fraction of a second, and it was then that something smashed into his face, crushing his nose and sending a tsunami of pain and nausea through his body. Through blurred vision he saw the girl pull back her hand, and realized that the fan was not a fan at all – it was a heavy metal bar disguised as an everyday object, a classic ninja trick.

But how—?

The girl struck again with the bar, and the ninja easily blocked, feeling a new surge of confidence as he finally managed to free his sword and swing it in an upward arc, calculated to shatter the jaw and cut the arteries in the neck and—

The girl somehow turned out of the sword's path, bringing the fan-turned-club down on the ninja's wrist. The man felt his wrist shatter and the sword drop to the ground just as a fistful of sharp jewels destroyed his left eye.

Not rings. A knuckleduster.

His legs gave way, and he sank to the ground. But it wasn't over. It was never over. He would heal, in time. Not his eye, of course, but the rest…

Then the girl stood over him and drew a brutal *wakizashi* from her kimono, the short-sword's blade so sharp it shimmered as if surrounded by heat. She whirled it round her fingers expertly.

And then the ninja knew that it was over.

'Tell Lord Tokugawa that if he continues to send me assassins, I will continue to send him corpses,' she said. 'Let him set the world against me, and I will kill the world. Tell him that. And tell him if he wants me to spare his life, he had better send Taro next time, not some weakling of an ordinary ninja. That boy owes me a death.'

The ninja looked up at her, faint hope in his one working eye. 'You're allowing me to live?'

The girl paused. 'Ah. My mistake.'

The ninja tried to smile.

Then she struck, hard and true, at his heart. 'I'll just have to tell Tokugawa myself.'

Yes, this was not a good place to be out at night, all alone.

Especially if you were a ninja.

TARO STRAIGHTENED UP, took a deep breath, and pulled back the string of his bow. There was a familiar twinge from his left shoulder, where a thin silver scar traced a semicircle from chest to back, at intervals punctuated by darker circles suggestive of large tooth marks.

This was not surprising – they were tooth marks.

Taro ignored the old pain and lined up his arrow with the fleeing rabbit. He held his breath, concentrating on making the bow an extension of his own body. From an early age he had taught himself to make firing the bow a kind of meditation, believing in his mind that the arrow was already sunk deep in its target, that the only thing required was to loose the string and let it fly.

He loosed the string.

The arrow arced over brown summer grass and met the rabbit as it jumped over a tussock, driving it to the ground.

Taro walked over to the dead rabbit. He knelt and removed the barbed tip, then wiped the arrowhead on the grass before returning the arrow to his quiver.

Taro dropped the rabbit into his shoulder bag and turned for home. He wasn't far from Shirahama, the coastal village where he'd grown up: he'd come only as far as the first way marker showing the road to Nagoya. He had kept the sea in view, however, and now as he rounded the headland, he could see Shirahama bay, cradled by tall mountains whose flanks were heavily forested with cedar, chestnut, and pine. The simple dwellings of the village nestled on the side of a hill overlooking the sea. The sun was setting, and already a few plumes of smoke rose from houses. It was warm, but there was always fish to smoke, and seaweed to dry for its precious salt, so the fires were always burning.

The air that Taro breathed as he walked through the trees was scented with pine oil and the salt of the sea. Like most of the other coastal settlements in this part of Japan, Shirahama was entirely dependent on the sea. The men went out on fishing boats, the women were ama divers, and both men and women joined great gatherings of seaweed in the autumn, so that from the slimy, bubbling stuff could be burned salt to sell to the nobles.

Taro was not like them. He loved the earth as much as the sea. He had no desire to grow rice, like the peasants of the interior, but he liked to hunt using his bow. As he walked, he cradled the arc of smooth wood in his hand – it was slender and fine, but filled with taut, latent energy. His father had made it for him when he was too young even to hold it, but since then he had grown fearsomely accurate with it, and often employed it to supplement the family's food stocks with a rabbit or a fat wood pigeon.

The village people didn't like that – well, except for Hiro.

But the others said hunting was only for samurai, and that peasants like him should content themselves with the bounty of the sea. They said that to kill four-legged creatures angered the *kami* who walked the woods, Shinto god-spirits who were everywhere in these parts, though the Buddha was supposed to have chased them from all of Japan.

People said a lot of things about Taro – jokingly, and otherwise. They said he was half *kami* himself, his delicate features and perpetually pale skin out of place in a simple village where rough faces and sunburn were the norm. They said his skill with the bow was supernatural; they said his parents must have gone into the mountains and swapped him with a god at a shrine somewhere. Taro hated it. It wasn't his fault he didn't look like anyone else, or think the same way.

And anyway, the villagers were hypocrites. Taro didn't see why the Buddha should accept the killing of fish and sea creatures but condemn the murder of a rabbit. There was also, deep within him, a dream he could never have shared with the other villagers, nor even completely admitted to himself.

He dreamed that one day he might actually *be* a samurai; that he might leave this little village to enter the service of the great Lord Oda, fall in love with a beautiful samurai woman, and finally die gloriously with a sword in his hand, refusing all mercy, and tendering no surrender.

There was only one other person in the village who shared Taro's enthusiasm for tales of war and honour and duels, and that was his closest friend, Hiro. So Taro was pleased when he came out of the woods onto the Nagoya road and saw Hiro there.

On the dusty road that led into the village, Hiro was standing, bowlegged, in a posture of defiance. His massive body glistened in the failing sunshine, naked but for a white loincloth. A heavily muscled traveller was stripping off his kimono and squaring up. By the way he carried himself, he had to be one of the wave-men

– ronin – who had been left without allegiance after the colossal defeat of Lord Yoshimoto's enormous army by the cunning Lord Oda Nobunaga.

Having been conquered in battle, *ronin* served no lord, followed no code of loyalty, and thus were as the waves – many and masterless, with no purpose and no end. Most of the *ronin* in these parts had served Lord Yoshimoto, once, but their very existence proved they had refused seppuku after Lord Oda's victory, and so had lost themselves the status of samurai.

Taro smiled as he watched Hiro limbering up. His friend loved to challenge passing strongmen to wrestling matches – and despite his apparently fat body, he rarely lost. This particular *ronin* didn't know what Hiro was capable of – and Hiro was relying on it. The man and his companions would have placed heavy bets on the bout, confident of victory over the chubby peasant.

Taro sat down, ready to enjoy the show.

As Hiro and the *ronin* circled each other, looking for weak points, the *ronin*'s companions stood to one side. Taro watched them, curious. Unlike the usual onlookers, they didn't seem all that interested in their friend's performance, though from their armour and swords they were clearly *ronin* too. Instead, they appeared distracted. Taro scooted over a little closer to where they were standing.

'…two puncture wounds, on the neck,' said one.

'And this was where?' replied the other.

'Minata. Just down the coast. The peasant was drained of all his blood.'

The first traveller whistled. 'A *kyuuketsuki* on Lord Oda's land. It's a bad omen.' Then, suddenly noticing Taro crouching near him, the man glared and turned back to the fight.

Taro turned away from them as if he had not been eavesdropping, and watched as the wrestling *ronin* stepped forward and lunged, grabbing Hiro round the neck and waist. But Taro's attention was now elsewhere, and he watched the fight as distractedly as the two *ronin*. A man had been killed, that much was obvious. And the *ronin* suspected a *kyuuketsuki*...

Taro had thought that the bloodsucking demons were only storybook things, meant to scare children into obedience, not real killers that could step out of the shadows and kill peasants only three *ri* from his home.

He felt a shiver run down his spine, and a sense that danger had landed in Shirahama, as large and ponderous and unshiftable as a beached whale. Then he shook away the feeling. No, he was safe there, with his best friend, and there was no such thing as a *kyuuketsuki* – not outside the old folktales, anyway.

Before him, the *ronin* threw his weight forward, trying to pull Hiro off his centre of balance. Hiro fell backwards, and the man gave a roar of triumph, which died in the air as Hiro tucked his legs in, placed his feet on the attacker's chest, and did a rolling kick, sending his opponent flying across the road. Hiro flipped back onto his feet as the traveller came running at him, his humiliation at the hands of a countryside oaf turning into an anger that blinded him to caution.

The traveller leaped into a jumping kick, aimed at the chest, that would floor even the strongest warrior. Hiro sidestepped neatly, grabbed the traveller's foot, and twisted, sending his body spinning to the ground. This time the challenger was much slower to get up, and when he got close enough to try a lock, Hiro pinned him easily to the ground. The man smacked his palm on the ground, indicating surrender.

Taro stood and walked over to the improvised wrestling ring. Hiro grinned and pulled him into a hug, which drove the breath from Taro's lungs.

'All right, big man,' said Taro. 'No need to kill me.'

Hiro pulled away, but, as always when Taro's shoulders were uncovered, Hiro glanced rapidly at the scar running round the top of Taro's arm, then looked away again, both of them pretending not to have noticed.

Behind his friend's broad back, Taro saw two of the *ronin*'s companions muttering, then heard the unmistakable *hiss* as a sword was drawn. Spinning away from Hiro and round again to face the men, Taro drew an arrow from his quiver and notched it, all in one smooth motion. He aimed the arrow straight at the nearest traveller, who stood with a half-drawn sword and an open-mouthed expression of surprise. 'Go,' Taro ordered. 'And leave your bets here on the ground.' The men frowned sourly but dropped a money purse and walked away, following the road to Amigaya territory.

'Some day,' Taro said, turning to Hiro, 'you're going to pick a fight with the wrong *ronin*.'

'There's no such thing as a right *ronin*,' said Hiro, laughing, his voice deep and sonorous. Both boys were keen admirers of the samurai – noble, upstanding warriors who protected the nation's lords, who were themselves samurai. They had grown up on tales of bravery and honour; tales of samurai victory against heathen and bandit alike. Many times they had spoken of how one day they would take up swords together.

Yet Taro knew that for Hiro this dream of leaving could remain safely that – a dream, passingly entrancing and then gone, like cherry blossoms in summer. Even though Hiro was the son of landlocked refugees, he belonged there, by the sea, fishing and wrestling.

Hiro had come from the interior, where peasants were grown

stockier and heavier than the seaside variety; yet still it was Taro who felt a foreigner in his own land. Hiro entertained a mere fantasy of being one day a samurai. But Taro fervently wished it.

'And anyway,' continued Hiro, 'we'll always be there to protect each other, won't we?' He gave Taro a look so open, so innocent, that Taro was forced to look away. Hiro was unable to imagine a future where they were not friends and protectors to each other, but Taro feared that to make his way in the world, he might one day have to leave the village. His delicate features had, with age, only become more pronounced and noble-looking, setting him apart from everyone else, much as he tried to be friendly. Hiro, with his ruddy complexion and brawny body, was much more the village type.

Taro knew that Hiro would follow him anywhere. The problem was that deep down, Taro wanted to be anywhere but Shirahama.

'Did you hear what the other *ronin* said, about the *kyuuketsuki*?' Taro said finally, breaking the uncomfortable silence.

Hiro looked blank. 'A bloodsucking spirit?'

'The *ronin* said that a *kyuuketsuki* had killed a peasant near here.'

'Just a silly rumour, I expect,' said Hiro. '*Kyuuketsuki* don't exist. And anyway, travellers are always telling outlandish tales.' He set off towards the village. 'Earlier, before those *ronin* showed up, there was a merchant passing through. Your mother was here – traded him some pearls for a bag of rice. He told us a story about a family just down the coast who were killed by ninja. A fisherman, his wife, and their teenage son. Claimed the villagers found throwing stars embedded in their bodies.'

Taro hurried to catch up with his friend. '*Ninja?*' he asked, incredulous.

The secretive group of black-clad assassins were, unlike the *kyuuketsuki*, thought to be real. They had been blamed for several assassinations, and it was said that Lord Tokugawa – Lord Oda's strongest ally – used them often for clandestine missions. But the thought that these well-trained and deadly killers might take the trouble to erase from the world a fisherman's family was absurd.

'That's what they said,' Hiro replied. 'Like I told you, travellers are forever coming up with ridiculous stories. We're far into the countryside here – rumours have a lot of space in which to grow and change before they reach our ears.'

Taro grunted assent. But something about this conjunction of claims struck him as peculiar – the idea that, in a single day, there should be talk of both evil spirits and ninja near their quiet little village. 'I don't like it,' he said. 'I have a bad feeling about all of this.'

'Like mother, like son,' said Hiro.

'What do you mean?'

'When the merchant told that story, your mother went pale. Ran off back to the village. She would have forgotten the rice, if I hadn't chased after her.'

Taro frowned. It wasn't like his mother to overlook something like that, especially where food was concerned. She took great care of the flow of goods into and out of the house, always making sure not to pay over the odds for anything.

'You know what I think?' said Hiro. 'I think the *ronin* want to stir up unrest. You spread a few stories about peasants getting killed by imaginary monsters, and pretty soon no one feels safe. They want to make things difficult for Lord Oda.'

'You're probably right,' said Taro. 'A lot of them served his enemies.' The *ronin* were known to despise Lord Oda, and to blame him for the loss of the their honour, when Oda's troops destroyed the armies belonging to Lord Yoshimoto. That war had affected everyone – even Taro and Hiro. It was fleeing the violence inflicted by Lord Yoshimoto's samurai that had brought Hiro's parents to the village of Shirahama, like so many other peasants of the interior who'd been forced outward to the coast, and a new life of fishing that they had had to learn quickly, or perish.

But Hiro's parents had not learned quickly enough, and that was why they were dead.

Taro felt a little better now. Of *course* the *ronin* were seeking to destabilize Lord Oda. He was the strongest daimyo the Kanto had ever known, and strong samurai always made bitter enemies. His heroism, his extraordinary ability with the blade, and his genius for the tactics of battle had made him a god to his people, and a demon to those he had defeated. It was said that when he was first named a *kensei* – a 'sword saint' – in recognition of his mastery of the *katana*, he barely went a day without being challenged by some samurai desperate to make his name ring out over the land. All of them had died.

And when Lord Oda had lost the use of his right arm in battle, he had simply switched his sword to the other hand, and become once again a *kensei*.

Yes, he was the kind of man who could provoke the weak to make up silly rumours.

Taro shouldered his bow, clapped Hiro on the back, and set off towards the village. He didn't know that later on that night he would get all the adventure he wished for, or that real adventure was not like the feats he had heard of in stories.

Real adventure involved pain, loss, and blood. Sometimes all at once.

CHAPTER 2

Tʜᴇʏ ᴘᴀssᴇᴅ Hɪʀᴏ's hut first.

When Taro's father had brought him back to the village after the death of Hiro's parents, Taro had been so badly injured that he had almost died of blood loss. Seeing what Taro had risked to save the chubby little boy, his parents had taken Hiro in, lavishing all the care on him that they wished they could give to their son.

But Taro had been in the healer's hands, and the Buddha's, and they could do nothing for him. Finally, on the seventh day, Taro awoke from fever dreams. His wound was already healing and, miraculously, infection had been held at bay. He returned to find a new brother in his home.

A couple of years ago, though, Hiro had earned enough from his wrestling and fishing to acquire a small shack only a few hundred meters from the sea that had taken his parents. Hanging from a wooden nail above the door was the open jaw of a shark, white against the dark wood.

Even now, when Taro saw the jaws and their serrated teeth, he would sometimes shudder. But Hiro would never get rid of the thing. It was a talisman, almost, of their friendship – a tangible reminder of what Taro had done for him.

That day itself was a little blurred in Taro's memory, by time and also because for many days afterwards he had been unconscious, first from blood loss and later from fever. It had been a bright summer's day, the breeze bringing scents of pine and dry seaweed. Taro had been up on the headland, playing with his bow. The first he had known something was wrong was when he'd heard screams, and looked down to see a little boat in the bay, people splashing round it.

He'd seen the blood next.

The villagers had warned the refugees from inland about the *mako* who patrolled the waters, the sleek, large sharks that followed the tuna. But the inlanders must have thought it just a superstition, or a story made up to frighten them, perhaps because there were no monsters to kill people where they came from, only samurai and wars.

Hiro's parents, ignoring the warnings, had cut up their fish and thrown them into the water round their boat, thinking to attract more fish into their nets. All they had attracted was a *mako*, and it had capsized their boat with no trouble at all.

Of course, Taro hadn't known any of that then. All he'd known was that someone was in trouble. He ran down to the beach, threw himself into the water, and swam out, not thinking for one moment of his own safety. Diving into the murk, he found a chubby young boy, drowning. He seized the boy and dragged him back to shore.

'My mother!' gasped the boy when Taro dragged him onto the sand. 'Did you see my mother?'

Taro shook his head, winded.

'A monster came from the sea and… *bit* her,' said the boy. 'I tried to find her, but I can't swim, and my father can't either…'

Taro looked out again at the dark slick on the sea, and pursed his lips grimly. A *mako* attack. The boy's parents were surely dead. But he couldn't just leave it at that. Without a word to the boy he checked that his knife was in his belt and dived again into the waves, swimming out towards the slick.

He didn't find anything, but when he was swimming back to shore, he did feel a rough impact against his side, and then the shark was circling and coming for him again, its mouth open. The salt water stinging his open eyes, he fumbled the knife from his belt, and that was when the shark collided with his shoulder, biting down, and he felt pain flooding his chest.

Blood ribboned from his wound into the clear water. He was surprised that alongside his pain he felt no fear. Only an all-consuming fury at this beast that had orphaned the boy on the beach, and looked like it was going to kill him too. Dizzy from the bleeding and the pain of moving his arm, Taro snapped his hips aside on the shark's next pass, threw his arms round the coarse, rough body, and stabbed down with his knife.

After that, Taro's memory failed him, but he must have fought like a demon from Enma's hell realm, because his father said the shark was more wound than flesh in the end. When it was dead – and this was the part Taro could never remember, but that had bonded Hiro to him forever – Taro dragged its weight into shallow water, then hauled the carcass up onto the sand.

Collapsing to his knees in front of Hiro, he gestured to the dead shark. 'There,' he said. Then he passed out, and Hiro ran screaming for help, and it wasn't till three days later that Taro awoke and asked how the little orphaned boy was doing.

Now the two of them never spoke of that day. Hiro kept the jaws on his hut, Taro kept the scar on his shoulder, and that was that. The two boys had grown up as brothers, and even now that

Hiro lived on his own, they spent most of every day together. Taro's mother had wept when Hiro had left their home, waving smoke from the cooking fire away from her face, impatiently, as if it were that which had made her eyes water and not Hiro's going. But it was a small dwelling place for four, especially when one of them was as big as Hiro. The best way to repay them their kindness, said Hiro, was to give them their home back.

As the two friends entered the village, the sun dropped below the mountains to the west, setting fire to their peaks.

'Well,' said Taro. 'Another day gone. What shall we do tomorrow?'

'I had it in mind that I might visit some friends for tea,' said Hiro.

'Ah. I was going to have a new kimono made. I thought perhaps a pattern of peony flowers and birds. Then I might visit my sword smith and pick up my new *katana*.'

None of these things would happen: Taro would spend the next day hunting with his bow, as always, and Hiro would spend the day wrestling strangers, as always.

Taro and Hiro walked past the wooden houses of the village, light spilling from the paper shoji windows onto sun-dried ground. But no light shone from the hut Taro shared with his parents, and as he approached it, he frowned. His mother should have been back by now, lighting the fire, preparing food. He had been looking forward to showing her his rabbits.

Taro glanced at the bay, scanning it for the forms of the ama, black against the now-dark water. When he saw the boat, he let out a sigh. He could see his mother's little boat over on the far northern side of the bay, below the promontory on which stood an ancient red *torii* shrine, its sweeping roof resembling a dragon's back. The other amas were nowhere to be seen –

perhaps they were on the other side of the finger of rock, diving near the shrine to the Princess of the Hidden Waters, who protected the amas from harm.

But even the Princess of the Hidden Waters would be no help to Taro's mother if she got into trouble in those waters.

'What's wrong?' said Hiro, sensing Taro's anxiety.

Taro pointed to the boat. 'My mother. She's very near the wreck.' As he spoke, he saw her head break the surface, her dark hair matted to her scalp as she pulled herself into the boat and took up the oars.

'Gods,' said Hiro. 'What's she doing?'

'I don't know,' said Taro. 'She told me she wasn't going to dive there any more.'

Everyone knew that the part of the bay in which his mother was diving was unsafe – *especially* the ama. It was his mother and her friends who had told Taro about the royal ship that had gone down there centuries before, and how its wreck had cursed the waters. They spoke of the hungry ghosts of its sailors – *gaki* – that had been left by the suddenness of their drowning forever barred from enlightenment, and could only now relieve their eternal hunger by causing others to drown as they had drowned.

The amas spoke of an enormous octopus, which had stolen one ama away, and made a wife of her corpse.

But above all, they spoke of the dangerous, unnatural currents, and the possibility of death for anyone who dived there.

Taro turned to Hiro. 'You go home. I want to make sure she's all right.' He hurried down the hill towards the shore.

It was bad enough that one of his parents should be dying, without his mother killing herself too.

CHAPTER 3

Taro watched his mother's every move as she put some rice on to boil. He kept his eyes on her movements all the time. He knew that amas could be hurt by diving too deep and coming up too quickly, and he didn't like the pallor of his mother's skin. A couple of times recently he had seen thin trickles of blood coming from her ears, which she had wiped away quickly, refusing to answer questions about it. He feared that there might be more blood too, when he wasn't looking. Amas could dive only so long – eventually even the strongest went deaf, or worse, as the coral of the sea took root in their ears.

She turned to him, her eyes dark pits of shadow in the dim light of the little hut. With the glow of the fire behind her, she seemed ghost-like, thin, weak.

'I'm not going to break, you know,' she said. 'There's no need to worry about me so much.'

Taro shrugged. 'I don't like it,' he said. 'You told me you wouldn't dive in deep water.' He didn't say, or near the wreck, but the accusation hung between them anyway.

'I needed some pearls,' said his mother. 'With your father ill…'

Taro glanced over at her diving bag. He'd seen her take out

some abalone – not much, in fact – but no pearls. 'You didn't find any?' he asked.

His mother looked up quickly. 'No,' she said. 'Sometimes the sea takes but doesn't give.'

'Takes what?' said Taro.

His mother shook her head. 'Nothing, Taro. Nothing.'

But Taro knew it was *not* nothing. What the sea took, eventually, if you dived its depths for long enough, was your hearing, your sight, eventually your life. It worked its way into you, calcifying you, making you slowly into rock or reef.

Taro's mother busied herself with the rice, averting her eyes from his, clearly wanting to avoid further discussion of her diving. On the other side of the curtained partition, Taro could hear his father's heavy breathing. Leaving his mother's side for a moment, he went to peer in to where his father lay. The old man snored, oblivious – he had been bed-bound by illness for months now, his body clinging to life even as his spirit seemed to have made up its mind to depart the human realm. He lay on his back, mouth and eyes wide open, but no sound issued from the former and no light of understanding from the latter.

As Taro looked down at his father's frail frame, he couldn't believe that this was the same man who had taught him spearfishing, who had showed him how to keep his ears from popping when diving right down to the floor of the bay. Steeling himself, Taro knelt by the bed, and kissed his father on the forehead. He made a prayer to Amida Buddha, to fish his father's soul back from whichever dark depths it swam in. 'Come back,' he said. 'You are the only father I have.' Even as he said it, he knew it was childish, stupid.

Taro's father was older than his mother – older than almost anyone else in the village, in fact. But it seemed cruel that this illness had taken him down into sleep and forgetfulness, before Taro and his mother could say goodbye. Taro just hoped now that his father would recognize him – only once – before he died, and they could speak before his shade went to the next realm.

Taro touched his father's wrinkled hand – cold, and hard – then kissed him again on the forehead. He had been worried about losing his father for a long time. And he felt like he might at any time lose his mother too – she could have drowned there by the old wreck, or worse – been possessed perhaps by some vengeful spirit. A chill passed through his body. He didn't know what he would do if his parents were taken from him.

Returning to the main room, Taro sat down again as his mother passed him a bowl of rice.

'He's asleep?' she asked.

Taro nodded. It was a pointless question – his father was always asleep.

They ate, after that, in silence, but the warm food seemed to have a restorative effect on his mother, who got up with some of the old springiness in her body, and began to clear away.

She seemed now as strong as ever. Her face was lined by the years and the harsh water of the sea, but there was still prettiness in the sparkling eyes and the pleasingly oval line of her jaw. She smiled and was illuminated almost by a kind of inner light that only the kindest and wisest of people possess. She gestured to a bowl of mussels. 'I brought up some abalone too. I should be able to sell it to the trader, if he comes tomorrow.'

Taro in turn pointed to the brace of rabbits where they lay in the corner. It was a ritual of theirs to show each other their day's gatherings. 'They're fat,' he said. 'Must have found some green grass somewhere.'

His mother nodded. 'Your father stirred, this afternoon. I

thought he might wake, but he only mumbled and then slept again.' Her eyes flashed to the shoji screen that separated off the sleeping area. The whole shack was no more than six tatami mats in size, and the restricted space did not allow for much privacy.

'Do you think he'll die?' Taro asked, his voice cracking as if giving way under the weight of the question.

Taro's mother looked up, startled. When she spoke, it was with childish force. 'No. Never. He wouldn't leave us alone like that. He never has.'

Taro looked down, abashed. 'Of course. It's just… painful. That's all.'

His mother looked at him, her eyes kind. 'Yes. But what do I always say?'

Taro smiled. '*Ame futte ji katamaru.*'

Land that is rained on will harden. Suffering makes us strong.

Taro's mother nodded, as if that settled it, but Taro pursed his lips. He was suffering; so was his father. But no good would come of it.

His father would only die, and soon. Taro knew it.

It was now fully dark outside and the room was dim, lit only by the fire and by a couple of whale-fat candles. The people of the village didn't kill creatures of the land, preferring to subsist on the fruits of the sea and avoid killing as the Compassionate One had taught.

But if a whale beached itself on the shore, every available man, woman, and child would be summoned to strip it of its natural bounty: meat, bones, and blubber would all be taken and put to good use.

Taro wasn't quite ready for sleep yet, so he reached over and picked up his bow, running his hand along its smooth wooden belly, checking the tautness of the string.

'It's still as good as new,' Taro's mother said, looking at the weapon in Taro's hands with a strange, wistful expression. 'Just like he said it would be.'

'Like who said?'

The wistful expression left his mother's eyes and was replaced by a hard, flat look. 'Oh, your father, of course.'

Taro balanced the bow in his palms. It was beautiful – curved like a beach, smooth like pebbles washed by the sea, as hard as whale ivory. On the inside of the bow, hidden from casual view, was carved a tiny insignia: three hollyhock leaves inside a circle, pointing to the centre. Taro's father had made the bow when Taro was a baby, sensing somehow that he would need it. But when Taro had asked about the insignia – which was not repeated on any of the tools his father had made – he had only shrugged. 'I felt like carving leaves,' he'd said.

Taro's mother was still looking at him strangely, as if about to tell him something. He frowned. 'This bow,' he said. 'I have never seen Father make another. I've never seen him carve *anything*. Did he not—'

She cut him off with a sharp gesture, turning at a sudden sound from the other side of the screen.

Taro stood very slowly. It sounded like someone was moving very quietly in the part of the hut where his father slept. Just as he began to move towards the screen, he heard a dull thud as of a body falling.

Father.

Taro walked round the screen and stifled a scream. His father's body lay at an angle on the sleeping mat…

…and his severed head lay on the ground beside it.

CHAPTER 4

IN THE SEMI-DARKNESS the blood surrounding Taro's father was black on the ground.

Then, as if forming itself from the pool of blood, a figure dressed all in black moved quickly forward, drawing a blade that gleamed in the darkness like a fish glimpsed in deep water. He wore a black mask that revealed only his eyes.

Ninja.

Taro had time to fix his eyes on the dagger moving towards him, before another blade burst through the man's chest. The assassin coughed, looking down at the sword point in wonder. Blood bubbled out of his mouth and down the folds of black cloth that masked his face.

He fell, and as his body slumped, another man in black who stood behind him slid the blade from his torso, with a grunt of satisfaction.

Taro blinked. *That ninja just killed that other—*

Just then, his mother screamed.

Taro turned and saw a third dark-clothed figure crouched behind his mother. The ninja moved his arm almost imperceptibly, and a knife appeared in his hand. He went to slit Taro's mother's throat.

'N—' Taro screamed, his cry cut off by a hand that came from nowhere and covered his mouth. The figure at Taro's side pushed him to the ground, just as he pulled something from his cloak and threw it at the man who knelt behind Taro's mother. Taro saw a gleaming star stick in the man's masked face, then the ninja fell soundlessly to the ground. Taro had never seen a throwing star before, but he knew this was the legendary weapon of the ninja – the six-bladed *shuriken*.

'Wha—' started Taro.

'Shut up,' said the man in black beside him. 'First, do you trust me?'

'No.'

'Good. That would be stupid, as you don't know me. But I'm afraid you'll have to try. Otherwise you will die. Come here.' He stepped over to Taro's mother, who sat still, her eyes wide and staring.

'You're… not going to kill us,' she said. 'I thought, earlier, when I heard what the merchant said…' She trailed off.

The ninja looked at her blankly. 'No, I'm not going to kill you. I'm going to leave, with your son.'

She opened her mouth to speak, but the ninja interrupted. 'Don't worry. I'll keep him safe. I'm sent by a friend.'

Taro's mother's eyes opened wide, then she nodded.

'You will need to lie absolutely still,' the ninja continued. 'We are going to make it look as if you are dead. Lie here until there is complete silence, until the screaming stops. Then get up and run. Go to a monastery, go anywhere you like, as long as there is no one there who knows you. Take a different name. Take a vow of silence. But *disappear*. Do you understand? You may never see your son again, but you will live.'

She nodded, mutely, tears streaming down her cheeks. The

ninja arranged her on the ground, then took a stick of some dark red substance from his sleeve and drew a cut across her neck. He followed this with blood from a vial concealed under the folds of his mask. Then he turned to Taro. 'To you, she is dead. Yes?'

Taro shook his head, tears welling hotly in his eyes.

The ninja slapped him. 'Do you want her to die?'

Taro shook his head again, still crying. 'I c-can't leave her,' he mumbled. There was also his father's body, lying headless on the sleeping mat it had occupied for so long, getting stiffer and colder by the moment. Taro was sickened by what had happened to his father, by the way that this once strong fisherman had been laid low by illness, then dispatched into death by an assassin who had not hesitated to murder a sleeping man. Would anyone even mourn him, if Taro and his mother were gone?

The ninja sighed, appearing to hesitate. Then he unshouldered a light fabric bag, as black as his clothes, and withdrew from it a pigeon, its wings tied. The pigeon cooed lightly but seemed undistressed – Taro guessed that it was an experienced messenger.

'I had this for an emergency, but I suppose this counts as one, since if your son doesn't come with me, you will both die in the next few moments.' The ninja tucked the bird into Taro's mother's robe. 'When you are safe, write a note for your son. Tell him where you are. The bird will reach me.'

'Thank you,' whispered Taro's mother. The ninja grunted, irritably, as if he were conscious of making a mistake, and annoyed with himself for being unable to resist it.

Then she gave Taro one look – one single look in which all her love was encompassed. Taro almost cast his eyes down, embarrassed – for she looked at him as if he were a scroll containing the words that would save her soul.

She turned away. The ninja looked at Taro, and sighed again when he saw Taro's eyes cut to the screen behind which lay his father's body. 'He's dead,' said the man. 'You will do him no honour by joining him.'

'But...' mumbled Taro. 'I shouldn't just let him lie there. I should help his soul by—'

The ninja raised a peremptory hand. 'Help his soul by taking vengeance on his killers,' he said. 'Not by dying with him.'

Numbly, Taro nodded. He looked one last time at the screen, then gripped the bow in his hand.

The ninja looked at it. 'Do you know how to use that thing?'

Taro nodded.

'Good. There are others coming. We will need to fight.'

Taro looked at the dead man behind his mother's seeming corpse, then at his saviour. They were dressed identically, in loose black robes and with black scarves covering their faces, leaving only the eyes visible. 'You are with them,' he said wonderingly. 'And yet you save me.'

'Yes,' said the man simply.

'Did you kill my father?'

'No. Enough questions.' He pulled out a short-sword. Less elegant than a samurai's *katana*, it nevertheless had a brutal, businesslike air. Then, without warning, he slashed at Taro with the sharp edge. It was a trap! Taro dodged backwards, felt the blade slashing his kimono, had time only to think *I can't die now—*

—And the black-clad man stepped back, holding a piece of Taro's robe. 'We don't have much time,' he said as he stepped over to the doorway and pinned the scrap of robe with his sword to the wooden jamb. The fabric was positioned so as to be visible from the outside. 'They'll soon wonder why we haven't come out.

Get over here and draw your bow. Get ready to fire.' He beckoned Taro, positioning him on the side of the door opposite the scrap of robe. 'They'll think you're waiting to ambush them on the other side.' And with that, he crouched, putting his finger to his lips.

Sure enough, a moment later another ninja whirled into the room, the blade of his sword making a silvery circle in the air as he brought it down where he thought Taro was standing. The sword met only thin air, and the man let out a grunt as the sword struck the side of the door, where the scrap of silk fluttered in the breeze.

Taro didn't hesitate. He let go of his arrow, and it crossed the narrow space at the speed of thought, burying itself in the man's neck. The ninja dropped to the ground.

'Good,' said the crouching ninja. 'A true warrior's instinct.'

Taro looked down at the dead man, and suddenly a terrible sickness rose in his throat. He doubled over and was sick. He had never killed a man before – and he had done it so easily! He had barely paused. He was a monster!

'Ah. A warrior's instinct but not a warrior's stomach. Come, there are still more and we must hurry.' Quickly, the man crossed the open doorway – shimmying to the side as a silver star sang through the air at body level – and took back his sword from where it had bit into the wood.

He grabbed Taro's arm and pulled him to the back of the room. 'We'll break out through the shoji,' he said.

The ninja kicked a hole in the thin wooden wall and stepped through, pulling Taro behind him. Outside was black as ink, the only sound the beating of the waves on the rocks below. Then the light of a torch flared nearby, and a voice called out. 'Hello? Is everything all right?'

The huge form of Hiro loomed out of the darkness. The ninja beside Taro reached for something in his robes, but Taro put a hand on his arm. 'No. He's my friend.'

The ninja stilled his arm, but just then another dark figure appeared out of the night and launched itself at Hiro, short-sword whirling. Hiro ducked below the sword's trajectory and brought his fist up hard, smashing it into the man's solar plexus. The ninja slumped, and Hiro, not hesitating even a fraction, stooped to pick up the sword and then stabbed it downward, cleaving the attacker's neck.

He straightened up, holding the torch and the sword, turning his head searchingly.

'Over here!' said Taro, as loud as he dared.

Hiro moved towards him, picking his way across the rocky ground. Then Taro saw a black shape rising in front of his friend.

Ninja!

The ninja threw something – like a black stone – and before Hiro could move to avoid it, there was an explosion in front of his face, and as Hiro was distracted by the flash, the ninja brought up his *wakizashi* and knocked the stolen sword from Hiro's grip. The torch Hiro had been holding in his other hand fell to the ground and guttered there, vacillating in the wind. In the flickering light the ninja stuck out a hand and jabbed a finger into Hiro's neck. Hiro's legs crumpled and he collapsed to his knees.

Taro started forward, reaching behind his head for an arrow even as he kept his eyes fixed on the black figure as it drew its sword and raised it, ready for the killing stroke—

Taro armed the bow and let the arrow fly in one smooth movement, and the black figure paused, seeming to stare down at Hiro. Then he tumbled forward. Taro grabbed Hiro's arm and helped him to his feet. Beside him lay the ninja, an arrowhead protruding from his mouth, like an obscene tongue, and his eyes rolled back in his head.

Hiro picked up his sword and torch. 'Good shot,' he wheezed. Then he saw the ninja who was helping Taro, and his eyes went wide and he raised his sword. Taro held up his hands.

'No! This one's on our side,' he said. 'He's a good ninja.'

Hiro raised his eyebrows in suspicion but lowered the sword.

'Gods,' said Taro. 'You're wounded.'

Hiro moved his hand to his face. He grimaced, and Taro knew that his old friend was in agony. For Hiro to succumb to the pain enough to acknowledge it in any way was a bad sign. The boy's left cheek was split open, blood spilling from it thickly.

'It will heal,' said Hiro.

Taro nodded. They would worry about the cut later. 'Are they gone?' he asked, turning to the ninja. The man shook his head.

Into the circle of light cast by the torch, a black figure stepped, his weapon raised. 'You are turned traitor, I see,' he said to Taro's rescuer. 'But now you must give yourself up. And the boy, too. You are outnumbered.'

Then something happened that Taro could never afterward remember clearly.

A pale movement flashed in front of him, light gleaming on something long and thin.

Then a sword hilt was sticking out of his stomach, like a grotesque growth. Taro stared down at it. Blood was soaking through his cloak, and dripping down his trousers to pool in the crevices of his toes.

'What—' he began.

And then the pain hit.

He doubled over, gasping, unable to breathe, feeling the burning metal that had pierced his organs and – he knew without checking – burst out through his back. At that moment, his knees gave way, and it struck him with a horror that crawled on his skin that his spine might have been severed.

But I can't just die, he thought. *I was going to be a samurai . . .*

His vision blurring so that it seemed the scene was darkened by rain, he just made out the good ninja as he swiftly slit the throat of the man who had stabbed Taro. For a moment he was a tearing, spinning thing, a whirlwind, and then there was a calm point in the storm.

Ahead, Hiro pushed back the ninjas, who had fallen away, retreating from the good ninja's onslaught.

Then a hand clasped his shoulder. The ninja. 'Taro,' he said – but had Taro given him his name? He couldn't remember. 'You're dying. There is only one chance to save you. But it will mean living your life in secret, in the darkness, hiding with me. You may never see your mother again. Do you agree? Answer, quickly. If you do not agree, both you and your mother die.'

Taro stared, unable to respond.

'You will die now if I do not do this, and so will your mother. I said, do you agree?'

To never again see his mother? To never again witness her smile, which was like the rising of the sun to him?

And yet if he did not agree, he would die, and she would be killed too.

The fear for her mixed with the pain in his belly, striking him through with agony.

'I—I agree,' Taro stammered.

The ninja drew back his lips, revealing a pair of long, sharp canine teeth. Then he bent his head and bit deep into Taro's neck. Hiro yelled, 'What are you doing!' and turned from the attackers, but the ninja pushed him back easily with his free hand and sprang back, releasing Taro.

Taro swayed. His blood hammered in his chest. He felt light-headed, his thoughts were swirling – bright lights burst in his vision. He heard the ninja speak urgently to Hiro. 'If you wish for your friend to live, keep back and do nothing.' Then the man's face swam into view, close up. 'Taro,' he said. 'I know you're feel-ing strange, but I need you to bite my neck.'

Taro felt a need to obey. Still swaying, he opened his mouth and leaned forward. The other man guided his teeth towards his exposed neck, white in the moonlight. Taro bit down, and warm blood filled his mouth, while a warm light filled his mind and his body, making his muscles sing, making every feature of the scene spring into vivid detail. The pain in his belly left, replaced by a feeling of warm energy.

He stood. As if in a dream, he slid the sword from his own flesh and watched as the wound closed over.

He saw Hiro, looking on in astonishment. He saw the ninja step back, smiling sadly.

Taro turned, exquisitely aware of every muscle and tendon in his neck, and faced the darkness. A dozen black-clad figures melted out of the night and stood before him, a semicircle following the line of the circle cast by Hiro's torch. Absently, he reached out with his left hand and pushed Hiro behind him, where his friend would be safe. He was aware on some level that he shouldn't be strong enough to push Hiro anywhere, let alone with his left hand. But the strength felt good and right.

He saw his enemies approach him, and he was glad.

He saw *shurikens* fly, and he ducked and weaved, avoiding them, plucking them out of the air even as they headed for Hiro.

He saw his own hands as they flew between bow and quiver, knocking ninja after ninja to the ground, every shot perfect, whether he aimed at eye or chest or hand raised to throw.

He saw the ninja beside him, his blood master now, draw a long and perfect samurai sword from a concealed scabbard that ran down his spine, under the black cloak. Taro saw the wave-like pattern of sand-cooled steel down the sword's blade and knew that it was a masterpiece. And he saw the symbol etched into its base by the handle.

It was a circle containing three hollyhock leaves – exactly like the one on Taro's bow.

CHAPTER 5

A FARAWAY PART OF Taro's mind was aware that he had been bitten by a *kyuuketsuki*. He realized too that the other ninjas were also *kyuuketsuki*. One of them, when Taro shot an arrow through its shoulder, bared its sharp canine teeth in a growl that was more animal than human.

It was impossible: a ghost story come to life. But as impossible as it was, it was also *happening*.

Kyuuketsuki could be hurt, Taro knew that. They bled like ordinary men. But he wasn't at all sure they could be killed, at least with conventional weapons, and they were many times faster and stronger than humans. Their weakness – the price they paid – was that they could walk abroad only at night.

Taro glanced up at the moonlit sky.

Morning was a long way off.

He turned to the left, narrowly avoiding a sword strike that would have taken off his jaw.

'Stay by me,' said the good ninja, as his sword traced silver loops and butterfly wings in the night air. 'You're stronger than them, at least while my blood flows in your veins, but they are more experienced.'

The wickedly barbed wheel of a *shuriken* whined through the air past Taro's head, nicking his ear. He fired an arrow that went wide, just as the good ninja's blade struck in front of him, as quick and lethal as a snake, gutting a man who had been about to stab him with a dagger. Taro felt that the world and the air surrounding him had grown sharp edges, and waited only for him to fall on them.

And yet still Taro moved with strength and grace. He could feel the other man's blood in him, singing in his veins, doubling his power – for there were two of them animating this body, lifting and twisting its muscles and bone, as two men carry a weight more easily than one.

But then another *shuriken* flew and he didn't move quickly enough: it stuck in his left bicep, going deep enough to jar against the bone. Taro gasped. Next to him, the good ninja whirled round. 'We need to go,' he said, while his left hand snapped out and hit one of the assailants in the neck, dropping him instantly to his knees. The good ninja's sword arced in his right hand, describing a flashing silver oval that ended deep in another man's shoulder, cutting his arm and half his chest clean off. 'Let's head for the beach. There should be boats, yes?'

Taro nocked another arrow; let it loose. There was a scream. 'Yes,' he replied, too short of breath to add anything else. The ninjas were pressing in now. They had suffered heavy losses, but there were just too many of them, and they were stronger than ordinary men. They kept trying to circle round Taro and the good ninja, which forced them farther and farther back against the paper walls of the house, to protect Hiro.

The good ninja turned to Hiro. 'Ready to run?'

Taro's big friend clutched his bleeding cheek – with the other he had formed a fist, ready to defend himself to the last.

He nodded.

There was no signal, no warning. The ninja simply turned and ran, stumbling in his speed as he headed down the steep hill towards the sea. Taro grabbed Hiro's arm and ran too. He felt something small and sharp penetrate his back, but as with the *shuriken* still lodged in his arm, the pain felt distant – not gone, he sensed, but saving itself for later. He grimaced and kept running.

Taro ran as fast as he ever had. Hiro, who had never been fast on land, struggled to keep up with him. Twice he stumbled to his knees, and Taro, who had never been strong, lifted him easily to his feet with one hand.

Whatever the ninja *kyuuketsuki* had done to him when he'd bit him, it had made him powerful.

Finally, they crashed through a bush and went sliding down a dune onto the beach. The moon shone down on the blue-black sea, which gleamed, glassy and still. 'This way,' Taro shouted, pointing to the right, where the boats were moored just offshore. He saw the ninja jag to the right to follow his pointing finger. The three of them ran full tilt towards a small fishing boat that had been tied up and was bobbing maybe a quarter of a *ri* from the shore. Further along the beach were two or three similar boats.

Taro turned, still running, and saw a dark group of pursuers close behind them. The ninjas were gaining quickly, and occasionally stopped to loose an arrow that would strike the sand near their feet. Twice Taro ducked as arrows sliced over his head.

The good ninja turned, pausing to allow the first of the pursuers to catch up. Then he spun round, ducking simultaneously, bringing his sword round in a low circle that severed the man's legs at the ankles. The man fell, screaming, his feet sitting on the sand like shoes.

The man coming up behind stopped, for a split moment, to

draw his sword, and Taro had time to fire an arrow that took him in the throat.

The good ninja stooped, slashing the tie rope that kept the first boat from floating away. Still running, he cut the second one too. That left only one boat tethered to land.

Taro whirled round to loose another arrow at the dark figures chasing them along the beach. He heard an angry *hiss* as the point found its target.

'To the boat,' said the ninja. Without waiting for a response, he cut to the left and dived into the waves. Taro slung his bow and quiver over his shoulder – he'd have to restring it again after this – and followed him. He heard the splash from behind as Hiro leaped into the sea.

In minutes they had reached the boat, and they pulled themselves, dripping, cold, and panting into its slick, wet carapace. Just in time. An arrow thudded into its wooden side just as they slid into the bottom.

Taro looked back at the beach. From this distance he had to strain his eyes, because there was a thin cloud covering the moon like a silk death shroud, but he could see the ninjas gathering at the shore. Some of them were still firing arrows into the water. The moon was behind them, and they clearly couldn't see that their quarry had already reached the boat.

'Why don't they swim?' Taro asked.

'They can't,' said the ninja. 'They come from the mountains in the north country. Not much cause to learn.'

'So what do we do?' said Hiro. 'Wait here for them to leave?'

The ninja was about to reply, but then his gaze flew back to the huddle of desperate-looking men as something fluttered up into the air. Taro turned to look, narrowing his eyes, trying to make it out.

Then it split into two, resolving into two birds that forked, flapping their wings, into the sky.

Messenger pigeons.

The ninja cursed. He looked at Taro's bow. 'Can you hit them?'

Taro felt the wetness of the string, saw the almost indistinguishable flickering of the birds against the dark sky, already dwindling to small pale points like dim stars. 'What do you think?'

'Right,' said the ninja. 'We need to move, before those pigeons bring reinforcements. Where's the nearest village?'

'Minata. Two or three *ri* to the north.' Something tugged at the back of his mind, and it wasn't until much later that he remembered what the *ronin* had said – about the peasant who had been killed in Minata by a *kyuuketsuki*.

The ninja leaned back in the boat, looking at the sky, and for a moment he all but melted into the darkness as his eyes disappeared from view. He wore loose black *hakama* trousers, a short black robe, and black silk coverings over his face. Soaked with water, these garments had gone an even deeper black, merging into the night.

'The north star,' he said, pointing. 'Row that way. Along the coast.'

Hiro smiled as he picked up the oars. 'Yes. We could have told you that.'

Far above them one of the pigeons winged its way towards a distant castle, there to communicate news of the wretched boy's escape.

The other flew north.

CHAPTER 6

Walking, they could have covered the distance in an hour or two at most, but north of Shirahama the waves were high and the wind stiff, and they made slow progress over the sea.

Taro had been impressed, when he'd pulled out the *shuriken* lodged in his arm, to see his flesh heal over quickly. It was sore, but there was soon little sign of the wound – just a raised pink line, hardly more than a welt.

No boat had followed, and slowly the ninja, who had remained tensed for action, began to relax. To the east they could make out the grey silhouettes of mountains, the darker rocks of the shore. The bright moon ahead of them lit a silvery path on the water, as if showing the way to a more marvellous world.

The ninja still wore his mask. When Taro had suggested he take it off, he had refused curtly.

But now that they seemed safely away from their pursuers, Hiro stilled the oars, an expression of grim determination on his face. 'I think you should tell us what's happening,' he said to the ninja. 'What did you do to Taro, back there? What did those men want?'

The ninja took a deep breath. 'I can't explain everything.'

'Try your best.'

Taro held his hands up to his friend in a placating gesture. 'He's with us, Hiro.'

'How do you know?'

'He saved my life. He saved my mother's life.'

Hiro caught the unspoken implication. 'Your father…'

'Is dead. This man' – Taro nodded to the ninja – 'killed the one who did it.'

'Gods, Taro,' said Hiro. 'I'm so sorry.'

'So am I.' Abruptly, Taro's eyes stung. His father was dead. He'd been ill, of course – and Taro had known that soon he would die. But now he had been killed by cowards and Taro would never have the chance to speak to him again before he departed for another realm of samsara, would never be able to tell him he loved him. Tears welled up as he remembered his father before the illness – his strength, his courage, his humour. He remembered the man who had told him stories as he faded into sleep, of samurai warriors and their Bushido ideals of honour, valor, and loyalty.

And then there was his mother – his kind, beautiful, brave mother. The ninja had faked her death and told her to run away. Would Taro ever see her again?

Hiro looked away, embarrassed, as Taro cried. He narrowed his eyes at the ninja. 'Why did they kill Taro's father?'

'They wanted Taro dead. I was sent to stop them.'

'Who sent you?'

The ninja looked down. 'I don't know,' he said.

'You don't know?'

'I'm a ninja. The people who seek to hire ninjas don't often want their names involved.'

'So you just… do whatever you're paid to do?' said Taro. He

was horrified. That would mean... Well, it would mean killing for profit, not for honour. He felt his admiration for the person who had risked his life to save him warring with his disgust that it had been only an assignment.

This was not such a good ninja after all.

'Yes. All I know in this case is that I was sent to infiltrate a group of ninjas, and stop them from killing a boy from the village of Shirahama. You, Taro. I don't believe *they* even knew why you were to be eliminated.'

Taro wasn't quite listening any more – he was focusing on something the ninja had said. 'I never told you my name,' he said.

'Ninjas always know their targets' names,' said the ninja. 'Even if they don't know why the target was chosen. It helps to not kill the wrong person.'

'Oh,' said Taro. 'Well, you know my name, so perhaps we should know yours.'

The ninja bowed, slightly. 'Shusaku. At your service.'

Hiro leaned forward. 'You're telling us that all those ninjas were there to kill little Taro?'

'Yes.'

'And yet there was only one of you. How could you have thought you would succeed in saving him?'

'Because I'm the best,' said the ninja. He spoke without boastfulness – as if merely stating a fact. 'And anyway, I did succeed. Taro is still alive, is he not?' He paused, and his eyes closed for a moment, as he sighed with what seemed like the admission of an error. 'At least, in a manner of speaking.'

Hiro grabbed him now. 'What do you mean, a manner of speaking?'

Again Taro moved to calm his friend down. 'I think I know.

He means that I am a *kyuuketsuki* now.' He looked at Shusaku. 'That's true, isn't it?'

Hiro's eyes went wide, and Taro realized that he must not have understood the bite, the exchange of blood – perhaps he hadn't really seen the sword that had run Taro through either.

Shusaku sighed. 'You might say that.'

'And you... and all the other ninjas...'

'Also vampires, yes.'

Hiro's mouth was open now. '*Vampires?*'

The ninja put a hand on Taro's arm. 'Show your friend your wound.'

Taro held out his forearm, showing the pink scar where the *shuriken* had pierced the skin and muscle. Then he held up the throwing star he had taken from it. The points were still wet with his blood.

'Those ninjas were trying to kill him,' said Shusaku. 'By turning him, I made their job harder. I wish...' He took a long breath. 'I wish I had not had to do that. But there were too many of them.'

'But...' said Hiro. '*Kyuuketsuki* aren't real.' He was staring at the miraculously healed flesh, though, and Taro could tell that he was having trouble reconciling his deep-held beliefs with the evidence before his eyes.

Shusaku's eyes sparkled, and Taro thought he might be smiling. 'Had you ever seen a ninja before tonight? And yet you can't deny that they are real.'

Hiro shook his head in disbelief. 'But... ninjas are different from *kyuuketsuki*... I mean, ninjas are men, and vampires are—'

'Actually,' said Shusaku, 'they're not different. All ninjas are vampires.'

'*All of them?*' said Taro, incredulous.

'Of course. Vampires are faster than ordinary men, stronger and more agile. And have you ever heard of a ninja doing his work by day? Never. They operate only by night – silent, stealthy, deadly. It makes perfect sense that ninjas should be vampires.'

Hiro looked bewildered. 'And now… Taro is…'

'One of us, yes.'

'What does that mean?' said Taro. 'I mean, I know that I can heal quickly, but… vampires suck blood, don't they?' He felt sick at the thought of it.

'Yes. We do. But not all of us are killers.'

'Not all of you?'

'Our friends on the beach have a somewhat different code from the one I live by. They belong to what you might call a different clan. When they feed, they kill their victims.' Taro thought of the villager who had been drained of his blood, the one the *ronin* had mentioned. 'Me, I take only enough blood to survive. I will teach Taro to do the same. I believe that killing my food is inexcusable. You might say that I am a better Buddhist than most villagers. They don't hesitate to kill fish. Me, I kill nothing!' He laughed.

'You kill ninjas,' said Taro, not sharing the man's amusement.

'Well, yes,' said Shusaku, almost like a scolded child. 'That's different. I was doing it to save you.'

'If they're not your clan, then why were you with them?' asked Hiro.

'Some of their number recently died of a terrible accident. Their leader was left in need of ninjas to complete the mission. I volunteered.'

'An accident?' asked Taro.

'Yes. They fell on their swords.'

There was silence for a moment. Taro's father had been

killed, his mother was gone who knew where, and he had been turned into a monster from a story. Now he sat in a boat with a ruthless killer who had thought nothing of gutting a man from behind with his short-sword. Could a *kyuuketsuki* ever become a samurai – ever become a hero? He thought it unlikely.

But, least likely of all, he found that he quite *liked* Shusaku. The man seemed neither good nor bad – and Taro was beginning to wonder whether the black and white world of the samurai stories he had loved was only that – stories, told to children, to convince them that there were such things as heroes and monsters in the world.

Perhaps, he thought, the two were sometimes combined in the same creature.

And anyway, the man that Shusaku had so dishonourably killed in Taro's hut had only moments before cut off the head of Taro's sick, defenceless father – so the manner of his death seemed appropriate. It struck Taro that this world of violence and action was far from the glamorous arena of duels, honour, and romance that he had imagined.

He licked his lips, feeling the sharpness of his canine teeth. It was only when he saw Hiro looking at him with a distinctly nervous expression that he realized how different he must look. Hiro backed away a little. 'Will he... bite me?' he asked Shusaku.

'I doubt it. You two are friends, are you not? I'm sure he can resist the lure of your blood. You eat fish, but that doesn't mean you are compelled to eat every fish you encounter.'

Hiro had gone pale.

'But, if you wish, you can leave us when we go in to land. My task is to keep Taro safe. You are free to leave.'

Hiro shook his head. 'Never.'

'You're very loyal to your friend,' said Shusaku. Taro thought he sounded impressed.

'He saved my life twice.'

Shusaku nodded gravely. 'Such things breed loyalty, it's true. Very well, you will come with us.'

'And where are we going?' asked Taro. 'We should search for my mother. I'm sure she—'

'Of course,' said the ninja, interrupting him. 'But first things first. We must get you to safety.'

'And then we find my mother?' said Taro.

'Yes.'

Shusaku turned to look out to sea. A dim glow was beginning to accentuate the line of the horizon, the first light of dawn dividing sea from sky, where before the darkness had blurred them into one. 'In the meantime, we need to row.'

'Why?'

'There's something else you need to know about vampires. The sunlight kills us.'

IN THE BRIGHT, early morning light, Lady Oda no Hana patted her horse's neck and leaned back in the saddle. She held her left arm very still so as not to startle Kame, the beautiful chicken hawk that stood on a leather bracelet encircling her wrist. The hawk was still hooded – she cocked her head, listening to the sounds of the woods. A small stream babbled nearby; from the distance came the call of a cuckoo.

Hana stroked Kame's head with a hand that bore the scars of taming. The hawk made a little throaty noise and pushed against Hana's hand, strutting a little on her leather perch.

She was eager to be free – and Hana knew how she felt.

But Hana wasn't quite ready. Kame was a short-range hunting hawk, not a peregrine like Hana's father's. It was necessary to wait for prey to come close enough before letting her go. Otherwise the hawk might fly off, never to return. Of course, that was always a risk with a hawk. It was not loyal, like a horse, and Hana respected Kame for that. You knew that the bird remained with you, and did your bidding, only with its consent and tolerance. It was a killer, a weapon, content for a short time to bear the touch of a human hand, but certain to one day take its leave.

If a sword could think, Hana said to herself, *it would not be so different from a hawk.*

Hana breathed in the scent of the pine forest. She was not far from the castle where her father, Lord Oda no Nobunaga, ruled his fiefdom, but she was alone in this clearing, and for once could simply enjoy the feel of the horse beneath her, and the clear country air round her. Her father had no sons, but sometimes he joked that Hana had inherited his male spirit, even if she could never inherit his title of daimyo and rule over the Kanto when he died.

Judging that a sufficient time had elapsed since she had entered the clearing, Hana removed Kame's hood. The hawk cast her sharp eyes over the surrounding trees, then looked up at Hana and gave an excited cry – *ki, ki, ki*. She strained against the leather leashes that bound her to Hana's wrist.

Just then, Hana saw a shape moving fast over the trees – a pigeon. With practised smoothness she untied the leather thongs and thrust her left hand out, as if striking out with a sword. Kame shot forward, wings folded, then lifted into the air with a snap of feathers. Hana watched, proudly, as her hawk rose quickly over the trees.

The pigeon banked when it saw the hawk, but much too late. Kame was bred for this. She was as perfect in her efficiency of purpose as a well-honed weapon, all muscle, claw, and sharp eyesight. As the prey dropped and turned, Kame uttered another harsh cry – *ki, ki, ki, ki* – and, folding her wings, plummeted as straight and true as an arrow at a pocket of clear, empty air—

(Hana held her breath.)

—that a heartbeat later contained the pigeon, following a trajectory the hawk had seen and calculated before she'd committed to the attack.

47

There was a startled coo and a flipping and flapping sound like clothes drying, as the hawk and the pigeon spiralled and tumbled through the air. Kame struggled to get a grip on the heavy bird as she fell, but soon enough she got it under control and was falling gracefully to earth, the limp pigeon held between her claws.

Hana squeezed her heels against the horse's flank and trotted forward under the trees. Kame looked up at her from where she stood on the body of the pigeon, next to a broken branch on which grew dense moss, making Hana think that when she returned to the castle, she would pick up pen and ink, and render the scene on paper. The drama of death, the grace of the hawk, the elegance of the twisting branch.

Kame shrieked with pride. *Krrriiiii, ki, ki*.

'Well done,' said Hana. She held her hand down, offering the leather guard to the hawk. As always at this moment, she caught her breath. Would this be the time that…? But Kame hopped lightly onto her wrist, and Hana gave silent thanks to the kami of the sky. She looped the thongs quickly over Kame's feet, binding her to the gauntlet.

Now for the tricky bit.

Holding the hawk still, Hana kicked her right leg out, swinging it in the same movement behind her, as if executing a spinning kick. As her weight turned in the saddle, she tucked her left leg at the knee, bringing it round to the right over the horse's back, so that she spun almost in a full circle, and dropped lightly to her feet next to the horse. Kame did not even stir.

Hana bent down and picked up the pigeon. She tore off one of the wings and gave it to Kame. The hawk fell upon it greedily.

It was then that Hana noticed the scroll tied round the pigeon's leg. She cursed. A messenger pigeon. At least it had been flying towards the castle, and that meant it probably didn't belong to her father. Hana dreaded to think what would happen if she brought him one of his pigeons, its neck broken by her hawk. Already his patience with her hunting and riding was growing thin. He was beginning to think about her marriage, and the alliance he could seal with it.

Hana unfurled the scroll. She would take it to her father, and bear his wrath – which, because the bird was not his property, and because he was still receiving the message, would almost certainly not be terrible. (Almost. His temper was legendary.) But first she wanted to see what it said. Could it be the news she had dreaded – an announcement of her marriage to some daimyo of a distant province, necessary to her father in his endless quest to be shogun and rule over all of Japan?

But it wasn't that at all.

It was a single line of script, the calligraphy done in an uncertain hand, not at all the way a noble would write. Hana stared at it, puzzled.

The boy lives.

She leaped lightly onto her horse and turned round, galloping back to the castle. A nameless misgiving stirred in her breast.

As it turned out, she was right about one thing: Her father was wrathful. She was wrong about another: She did not have to bear it. In fact, he turned from her almost as soon as she handed over the message, and she did not see him again for some days.

CHAPTER 8

Behind them was a line of red fire on the horizon, and
before them loomed the dark embrace of the shore. Just dimly
visible above it was the twin-peaked promontory that marked
out the bay of Minata. Taro pulled hard on the oars, amazed by
the new strength in his arms. He was rowing almost as quickly
as Hiro had done, and Hiro was the one with all the muscles.

'Quickly,' muttered Shusaku, glancing at the encroaching
sunlight.

The safety of land seemed too far away, but Taro kept his
mind on the rowing, making the rhythm of the oars into a sort of
mantra: *out, down, pull, out, down…* Even he could see that the
light in the east was growing faster than the land was approaching, and he could sense the ninja's tension in his rapid breathing.
Hiro, beside him, was scanning the horizon worriedly.

Taro's fingers tightened on the oars, his hands clinging to the
wood like pale starfish. His arms ached, his eyes burned with
salt. His robe was beginning to chafe against his inner arm and
chest, which were being rubbed raw by the wet fabric. But
ignoring the discomfort, he continued his rhythmic mantra.

Up, back, pull, up…

Then, surprised, he felt the gentle shock as the boat slid up onto sand. He had been so focused on rowing that he had barely noticed the beach expanding, until instead of a far-off line of darkness it had become an embracing enormity of trees and rocks and mountains, and they had passed from the realm of water into the realm of land.

Shusaku leaped down into the shallows. 'We need to find shelter, fast.'

Taro scanned the hills. Minata's simple huts were too far away – their lights shone on the upper slopes, so distant as to resemble fireflies. But then he saw it: the sweeping red gate of a *torii* temple on the mountainside. Beside the temple was a small wooden hut. Taro showed it to Shusaku, and the three companions began to run.

Over the sea, the flames of sunrise began to burn the clouds. As the still-weak light reached them, Shusaku gave a little grunt of pain, despite the dark clothes he wore. Taro wasn't sure if he could feel anything, but he was aware of the burning in his muscles as they raced for shelter.

The door of the hut was shut, but Hiro barged it open. Shusaku cast his eyes round. He ran his fingers over the joints between the wooden planks of the walls. A rake leaned against one of these, and Taro thought that the hut must serve as a storeroom for the person responsible for maintaining the temple.

After circling the room, the ninja nodded, apparently satisfied. 'We'll be safe till nightfall,' he said. Wearily, he sat down.

'What do we do now?' asked Taro.

'We sleep.'

'But it's daytime.'

'Indeed it is. You're going to have to get used to it,' said the ninja.

Hiro was pacing up and down. 'I'm hungry,' he said.

Shusaku smiled. 'You of course are free to leave the hut – just be careful when you open and close the door.'

Taro felt a tingling in his stomach. 'I'm hungry too.'

'I'm afraid *you* will have to wait. Unless you wish to feed on your friend.'

Taro looked at Hiro and for a moment he was acutely aware of the vein that beat in the other boy's neck, the blood welling in the wound on his cheek, and he felt hotly ashamed of it while at the same time thinking how good it would be to sink his teeth in and—

He turned away, breathing deeply.

'Hunger is one of the disadvantages to being a vampire,' said Shusaku.

'And the advantages?' said Taro, hoping there were some. He could smell Hiro's blood and it was making his mouth water...

'Those you know already. Speed. Strength. Agility.' Shusaku smiled. 'I'll answer all your questions, I promise. But first, I think we should tend to your friend's wound, before you lose control and feed on him.' Taro swallowed, flushing with embarrassment. He had been so fixated on the blood, its rich, delicious smell, that he had forgotten his friend was hurt.

Shusaku sent Hiro out into the daylight to gather some wet seaweed from the beach, as well as some dry wood and twigs from the forest. Then he set Taro to lighting a fire in the middle of the small hut, to dry their wet clothes, while he created a seaweed compress that he put over Hiro's cut. He tore a piece of his black shirt and used it to bind the salve onto the wound.

When Hiro's cheek was safely bound, Taro and Hiro sat cross-legged on the bare, hard ground before Shusaku. Hiro cleared his throat, then said, 'So are you a demon?'

Shusaku laughed. 'Hardly. Some say that vampires are descended from the *kami* of night, and that is why we cannot go abroad in daylight. But you have already seen that one vampire can create another – the ability is passed by the sharing of bites, not by parenthood. So I wonder if that story can be true.'

'And all ninjas are vampires? Is *that* really true?'

'Yes. Though the reverse is not. There are vampires who are not ninjas, such as yourself. But a person cannot become a ninja without being turned. Usually we train the young until we feel they have reached a sufficient… maturity, and control of their powers. Then we turn them. With you, it was somewhat different.'

'You did it to save my life.'

'Yes.'

'And now what?'

The ninja stiffened, and Taro could almost have believed that, for once, Shusaku was unsure of himself, worried, even.

'I will take you to the home of my clan,' he said. 'It's the safest place for you.' He spoke these words as if to convince himself as much as the boys, and Taro frowned. Something was making the ninja uncomfortable. What was it? 'And anyway, I have received no instructions beyond saving your life. I must go back to await further information.'

Taro bit his lip, feeling impatient. 'And how long will that take? I want to find my mother. You said when I was safe, we would look for her.'

It was only in saying this that he realized, with a lurch in his heart, how much he already missed her. He wanted to curl up in her arms so she could make all of this go away, like a childhood nightmare.

But then, unbidden, his final image of his father swam into his mind – the body, divested of its head, lying in a pool of blood.

And this was no nightmare he could awaken from.

Surrounding his grief, like the sharp edges welded to the shaft of a sword, was a murderous desire for revenge. Taro knew that, as much as he missed his mother, he also wanted to avenge his father. 'And then we find the person who sent those ninjas. The person who killed my father.'

Shusaku made a weary gesture. 'As for your mother, she is even now seeking out a place to hide. You will not find her alone. We must wait for the pigeon I gave her.'

'Good. Perhaps it will come soon.'

The ninja snorted. 'It is a clever bird but not that clever. It cannot find me wherever I happen to be. It will fly to my home. So you must return with me there.'

Taro twitched, impatiently. He wanted to find his mother now, but he could see that the ninja talked sense. 'My father, then. We will find his killers. Take vengeance.'

Shusaku sighed. 'Yes, of course. But what would you do, a boy, on his own, with little idea of how to use his powers? Even one fully trained ninja would slaughter you like a pig. And whoever is after you, they are *very* serious about killing you. The services of ninjas do not come cheaply. I've never seen so many sent against one target. The cost would usually prohibit it. And anyway, for most missions one of us is sufficient.' He said this with an unmistakable measure of pride – as if the assassinations of unarmed men were an impressive thing, as if putting on a disguise and killing people before they even knew they were under attack were an act on par with a samurai's bravery in battle.

But there were some advantages to being a ninja.

'I'm a vampire now,' said Taro. 'I'm strong.'

Shusaku pulled a short-sword from his cloak. He smiled at

Taro. Then, with no warning at all, he lashed out at Hiro's neck.
Taro didn't think. He snapped forward, hand flying out, closing
the distance between himself and his friend in a fraction of a
heartbeat. His fingers closed on the ninja's wrist, stopping the
blade just as it neared the skin—

No. It was no longer a blade.

Shusaku waved the thin sapling branch that he was holding
next to Hiro's throat. Hiro looked down at it with wide eyes.
'Turn round,' Shusaku said to Taro, who was still gripping the
older man's wrist. 'Look behind you.'

Taro turned. The sword was now in the ninja's other hand,
and it was so close to the back of his own neck that he could feel
it touching the small hairs there.

'You're fast,' said Shusaku. 'You probably were before, but
vampires have quicker reflexes, and greater strength, than ordinary humans. Yet you have a lot to learn. Imagine if it were one
of your father's killers attacking your friend. You would have
saved him from a green branch, not even fit for the fire, and your
spine severed for your trouble. You will come to the sacred
mountain that is home to my clan. And then we will see about
your mother, and your father's avenging.'

Taro sighed, and sat back, releasing Shusaku's hand.

'Your home. How far is it?'

Shusaku spread his hands. 'If we weren't hunted, and had
supplies, spare clothes? A day or two. As it is we will need to
stop. There is a woman I know – she is part of our network, and
she is wiser than anyone else I know.' His eyes crinkled with
what seemed like humour. 'She has two rather pretty girls in her
charge. She lives on the way to the sacred mountain. We'll go to
her, rest for a while in a place where the sun can't reach us. She
can give us clothes, too – string for your bow.'

'When we get to your home,' said Taro, 'the sacred mountain, what will happen?'

'I hope your skills will be sufficient that you may one day become a full ninja. You're a vampire already – that's part of it. But being a ninja isn't just about being bitten. It's about clan, discipline, and loyalty.'

Strange, thought Taro. *He speaks of ninjas as if they were samurai.*

Shusaku grimaced. 'There is a small problem,' he went on. 'Usually a young acolyte is turned and made a full ninja at the same time, in the same ceremony. That you are already vampire will cause a certain amount of… resentment.'

'Sounds wonderful,' said Hiro.

Taro thought about what Shusaku had said. The ninja spoke as if the choice of where they went was left to him alone – as if he and Taro could decide together where to go and what to do. But surely his employer – whoever had sent him to rescue Taro – had to have a say?

He leaned forward. 'You said that you were ordered to save me. Yet you had no instructions at all as to what to do with me once I was saved?'

'None.'

Taro looked at the man's eyes, and they did not waver – cold, implacable. Taro had no idea whether he was lying or not.

'You also tell me you don't know who employs you. I don't believe you.'

The ninja spread his hands. 'My orders are sent anonymously. It's safer that way. As for believing me… that is your own decision to make. But I *did* save your life.'

Hiro edged forward. 'And what about me? The ninjas we fought know me now. If I go back, I might be killed.'

Shusaku nodded to him. 'You fought with great skill and bravery. You will come too, should you desire it. And if you are good enough, you too will become a ninja.'

Hiro looked a little pale. 'A ninja... yes. But a vampire... I'm not sure.' He glanced down as if ashamed. Then he looked at Taro again. 'But I'll come with you both if you want me.'

'Of course,' said Taro and Shusaku simultaneously.

'The things you will teach me,' said Taro to Shusaku. 'They will make me strong? Skilled? Enough to avenge my father?'

'Certainly.'

Taro thought about this. His father was dead – the pain of it blossomed inside him constantly, like a flower that is always opening. And he had been forced to leave his mother behind. Half of him wanted to run, now, while it was light – and return to Shirahama. Another part of him wanted above all to begin a new life somewhere far away, with Hiro – to forget that any of this nightmare had happened.

But he felt too a burning desire to strike at those who had hurt him and his own – something he knew he could do better if he were a ninja. And he felt a desire to return, one day, to his mother, when he knew where she was.

And when he had burned the shame from him by honour, by vengeance, and could stand proud in front of her – a demon, but a demon who had acquitted his father's murder.

Yes. It would hurt, it would burn, but what was left of him in the end would be good and pure – like the fire that destroys the wet stickiness of seaweed, leaving behind only hard salt, more valuable but hidden until then by soft flesh.

He leaned back, sighing. He would go with Shusaku and learn what he could – and then, when he was strong, he would bring the fight to his enemies.

'These girls you mentioned…' said Hiro to Shusaku. 'The ones who live with the wise woman. They're really pretty?'

'As cherry blossoms.'

Taro still felt anger pressing on his chest like a stone, but he couldn't help smiling at his friend, who now put an arm round Taro's shoulders. 'I promise you,' he said, 'as soon as we can, I will help you to find your mother. And I'll help you wreak vengeance, too.'

Taro smiled. 'Thank you, Hiro.'

'But first,' said Hiro, 'we'll meet these pretty girls.'

Taro laughed, play-punching Hiro's arm.

'Now, now, boys,' said Shusaku, 'go to sleep. Tiredness kills almost as easily as I do.'

CHAPTER 9

T ARO WAS STARVING.

Hours had passed, and the cicadas were singing. He thought that the sun must have gone down by now. He looked at Hiro, sitting against the far wall of the hut, gathering his few possessions, and saw a vein beating in the boy's meaty neck. Shusaku was still snoring in the corner.

He licked his lips, his tongue raking over his sharp teeth.

Just one bite.

He dug his nails into his palms, sickened. *Is this what it is to be a* kyuuketsuki? he thought. *Will I turn on my friends?*

But then Hiro looked up and smiled at him, his cheek covered by a makeshift bandage, his face stained with blood from defending his friend, and Taro felt a rush of love for the big wrestler who had not hesitated to take on multiple attackers when the time had come; and the redness that had come upon the world when he saw the throbbing of that vein was lifted, as mist at sunrise.

Taro realized that if he was hungry, Hiro must be hungry too. The seaweed he had gathered, dried, and eaten the previous night would not be enough to sustain him for long. He stood and opened the door a crack – full dark.

'Going hunting,' he said. He stalked through the trees, notching an arrow into his bow. The gut bowstring was wet and had probably lost some of its elasticity, but he hoped it would suffice for a close-range shot. Keeping his footsteps silent, concealing his shadow by moving from tree to tree, he had only gone a short distance before he saw a squirrel sitting on a branch. He lined up the shot and fired. The arrow flew true, if not with its usual power. It struck the squirrel behind its shoulder and knocked it from the branch. But it didn't pierce far enough, and Taro had to break its neck as it lay there on the ground.

Taro carried the squirrel back to the hut and, skewering it on a thin green branch, roasted it over the fire. Then he handed it to Hiro. 'Thank you for helping me,' he said.

'I swore to serve you always,' said Hiro. 'And anyway, I enjoyed the fight.' He laughed, but his hand went up unconsciously to worry at the fabric covering his wound.

When he had taken a few bites, he handed the roasted squirrel to Taro, who took it gratefully. He bit into the tender flesh of the leg, chewed, and swallowed.

And immediately gagged.

The meat seemed to have turned in his mouth into something sharp and raw, tearing at his palate and tongue as if barbed. He coughed and spluttered, spitting out the piece of food, clutching his throat.

Choking, he thought. *Dying.*

Yet he couldn't feel the meat in his throat. He was sure he'd spat it out…

And that was when Shusaku clapped him on the back, roaring with laughter. 'You think you can eat ordinary food?' the ninja asked. 'You're part spirit now. You can feed only on blood, for that is where the spirit lies.'

Taro took a deep breath, controlling his convulsions. '*Human* blood?' he said.

'Not necessarily. We can survive on animal blood. But human is better.'

'You said you don't kill,' said Taro.

'And I did not lie. Tonight, if we are to keep our strength, we must find someone to ambush. But we will take only as much as we need to survive – no more.'

Taro saw Hiro shiver and cast down his eyes, and once again he was filled with fear that his oldest friend might reject him, now that he had become a monster.

He looked at the ninja, who was still chuckling about Taro's misfortune with the squirrel. 'You could have warned me,' he said.

'Yes, I could,' said the ninja. 'But think how much better you have learned the lesson this way. You won't eat flesh again.'

Taro scowled. 'I'm going outside for a moment.'

Hiro began to stand, and Taro added, 'On my own.' Hiro sat again, looking hurt, and Taro hated himself for it. But Hiro had not been inside Taro's head just then, had not felt the thirst for blood. Hiro would doubtless feel differently if he knew how hard it was for Taro to resist the throbbing of those prominent blue veins.

'I just… need a little time, that's all.'

'We should be going,' said Shusaku. 'We need to use every hour of darkness we can.'

'I'll be fast,' said Taro. He walked down the beach to the water, sat on the hard sand just before the surf and hugged his knees.

In the distance he could see an island, silver against the blue water as if it really were a drip from the sword that, it was said, had created the islands of Japan.

Now, Taro supposed, the island he could see was probably crawling with pirates, who since the fall of the emperor preyed increasingly on coastal vessels, fishing boats, and the merchant ships of the Portuguese, and had grown rich from the weakness of the shogun.

Yes, it shone from here, that island, in the moonlight – seemingly made of a rarer element than base water or rock. But up close you would see the ash of cooking fires, the rough, functional weapons of the pirates; you would see the stolen goods and the hostages and the dead.

Taro's dream of leaving the village had shone once too, his idea of taking up weapons and serving a samurai lord and one day marrying that lord's daughter. This, though, was the reality of adventure – a dead father, a lost mother, a newfound physical strength that also made him look at the veins throbbing in his friend's neck, and want to drink the blood inside.

The island swam, disappeared, as if sinking into the sea, as Taro's eyes welled with tears. He clutched his knees, feeling as though he would melt and run down the sand into the waves. His chest heaved, his breath rattled and gasped. The tears spilled from his eyes and ran down his cheeks. He had never cried like this, and felt as though the moisture would be all wrung out of him, leaving him a dried husk on the beach, twisted driftwood.

Father, he thought. *Mother*.

He missed them the same, and in that moment he didn't know which was worse – to never again see the one who was dead and beyond the torments of this world, or to never again see the one who lived and who languished somewhere in fear and hiding.

Surrounding this thought, wrapping it as leaves wrap a flower bud, was a sneaky fear that spoke its terrible question to

Taro over and over. *Even if your mother lives, would she wish to see you now? You're a demon. A* kyuuketsuki. *She is a simple woman, an ama; she will spurn you. Perhaps even now your father wanders the land of hungry ghosts, his soul made restless by his son's affront to the Buddha.*

And only barely acknowledged, crouching at the back of his mind like a weevil in rice, the worst thought of all. *What if it's all my fault that Father is dead and Mother is gone? If it weren't for me, the ninjas would not have come.*

He held his head, and he cried for them, and he did not melt into the sea but sat, aching, in the glowing moonlight – for in the end our bodies know only how to carry on surviving.

Sighing, Taro wiped the tears from his cheeks. It was time to go back to Hiro, and Shusaku. It was time to get moving. Perhaps that was all he needed – to move, to *do* things. He stood up and began to walk back up the beach.

When he put his hand on the door to the hut, he felt more than heard a *thwip* in the air, and then there was the shaft of an arrow protruding from his shoulder. He gasped, whirling round as another arrow struck his upper arm on the other side. Shadows moved in the trees surrounding the hut.

Taro blundered into the door, pushing it open, falling inside. The places where the arrowheads were lodged inside him were burning now, and as he staggered inside, one of the shafts caught on the doorjamb and snapped off, tearing his flesh. He screamed.

Shusaku was already up and clutching his short-sword. 'Ninjas?' he asked. Hiro rushed towards Taro and caught him before he could fall. He eased Taro down to the ground.

'I—I think so,' stammered Taro. 'Dark shadows. In the trees.'

Shusaku considered a moment. 'They don't know I turned

you. Any ninja knows that it's not an arrow or two that will kill a vampire. And that must also mean they don't know I'm with you.'

'But… they were there, on the beach.'

'I don't think so. I think these are others. Probably there are ninjas in every village surrounding Shirahama, waiting for you to show up. I should have thought of it. But this kind of operation, for a mere boy… it's unusual.'

'Unusual?' said Hiro angrily. 'That's what you call it? We're going to die! Taro's badly hurt.'

The ninja shook his head. 'We'll get those arrows out in a moment. They won't kill him. In the meantime, we have one slim advantage.'

'What's that?'

'They don't know *I'm* here.'

With that, Shusaku slipped out through the door. Taro had sunk to the ground just inside the hut, and he found now that by turning his head and shoulders he could watch as Shusaku glided out into the night. Arrows flew, but he ducked and weaved, avoiding them.

From the trees, holding wickedly gleaming swords, came the ninjas.

Then, so unexpected it seemed a dream, Shusaku began to twirl off the black silk wrappings that made up his mask. Continuing to move gracefully to avoid the arrows that flew towards him, he stepped out of his *hakama* and his robe.

Taro stared, gaping.

Where there had been a ninja – Shusaku – in dark clothes, and holding a *wakizashi* short-sword, now there was only a sword, shining in the starlight.

Shusaku had disappeared.

Yet his sword bobbed and danced in the air, advancing on the group of enemy ninjas, as if invested by a magician with the power of locomotion.

The ninjas who had advanced from the trees stared at the floating sword, and Taro heard them murmuring, nervous.

Then the sword fell to the ground and lay still.

There was a commotion among the attacking ninjas. One of them pointed at the sword, and another shouted something. Taro thought he heard the word *akuryou*, 'evil spirit.'

The ninjas all took a step back.

Just then, one of them, standing farther back than the others, near the trees, suddenly fell to his knees. He pitched forward, the gleaming hilt of a dagger sticking out of his back.

'What was that?' said Taro, shocked.

'You didn't see?' said Hiro. 'Shusaku sneaked up behind him and stole his dagger, then stabbed him with it. I'm not sure why he dropped his sword, though. And I don't know why he didn't want his clothes.'

Before them, the ninjas argued among themselves, brandishing their weapons at nothingness, backing up until they were facing outward in a tight-knit group, like a deadly hedgehog.

Suddenly one of the men dropped to the ground, with slack finality.

Again the ninjas panicked, jostling against one another, shouting.

'What in the gods' name?' exclaimed Taro.

'It was him again,' said Hiro. 'He smashed that one's head in with a rock. Is something wrong with your eyes?'

'I can't see him,' said Taro, wonderingly. 'Where is he?'

'Walking round them. He's *naked*. But his body is covered in something... tattoos, I think.'

Taro searched the scene ahead of him. He could see nothing but scared ninjas.

One of the men stepped forward from the group, and all of a sudden his sword hand jerked up. The sword sprang from his grip but didn't fall to the ground – instead it hung in the air, pointing towards him. Then it slashed out violently as if of its own accord, and gutted the man.

Taro gasped. What was happening?

Smoothly, in a continuation of its previous motion, the sword spun in the air and took off another man's arm and shoulder. Then the sword dropped to the ground. The men backed away from it, as if it were infused with dark magic.

One of the ninjas ran then, but he had not gone far when one of his fellows was divested of his spear, and that same spear moved bobbing along the sand, hovering at waist level, and plunged into his chest. The ninja ran on for several steps, then went down face first.

That was it for the other ninjas. In chaotic concert they dropped their weapons and ran, dispersing in all directions.

Most of them escaped.

The spear rose magically from the back of the man it had killed, before arcing through the air as if thrown with some power, and hitting one of the fleeing men in the back of the neck.

Moments later, he and the other dead were the only figures visible. Taro felt sick. He didn't understand how those men had died, but he understood one thing: It was a slaughter of those unable to defend themselves.

'This isn't possible…' said Taro. 'Who threw that spear?'

'What are you talking about?' asked Hiro. 'It was Shusaku. He killed all of them. But it was like… like they couldn't see him.'

Taro turned to his friend. 'Hiro,' he said. 'I can't see him either.'

CHAPTER 10

ODA NO HANA cursed her calligraphy master.

Not out loud, of course. That would have been unladylike.

Sunlight shone through the open window, accompanied by a light breeze. The day was warm, so they were in an upper room of the castle where the windows were not covered with shoji paper. This was the calligraphy master's one concession to Hana's preference for outside pursuits. The windows of this upper room were narrow, so that an archer could fire from behind them without being hit. A shaft of light illuminated Hana's desk.

She knew that the master meant well, but this was pure torture! The sunlight, unfiltered by paper blinds, only made her long more keenly for that which she couldn't have.

Lady Hana would have liked to be outside, honing her skill with the sword. She trained with a bokken, but her skill was already a matter of public knowledge, and it had been whispered – sometimes in her presence – that she would one day be a sword saint just like her father, a *kensei*.

But Lord Oda did not want a sword saint. He wanted a gift, a bargaining piece, a pliant bride he could offer to whichever nobleman he most needed to forge an alliance with – whichever of his vassals or enemies he could bind closer to his person by marrying them to his beautiful daughter.

The times when Hana was able to escape the castle and practise her sword moves were very few indeed, and since she had given her father the message from the dead pigeon, they had stopped almost entirely. Her father, on the few occasions she had seen him, had appeared distracted, angry, and – yes – worried. She would not have believed it of the sword saint daimyo, whose eyes and will were made of the same steel as his swords. But he was afraid. And lately he would not allow her to leave the castle under any pretext. These last days, Kame had been confined to Hana's room, submitting with increasingly poor grace to the indignity of food she hadn't killed herself, its blood no longer flowing in its veins.

Hana gazed out of the window, looking at the oblong patch of sky above the main gate of the castle. A few wispy clouds drifted by, against the pale blue.

The calligraphy sensei rapped Hana on the knuckles. 'You're miles away! Concentrate, girl! You're worse than the Tokugawa boy.'

The Tokugawa boy, who was sitting right next to Hana at the adjacent desk, looked up from where he was scrawling a messy spiral on his paper with a wet brush. 'I hate you!' he said. 'Calligraphy is *stupid!*'

Lord Tokugawa's son was a ruddy-faced boy of round four – far too young for calligraphy, of course, and Hana didn't quite see why he had to sit there with her. She strongly suspected that it was meant to teach her some sort of salutary lesson, useful one day for her management of a samurai household. Patience, perhaps. Or the fortitude required not to gut an obnoxious four-year-old boy with one's sword.

Little Tokugawa loved mud, frog spawn, and stone fights, and hated anything to do with sitting inside. On that point, Hana was in complete agreement with him – though on that point only. He was an arrogant brat, and she tried to keep her contact with him to a minimum. Some days she worried that her father might try to marry her to him. A four-year-old boy! She wouldn't put it past Lord Oda.

The lesson crawled along slowly, like a dog with three legs. Hana applied herself to several new characters, deriving – despite herself – a certain pleasure from the brush's progress across the white paper.

Suddenly there was a cough from behind her, and Hana turned, startled, her brush sketching a wild, unplanned stroke. Kenji Kira had entered the room, his tabi shuffling lightly on the polished   wooden floor, as he placed his weight on his uninjured leg, dragging the wrecked one behind him.

Not that there was much weight to place – the man seemed thinner every time Hana saw him, as if a hungry ghost from the lowest realm of samsara were feeding on his flesh. She had never seen him eat anything but rice, and he drank only water. She wondered how he remained alive. His eyes were sunk in dark pools, surrounded by bruises; his bones showed through his near-translucent skin like sticks bundled in a sack.

He bent over Hana's desk and greeted her respectfully. Hana would be more grateful for the man's respect if he didn't convey it with such terrible breath. The man's every word carried a scent of decay, as offensive to the nostrils as unconvincing to the ear.

In truth, she trusted nothing Kira said.

He was her father's head of security – his spymaster, as

Hana's indiscreet maid Sono called him – and he had a wide remit of responsibility. Hunting fugitives, interrogating prisoners, quelling insurrections – he had done them all. There was, however, one insurrection he was powerless against: Hana did not return his obvious admiration.

Kira leaned his long, emaciated body over hers, forcing her to squirm aside, and plucked up her sheet of white paper. He examined the image she had drawn there, the character for 'crane'.

'Your strokes are too bold,' he said in his nasal twang. He tutted at the mistake she had made when he'd surprised her. 'You must aspire to a more feminine line if you wish to make a fine match for a desirable nobleman.' He smiled at her, revealing rotten teeth, and red, bleeding gums. 'Unless, of course, you already have your eye on someone…?'

Hana shook her head. 'Even if I did, it would be futile. I will marry whomever my father wishes me to marry.'

Kira bowed. 'Indeed. Let us hope that he makes the choice wisely.'

Hana's calligraphy master cleared his throat. 'Sir Kira – did you wish me to end the lesson?'

'No. I merely came to inform Lady Hana that I am departing on a mission for her father, a very dangerous mission to recover a lost asset. It is a great honour, of course, that I have been entrusted with a matter of this magnitude.' Preening proudly, he ran his fingers through his greasy hair, which in the samurai way was long and tied back.

A man who boasts about his honour, thought Hana, *doesn't have much of it*. But she said, 'What is the… asset which you are sent to recover?'

Kira put a finger to his lips. 'It is some– something Lord Oda wished above all to possess. But those he sent to find it failed him. I will not. And when I return with it... who knows? Lord Oda will no doubt wish to reward me, his loyal servant.' He bowed once again to Hana and fixed her with his milky eyes. 'Maybe, when I come back, our relationship will be set on a closer footing.'

CHAPTER 11

BLACK CLOTHES FLOATED into the hut, apparently moving of their own volition.

Taro stared as the clothes dropped to the ground. Then, shocking him, a pair of eyes appeared suddenly in the air.

'You don't see me?' said Shusaku's voice.

'I see– see your eyes,' stammered Taro.

The eyes bobbed up and down.

Taro stared blankly.

'Oh, I apologize,' said Shusaku. 'I was nodding.'

Taro continued to stare. Hiro turned to him. 'What's going on? You don't see him? He's right here. He has black writing all over his body. Kanji.'

Taro shook his head. 'No, I don't see him.'

He saw the disembodied eyes turn to the pile of clothes. A pair of *hakama* trousers rose into the air, followed by a cloak. They floated into position round a pair of legs and a torso, which Taro now saw clearly, beneath a pair of eyes that hovered in empty space.

A long, black scarf now drifted up into the air and wrapped itself round the invisible head several times, until what stood in the hut before Taro was again a man dressed all in black, with only his eyes visible. He knelt by Taro and gripped the arrow in his shoulder. 'This is going to hurt,' he said, before pushing the point right through and out the back. Taro gagged, just as he did for the second arrow. But again, on looking at the wounds, he was amazed by how quickly his flesh healed over.

When the pain had died down, he looked hard at Shusaku. 'Why couldn't I see you, just then?' he asked. 'Is that a ninja trick?'

'Not quite. It's a trick *against* ninjas.'

'How does it work?'

Shusaku narrowed his eyes at him. 'You can't guess?'

'The tattoos,' said Hiro. 'They protect you.'

Shusaku nodded. 'Did you read them?'

'No. I can't read.'

The ninja shook his head, as if disappointed. He turned to Taro. 'And you?'

'No.'

'A disgrace.'

'I can't *see* your tattoos,' said Taro. 'And anyway, none of the villagers can read.'

'Precisely,' said the ninja. 'The villagers are uneducated peasants.' Taro wondered what the man expected – he and Hiro were peasants too. Shusaku sighed, then rolled up a sleeve. The effect was disconcerting. For Taro, the man's arm simply disappeared.

But Hiro could obviously see something. He leaned forward, as the ninja traced a gloved finger along empty air.

'*Shiki fu i ku, ku fu i shiki, shiki zoku ze ku, ku zoku ze shiki.* Form is emptiness and emptiness is form. Form is not different from emptiness, and emptiness is not different from form. It is the Heart Sutra. An old teaching of the Buddha. For spirits, it acts

like a spell. It reminds them that form and emptiness are equal –
and so it conceals my form. Evil spirits, like good spirits, are
incapable of denying Buddha's truths.'

'But I'm not a spirit,' said Taro.

'You're a vampire now,' the ninja explained. 'And so you are
part spirit. We vampires trace our lineage back to the days when
the spirits were everywhere and walked and lived with men.
Like I said before, there are people who say we are descended
from the *kami* of night.'

Taro could think of nothing to say to this. So many years the
villagers had joked that he was part *kami* – a descendant of the
god-spirits that inhabited the streams and woods and mountains
of Japan – and now Shusaku was saying that this might actually
be true! He knew there had been more *kami* in every wood and
seaside cove, before the Buddha chased them away, but…

Taro let these thoughts, which struggled against him like fish
on a line, swim away for the moment. For now, he would stick
with simple questions. 'You're a vampire,' he said. 'And' – he
took a breath – 'you made me one too. Why would you make
yourself invisible to your own kind?'

'So that I could kill them. And now we should be going.
There are not many hours of night left, and we must reach the
house of the woman I spoke to you about.'

They left the little hut and began to walk through the woods,
Shusaku checking always to left and right in case any of the
ninjas had been brave enough to stay.

'We must pass close to Nagoya,' he said, 'to get to the
mountains where the woman I spoke of lives. We must be very
careful. If possible, we should find some sort of conveyance in
which we can conceal ourselves. A cart, perhaps, or a palanquin.
If he sees us like this, exposed, Oda will kill us in a heartbeat.'

Taro and Hiro both gasped. Lord Oda Nobunaga was a legendary figure in the Kanto. Both the impolite shortening of his honourific name – 'Oda' instead of 'Lord Oda' – and the idea that this upholder of the samurai ideals might want to kill them shocked them profoundly.

'But Lord Oda is a great daimyo!' said Taro. 'Why would he want to kill us?'

Shusaku paused. 'He… does not take kindly to strangers. Two peasants and a ninja? It's a suspicious combination.'

Taro laughed. 'A samurai does not kill strangers for no reason. Lord Oda is a man of honour.'

Now it was Shusaku's turn to laugh. 'You think a man can hold on to the title of sword saint for so long if he fights honourably?'

'I think he probably doesn't kill people who can't defend themselves,' said Taro bitterly. 'People who can't even see him.'

Hiro drew in a breath at the insult, but Taro didn't care. Who was this ninja to speak to him of honour? He was little more than a paid assassin, and he was content to murder defenceless men in cold blood. Hadn't Taro seen him run someone through from behind; hadn't he watched him prey on blind enemies, who had whirled round hopelessly, panicked, oblivious to where he stood?

The man seemed to have no conception of fairness, and Taro wondered if he was doing the right thing by going with him. Once that pigeon arrived, and he knew where his mother was, he could of course take Hiro and leave. He didn't know if he could trust Shusaku, but he *did* trust Hiro. For now, he would tread cautiously, bide his time.

Shusaku walked on in silence in front, not responding to Taro's cruel words. The ninja held his head down, studying the terrain, and Taro could almost feel sorry for what he had said, but every time he was about to say something, he remembered what Shusaku had said about Lord Oda. The protector of Kanto Province, dishonourable! The effrontery of it repulsed him anew every time.

None of them spoke for a while. They simply moved steadily towards Nagoya, keeping always to the hidden ways and barely visible paths used by peasants and wild animals.

'Always avoid the roads,' said Shusaku finally, his tone even. 'To a samurai or a ninja, a peasant or a wild animal are of roughly the same importance, and that either may have ways and passages beyond the knowledge of civilized men is unthinkable to them. It gives us an advantage, because there will be ninja looking for us, you can count on it. Maybe even samurai, too.'

'Samurai do not kill peasants,' said Taro.

'No,' muttered Shusaku. 'They just send them into battle armed with farming utensils.'

Taro ignored him.

Nagoya lay only round five *ri* away, but they had to creep at a slow pace through fields and across rice paddies, avoiding the roads where nobles, samurai, and *ronin* rode from town to town.

The weather, at least, was clear, and though their ankles soon became wet from rice water, the evening was cool without being cold, and the moon illuminated their way without being so bright that anyone would see their silhouettes from far away.

After walking for half the night, they came at last to a low hill overlooking Nagoya. They were hidden by a small copse of trees above the road into town. The road itself curved when it met the hill, creating a bend that was not visible from the town. Paddy fields descended in even steps on all sides of the rounded hill topped by Nagoya, their water flashing silver in the moonlight.

Atop the rough wooden shacks of the bulk of the town rose the elegant curves of a palace, the sweep of its many red roofs suggesting dragons crouching on the town or, if you squinted, a flock of herons in flight.

The night sky was darkened only by the smoke that rose from the many chimneys. On the far side of town, a section of Lord Oda's army had camped and was engaged in military exercises. The trio could see their armour flashing from where they stood, and hear low grunts and metallic clashes, which seemed plucked in concert from the soldiers by a greater intelligence, as an expert player derives music from the varied strings of the koto.

Shusaku gestured at the scene before them. The hill on which Nagoya stood was a single low dome in a wide, shallow valley. On the other side, past the town, mountains rose up into a cloudless, starry sky, as if reaching for the heavens.

'We have to get to those mountains,' said Shusaku. 'But the valley is all farmland. No hidden paths. There is only one road we can follow.' His finger traced a pale, sinuous line that cut across the great low valley like a scar. Crossing it was another road that led to the gates of Nagoya itself, and Lord Oda's castle. This was the road that led to the low wooded hill on which they had stopped. 'There will be traffic entering and leaving Nagoya, even at night,' he said. 'We should not have too long to wait.'

Then he turned to Taro. 'What do you see? Any obvious risks?'

Taro stared at the landscape before them. 'I don't know... the brightness of the moonlight?'

Shusaku tutted. 'Hiro?'

Hiro narrowed his eyes. Then he pointed to a spot just beyond the town, at the base of the hill's broad flank. It was a place where the road narrowed to cross a wide river. 'Those soldiers. They're not involved in the exercises.'

Taro squinted. Ah, yes – he could see it now. Camped beside the road on either side as the route left the river and entered the endless rice paddies beyond the town, was a small group of well-armed samurai. Anyone approaching them would have to come across the bridge – unless they were willing to swim the river – and so the samurai had a stranglehold on the road's traffic.

'A checkpoint,' said Shusaku. 'They're watching the travellers heading for the mountains.'

'Or the travellers *coming* from the mountains to the town,' said Taro. 'Perhaps Lord Oda fears attack.'

'Perhaps,' said Shusaku. 'But I don't know if Lord Oda fears anything but failure.' He turned his attention back to the branch of road beneath them. 'The checkpoint is a hindrance. It means a cart will be of no use. They'll thrust swords into rice, or hay. We'll have to wait here in the woods for a palanquin to come along, then we'll ambush it.'

'How honourable,' murmured Taro.

Again, Shusaku ignored him. He led Taro and Hiro to the other side of the hill, where they could watch the traffic.

It was thin. The hour was late, and few people would venture outside by moonlight, now that *ronin* were so numerous in the countryside of Japan. The three companions waited a long time – enough for several incense sticks to burn to the end.

Finally, Shusaku pointed. Two men were approaching from the town, bearing a palanquin that befitted the station of a minor noble. Shusaku took a long, slim tube from his cloak. Taro could not imagine where he had hidden it. The ninja conjured a small dart with his fingertips, seemingly from nowhere, and fitted it into the tube. 'It will only make them sleep,' he said, anticipating Taro's question.

Taro nodded. 'Just don't kill them.'

Shusaku crept down the hill. Even Taro, who knew where Shusaku was, found it difficult to spot him after a while. And yet he was fully clothed this time. He glided between the bushes like a ghost.

There were two light puffs. The men carrying the palanquin dropped to their knees, causing the covered chair to fall abruptly to the ground. Taro heard a startled shout.

Shusaku surged forward, reaching the palanquin in a few bounds. He reached inside and pulled out a fat man in an opulent kimono. Before the man could protest, Shusaku did something with his fingers to his neck, and he crumpled to the ground. Shusaku began to search the man's clothes, then called to Taro and Hiro. 'Come down and help.'

They went down to the road and assisted him in pulling the bodies into the bushes, where they laid them down, concealed from sight. Shusaku used the tie strings from their kimonos to bind their hands and feet. Then he pointed at Taro. 'Bite one of them. Drink his blood. I will tell you when to stop so that you do him no lasting harm.'

Taro stared down at the unconscious men. It seemed dishonourable, appalling even, to feed on a man who couldn't resist. But he was so hungry…

'Hmm,' said Shusaku, holding up a scroll that he had taken from the nobleman who had been riding in the palanquin. 'This is both good and bad.'

'What is it?' said Hiro.

'This man's a messenger. He bears a note from Lord Oda to the shogun. The bad news is that we've ambushed the palanquin of someone very important indeed.' He smiled. 'And that is punishable by death. The good news is that we'll be carrying a message to the shogun, and that should get us through any checkpoints. He may only be a lad, but the office invested in him is a powerful one, and people remember his father's strength.'

The shogun was the true ruler of Japan, holding all the military and financial power that was denied to the emperor, who had been reduced to the role of a figurehead. The current emperor was a sickly young boy, ruler of a pleasant palace and very little else.

The problem was, so was the current shogun.

Ever since the previous shogun had died, his young son had been protected by six lords, the daimyos, each of them charged with keeping the boy shogun safe. The dying shogun had reasoned that each would prevent the others from rising up against his son – that their rivalry would result in a fragile balance. So far, he had been proven right, thanks to a lasting alliance between Lord Oda Nobunaga, daimyo of Taro's province, and Lord Tokugawa Ieyasu, the cunning and equally powerful daimyo of the Northern Territories. Since Oda's victory at Okehazama, he and Tokugawa had merged their armies to protect their neighbouring territories from smaller lords, and to enforce the shogun's rule.

Shusaku cuffed Taro round the ear. 'Drink. Now.'

Taro wavered. In his mind his mother's expression echoed – the one she had used when he was learning to swim, and swallowed salt water; the one she had used when he lay in the healer's shack, his shoulder bleeding black and sluggish blood from the wound where the shark had bit him.

Ame futte ji katamuru.

Land that is rained on will harden.

Like a charm, the words lifted the darkness that had settled on Taro's spirit, the tremble that had set into his legs. He looked down at the man. *I will be rained on*, he thought. *It is in the nature of revenge to suffer. But I will grow strong, and I will use my strength to find my mother and avenge my father.* Filial piety was the perfection of Bushido ethics, and the greatest gift a son could give his father was revenge on those who had wronged him. Just as the great hero Yomato Takeru had slaughtered his father's enemies in numbers like locusts, so Taro would lay low the men who had killed his.

Taro bent down and lifted the surprisingly light wrist. *The man must have the bones of a bird*, he thought. The wrist was narrow, and the bones and muscles impossibly small and delicate beneath the wrinkled, loose skin. Taro felt a comforting hand on his shoulder. Shusaku.

Suppressing the urge to gag, Taro raised the arm to his lips. He felt a strange movement in his mouth – *my teeth lengthening?* – and then bit. Then there was only the urge to bite, the biting, the sinking of teeth into flesh, and the hot burst of blood in his mouth – and Taro was surprised to find that it tasted good. More than that, it *felt* good, the same way that water feels good when you're hot and thirsty and your tongue is a squat toad in your mouth – and then he was aware of nothing more than sucking down that hot, vital life force and wanting it to go on forever, and he could feel his own blood rising to meet it, beating more forcefully than he had ever known it, and—

Rough hands pulled him up, wresting his mouth from the man's wrist with a popping sound.

'Enough,' said Shusaku. 'You will kill him.'

Taro looked down at the man. His skin looked a little blanched, as if the colour had been drained from it. Taro felt sick, but also alive and quick. Smooth power flooded the much-abused machinery of his strength, loosening his every joint.

'Come on,' he said. 'Let's go.' He ignored Hiro, who was looking at him with something approaching horror. He had never felt such energy, such focus.

Shusaku nodded. 'You will ride in the palanquin. Hiro and I will carry it. You had better take the letter.' He handed Taro the scroll, on which was a wax seal bearing the petals-within-petals *mon* of Lord Oda, and the crossed-sword *mon* of the shogun.

'You will also wear his clothes,' continued Shusaku. 'The ambassador's, that is. We will hope that, in this age of boy emperors and boy shoguns, a boy ambassador will raise no suspicion. Strip him, please.' As he said this, he was stripping the simple clothes from the smaller of the two servants. He took off his own black ninja's clothes – for a second he disappeared from sight – and then began to pull on the simpler garments. 'Only ninjas wear black,' he added.

'What about your tattoos?' asked Hiro, as Taro took off the rich man's clothes and began to substitute them for his own.

Shusaku had uncovered his face, and for Taro, the man's eyes were floating again in thin air.

'No human will question them. They will think I was once a criminal, a member of the thieves' fraternity. If we encounter a vampire… that would be more awkward. They may not know what it means, but they would see, as Taro sees, a pair of eyes bobbing about unsupported. That would be enough to make anyone suspicious, and ninjas are suspicious folk by temperament.'

Shusaku looked at Taro, who was bedecked now in the opulent clothes, and whose feet had disappeared entirely beneath a flowing pool of silk on the ground, his hands concealed by great wide sleeves.

The ambassador was a lot bigger than him.

Shusaku adjusted one of the sleeves. 'Hmm. Well, it might do, if you're sitting down.'

He beckoned Hiro forward. 'Bend your neck,' he said, then began to wrap his scarf round Hiro's face, leaving only the boy's eyes uncovered.

'What are you doing?' asked Hiro.

'We may not need it,' said Shusaku. 'If they believe that Taro is who he is supposed to be. But if you hear me say the word "balance", straightaway you yelp as if in pain and drop the palanquin. Do you understand?'

'Yes, but—'

'Good.'

Shusaku bent down to the larger of the prone servants. He flourished a knife that seemed to have been conjured from nowhere. 'I'm sorry,' he muttered, then cut off the man's left little finger. The prostrate man did not stir, still sleeping soundly from the drug in the dart.

Taro could hardly believe what he had just seen. 'Hey!' he said. 'What are you doing?'

Shusaku weighed the finger in his hand. 'It is not much to him, the smallest finger of his left hand. Its loss will not prevent him from wielding a sword, or a pen.' He reached inside his kimono and removed a gold coin. Once again, Taro wondered how the ninja was able to secrete such things about his person, as if his clothes, whether borrowed or not, were capable of producing on demand the items of his requirement. Taro had seen Shusaku replace his clothes after swimming to the small boat the previous night – and had seen no evidence of the swords, blowpipes, coins, and gods-knew-what-else that the man apparently carried.

Shusaku cut a length of black fabric from his robe, bandaged the servant's stump with it, then curled the man's fingers over, like a small octopus closing over its prey, and slipped the coin into the grip so created. 'A small compensation for your loss,' he murmured to the unconscious man.

Taro was impressed by the ninja's generosity, even if he *had* just maimed a man for no clear reason. A gold coin of that size could buy a smallholding of several square *ri*.

Shusaku ignored him, handing the finger to Hiro. 'When you drop the palanquin, you also drop this, all right? And you look at it, so as to make sure that others notice it too.'

Hiro took the finger with a disgusted expression and tucked it into a pocket in his robe. 'If you'll just tell me why I must carry this finger and cover my face, then—'

Shusaku put a finger to his lips. 'An old man must have his secrets,' he said.

Shusaku moved towards the palanquin, stretching the muscles of his arms and shoulders. Taro climbed inside the little carriage, and felt it rise into the air. He sat back. He was proud of Hiro's strength, and grateful for it. If Hiro had not been as large as he was, Taro didn't know how they would have disguised themselves to get into the town.

Two slits had been cut into the front of the palanquin so that the person inside could see out, without anyone being able to easily see in. Taro looked through these eyeholes as the palanquin turned round, and he saw the bodies of the men Shusaku had knocked out.

'Wait,' said Shusaku. 'Put the palanquin down.'

Taro leaned out of the door. 'What is it?'

Shusaku had lifted up one of the bodies by the armpits. 'Help me hide these in the undergrowth,' he said to Hiro. 'They won't stir for many incense sticks, but we don't want anyone seeing them. With any luck, they'll realize what happened and get safely away before Oda finds them, and punishes them for letting us overpower them.'

Taro rolled his eyeballs. 'Lord Oda is merciful,' he said. 'They're just servants. They can't be expected to defend themselves against a trained ninja. A person cannot be killed simply for failing in the face of impossible odds.'

Shusaku came back for the third man, the ambassador himself. 'Usually,' he said softly, 'that is *just* what gets people killed.'

Iто Kazei walked down the long corridor, the echoes of his tabi on the stone floor seeming to measure out the remainder of his life. He would have liked dearly to dawdle, but when Lord Oda Nobunaga requested one's presence at one's soonest convenience, it was a request in name only, and was rarely convenient. It was said that when a distant family member had been too slow to offer his condolences at the funeral of Oda Masahine, Nobunaga's father, Nobunaga had forced the miscreant to commit seppuku right there, disembowelling himself with his own ceremonial sword.

Ordinarily, a samurai committing this most sacred of ritual acts was accorded the courtesy of a second – another samurai who would stand behind and decapitate him as his blade cut through his guts, allowing him to escape much of the terrible pain.

Nobunaga always refused.

Many had wailed for Nobunaga's father that day. But their sobs had been drowned out by the cries of the dying man, who'd knelt by the pyre with his guts at his feet for hours before death had come for him, too.

Ito was carrying the sword as he walked – not sheathed, as

that would be an unforgivable presumption, but wrapped in oiled cloths and cradled in his arms. He increased his pace, careful not to drop the precious package. This sword had cost him several months of work, with him beating and re-beating the three steel bars that made up the blade, hammering and cooling them with great precision in order to achieve a shinogi line that undulated along the dull edge of the blade, a pale blue wave against the gleaming silver.

It was the finest blade Ito had ever made. And he had instructed his artisans to create the finest *tsuka* hilt and the most beautifully decorated *tsuba* hand guard ever produced, to complement the sharp metal and create a weapon of the most extraordinary beauty. An excellent nobleman's sword might take several days to make. Lord Oda's had been three months in the workshop.

When one of Lord Oda's retainers had presented himself to Ito and asked that he make a sword for the daimyo, Ito had been proud of the skill that he had spent so many years honing, perfecting it as the blade is perfected by the hammer and the forge. For his reputation to have reached the ears of the lord was praise indeed.

But he had also been terrified. Oda was known to have acquired the title of sword saint, or kensei. Various sword masters from the length and breadth of the country could attest to his skill – if they still lived. But everyone who had ever duelled with Oda was dead, and they had been many too.

A door opened ahead of Ito, and a girl's face of astonishing beauty looked out. Ito almost gasped out loud. He had heard of the legendary looks of Hana, Lord Oda's only daughter. But he had assumed them to be exaggerations – obsequious flattery disguised as gossip, in order to keep the lord happy. Ito stopped, without even being aware of it. He stared at the girl. She truly was exquisite: her dark, limpid eyes were as midnight pools, and her long eyelashes strands of weeping willow. Her skin was white with blushes of pink, like the blossom that was her namesake. There was a nervousness about her, a restless kind of grace, but this only made her more attractive. Ito had heard that Lord Oda feared for her safety. He wondered what could possibly threaten this beautiful girl, what kind of man – or demon – could possibly want to hurt her.

He was not aware that he was staring at her. She cast her eyes down, her cheeks flushing, and retired into the room. The door shut behind her. Ito, who had not even been aware he was holding his breath, let it out. He continued on his way.

The end of the corridor arrived too soon, and Ito could no longer delay. He stood in front of the heavy wooden door. Voices came from the other side. 'Where is the boy?' Ito heard Oda say, in his unmistakable gruff voice. Ito had seen the lord only when he and his retainers had ridden past the workshop on one or other of their hunting expeditions, but he had learned quickly to distinguish the man's authoritative tone and deep timbre.

There was an indistinguishable mumble from someone else, then a clattering sound of metal on stone. 'I sent you for the boy,' shouted Oda. 'And you return with nothing but excuses. He's nothing but a child! Children are easy to kill. It is one of their advantages.'

Then one of the other voices said, 'The traitor ninja turned him, Lord Oda.'

'Turned him?' said Oda, horrified.

'Yes. It's much harder to kill a vampire child than a human child.'

There was the sound of a person sucking on their teeth,

thoughtfully, then a sigh. 'Still,' said Oda. 'You failed, whether the boy was turned or not. You have shamed your clan, and my family name.' There was a loud slashing sound, then screams, then silence.

Ito stood for a long time, worrying. He had been summoned; he was expected quickly. And yet Oda was clearly involved in some kind of dispute, perhaps with his retainers. Perhaps it would be best to come back later? No. His presence was requested. Ito swallowed, and found that his throat was constricted and dry. He raised his hand and knocked, lightly, on the door. A small part of his mind hoped that something was wrong, that he would be sent away and told that Oda was not available today. Then he could polish the sword a little more, work on the etching to the hand guard so that it caught the light just so.

'Come in,' said Lord Oda.

Ito entered, keeping his eyes low so as not to cause offence.

'Look up,' said the lord.

Ito looked up and saw, to his astonishment, that Lord Oda was smiling. The daimyo stood in front of a tall shoji window from which the paper had been ripped, so that he was lit by a shaft of light as sharp and narrow as the sword in Ito's hands. Several retainers stood against the walls, watching. In the middle of the room was a shaven-headed man who stood with his hands bound behind his back, keeping his eyes fixed on the floor. He was trembling.

Lying on the ground, curled in various attitudes of agony, were a number of men in black clothes, obviously dead, their faces obscured by black silk scarves and hoods. Smoke rose in lazy spirals from their bodies and hung in dark motes in the bright light.

Ninjas.

'Don't look on them,' said Oda. 'They are unworthy to be looked on, or remembered. They failed in their duty to me. I trust that will not be true of you. They say you are the best sword smith in the region. That had better be true.' He waved a hand, and retainers began dragging the bodies from the room.

Oda held out his left hand to Ito, and for a moment the sword smith just stood there, mouth open, staring at the lord's shrivelled right arm, which hung uselessly at his side. Ito saw that the rumours were true: Lord Oda was lame. They said he had been struck in the shoulder with a sword while fighting in the glorious rout of Yoshimoto's larger army. The wound had severed tendons and nerves; now the arm was thinner than the other and Nobunaga couldn't use it.

Someone had told Ito that it was a woman who had wounded Lord Oda – a ninja woman, at that. But he tried not even to *think* this idea, so blasphemous was the suggestion that a mere woman could inflict such harm on the great daimyo. Already, he had half-convinced himself that the report had been a dream.

It was also said – and Ito still remembered this part – that the lord's private physician had begun the preparations for an amputation, Oda himself being unconscious at the time. When the unfortunate doctor began to cut into the flesh of the damaged arm, Oda had awoken suddenly and flown into one of his legendary rages. Taking his sword, with which he had killed so many sword masters in so many duels, granting him the title of sword saint, he had chopped off each of the physician's limbs, leaving only his head and torso. Then he had cauterized the wounds with a brand from the fire, and instructed his servants to bring the doctor back to the castle, there to prop him on a seat behind a curtain and feed and water him whenever required. In this way, said Oda, he would have the perfect physician: one capable of dispensing advice but not action. For action was the preserve of the samurai class, and was only to be entered into on the express orders of the lord.

After that, Lord Oda had cancelled all his activities other than the most essential, such as eating, sleeping, and torturing informants. He had dedicated his waking hours to training his left arm, making it as strong as his right had been. After a month, the great sword fighter Musashi had sought Oda out, thinking the time had come for the greatest of sword saints to be brought low. Oda had disarmed him, then dishonoured him by ordering him to remain alive, and refusing him the release of suicide.

The sword saint had discovered something new: His left hand might be weaker, but it was faster.

Lord Oda coughed, and Ito, startled, raised his eyes from the wasted arm to the lord's face. Oda glowered at him, proffering his hand, and Ito understood that the lord wished him to hand over the sword. He unwrapped the soft oiled fabric and took out the sword, giving it to the daimyo.

'A sword of blood, or a sword of peace?' asked Oda. 'Should I find a stream in which to test it?'

Ito thought how to answer. He had trained under the great sword smith Muramasa, who was known for creating bloodthirsty blades. But Muramasa himself had trained under Masamune, known for his peaceful weapons. It was said that one day Muramasa grew too bold and claimed that he was as good as his master. So Masamune took him to a stream in the mountains, next to a forest of great fir trees. He lowered his best sword, Yawakara-Te, or Gentle Hands, into the water, and bade Muramasa do the same with his own blade, Juuchi Fyu, or Ten

Thousand Winters. The pupil's sword cut everything that flowed towards it. Fish, leaves, twigs were all severed and split asunder. Yet nothing was cut by Gentle Hands – indeed, the leaves and fish simply swished round it, unharmed. Even the air hissed as it glided gently past the blade.

After a while, Muramasa began to scoff at his master: surely no one could claim to be a great sword smith, whose swords would cut nothing, not even the air. But just then a monk was passing on the opposite bank. Masamune hailed him, keeping Gentle Hands all the while in the current next to his pupil's sword.

When they had exchanged pleasantries, the monk asked Masamune if he knew of a way to cross the stream, for it was very deep in parts and not easily traversed. 'I'm afraid not,' said Masamune. 'But please, tarry awhile to judge a contest between myself and my apprentice. Which of these swords would you say is greater?' The monk kneeled on the bank and watched as Ten Thousand Winters sliced through frogs, fish, and leaves, and Gentle Hands only stirred up eddies in the water. Threads of blood billowed in the water from Ten Thousand Winters, as if red silk ribbons had been tied to the blade.

'That sword is greater,' the monk said, pointing at Gentle Hands. 'The other is a brutal sword, good only for killing, and indiscriminate. It will cut a butterfly as happily as it will sever a head. But this sword' – he gestured again at Gentle Hands – 'is more thoughtful. This is a sword that would hesitate before cutting that which is innocent or undeserving of harsh treatment.'

Muramasa scoffed again and drew Ten Thousand Winters from the stream, sheathing it. 'My master has simply made a sword that is blunt,' he said. 'Anyone could do that.'

At that, Masamune turned suddenly and whipped Gentle Hands round in a circle. The blade passed through the trunk of a great oak tree behind the pair, as if the trunk – which was as wide as two men standing side by side – were made of water. Masamune sheathed the sword, then walked to the other side of the tree and, very gently, pushed. It fell over the stream with a loud crash, its trunk neatly severed. The monk bowed, and used the new bridge to cross to the side where the two sword smiths stood, one a little more flushed than the other.

Lord Oda blinked, and Ito realized that he had taken too long to reply. A sword of peace, or a sword of blood? If he said 'peace' he would be true to the legend about his master and his master's own master, for had not Masamune won the contest with his sword of peace? And had not Muramasa changed his style of construction in the years following, to make his blades more careful? Yet Oda was a fearsome general and known for his martial prowess. He might be insulted to be given a peaceful weapon. Worse, though, would be to call it a blade of blood and risk insulting the lord even more, for as a Zen Buddhist, Oda was supposed not to kill anyone.

Ito took a deep breath. 'It is neither, my lord. That is to say, it is either. Whatever you wish it to be, this sword will become. If you wish it to kill, it will kill. If you wish it to be just, it will be just.' Ito was a craftsman, and saw no point in lying about his skill. 'It is the greatest sword I ever made.'

Oda grunted and lifted the blade, examining the whole length of gleaming steel. He hefted it and gave it a tentative spin in his hand. Then, without warning, he turned and decapitated the prisoner standing in the middle of the room. The man's body crumpled to the ground. His head hit the floor and bounced, surprisingly loudly, to the wall. When it stopped, the eyes were facing Ito. The sword smith saw them blink several times, even with the head separated like that from the body. Blood gushed from the neck. A thin line of drool hung from the lower lip. Then the eyelids froze and the open, staring eyes fixed Ito with a look that was part shock and part acceptance.

'Sharp enough,' said Oda. 'How much do you want for it?'

Ito looked round wildly, yet everywhere he looked the eyes of the severed head seemed to follow him, challenging him to come up with an acceptable reply.

This was bad.

The retainer, when he had come, had agreed on a price, of course. This was why Ito was stumped. He had thought the deal was done.

An architect in Oda's employ, hired to rebuild a shrine on the Oda land, had been stabbed to death when he'd requested an insultingly high price. A merchant had been killed for offering Oda a silk kimono for his wife that had previously been offered to Yoshimoto's concubine.

If Ito asked for too much, he would be considered grasping, and Oda would consider it his right to demand his life. He was no samurai, either, so could expect no second to take his head. Yet if he asked for too little, he might insult the lord by suggesting that he couldn't afford the best, by undervaluing the perfect sword that even now was spinning in the daimyo's hands.

What to do? There were only two choices, and both were impossible. He had to think of the exact right price, one that would match the quality of the sword but not appear greedy... and one that would please his wife. Ito had it in mind to buy her a beautiful painted fan, of the type that she had admired on their last visit to Edo.

'You're wasting my time,' said Oda.

Ito wasn't even aware of the sword cutting through his neck, and the first he knew that it had been severed was when he was suddenly looking up from the ground at his headless body, which fell first to its knees, then toppled forward and hit the stone floor with a soft poof sound.

There had been a third choice all along, Ito realized before everything went black. He should have answered more quickly, naming the first price that had entered his head.

CHAPTER 13

T ARO WATCHED THROUGH the twin slits as the palanquin turned onto the road for the mountains. Soon they were skirting Nagoya's hill, the road almost seeming to turn away deferentially from the majesty of the castle, and the formidable reputation of Lord Oda.

After a short distance they crossed a stone bridge over a swift-flowing river. Next to them walked an ox, being jostled along by a peasant in a wide-brimmed hat.

Suddenly they stopped. In front of them were two richly dressed samurai, each heavily armed and bearing the Oda *mon* on their armour.

The checkpoint.

The larger of the two guards spoke in a loud, deep voice. 'Halt. State your business.'

Shusaku supported the front end of the palanquin. He bowed as best as he could. 'My master bears a message from the shogun to Lord Oda.' He paused for the gravity of this to sink in. 'It is *quite* urgent.'

The samurai – his features were long and fine, and he wore a tight topknot that pulled the skin of his face back to accentuate the sharp teeth and thin lips – nodded curtly. 'I am quite sure it is. Indeed, we have been expecting you. All the same, we will have to take a look inside and verify that your master is... accounted for.' He looked Shusaku up and down. 'I see that your face is marked. We live in dangerous times, you know. There are vicious people about. Disgruntled *ronin*. Angry peasants. Ninjas. For all I know, you could be a man of... limited scruples. You may even have kidnapped Lord Oda, and have him stashed in that palanquin. And it wouldn't do if I let that pass, would it?' He laughed, to show that he was joking, but his eyes stayed cold and hard.

Taro pulled back from the eyeholes. Had this man seen through their disguise?

But Shusaku only echoed the samurai's laugh. 'Please don't confuse me for a peasant. My master's elevated class excuses him from this kind of irritation. You will let us past.'

The samurai bowed. 'Ordinarily I would agree. However, the order to search comes from Lord Oda himself, and he is of a *sufficiently elevated* class to impose whatever he wills. Besides, it will be a matter of a moment. The ambassador we have been expecting is a grown man. The criminal we seek is too young to shave. I imagine that even men of our class can tell the differ-ence.' He put a strong accent on the words 'our class', and Taro could feel the tension and violent potential in the air.

Taro tried to control his heartbeat. *They're going to look inside*, he thought. *And then we'll be done for*.

Shusaku sighed, then jerked his head back to indicate the palanquin. 'Very well. But please don't detain us too long.'

What? Taro sat back as far as he could in the seat, as if he could disappear into the fabric.

The samurai motioned for his companion to go forward. This man – his features were coarser, suggesting a lower rank –

stepped towards the curtained door of the palanquin. Taro, thinking of nothing else to do, pushed the scroll out through the curtain, hoping that the man would see the seals and leave it at that, satisfied.

It almost worked.

The scroll was taken from Taro's hand, then returned to it. He allowed himself for a moment to hope, but the curtain began to twitch open and—

'Balance, Hiro!' said Shusaku, using the signal they had agreed on before.

As instructed, Hiro dropped his end of the palanquin. Taro fell backward, striking his head on the wooden board of the vehicle, cursing. The samurai called out in surprise.

Taro heard the man step up to Hiro. 'What's wrong, man?' he demanded. There was a pause. 'What's that you're looking at?' Then there was a cry of disgust. 'Gods, it's a finger! What the—'

'Hey,' said the higher-ranking samurai. 'What's going on here?'

Taro heard Shusaku say, in a calming voice, 'All is well, guard-*san*. My friend here is a leper, that is all. I thought his condition was improving, but... Well, you see how his face is wrapped. It is a terrifying sight when that scarf comes off. Boy,' he continued, his voice modulating from placatory wheedling to indulgent reprimand. 'Please pick up your finger and apologize to the samurai for startling them.'

The higher-ranking samurai grunted with revulsion. 'A leper? And you use such a man to carry an important official?'

'Charity,' said Shusaku, 'is of great importance to the ambassador.'

Taro pressed his face once more to the crack and saw the samurai guards stepping back, wary of infection.

The leader gestured irritably. 'Be on your way,' he said gruffly. 'I don't want you leaving body parts all over my bridge.'

Taro felt the rear end of the palanquin lift into the air, and then they were moving again. He looked through the eyeholes. They were passing between rice paddies, over which peasants' cottages stood on stilts. It was drawing close to the annual *obon* festival, when the spirits of the dead walked the earth, and many of the cottages already bore blue lanterns, swinging in the breeze.

This was the time of year when the spirits were able to leave, for one week only, the confines of the lower realms of samsara, known collectively as *annoyo* – the realm of hungry ghosts, or any of the other circles of hell. For this one week they could return to their families, and the *obon* lamps would guide their way. Then they could feast on the offerings of rice that were left for them, assuage for a short time their hunger, and perhaps progress further to enlightenment in a subsequent life, thanks to the prayers of their family.

When the dead of the family returned, these lanterns would help light their way home.

'We must find somewhere to shelter,' said Shusaku, turning as he supported the weight of the palanquin's front bars. 'We've lost time, with waiting for the ambush.'

'All right,' said Taro. The light was already spreading on the tips of the now closer mountains, as if they had been dipped in gold.

'Have you seen how many cottages are not displaying *obon* lights?' the ninja asked.

'Yes,' said Taro. He *had* noticed it, actually, and found it strange. Only a few blue lanterns had glowed in the windows of the villages they'd passed.

'Many peasants were killed in the battles against Lord Yoshimoto. Many others were forced out of these areas.'

'My parents included,' said Hiro.

'Ah, I'm sorry,' said Shusaku. 'Anyway, we should be able to find an abandoned hut without too much difficulty.'

Just then, Taro saw a flicker of movement over to the right. Bushes lined the side of the road, obscuring the fields from view. 'What was—'

The words stopped in his mouth, as two black-clad figures stepped out of the undergrowth in front of them, blocking the road. They wore masks that covered their faces, all but the eyes – and their swords were short and businesslike in their strong-looking hands.

'Didn't I say,' said the one on the left, 'when we saw those two eyes bobbing along in the air before that palanquin there, that we may have happened upon our quarry?'

'You did,' said the other man, running his fingertip along the blade of his sword. 'Your powers of discernment remain un-dimmed by your recent bludgeoning.'

'Thank you. You, too, appear unaffected in your mental capacities by the painful evisceration you only this night received.' He snapped his wrist to make a heavy wooden stick drop from his sleeve into his hand.

Shusaku stammered. 'We're just – just travellers… We have no money.' Taro couldn't tell if he was really scared, or just feigning terror to buy time.

The ninja on the right laughed, palming a dagger into his left hand, and turned to his companion. 'Oh, our master will forgive us *now*, don't you think?'

His friend nodded, flipping his heavy stick.

The ninja who had spoken first pointed his sword at Shusaku. 'You *gutted* me. From behind! It took me an age to push my entrails back inside.'

'You bashed my head in with a rock,' said the other. 'Luckily, I was ugly to begin with. But it *hurt*.'

Taro stared at the hooded figures. *These are the men Shusaku killed when he was fighting invisibly.* Shusaku was not wearing his mask now, and so to a ninja his eyes would appear to hover in the air. *Yet they live. How is that possible?* He had seen Shusaku kill them, with his own eyes.

Taro felt behind him, and his fingers touched the smooth curve of his bow. The string had lost much of its elasticity from the seawater, but the two ninjas were not far away. He held his breath as he held up the bow, nocked an arrow, and aimed through the eye slit. The point of the arrow wavered over the closest ninja's chest, as if it were marking him out, eager to leap into his flesh.

But it's not the arrow marking him out, Taro told himself. *It's you*. He felt his soul withering within him, as he contemplated shooting this man from concealment. But he knew he would do it, to help Shusaku.

'What are you doing here?' Shusaku asked. 'On this road?'

'Sneaking away,' said Sword-and-Stick. 'Our master is a man of iron principles. He would not view our failure with indulgence. Let the others go to him if they like. We are better off alone.'

Sword-and-Dagger hissed at him. 'Enough,' he said.

Taro cursed him. The talkative one may have revealed the name of their employer, given a little more time.

Suddenly Sword-and-Stick sprang forward and, spinning in the air, punched Shusaku in the throat with the end of the stick. Shusaku dropped the palanquin, coughing, and now Taro was looking up at the scene, holding his breath.

The ninja landed and was turning on his foot even as he hit the ground, coming round again with his sword blade glinting –

Then something flew up from Shusaku's waist and burst in front of the attacking ninja's face – one of the little bombs Shusaku carried, packed with gunpowder from China. The ninja screamed as flames ate at his scarf. He spun round, flapping at his face with his sleeves. Shusaku plucked the man's sword from his hand as he flailed ineffectually at the flames, as easily as removing a cherry from a low-hanging branch.

The other ninja fared little better.

With ample time to react, he also had the advantage of approaching Shusaku from the side as Shusaku was occupied with throwing his bomb. That meant that he was able to launch a well-aimed strike with his sharp-looking dagger.

But by the time the blade was in motion, Shusaku had already pirouetted out of the way, leaving the steel to penetrate the wall of the palanquin. Taro fell back, as the point shivered just a hand's breadth from his face.

Outside, the ninja tugged on his knife, trying to free it. Taro closed his eyes for a moment, then fired.

The ninja had of course not anticipated the arrow that sprang forth from the palanquin, as if the vehicle itself wished him harm. His dagger forgotten, he stared at the shaft protruding from his chest. It had not penetrated deeply. Taro had known the string was not strong enough, but as the attacker pulled out the arrow, Shusaku moved liquidly from the side.

The unfortunate ninja's hands still clung to the arrow as his head fell past the slits in the curtain, turning in the air.

Before the head left the shoulders, Shusaku was already moving at the other man. Hiro, too, had rushed forward, when the palanquin fell, and now the big wrestler grabbed the ninja's arms and pinned them behind his back. Sword-and-Stick had managed to put out his scarf, and now it only smouldered, giving off little wisps of grey smoke.

He struggled against Hiro's grip.

Taro dragged himself out of the palanquin, stumbling to his feet at the side of the road. 'Wait!' he shouted to Shusaku, who was advancing on the ninja with his sword twirling in his hand. 'He might know something about who wanted me dead!'

But his words were still forming in his mouth when Shusaku gestured at Hiro to let go, and plunged his sword into the man's heart. The ninja swayed a moment on his feet, as if pinned to the air by the blade, then crumpled to the ground.

Taro put a hand on Shusaku's arm. 'You killed them.'

'This time, yes. I could not risk any less. We should move, right now. Get off the road and into the fields, if we must.'

'But in Minata, then, and on the beach – you didn't kill them?'

'No. A vampire can survive any kind of insult to his body, unless he be decapitated or cut through the heart or exposed to bright sunshine, of course.'

Taro looked at the man's floating eyes. He could see Shusaku's body, clothed in the servant's garb, yet the face was invisible. The effect was disconcerting. 'Yet you let me believe that they were dead. Why didn't you tell me they lived?'

Shusaku's eyes glimmered with what Taro thought might be a smile. 'I didn't tell you they *didn't*. But better that I lie to you, if it forces you to see that sometimes we must be practical, not merciful.' He pointed to the fields that lay glittering in the encroaching grey light of dawn. 'Come on. Look for a hut with no light in the window.'

Taro looked at the ninja, then at Hiro. He nodded, and they left the road, following as Shusaku led the way through shallow reed beds, disturbing frogs that leaped away, croaking. A smell of damp vegetation rose from the waterlogged ground. Luckily for them, the moon was now covered by ragged clouds, and so despite the rapid onset of dawn, their movements were obscured by darkness.

As they skirted what looked like an inhabited village, Taro watched Shusaku. The older man had wrapped his face again, using silk scarves he appeared to have secreted in his clothes, and his dark clothes made him a shadow in the night.

They crept in this manner across a *ri* or more of farmland, and Taro was acutely conscious of the orange light that tinged the mountains – both because of the threat it posed to his physical safety and also because when the sun rose, it would reveal them starkly against this flat, featureless landscape, devoid of woods and concealed animal paths. Anyone looking for them would spot them immediately from the road.

If the sun didn't kill them first.

So it was with a sigh of relief from Taro and Hiro that Shusaku peered through a grimy shoji window of a hut just at the edge of one of the villages. Already they were in the foothills that had seemed so distant from Nagoya, and the ground was less wet underfoot, as rice paddies gave way to orchards and beehives.

'This one,' he whispered, and Taro stood beside him to look into a dust-covered and sparsely furnished hovel, only a couple of tatami mats wide. 'We'll have to hang up cloth in the window, to block out the sunlight. But it will serve for today. As long as the light is not too bright and our skin is covered, we will survive.'

Later, when they had barricaded out the fingers of sunshine as effectively as they could, and were sitting in the corner of the room, Taro put his hand over his heart in the old gesture of sincerity. 'I apologize for questioning your honour,' he said to Shusaku.

The ninja snorted, but Taro could see that his eyes glinted with pleasure. 'It's not the first time it's happened to me,' he said.

'Back in Minata,' said Taro, ignoring the ninja's joking tone. 'You could have killed them, if you'd wanted to. It would have been more practical, as you put it. But you didn't.'

Shusaku leaned back, his hands behind his head. 'I told you I don't kill anyone if I don't have to. Even ninjas. Especially ninjas. We are in a very dangerous business, and our skills mean that occasionally we find ourselves fighting for different sides. Long ago, the founders of our clans laid down a single law – a ninja must never kill another ninja, or even attempt it. To do so is punishable by death.'

'But you just did.'

'Yes, well. That was unavoidable. We must get to the mountains safely. I gave my word of honour that I would keep you alive, and I would not break that word.'

'Yet you talk of honour as if it were a joke,' said Taro.

'No,' replied the ninja. 'I don't mock the notion of honour. The honour of the samurai is no joke. It is lethal. That is why I don't place much faith in the word.' He spoke seriously now.

'I don't understand.'

'Tell me, then,' said the ninja. 'What does the Bushido code of the samurai teach about honour?'

'To be brave. To be loyal. To act as if each moment were your last.'

'Precisely. The heart of honour is to obey, and to die when required. To be loyal to the lord, to the daimyo, to the shogun. Everything else is meaningless. The lords talk about honour, but they wish only for their samurai to submit themselves totally to their authority, to be always prepared to die in their name. They themselves have no honour, only practicality. How did Oda Nobunaga defeat Imagawa Yoshimoto at Okehazama, when he had only three thousand men and Yoshimoto had forty thousand?'

Hiro interrupted. 'He and his men overtook Yoshimoto's army and ambushed them.'

'How?'

Hiro smiled. The story was an old one, and was hugely popular in Taro and Hiro's village and indeed the entire Kanto. 'That night, Lord Oda's samurai set up a false army of straw-headed dummies on the mountain pass, to make Yoshimoto think that they were up there. Then they climbed down into the valley under cover of darkness and concealed themselves in the woods. They hid among the trees, waiting for Yoshimoto's army to take their rest. Soon a storm broke, forcing the enemy into their tents. As the rain fell and the lightning struck, Lord Oda and his men sprang from the trees and killed Yoshimoto's men as they slept, or as they stumbled in disarray. It was a great victory.'

'They slaughtered a superior army as it slept,' said Shusaku. 'It was not a great victory. It was simply a victory of cunning over your so-called honour. They tricked Yoshimoto with their dummies, then they executed him and his men. But did Oda's men question him when he gave the order? Of course not. Honour is different things to different men. To the samurai, it is the code that binds them by unquestionable loyalty to their lord. To the lord, it is a useful tool to exploit their samurai and their peasants. But a lord has no conception of loyalty. A lord is happy to use ninjas to do his dirty work.' He seemed about to say more, then stopped. 'The fact is that Oda's victory was a despicable act of cold-blooded murder. Yet sometimes despicable acts of cold-blooded murder are necessary.'

'It wasn't murder! It was an audacious act by a vastly out-numbered army!' exclaimed Taro. The people of the Kanto were great supporters of Lord Oda's, and Taro saw him in his mind still as the epitome of a samurai, despite the empty villages he had seen, the devastating effects of war on the peasant pop-ulation. 'And anyway, there is honour in victory. Lord Oda won a great rout against an army superior in number. That makes his tactics excusable.'

'Ah,' said Shusaku. 'Now you're learning.'

CHAPTER 14

WHEN NIGHT FELL, they continued westward into the foothills, leaving behind the broad valley, which stretched like a great flat bowl behind them.

Often they passed abandoned huts, and Taro was starting to realize the effects of the expensive wars Lord Oda had fought against Lord Yoshimoto and others. He saw the effects in the cowed population, the lack of young men – most of them killed or recruited by passing armies – and the painful malnutrition of the children. Shusaku had explained that Lord Oda had only recently raised his tax on rice yet again to pay for a new campaign against a minor, rebellious daimyo, and for many peasants this meant handing over their entire crops, leaving them with nothing to eat.

Shusaku led the boys through the woods, following fox or deer trails, keeping constant watch for the wider trails that might indicate human passage. Taro found that his sense of smell was more acute than ever before. In the darkness he could see little, but he was aware of the scent of wild garlic, tree sap, and deer scat.

They paused at an open clearing in which a luxuriant meadow grew, fed by a clear mountain stream. Shusaku pulled up some wild orchids and handed the roots to Hiro, who accepted them gratefully and chewed them as they walked.

'Only one more valley before we reach the village where the abbess lives,' said Shusaku. 'We should arrive tonight.' He stopped to check some tracks in the moss. 'Only a stag,' he said. Then he looked up at the sky. 'You'll like the girls. They will make good allies for you in your coming life.'

'Allies?' said Taro. 'Don't you mean friends?'

Shusaku smiled. 'The two are the same.'

Soon they began to climb quite steeply, and maples and oaks gave way to pines that clutched on to the soil and rock with gnarled old-man fingers. Shusaku began to skirt round the mountain, heading for a narrow pass that led away from the lowlands and into the wilder country of the west. The going was hard. Many times Taro slipped and grazed his knees or palms, and he suspected that this didn't hurt him as much as it did Hiro, who was also prone to falling. Nevertheless, the big wrestler kept going doggedly, never complaining.

Shusaku, of course, leaped nimbly from rock to rock, never losing his balance once.

They crossed the pass round the middle of the night, keeping always against the rock since they had passed out of the tree line and their silhouettes would be visible to anyone even far below.

They followed an easier way down the other side, in the bed of a nearly dry stream, and soon they were in the trees again. The scene was framed now by mountains to the east, and from these began to emanate a pale grey light, as morning crept towards them on its relentless westerly voyage.

As they crept through the forest, their footsteps silent on the mossy ground, Shusaku once again held out his hand and they came to a stop. The ninja made urgent gestures with his hands, instructing Taro and Hiro to hide behind trees. They did so, and saw before them a wide path that cut through the soft, loamy ground and snaked up the hill towards another, wider pass.

Taro turned back and saw Shusaku gesturing for them to get down. He crouched.

A stooped figure appeared on the path, walking towards them. It was an oldish man, though Taro thought his hunched back probably owed more to hard work than to old age. The man walked on till he was facing a large maple tree near the trio's hiding place, then began laboriously to climb it, until he was standing on a wide, low branch and hugging the trunk with his arms.

Taro, Hiro, and Shusaku stayed absolutely quiet while the man felt at the tree trunk. He came to a hole in the tree and shuffled himself round to face it. Then, bracing himself against the tree with his knee, the muscles of his leg trembling, he took a thin taper from his robe. Using what Taro supposed was some smouldering moss, wrapped up in wet leaves to keep it alive, the man lit the taper and held it to the hole. Taro smelled pine smoke.

Gingerly, the man reached into the hole with his free hand, his thigh still shaking alarmingly with the effort of keeping himself upright. He extracted a large honeycomb from the hole, which he dropped into a bag at his waist. Then he climbed down awkwardly from his perch.

Just then, the sound of hoofbeats approached from down the hill. Taro turned to see a small group of samurai, in heavy armour, mounted on impressively large horses. They wore long *katana* at their waists, in ornately decorated *sura* sheaths. As they passed, Taro saw the Oda *mon* embroidered on the men's backs. What were Oda's samurai doing on this path in the early hours of the morning?

Whatever they were doing there, the samurai were magnificent. Taro gazed in admiration at the gleaming metal of their armour, at the gorgeous inlaid lacquer work of their sword sheaths. Unconsciously, he took a step towards the men. Each man wore the full, expensive samurai garb: kimonos stitched with beautiful designs of flowers, birds, and mountains; *nodowas* to shield their throats; *sode* protecting their shoulders. Full, fitted *donakas* guarded their torsos.

'You, peasant,' said one of the leading samurai to the old man, who had frozen by the side of the path and was staring at the sudden apparitions in front of him. Taro stepped back behind the tree. Something about the man's voice frightened him.

The samurai's horse pawed at the ground as if finding it hard to stay still. It gave an impression of barely contained power. The samurai who rode this noble beast was a very thin man, his moustache and beard straggly and greasy. His skin was very pale, and criss-crossed with broken veins, which fluttered weakly. He looked as if he were being consumed from within by small crawling things.

'I said "You, peasant",' the samurai repeated, his tone threatening.

The old man still did not reply, seeming struck dumb by shock. A mountain man like this, Taro thought, would not have seen many fully armed samurai in his life. The old man's mouth flapped open, as he tried to speak.

'What's that in your bag?' asked the samurai.

The old man opened the drawstring and took out the honeycomb. He showed it to the soldiers.

'Ah,' said the samurai. 'Honey, stolen from Lord Oda's forest. Why don't you hand it over? Let's consider it a tax. We've been riding all night, and we could use some sustenance.'

'B-b-but th-this is the open forest. I pay my taxes in rice.' The old man's voice was shaky, his eyes wet with tears.

'The open forest is also Lord Oda's. Would you deny that the province is his to command? Your rice levy is not a tax or a payment, it is simply a giving back of something that belongs already to the lord. Just as you belong to the lord, and just as this forest belongs to the lord, and those bees in that tree just there. You have stolen this honeycomb from Lord Oda.' The samurai leaned down in the saddle and grabbed the honeycomb, which he tossed to one of his companions. 'And to add insult to injury, you fail even to bow to us, your superiors.'

The old man babbled an apology, while bowing low – as low as would be expected even in front of a lord.

But it wasn't good enough for the samurai. 'Lower,' he commanded. The old man knelt.

Taro, watching, felt a sickness in his stomach. For a moment the old man's face flickered and became Taro's father's. In that moment Taro felt a burning moment of pure hatred for Shusaku, who had not prevented his father's death, and who now was doing nothing to help this poor peasant. He began to reach for his bow. But something struck his arm, and he turned to see Shusaku, who was shaking his head vigorously. Taro turned away, ignoring the ninja, and raised his bow once again. He aimed at the leading samurai.

Then Shusaku – who had been the width of two tatami mats away – was suddenly behind him, holding his hands behind his back. He struggled and was about to call out when a scarf was pulled tight over his mouth. Yet his hands were still immobilized behind him. Shusaku must have bound them, somehow, but how had the ninja done it so quickly?

Taro could only watch, his blood boiling, as the samurai humiliated the peasant.

'Lower,' he commanded once again, as the man tried to bow even deeper. He was on his knees by now. 'I am Kenji Kira of the Kira clan, and I would see you eat the dirt at your feet to erase this stain on my honour.'

The old man lowered himself still farther, till he was lying face down on the ground. Kenji Kira laughed, then turned to his men. 'Give me some of that honeycomb,' he ordered. One of the samurai handed it to him, and he sniffed it. 'Hmmm,' he said. 'It smells good. As I'm sure my lord would agree, since the bees and the flowers that made it belong to his ancestral fiefdom.' Kira threw the honeycomb to the ground. 'And now' – he drew his sword with a flourish – 'you die.'

But rather than use the sword on the old man, Kira slid it back into its sheath with a loud *thwock*. 'Wait. Look up, peasant.' The old man looked up. 'Have you seen two boys and an older man pass through here? One of the boys is a leper.'

'N-n-no,' the old man stuttered. 'I'm the only one as comes this way, for the honey. I have a little hut down the hill…'

The thin samurai began to draw his sword again, then slid it back into the sheath, sighing. 'No,' he said. 'I would not sully my sword with the flesh of your kind.' He grabbed the reins with his left hand, turning the horse to ride away. With his right hand he made a sharp, cutting gesture behind his back.

'Oh,' said the old man from the ground, where he had not seen Kira's gesture. 'Oh, thank you, my lord. Thank you for sparing m—'

One of the lower-ranking samurai cut through the man's

neck even as he spoke, and the head as it rolled along the mossy ground continued to utter a wheezy, whistley *eeeee* sound as it finished its final word.

The riders departed.

CHAPTER 15

Shusaku released Taro. 'Don't worry,' said the ninja. 'They're looking for us, but they're going the wrong way.'

Taro broke away. 'You think I'm worried for *myself*?'

'Then what—'

Taro turned away. He didn't want to see the ninja's cowardly face. He thought if he looked at Shusaku he would be sick. 'I'm thinking of this man, who died for no reason.'

'Now you know what the samurai you admire so much are really like,' said Shusaku.

'Really?' asked Taro, still not turning. 'Because he would still be alive if it weren't for you.'

Trembling, Taro walked over to the old man, still not looking back. He kneeled by the corpse and whispered '*Namu Amida Butsu*' eight times, hoping that this prayer to the Buddha of Compassion might help the old man's soul on its way to Sukhavarti, the Pure Land. The man had died suddenly, with no time to prepare himself. He would be lucky not to descend to the realm of the hungry ghosts.

For the past few days Taro had thought only of his parents – of finding his mother, of the pain of his father's loss. He had even started to warm to Shusaku a little, to admire him for doing a little more than would have been expected – giving his mother that pigeon, or how, as they passed through the blighted countryside, the ninja had stopped where an emaciated old woman sat by the road and handed her a coin. When Taro had commented on it, Shusaku had put a finger to his lips and shushed him. 'Don't go telling anyone,' he'd said. 'I might lose the respect of my fellow ninjas. We are an amoral sort, you know. Assassinations, secret missions, murder. A man has a reputation to uphold.'

Now, though, Taro saw in his mind only the old man falling.

Then, intruding on his consciousness, slow and warm as dawn, he began to notice the smell. Earthy and rich, with undertones of iron. It was the smell of life leaving a body, and it was delicious. He leaned forwards. What harm could one taste do? He knew it was bad karma to disturb the dead but…

As if it came from another world, he heard Hiro say to Shusaku, 'He was looking for us. And he wore the *mon* of Lord Oda.'

'Yes,' said Shusaku. 'I think they must have found the men from the palanquin. Lord Oda… doesn't like challenges to his power.'

'They're going to a lot of trouble to hunt us down,' said Hiro.

Shusaku grunted. 'It would seem so.' His tone did not invite further comment. Taro snapped upright and blinked. He looked down and saw a dead man again, not a meal.

Taro was surprised when Shusaku knelt beside him and began reciting the same prayer to Amida Buddha. Taro stood, tears welling up in his eyes. 'Why did you stop me from helping? We could have saved him.'

'Because we would have had to kill the samurai,' Shusaku replied, his voice as calm as ever. 'And a missing patrol would have raised suspicion, forcing us to kill whoever came looking for *them*. And what if one of them got away, to tell Oda that you live, still?' He clicked his tongue. 'Better that we keep you hidden, that you be thought dead, than have to kill all those men. And who says a farmer is worth more than a soldier? It is only your head full of romance and honour that tells you so. The leader, Kira, was cruel, I'll admit, but I would bet you that the others are only ordinary boys, far from home and without anyone to guide them. So which would you rather on your conscience – one dead farmer or six dead soldiers?'

'I would rather neither,' said Taro. Above the tops of the pines, a cloud moved to uncover the moon, causing a dull light to glow. It suffused the old man's corpse and the flowers, making the scene eerily beautiful.

'That is not your choice,' replied the ninja. 'We are not in a *monagatori* tale here, boy. Leave an old man to die, so as not to have to kill many more. That is the best we can do.'

Taro nodded. But he didn't agree. The best they could do was better than that, and he was going to find a way to achieve it. He would find his mother, and he would avenge his father.

And then he would go looking for those who preyed on the weak, and he would make them pay.

CHAPTER 16

Cلاحات LOUDS PARTED OVER the waning moon, illuminating the world with dull light.

Taro was growing to enjoy this itinerant life. His muscles were taut from walking, and the journey gave him a sense of purpose he had never before experienced. Shusaku pointed now to smoke, rising on the other side of a clump of trees. 'That is the village where the abbess lives. We'll stay there for a day or two. Then, from there, the mountain where I live is only a night's walk.'

Despite knowing that once they reached the mountain they would with luck learn where his mother had hidden, Taro couldn't help feeling a guilty pang of disappointment. He loved life in the open countryside. The blood of a rabbit sang in his veins, from yesterday's meal, not enough to tide him for long, but enough that hunger didn't stab his stomach; the land beneath his feet was springy, seeming to want to help him on his way.

As they approached the little village, they had no choice but to step out from the trees and onto the road, but they had left Kenji Kira far behind and travelling in the opposite direction. Shusaku was confident that they could enter the village safely –

and anyway, they needed a place to stay for a while before going on to his mountain home. Taro needed new string for his bow, and all of them needed new clothes. Taro was still dressed in the too-long trousers and robe of the ambassador whose palanquin they had stolen.

As they passed the first houses, Taro looked round at the blue lanterns. Where the plain round Nagoya had been half-emptied of people, this village seemed warm and welcoming. Smoke rose from the little houses, all of them seeming inhabited. *Gaku* charms had been hung on the eaves of the houses to ward off bad spirits, and the charms chimed softly in the breeze.

As they had walked, *obon* season had begun in earnest. In every window burned a light to guide departed loved ones home. Taro felt a pang of longing for his old life, for his mother, who always sought his help in collecting and arranging the food for the spirits, laying out bowls of rice on the *shoryodana* shelf, and lighting the *obon* lamp for the first time.

He wondered if anyone would light a lamp for his father in the hut by the shore in Shirahama.

Shusaku crept towards the outlying houses, navigating by the light of the lamps – these paper lights guiding a different spirit from the ones intended, as he slipped into the village.

Taro and Hiro followed. Their senses were improving all the time, and they could now walk almost as soundlessly as the ninja. Then a snatch of melody carried on the night air towards them – a girl, singing the *obon* song.

> *Obon* is a joyous season!
> On this day my beloved ones
> Who have departed—
> Even they return to this place.

Shusaku paused, listening to the voice. 'That's Yukiko,' he said. He led Taro and Hiro down a side alley and to a door set into a wall. Here the singing was louder, and Taro could hear another girl joining in. 'And that's Heiko,' said Shusaku. 'Her sister.' Glancing up and down the street to check that no one was watching, he took the long black scarf from a fold of his kimono, and retied his mask.

'I thought you said you knew these people,' said Taro.

'I do. But they don't know I'm tattooed. It's a long story.' Shusaku finished arranging the folds of black fabric, then pushed open the door gently.

Taro looked in to what seemed a scene from an *ukiyo-e* painting, and couldn't help letting out a soft gasp. In the moonlight the garden could have been a dream. A miniature landscape of pool and stream and trees, it seemed perfect and glowing in the bluish light, and Taro felt that if he stepped forward it might vanish, revealing itself to be nothing more than an illusion painted on the air by a playful spirit. Suffused with the light of the moon, the scene was also lit by candlelight that shone from inside the house, throwing a soft glow through tall shoji panels onto the grass and moss.

In the centre of the garden a heron stood very still in the middle of an ornamental pond, as if admiring its reflection, cast clearly onto the water by the moon. Across the pond a weeping willow touched the soft grass with its fronds. At the far end of the garden rose a rock garden that resembled mountainous scenery, even down to small bonsai pine trees.

Between the mountains and the pool ran a stream, its waters gurgling quietly. A bridge arced over it, elegantly curved, and on the bridge stood the slender silhouettes of three women – or rather, Taro realized, a woman and two girls.

As Taro watched, the girls knelt by the stream. They held oblong lanterns, windowed by shoji paper, each side painted brightly with a different primary colour to represent the four elements. The *shoryo-nagashi*, able to carry messages to the dead. Inside the lanterns candles flickered, casting coloured light on the cold water of the stream, and the mossy forest floor.

'I call on the spirits of my father and mother, and all un-resolved karma, to accept these messages,' said one of the girls, her voice a little choked. She placed her lamp in the stream and it floated, spinning, away. Speaking the same words, the other girl placed her lamp in the water, and it raced after its companion.

Taro felt a wave of pity. *They're sending* shoryo-nagashi *to their parents*, he thought. *They must be orphans.*

Having waited for the floating lanterns to spin away down the stream, and out of the garden through a hole in the wall, Shusaku stepped forward into the garden. The heron turned its head to look at him, then launched itself, ungainly yet somehow graceful, into the air.

Taro and Hiro followed Shusaku into the garden, as the taller of the girls turned and stifled a gasp. 'A ninja!'

Shusaku put a finger to his lips. 'It's me, Shusaku,' he hissed.

'Uncle Shusaku!' said the girl, no quieter than before.

Both girls left the bridge and ran over, and Taro saw that the one who had spoken – she seemed to be the elder – was slim and tall, with an intelligent, kind face. Her sister was more muscular, her hair shorter and her face more guarded.

Shusaku closed the door behind him as the girls walked over, followed by the most beautiful woman Taro had ever seen.

Shusaku bowed. 'Abbess,' he said.

'Shusaku. You have returned.' The woman's voice was

neutral, betraying no pleasure or pain. 'But why do you wear the mask in my home?'

Shusaku shook his head. 'I can't explain right now. Later.'

Taro stared. Could this really be the 'old woman' Shusaku had spoken of? She was so elegant, so smooth-skinned, so graceful…

But then the woman beckoned him forward, and Taro saw that her face was lined with fine wrinkles, and her hair was not dyed by the moonlight but was actually white.

The woman turned to Shusaku. 'The boy. It is he? It is the—'

'Yes,' said Shusaku, cutting her off. Taro wondered what she had been about to say about him. 'Is it so obvious?' he asked. 'How did you know it was not the other?' He indicated Hiro, who fidgeted, squirming with embarrassment.

The woman looked at Hiro, and laughed. 'No. He is a fine boy, but…' – she turned back to Taro – 'destiny clings to this one like smoke.' She examined Taro, then turned back to Shusaku. 'You have made him a vampire,' she said. It was a statement, but it was also a question.

'Yes,' Shusaku almost sighed. 'It was unavoidable.'

The younger girl – Yukiko – sucked in a sharp breath, frowning at Taro. He took a step backward, seeing the hostility in that look, but she composed her face into a smile, and he relaxed.

The woman nodded slowly. 'If you say so, then it must be so.' She looked at Taro. 'Later I will read his fortune. It should be interesting. In the meantime perhaps you had better tell me why you have come.'

'We needed a safe place to stay.'

'You will always have that here,' said the woman. 'But your mission was only to save the boy. Why bring him with you?'

'Things became… complicated. They sent many ninja against him. I had to turn him to save him.'

'So you said.' She spread her hands. 'Well, you're always welcome here, as I said. We have food and we have fresh clothes, and rooms to sleep where the sunlight cannot enter. Stay as long as you like. The girls will be pleased to spend some time with their uncle and protector.'

Shusaku nodded, then looked at the taller girl. 'Heiko. It is a pleasure to see you again.' He turned to the other. 'Yukiko. You have grown.'

'That is what girls do, is it not?' said the girl. She was pretty despite her more athletic build, and had a cheeky look about her.

'I suppose it is,' said Shusaku, smiling. Then he turned to Taro and Hiro, introducing them to the girls. Yukiko gave Taro a warm smile as she bowed to him, and he thought he must have imagined that sharp look when Shusaku had revealed that he was a vampire.

'We should talk alone for a moment,' said the abbess, putting a hand on Shusaku's arm. 'The young people can get to know one another.' She led the ninja into the house, leaving Taro and Hiro with the two girls.

'You don't *look* very important,' said Yukiko to Taro.

'I'm sorry?' he replied.

'Shusaku must think you're important, if he's already turned you. Usually people have to go to the mountain and train before they get to be ninjas.' Her words were tinged with a hint of bitterness.

'I was dying.'

She sniffed, and then her shoulders relaxed a little. 'Really?'

'Yes,' said Hiro. 'He was run through with a sword.'

'Well,' said Heiko, putting a hand on her sister's shoulder, 'in that case I'm glad Shusaku turned you. It would have been a shame if you had died before we met you.' She smiled.

'Thank you,' said Taro. 'And anyway, I'm not a ninja. Not yet, anyway.'

Yukiko looked him up and down, her gaze lingering on the point where his too-long kimono puddled on the floor. 'I have to admit you don't look the part,' she said, a touch of amusement entering her voice now.

'Yes,' said Heiko, a smile playing on her elegant features. 'Where *did* you get that kimono?'

Taro felt acutely conscious now of the absurd clothes swamping his body. 'I… borrowed it.'

'That means he stole it,' said Yukiko. 'Maybe he will make a good ninja, after all.'

DON'T WORRY ABOUT Yukiko,' said Heiko to Taro as they sat in the room that overlooked the garden. Occasionally, from óutside, came the sound of Hiro and Yukiko's wrestling. 'She wants so badly to be turned, but she likes you even if she mocks you – I can tell.'

It had been several incense sticks since they had arrived, and Taro had come to like both sisters, though Yukiko still seemed cautious of him, and every now and then he had seen her looking at his elongated vampire teeth.

Heiko, the elder, was tall and willowy, with pale skin and enormous eyes. He felt a little bashful in her company. Yukiko was shorter than her sister, and younger, with an impish smile. She was also stronger, with a muscular physique that reminded Taro of Hiro. Already she had attached herself to Taro's big friend, and had spent most of the time discussing holds with him, play-fighting, and exchanging tips for unbalancing an opponent. To Taro's surprise, Yukiko had even challenged Hiro to a wrestling match, and the pair had been fighting ever since. Taro wasn't used to girls and boys fighting, but Heiko had assured him that ninjas made no distinctions – a woman could scale a wall and slit a target's throat just as well as a man.

And besides, Yukiko kept winning.

'And you?' said Taro. 'You don't want to be turned?'

Heiko dipped her brush in the pot and drew a series of deft strokes across the paper. She had explained that Shusaku favoured calligraphy as an exercise for swordplay, and though Taro had initially been surprised that this scholarly pursuit should be considered a martial training, he could see now the way that Heiko's rapid hand movements – the brush dancing back and forth – could serve just as well to impel a sword.

She held up the parchment, then crumpled it up and threw it aside. Taro couldn't see what had been wrong with it. 'I will be a ninja,' she said. 'It's what I have always trained for. But I'm in no hurry to give up being a girl. To stop eating food, and live on human blood.' She made a face, then put her hand to her mouth. 'Sorry,' she said. 'No offence.'

'I wouldn't have chosen it either,' said Taro. He had drunk the pig blood that Heiko had given him – she and Hiro and Yukiko had eaten soup – and though it had restored his strength, he had dug his nails into his palms as the warm, slippery blood had run down his throat.

More pleasant by far had been the bath he and Hiro had taken, stretching their aching limbs in a tub of very hot water that the girls had run for them, before retiring, giggling, to another room. Taro hadn't bathed in hot water since he and his mother had gone to the *onsen* springs near Shirahama, a few days before her death, and he had enjoyed luxuriating in the bath while a small part of him, deep inside, had remained cold. He knew that it would not warm until he could see his mother again, could reassure himself that she was safe.

New clothes had been laid out for him and Hiro when they'd got out of the bath, and now Taro was sitting cross-legged on the floor in a kimono that, mercifully, was just about the right size. Taro hugged his knees, happy to be once again warm and clean. From outside, he heard Yukiko say, 'Tell you what, I'll go easy on you. If you can beat me one round out of five, I'll let you be my servant for the rest of the year. You can bring me tea and refreshments.'

Hiro tutted. 'Big talk for a weed like you.' But he was panting, and Taro smiled. Yukiko was obviously a fearsome opponent.

'She won't break him, will she?' he asked Heiko.

She grinned. 'No. But he may be sore for a while. Be glad you're in here with me. A bit of writing isn't likely to get you hurt.' She twirled the brush in her hand, then dipped it into the ink and began drawing the kanji character again.

'What does it say?' asked Taro.

'It says Shusaku. I intend to give it to him as a present. And to show how I have progressed.'

Taro nodded. 'He'll be pleased.'

'I hope so.'

'Is he… your uncle?' said Taro. He was sure Shusaku was not the girls' father, but his demeanour towards them was affectionate and protective, as if he stood in some relationship of familial authority towards them.

'No!' said Heiko. 'He saved our lives, when we were very young. He had just become a vampire himself. Before that, he was a samurai.'

Taro stared. 'A samurai? Shusaku?'

'Yes.' She held up the brush. 'How many ninja teach calligraphy, do you think?'

Taro rocked back on his heels. He couldn't imagine Shusaku being anything other than a solitary ninja, creeping round the landscape in darkness. He couldn't picture him on horseback, wearing armour, bearing a *katana*. 'But why would he become a ninja instead?' he asked.

'It wasn't his choice. He was turned to save his life, like you.'

'Turned? Who by?'

Heiko drew the brush across the page with a flourish, then smiled at the character she had drawn. 'This one will do.' She set it aside. Then she leaned a little closer to Taro, as if to impart a secret. 'He's never spoken of it. But the abbess says that it was for love.'

'He became a vampire for love?'

'In a manner of speaking. It seems that he fell in love with a ninja girl, and she with him. But he was injured in a great battle, and she could save his life only by changing him. Like a love story from a poem, isn't it? Of course, it all ended tragically too, just like a poem.'

'Why, what happened to her?' asked Taro

'She was killed.'

'*Killed?*' Gods, poor Shusaku. That explained why he had never mentioned any of this.

'Yes, a samurai killed her in battle, when she was with Shusaku.'

Taro nodded slowly. A samurai. Of course. It explained so much about his ninja rescuer's attitude towards the warrior class.

Just then Hiro and Yukiko tramped heavily into the room, smiling. 'I'm not sure if I want to be a ninja,' said Hiro, continuing a conversation from outside.

'But you should!' said Yukiko. Her eyes gleamed. 'Uncle Shusaku has already taught us some elements of the discipline. It's great. Well, not the meditation. That's boring. But the sword-fighting and the staff... oh, and the *shurikens*! I think when I'm a real ninja the *shurikens* will be my favourite weapon for killing with. We practised once on dead pigs, and when the throwing star hits the meat – *thwock* – it's such a satisfying sound!'

Heiko tutted. 'You would do better to concentrate on the more elegant disciplines. Lock-picking. Calligraphy.'

Yukiko scoffed. 'Calligraphy leads to madness and watering eyes. And anyway, careful and elegant doesn't save your life if someone is trying to kill you. Imagine if Shusaku had come to our rescue with a brush when we were babies. He'd have been slaughtered.'

Taro stared. He had never in his life heard a young woman talk so casually of violence. But Yukiko narrowed her eyes, and he looked down, realizing he was being rude.

'Shusaku rescued you when you were only babies?' he asked, ignoring the playful argument between the two girls.

'Oh, yes,' said Yukiko. 'We grew up in Lord Oda's domain. Our parents were killed by Yoshimoto's army. Shusaku found us when he was on a mission. We were hiding under the doorstep of a pleasure house in winter, shivering against the cold. Some bandits were hiding out in there, and Shusaku had been hired to kill them. But as he went inside…'

'I heard the crying of young children,' continued Shusaku, entering the room ahead of the abbess. Taro had the sense that this was an oft-told story. 'And so I peered under the step. There were a toddler and a baby, the one holding the other, both weeping with terror. So…'

'He picked us up, walked through the door with one of us under each arm, and killed the bandits using only his feet,' concluded Heiko. Taro noticed to his surprise that she was blushing.

'Well, that's not quite true,' said Shusaku. 'I bit out the throat of one of them.'

Taro looked at the ninja, thinking how little he knew the man still. He'd thought he was only a ninja – a dishonourable assassin – and now it turned out he had been a samurai, and he spent his time rescuing babies from bandits.

Shusaku walked over to the writing desk. 'Heiko. I see you're working on your calligraphy.'

Heiko presented him with the drawing of his name, and he smiled. 'It's beautiful. You have made much improvement.'

Heiko beamed with pride. But then she looked quizzically at the ninja. 'You still wear your mask.'

'Yes. I ought to tell you about that.'

'Are you injured?' said Yukiko. 'Burned?'

Taro looked at her, puzzled. 'It's just his tattoos,' he said.

'Tattoos?' asked Heiko, just as puzzled, and Taro remembered that the girls didn't know about them.

'Taro's right,' said Shusaku. Slowly he unwrapped the black scarf that concealed his face. As it came off, Heiko gasped. She ran to him, studying every detail of his face, and Taro almost wished that he could see it – could see the writing covering the ninja's skin.

All he saw was the eyes.

Then, shocking Taro, Heiko burst into tears, and ran from the room. The abbess reached out a hand to stop her, but Heiko jagged to the side with surprising speed and grace – in that instant Taro saw that to consider her more studious and still than her sister would be a mistake – and disappeared through the door.

'See?' said Yukiko. 'I told you calligraphy leads to madness and watering eyes.'

CHAPTER 18

H EIKO'S EYES WERE still puffy and red, but the abbess
had calmed her down, and now they were all gathered again in
the main room, Shusaku standing with his arm round Heiko.

'I'm sorry,' he said. 'It must have come as a shock.'

She touched his face. 'Why did you do it?' she asked. 'Two
months ago your skin was clear.'

Taro was as amazed as she was. Shusaku had done this only
two months ago? He had thought the ninja had always been
tattooed.

Shusaku sighed. 'It is the Heart Sutra. It protects me from
other ninjas, makes me invisible.'

'I know what it *does*,' said Heiko. 'You told me the story of
Hoichi yourself.' She sounded angry.

'Ah, yes. Of course.' Shusaku's eyes looked pained.

'I would have thought you would have thought twice, given
his example, about undertaking such a foolish course of action,'
said Heiko. She shook her head. She looked angry and upset,
and Taro felt that there was something he was missing here.
Who was Hoichi, and what did he have to do with Shusaku's
tattoos?

Now Yukiko stepped forward, glaring at Shusaku. Unlike her

sister, she remained composed, but Taro could tell that she was just as angry. 'What,' she said, 'could possibly have been so important that you were willing to cover your whole body in tattoos in order to pass unnoticed among other ninja? You realize, of course, that you will never be able to return to samurai life now?'

'I left samurai life behind a long time ago,' said Shusaku.

'That's not the point,' said Yukiko. 'The point is the *risk* you took. Why did you do it?'

But Shusaku only looked at Taro, and Taro realized with a silent groan why the ninja had done what he had done. He looked at Shusaku's floating eyes. 'You did this to rescue me, didn't you? You knew you would have to fight many ninja. You wanted to be able to turn invisible.'

Shusaku nodded. 'Yes.'

'Gods,' said Taro. He felt as though the ground were trembling beneath his feet, no longer able to hold him. 'But the pain… tattooing your eyelids and your face… You went through that for me? To save *me*? What could possibly make me so important?'

Shusaku spread his hands. 'Our enemies were willing to send dozens of ninja to kill a single boy. That alone is proof enough to me of your importance.'

'Perhaps,' said Yukiko, 'you should have just let them kill him, if they wanted to so badly.'

'Yukiko!' said Heiko.

'Perhaps,' said Shusaku in a conciliatory tone. 'But what is done is done. And now I'm hoping that your guardian will tell Taro's fortune. I believe it will support my belief that he will be crucial in the coming war.'

'What war?' said Hiro.

'The one that the daimyos will soon be fighting,' said Shusaku, 'to decide who will be the next shogun.'

'We already have a shogun. He's only a boy.'

'Yes, exactly. Boys are so fragile, so easy to kill. Most of them, anyway,' added Shusaku, with an ironic bow to Taro.

'No one will allow another war,' said Heiko. 'The one against Yoshimoto was so terrible, it would be madness to contemplate another.'

'Well, let us hope that is true,' said Shusaku. 'In the meantime we should try what we can to look into the future.' He turned to the abbess. 'I presume you will consent to look into the Tao for us? Then tomorrow evening we will leave you and continue on our way.'

'Of course,' said the white-haired woman. 'Allow me just to gather my things.' From the edges of the room she brought soft pillows, which she arranged on the tatami mats. Taro lowered himself gratefully onto one, and saw Hiro do the same. Shusaku remained standing, always alert. The two girls sat down together, whispering to each other. Taro could not hear what they said.

The old woman then went to the corner of the room and lit a small fire under a teapot that hung from the rafters. She lit sticks of incense that were placed all round the room. When the tea had boiled, she brought it over, and beckoned to Taro.

As he stepped forward, she smiled and took him by the arm, peering into his eyes. 'Ah, boy,' she said, 'you are set for greatness. Even thus, when I am awake, and separated from the Tao, I see it all about you. It lies on you and sets you apart, like the clothes of high office that you wear now.' She paused. 'Only your destiny fits you far better.'

Taro followed her glance to the arms of his kimono. It was not as vastly oversize as the ambassador's had been, but his hands nevertheless disappeared in the long, wide sleeves.

Then the abbess poured herself a cup of fragrant tea from the pot, but did not offer any to anyone else. She sat back on her heels in front of the sand tray and began to chant.

Taro watched her, curious. Suddenly he jumped – the woman's eyes had rolled back into her head, exposing only the whites, as when a whale rolls over and shows its belly.

She began to write on the sand with the metal rod. She wrote with a flourish, composing only a handful of characters, then gently put the rod down on the floor. Her eyes rolled back to their original position. She looked down at the message she had written and gasped.

'You are not surprised?' she said to Taro.

'He doesn't read,' said Shusaku, stepping forward so as to see the writing. He breathed out slowly.

'Astonishing,' said the woman. 'No wonder they took no risks in order for him to be killed.' She stood, her legs creaking audibly.

'What does it say?' asked Taro.

Shusaku looked down at the box of sand. 'It says, "This boy will be shogun".'

CHAPTER 19

S HOGUN?' SAID HIRO. 'Very funny. Come on, let's go.' He stood as if to leave.

' "The abbess never lies,' said Shusaku. 'She cannot. When she enters her trance, she is one with the Tao. She sees what our eyes cannot.'

'Well, *my* eyes can't see Taro being shogun,' said Hiro. 'He's just the son of a peasant and an ama diver.'

'The son of a peasant?' said Yukiko incredulously. 'And he gets to be a vampire before me? I've been part of the ninja world since I was a baby!'

'Shh,' said Heiko absently, but she was staring at Taro with mingled wonder and suspicion.

The fortune-teller was also looking at Taro curiously. 'Your mother was an ama?'

'*Is* an ama,' he replied. Or was she telling fortunes again? Was his mother dead already? 'She is still alive, isn't she?'

'I have no idea,' said the abbess, and Taro breathed a sigh of relief. 'But she is definitely an ama, nonetheless? This is important.'

'Yes. She is an ama. She dives for shells. Is that so unusual?'

'Actually, yes. But it is interesting for another reason also.'

She turned to Shusaku. 'Do you know the story of the first ama?'

He shook his head, and Taro did too.

'It's an old story,' said the woman. 'I had forgotten about it until just now.' She sat down opposite Taro. 'Would you like to hear it? I think you'd find it interesting.

Taro nodded. 'Please.'

'Very well,' said the woman. 'About a thousand years ago, when men were either brutish warriors or foppish lords, an elegant young man arrived in the coastal village of Shirahama during the *ume* blossoming of the spring, when the flowers of the cherry trees burst into pink mist. Nobody knew whence he had come, or what his purpose was in visiting this washed-out place on the sea, and to begin with, therefore, no one was sure if he was a common warrior or a lord.

'One night, as he was soaking in the *onsen* waters, a serving girl brought him some food, and later the same girl heard him composing a poem out loud. That settled it – any man who enjoyed poetry was obviously a lord and not a samurai.

'But in the village was a girl of common stock and uncommon beauty, the daughter of a simple fisherman, who dived sometimes for snails and seaweed. One day the lord went down to the beach and saw her coming back from one of her dives, carrying a handful of pearls.

'He fell in love instantly.

'Soon after that, they were married, and exactly nine months after that, they had a son whom they named Fusazaki, after a local shrine.

'For many months they were blissfully happy. But then a strange thing happened: increasingly, on his return in the evening from mysterious wanderings, the girl would find her husband crying. *This*, she thought, *is taking the poetic sensibility a little too far.*

'Eventually she could take it no more, and said to her husband, "You must tell me what is wrong. If you really love me, tell me what is upsetting you." And, seeing reflected in his wife's tears the pain he had caused her with his own, he told her the following story, revealing once and for all his noble origin:

'His real name was Tankai, son of Fujiwara Kamatari, the emperor of Japan. When his younger sister had married the T'ang emperor of China, she had sent three invaluable gifts from the mainland, to be buried with her recently deceased grandfather. One was a magic drum that, once struck, produced a continuous and beautiful tone, only returning to silence when covered in nine layers of silk. The second was an ink stone that, when rubbed with a stick, produced an inexhaustible supply of the finest calligraphy ink. And the last was a crystal ball, containing many images of the Buddhas, so that whichever way the ball was turned a Buddha would gaze out at the holder of the object. These objects, so rare and beautiful, would give their grandfather peace in his grave, and help him to a glorious reincarnation.

'But while the ship containing the presents was sailing the Shido sea, the Dragon King of the sea sniffed out the treasures on board as clearly as though they were blood, and decided he had to have them for himself. He immediately asked his ally Susanoo, *kami* of storms, to conjure an enormous thunderstorm, while he himself sent legions of sharks as living battering rams to gouge holes in the sides of the ship. The men fought valiantly, flinging harpoons into the roiling sea, but to their great terror the ship started to limp in the water, and they became convinced they were going to die. Thinking quickly, the captain seized the

Buddha ball and threw it into the sea. And it worked: the winds dropped, the rain stopped, and the sharks melted into the dark water. Even the family was happy: The remaining two gifts still made handsome grave goods for Grandfather Kamatari.

'But Tankai could not stop thinking about the Buddha ball, even though he had only heard it described. Setting off from home, he sailed to the site of the sea battle and dived into the water himself to try to recover the treasure. But the sharks were waiting, and as they closed in for the attack, Tankai's sailors hauled him out of the water, wet and undignified, in a tuna net. From there he sailed back to the mainland, and took to wandering the shores in shame.

'That was how he met his wife.

'Concluding the tale, Tankai gave a deep sigh. But his wife smiled with joy. "I am a diver! I could get the ball back for you."

'Tankai worried. "But what if anything were to happen to you?... I could not forgive myself." He looked at their son, Tankai's sea-wet eyes streaming tears.

'His wife stroked his forehead. "If I can get the ball for you, will you promise to recognize our son as your heir?" Tankai willingly agreed. He could already see the marks of greatness in his son's physiognomy.

'Early the next day they sailed out to sea. The wife tied a long rope round her waist and said, "Pull me up if I pull on this line. That means I have the ball." Her husband nodded and seized the end of the rope. Then, picking up a lead weight and dropping neatly from the side of the boat, his wife disappeared into the depths. Down and down she went, through the cold darkness, silently glad for the rope – since at least that had an end, while the sea seemed infinite in its depth. Eventually she reached a glittering palace of coral, guarded by eight sharks the size of boats, and two ferocious-looking dragons.

'For a moment she hesitated, seeing the indifferent ferocity in the sharks' eyes. But then she called on the Buddhas for protection, and swam into the palace, using her weight to speed her progress through the freezing water. Quickly she grabbed the ball, which had been set on an altar of seaweed in the middle of the great room. But the sharks raced after her, snapping their enormous jaws. One of them caught her a glancing blow with its tail, and another darted in under her arm as she flailed, biting a hole in her chest. Scenting blood, the other sharks went into a frenzy, but Tankai had felt the tug on the rope when the first shark had hit her, and he pulled now with all his strength.

'On the surface, Tankai couldn't believe the length of rope that came up, but eventually his wife's body came over the side, bloody and lifeless and without the ball. He held her in his arms and rocked back and forth, lamenting the loss of his two most precious possessions. Then, with her last breath, his wife whispered, "Look inside my breast."

'Reaching into the hole in her chest where the shark had bitten her, Tankai found the ball hidden inside – his own beloved wife forming the wrapping for the long-lost present. He clutched it, feeling its power.

'Then he threw his wife's body overboard and forgot her. The ball had taken over his senses, you see, and all he could think about was the control it gave him over everything in the world – because the Buddha ball is Buddha's own model of the world, and to possess it is to possess everything on earth and in the air and in the sea, and have them do your bidding.

'Some time later Tankai travelled back to the capital with his son Fusazaki, where he soon became emperor upon the death of his father, and ruled the country easily with the help of the ball.

With it in his hand, he could raise up storms, blot out the sun, cause famines to destroy his enemies' lands, and even – should he wish it – demand the death of the least of the country's creatures, for the ball would show him every detail of the world, down to a fly on a stalk of grass in the next province, and give him power over it.

'Many years passed, and Fusazaki grew to be a fine young man and a worthy heir. But only infrequently did Tankai think of, or mention, his wife and Fusazaki's mother. If ever the boy asked about her, his father would close like a clam, not even confirming if the mother still lived, and only giving the vaguest information about their romance. He never made their son his heir, preferring instead the son of one of his concubines, who for political reasons made a better choice.

'Then one spring, in the month of the rabbit, the boy was playing in the palace gardens under the cherry blossoms. Looking up at the trees, he saw a pair of birds keeping their eggs warm in the nest. Whenever the female would fly off to find a worm or a fly to feed to the chicks, the father would warm the nest. Thus, both parents took turns to nurture their brood. Seeing this, the boy was struck by *hosshin* – the desire for enlightenment – and knew that he must become a monk. But the sight of the female bird hunting for worms reminded him painfully of the biggest obstacle to his enlightenment: his attachment to a mother he did not even know. "Since the creation of the world, every creature – even those of the animal realm, and down to the lowliest lobster in the bay – has had two parents. How can it be that I, who am the son of the emperor, have no mother?"

'Hearing him, one of his serving girls broke down and wept. "If you wish to find your mother, you should seek her on the coast, near the village of Shirahama," she said. Fusazaki pressed her for more details, but fearing that she had already spoken too freely, she closed up like his father. Frustrated, Fusazaki set out the next day for the coast, determined to find the woman who had brought him into the world. At every village he visited he would ask about her, and whether a noble man had been there and married a local woman, but the people of the coast simply laughed.

'"If noble men came here and married our women, do you think we would be kneeling here in the sand, drying seaweed to make salt?"

'One day, though, Fusazaki met a young woman who flushed with recognition when he told his story. "I have a letter for you, from your mother," she said. Yet when Fusazaki reached out to take the letter, the woman disintegrated into a wet miasma of sea mist, saying, "I am the spirit of the ama who was your mother."

'Fusazaki read the letter: "Thirteen years have passed since my soul fled to the other shore. Many days and months have passed since the white sand covered my bones on the sea floor. The road of death is as dark as the deep water, and I cannot find my way – no one has mourned for me and my karma is heavy on me for the evil I brought to the world by giving your father the ball. My dear son, please return what your father and I stole to the sea and illuminate this darkness, which for thirteen years has surrounded me."

'Fusazaki found a local inn, comfortable enough for a long stay, and began the traditional obsequies. For forty-nine days he wore only the grey robes of mourning, and every seven days he paid tribute to the Buddhas and bodhisattvas at the local temple. Every evening he silently called the *nenbutsu*, imploring Amida Buddha to help his mother's soul find its way.

'After the mourning time was over, Fusazaki returned home and stole the Buddha ball, which his father kept by his pillow as he slept. Then he went again to the beach, where his mother appeared to him once more – this time as one of the *apsaras* of paradise, holding in one hand the *hokkeky*, the lotus sutra. She took the ball and dropped it into the sea. Then with thirteen graceful movements she danced the sacred *hayamai* dance, her feet light on the surface of the water. "Thank you for freeing me, my son," she said. "I look forward to the day when you will be emperor, for you are a fine boy."

'"But I will not be emperor," said Fusazaki. "Father has made another of his sons – my half brother – his heir."

'The woman stopped dancing. "What did you say?"

'Fusazaki repeated the information. His mother's face turned dark and angry. She was close to the gods then, and her magic was endless. "Then at this very moment I place a curse on the house of the emperor. No more shall the emperor have power over this country. Control shall pass into the hands of lords more prone to violence than poetry, and the bloodshed and war shall continue until the son of a diver like me rules this land."'

THE ABBESS SMILED. 'You see, it has long been prophesied that an ama's son would one day rule Japan.' She bowed to Taro. 'Perhaps you are that man.'

'Wait,' said Shusaku. 'You said this took place in Shirahama. Taro was born in a village called Shirahama. Is it the same place?'

The abbess shrugged. 'I don't know. But it seems a strange coincidence, doesn't it?'

Taro was shaken. He sat down on the cushions, his mind reeling. Was it possible? He couldn't read, he didn't even know how to act in civilized society, and he was a vampire. Surely such a boy could not grow to be shogun of Japan? Yet two details in particular had struck him. First, as Shusaku had said, the woman who'd married the emperor's son had come from Shirahama.

The same name as the village *he* came from.

Second, she had recovered the Buddha ball from a royal wreck off the coast. A wreck like the one he had, all his life, been told to stay away from. The one his mother had dived by just before they were attacked.

Taro frowned. Why had his mother been diving there? When

143

asked about it, she'd said something strange – what had it been? He searched his memory. Something about how they were always taking from the sea and—

Shusaku stepped forward. 'This changes everything,' he said. 'How extraordinary. I knew the boy was special, but this is…' He waved his hand in the air to indicate that he didn't know what it was. 'We need to leave, soon,' he said suddenly. 'Taro won't be safe until we're at the mountain.'

The old woman nodded. 'He would have to be eliminated before anyone else could make a play for the shogunate. That's if they are aware of the prophecy, anyway, and believe that he is the boy described in it.'

'Wait,' said Taro. 'You're saying people want to kill me because of some old story? I'm just a peasant.'

'I keep telling you that killing peasants is what daimyos do,' said Shusaku.

'No,' said the old woman. 'The boy's right. There is something more. Think about it. All those ninja, to kill one boy? It doesn't make sense.'

'What else, then?'

'It's all in the story,' said the woman. 'I shouldn't have to explain *everything*.'

Suddenly Heiko leaned forward. 'In the story the boy isn't the only powerful thing.'

Yukiko's eyes opened wide. 'The ball.' The old woman nodded, smiling.

'What?' said Shusaku. 'No – that's just a story. Everyone knows the Buddha ball isn't real. I mean, I've heard of it, but it's just…'

'A story?' said Hiro. 'That's what *you* said when I told you I didn't believe in vampires.'

Shusaku breathed out. 'Gods.' He turned to the old woman. 'You don't think it's real, do you?'

'I've seen the future,' she said. 'I know it's real.'

CHAPTER 21

T HE ABBESS YAWNED, tired from looking into the Tao, and
it was only then that Taro saw something in her mouth –
elongated canine teeth, sharpened to a point – and realized...

'You're a vampire,' he said.

'Yes. It is not only boys who play at assassins.'

Shusaku laughed at Taro. 'I wondered when you would
realize.'

'You may have noticed,' said the fortune-teller, 'that no lamps
or *gaku* hang outside my door. You see, I have no need to ban-
ish evil spirits from my home. *I* am already here. Of course,
the province has become more dangerous of late. Lord Oda is
fearful, constantly demanding that I tell his fortune. It is very
tiresome.'

'You still do his bidding?' said Shusaku, a little sharply.

'He protected me,' said the abbess. 'And I prefer not to take
sides.'

'What about the girls?' said Shusaku.

'You saved their lives. It is only proper you should choose
their loyalty.'

Shusaku nodded as Taro, bewildered, tried to digest their
conversation.

Then the abbess swept a hand over the sand in the tray, smoothing it. 'And now I think I should discover what I can see of each of your futures.' She beckoned to Hiro. 'Come. Sit before me.'

Hiro stood warily and moved over to where she sat.

The abbess took his hand, then sipped at her tea. She chanted for a while, the incense in the room seeming to pool strangely at ground level, then her eyes rolled back in her head. Putting down the tea and picking up the metal bar, she sketched a character in the sand.

'Loyalty,' said Shusaku.

Taro smiled at Hiro. The abbess's eyes rolled back to normal and she blinked at the big wrestler. 'You're a good friend,' she said. 'And I see that you will follow Taro anywhere. But the path will not always be easy.'

Hiro shrugged. 'I go with Taro.'

'Yes. Of course.' She turned to Taro. 'Might I see the scar?'

Shusaku watched Taro, confused, as Taro folded open the top of his kimono, revealing the semicircle of scar tissue running round his chest and shoulder.

'Gods,' said the ninja. 'How did you do that?'

It was Hiro who answered. 'I didn't grow up in the Kanto. I came from inland – from the plain below Nagoya. We fled when Lord Yoshimoto's samurai advanced on our land. My parents knew nothing of fishing. They borrowed a boat, went out into the bay. They threw blood into the water, to attract the fish. I was with them, and none of us could swim.'

'Ah,' said Shusaku.

'The *mako* knocked us out of the boat. My father was killed by the beast; my mother drowned, I think. But Taro was on the shore that day, playing with his bow. He saw the fin but he swam out into the bay anyway. He got hold of me and swam with me back to shore.'

'Extraordinary,' said Shusaku. 'Such courage.'

'I don't really remember it,' said Taro, embarrassed.

Heiko touched the scar gently. 'And this?'

'He went back, after he laid me on the shore,' said Hiro. 'He was looking for my parents. He had a knife with him…'

'You're not saying he fought the shark?' said Yukiko. For the first time Taro could hear a cautious respect in her voice.

'Yes,' said Hiro. 'And killed it, and dragged it up on the beach to show me. But the shark had bitten him. He fainted and I ran to the huts, screaming. His father carried him home.'

'I understand now why you wouldn't abandon him,' said Shusaku.

'Yes. My life is his.'

The abbess smoothed out the sand again. 'Of course, your loyalty will cost you dearly. You know that.'

Hiro smiled. 'Things that are worthwhile always do.'

'That is true.' She motioned for Shusaku to take Hiro's place. He hesitated.

'I'm not sure—'

'Come here, Shusaku.'

Shusaku appeared ready to resist, but didn't. He sat down on the cushion Hiro had vacated, staring at the fortune-teller with his hard, clear eyes. She drank another cup of tea, began chanting, and soon fell into a trance again. With the metal rod she scratched a message into the sand.

When her eyes opened again, she looked down at the message. She trembled lightly. Shusaku too read the character in the sand, then turned away quickly.

'What does it say?' demanded Heiko.

The abbess looked up, eyes brimming, her already lined face seeming to have aged another ten years in as many seconds. 'It says…' she began, her voice uncertain. 'It says, "Beware. Your eyes will betray you."'

She stared at Shusaku. 'Be truly careful,' she said, suddenly serious. 'I sense danger for you.'

Taro wondered what the relationship between this woman and Shusaku was. She seemed to really care for him.

'Nonsense,' said Shusaku, standing. 'I am in no danger at all, as long as I continue to be watchful.' Taro thought he seemed nervous, though.

'You can't tell us any more?' Taro asked. 'Help Shusaku to avoid whatever danger is coming?'

The abbess shook her head. 'Sometimes I see whole scenes, as when I watched you save Hiro from the shark. But sometimes it is only phrases, or ideas, that come through. Joining with the Tao is a bit like dreaming. Sometimes you dream in colour; sometimes you remember your dreams, and sometimes you don't. There are times when I write in the sand, and when I wake I have no recollection of doing it.'

'Which was it when you said I would be shogun?' said Taro.

'It was… in the flow of the Tao. I didn't see it, but I could feel everything in the world leading towards it. You can no more avoid being shogun than the moon can avoid circling the earth. Though I did see a single scene – you, wielding the Buddha ball. You were not much older than you are now.'

'I keep telling you,' said Shusaku. 'The Buddha ball isn't real.' But his voice lacked conviction, and Taro wondered if he wanted to believe it so he could believe too that he wasn't in danger. 'If it were real, wouldn't it have shown up by now? Something so powerful could not remain hidden so long.'

The abbess shrugged. 'They say that when Tankai died, his official son searched for the ball but could not find it. Fusazaki was suspected, of course. He was a dispossessed son, so he had cause to hate Tankai. And everyone knew that it was his mother who'd recovered the ball from the wreck. Yet when they found him, he was living in the little village of Shirahama near where his mother died, occupying a simple peasant hut, taking *onsen* baths, meditating, and eating raw fish.'

A funny tremor ran through Taro at this mention – again – of the village where he had grown up. Surely these momentous events could not have played out against such a modest backdrop?

'So he didn't steal his father's ball after all?' said Heiko.

'It didn't seem that way to Tankai's heir, or to the samurai entrusted with his security. But I don't know.' The abbess's eyes crinkled with what could have been a wry smile. 'Not everyone who comes into the possession of an object so powerful is tempted by it. Not everyone *wants* dominion over the world.'

The idea, for some reason, gave Taro a faint thrill – the thought that this enlightened noble son, this product of a lord and an ama, could have lived out his final days in a basic peasant hut, while all the while having in his grasp a ball that could allow him to bend the whole architecture of the world to his will.

The abbess yawned again, and Taro could see that the exertion had taken its toll on her. There were dark shadows under her eyes, and her skin was pale. She began to get to her feet, but then, with no warning or preparation, her legs let go and she fell. Shusaku rushed towards her, just catching her head before it hit the wooden floor. He lowered her gently onto the cushions. Heiko and Yukiko too were on their feet quickly, and went to kneel by their foster mother. Yukiko whirled accusingly on Shusaku. 'You've worn her out!' she said.

'No,' said the ninja. 'Look at her eyes. She's in a trance. She's seeing something.'

And that was when the woman's eyes snapped open, only they were white, like eggs, and her pupils had rolled up into her head.

She turned that ghastly blank stare on Taro with horror written on her face as clearly as the messages she had scrawled in the sand. Tears were running down her cheeks. She stumbled to her feet, keeping her eyes on Taro.

'Keep me from that boy,' she muttered. 'He brings death to all round him.'

Taro felt an overwhelming urge to run from her and keep running, as Shusaku murmured soothing words to the woman. Then, just as suddenly as her eyes had opened, they closed again. A moment later she looked at Shusaku, puzzled, and blinking as if she had opened a door from her bedroom onto the bright light of day.

'What's wrong?' she asked.

CHAPTER 22

T HE ABBESS – WHO clearly remembered nothing of her vision, whatever it had been – declared herself tired beyond endurance, and Shusaku led her towards her own room. Yukiko glared at Taro, then swept out of the room behind them.

Heiko gave him an apologetic look. 'She loves the abbess very much,' she said. 'It pains her to see her frightened.'

'I understand,' said Taro. His heart felt heavy in his chest, ponderous and slow. He had caused his father's death, and now it seemed he would be responsible for more devastation. He could not rid himself of the image of the abbess, staring at him with those boiled, empty eyes.

He sank onto one of the cushions.

'The things she sees… they don't always come about,' said Heiko. 'Sometimes the choices people make can change them.'

Taro grunted. Perhaps. But perhaps too he was just a poison – the price of his life the pain of others.

Hiro put an awkward hand on his shoulder.

'You could go, you know,' said Taro, not looking at his friend. He was looking out at the garden, and he concentrated on the blossoms that clung to the trees, the moon that shed light on the flowers. 'You heard what she said. I'm a monster. A demon.

You'll suffer if you stay with me. You may even die.'

'Where would I go?' said Hiro.

'I don't know. Anywhere. I have to go with Shusaku, otherwise I won't find my mother. But you…'

'Could leave and start a new life,' continued Hiro.

'Well, yes.'

Hiro sat down beside him. 'I have already started a new life,' he said. 'When you saved it.'

Taro nodded, feeling bleak. Nothing he could say would convince his friend to leave him, and that both warmed and chilled him. He was glad to have such a constant ally, yet he couldn't bear the thought of Hiro being hurt on his account. He also found, to his surprise, that the idea of Shusaku being hurt was abhorrent to him. The man had saved his life.

When he looked at Heiko, he saw that there was a tear in her eye.

'I couldn't bear for anything to happen to Shusaku,' she said. 'He saved my life.'

Taro nodded, startled to hear his thoughts echoed in her words. 'Mine, too. But don't worry about him,' he forced himself to say. 'He can look after himself. He fights with the grace of an *apsara* and the determination of a demon. I've never seen him show weakness of any kind.'

'Yes,' said Heiko thoughtfully. 'That's what worries me.'

Taro nodded. He really didn't want anyone to have to suffer because of him. Then he had an idea. 'It's still *obon*, isn't it?' He looked at Heiko. 'Do you have coloured paper left? Candles?'

'You would send a message?' she asked.

'Yes. My father. He was killed when Shusaku rescued me.'

She nodded. 'I'll get the things.'

A short time later Taro stood with Hiro and Heiko on the

bridge where they had first seen the girls. Taro held in his hands the oblong *shoryo-nagashi*. Leaning over the bridge, he lowered it into the water. The message inside was simple – though Heiko, being Heiko, had drafted it twice before seeming satisfied with the strokes of her brush.

I'm sorry, it said. *I miss you. Please protect my friends.*

Taro began to murmur the words of the prayer that would take his communication to the Amida Buddha, and from him to his father's soul, wherever it was. He hoped it had gone to the Pure Land of the Amida Buddha, not to the realm of the beasts, or of the hungry ghosts.

Taro was barely aware of Hiro and Heiko melting away behind him, leaving him alone with his grief as they retired into the house.

He stayed there a long time, listening to the murmuring of the stream, looking at the shadows of the trees and the strange, drained colours of the flowers in the moonlight. So still did he stand that the heron they had seen earlier returned, and stood, neck bent, in the stream, gazing down into its clear water.

Finally, he took a deep breath and turned for the house. That was when he heard a low babble that added itself to the noise of the stream. This, though, was not water. It was the sound of two people talking in quiet whispers.

He followed the voices to the left-most of the shoji screens. It gave onto a room smaller than the one in which the fortunes had been told, and Taro could see little of what lay inside through the transparent wall of the decorated paper, other than the shadows of two people who stood close together, conferring seriously.

Shusaku and the abbess.

Taro crept as close as he could to the screen, concentrating on keeping his footsteps as soft and silent as possible.

The abbess was speaking. '... now that Tokugawa has showed his hand with an attempt, there is—'

Shusaku gasped loudly, cutting her off, and Taro pulled back, convinced he'd been detected, so he missed the next thing the ninja said. But it was obvious Shusaku had been shocked by the abbess's words.

He put his ear again to the screen. '... long were you with those ninjas?' he heard the abbess say.

'No more than a month,' said Shusaku.

'Ah. Then it occurred after you left.'

Shusaku whistled. 'Tokugawa tried to have Oda *killed*? What about their alliance, which they want so much for people to believe in?'

Taro stifled a gasp. Lord Tokugawa was the daimyo of the western prefecture, and the greatest ally of Lord Oda, who controlled the eastern lands, among them the sea village where Taro had grown up. Both lords were among the daimyo chosen by the previous shogun to watch over his young son, keeping him in power, and so they possessed a shared purpose. They fought alongside each other to protect the shogun, shared the respect of smaller lords whose land abutted their own, were even married to two sisters.

That the one lord should threaten the other was unthinkable. But the abbess was claiming it nevertheless.

'Who did he hire?' asked Shusaku.

The abbess murmured something. The first part of what she said was garbled and quiet, but Taro just caught the end. '...while riding in the forest. Only Oda's peerless skill with the sword saved him.'

'*Ronin?*' exclaimed Shusaku. 'Has Tokugawa lost his senses?'

'I don't believe Tokugawa does anything without thinking

about it very carefully,' said the abbess. 'In this case he hired samurai whose lord fought on Yoshimoto's side in the great battle against Lord Oda. These men hate Oda more than all the demons. It was not difficult for Lord Tokugawa to provoke them into trying to kill the lord who stripped them of all their pride and privilege. Sadly, they had also lost their discipline, and they were caught and interrogated. It became obvious that Tokugawa had provoked them.'

'Gods,' said Shusaku. 'And Oda? What did he do?'

'Nothing.'

'Nothing?' said Shusaku. 'But...' There was silence, and for a moment Taro thought again that they must have become aware of his presence, but then Shusaku went on, and Taro realized that he had only been thinking. 'Ah, of course. He waited for Tokugawa to make his move.'

'Yes.'

'And?'

'Tokugawa blamed his elder son,' said the abbess. 'The boy had nothing to do with it of course, but—'

'He is samurai. He died for his father's gain,' said Shusaku, completing her thought. 'He took the responsibility of the assassination attempt, and so allowed Tokugawa and Oda to maintain their illusion of alliance.'

Illusion of alliance? thought Taro. He felt as though the world he had grown up in had been whisked aside, revealed to be nothing more than a painted shoji screen, and the precepts and history he had learned shown to be nothing more than shadows cast by figures more terrible and base than he could have imagined. Could it be true that Lord Oda and Lord Tokugawa were secretly fighting over who could become shogun? If *that* was true, then it meant the life of the boy shogun was in danger.

This was so blasphemous, so unthinkable to Taro, that he felt faint.

'Tokugawa himself acted as second,' he heard the abbess say. 'He decapitated his son moments after the boy slit open his belly. I was present. It happened between the two lords' castles. The boy didn't even blink. I'd call it brave, if it wasn't such a waste.'

'And the younger son?'

'Gone to Oda's castle,' said the abbess. 'With Tokugawa's wife. *Guests*, Lord Oda calls them.'

'Damn them both,' said Shusaku. There was a bang, as if he had struck the wood of the panel. 'So now Tokugawa has lost both his official heirs, and what has he gained? A moment of peace? Lord Oda's false trust in a show execution, one that has lost Tokugawa his greatest asset?'

'He has avoided war. That is their game, is it not?'

Shusaku said something in reply, but now they really had moved away, and it was lost to Taro.

So Lord Tokugawa had tried to kill Lord Oda. Unbelievable, of course, yet Shusaku had seemed convinced. Taro felt instinctive anger towards Lord Tokugawa. The Kanto, where he had grown up, was loyal to Lord Oda, and he was horrified that someone should threaten the great lord's life.

Yet the abbess had said, 'that is their game'. The suggestion was that both lords were involved, both as guilty as the other.

No, Taro told himself. If there was a hidden rivalry, it was obviously the fault of Lord Tokugawa. He had commissioned a cold-blooded murder. Then, when it went wrong, he killed his own son rather than admit to the attempt! What kind of a man could be so brutal? Tokugawa was clearly a snake, and a stain on the samurai class.

'And now,' said the abbess, 'I really must retire.'

Taro pulled back from the screen, his head swimming. *I should leave this place*, he thought. He remembered an ama who had cut her foot on coral. The wound had become infected, but she had not noticed until too late. The healer had said that if she had come to him right away, he might have been able to save her by cutting off the foot.

Taro felt like that foot. He had to be cut out – removed from the proximity of those who were healthy and happy and never visited in the night by ninja.

He had to go.

CHAPTER 23

W E HAVE TO go,' whispered Shusaku. He stood beside Taro's futon, a pale shape in the darkness of the room. Taro swung his feet to the floor. He saw that Hiro was standing already. Being abroad in the countryside had sharpened their reflexes, and dulled their capacity for deep sleep.

'What is it?' he asked, imitating Shusaku's low whisper.

Shusaku held up Taro's bow, which the abbess had taken away for restringing. 'I've also taken some food,' he said. 'Not much, but enough to sustain Hiro.' He glanced at Hiro's muscular bulk. 'Well, for a short time anyway.'

'We're leaving without saying goodbye?'

'It is the only way to leave. The abbess is a good hostess, and a good friend. She would not let us leave quickly.'

'And you don't think it's safe for us to stay here?' asked Hiro.

'No,' said Shusaku. 'I don't think it's safe for *them*.'

Taro nodded. He was glad they were leaving, and that the girls and the abbess would be safe, with luck. He hoped that now whatever the abbess had foreseen would never come about. And yet he'd miss the girls – Heiko, anyway. Yukiko was too sharp, too angular, and too suspicious of him.

Yes, he'd miss them. But he was a vampire now, and close to

being a ninja. He could not allow himself to form such attachments, and any time he allowed them to form he would be
punished by the deaths of those he loved, and his grief. Better to
leave them alive.

And so he crept through the dark house behind Shusaku,
and into the garden, and it was with silent movements that he
put a foot into Hiro's outstretched hands and was hoisted up
onto the wall, and thence out into the open vastness of the
country.

The stars in their infinite heavens were beautiful, but cold.

CHAPTER 24

Kenji Kira swept one of the bowls off the table and onto the floor, where it smashed into pieces. It was a gesture meant to intimidate, and it worked. The old woman looked up at him wide-eyed with fear. He saw again that despite her age she was beautiful, and he almost wished that he didn't have to kill her.

Almost.

He sucked on the cool, hard pebble he had tucked into his cheek before coming here, making an effort to keep his eyes from the stuff that was now scattered on the tatami mats at their feet. Because of course it had not only been a gesture of intimidation, smashing that bowl. It had also been necessary to remove the raw fish from the table, to no longer have to look at it.

Even now, Kira found himself glancing at the disgusting organic matter as it lay glossily on the ground. Another bowl still remained on the table, but it was empty, and although the grease of the flesh still clung to it, he could – just – bear its presence.

'You laid out food,' he said, trying to compose himself. 'Yet you feed on blood, do you not?' He poked the empty bowl. 'Who was eating with you, when we arrived?'

'I am under Lord Oda's protection,' said the woman.

'Not any more,' said Kira. 'You have harboured his enemies. I am authorized to deal with you as I see fit.' The woman trembled. He liked that.

'The bowls are for the spirits,' said the woman. 'I am a prophetess. I must set out food for them.'

Kira sighed. Perhaps it was true. There was no one else there, after all, and he could not believe that anyone could hide from his men in such a small house. And anyway, he needed to put the fish out of his mind. He made a hand signal to one of his samurai, and the man went to stand behind the woman, the blade of his *katana* resting against her neck. 'I know about your kind,' he went on. 'You can only be killed by decapitation, or a blade to the heart. Don't think I won't kill you if you fail to give me the information I need.'

'And what information is that?'

'I want to know where the boy went. And the ninja with him, and his fat friend.' He had a very bad feeling about that ninja, a sense that events were slipping beyond his control. He had interrogated some of the ninja who had attacked the boy in Shirahama – the circumstances of those interrogations strikingly similar to the current stand-off, the same samurai's blade against the necks of the miserable ninja who had failed Lord Oda – and they had spoken of two things that made Kira nervous.

The boy had been turned, and the ninja who had done it had borne a sword decorated with the *mon* of Lord Tokugawa.

'No one like that has been here,' said the woman.

'Yes, they have. They were seen entering the door in your garden.'

'Then perhaps they broke in for supplies.'

Kira was sure, in fact, that they had received supplies, but he thought the woman had given them willingly. 'What about the girls?' he asked. 'We are informed that two girls live with you.'

The woman flinched, and Kira smiled inside.

'They… are playing… in the woods,' she said.

'Then we shall wait here for their return,' said Kira. 'It will be such a pleasure to meet them.'

'No… please…'

Kira's internal smile turned to a grin, though his face remained impassive. Good. He would break this woman quickly, when the girls came back. If only he weren't so hungry. Blackness flickered at the corners of his vision, and he took in a deep breath, gripping the edge of the table.

'Are you all right?' asked the woman. 'You look very pale.'

Kira grimaced. He hated to show weakness in front of his men, and yet he had struggled to find vegetables in these parts, so many of the peasants' huts and fields having been left empty by the wars that had devastated the region years before. He had taken some rice, that morning, but his strength was ebbing away. He blinked, then nodded to the man holding the sword to the woman's neck. 'Tell me where they went. Or I give him the order.'

The woman ignored him, looking at him with a solicitude that he found more insulting even than her refusal to answer his questions. 'There's more fish, if you want it,' she said. 'I'm sure the spirits won't begrudge you it.'

Kira gagged – he couldn't help it. *She doesn't know what she's saying*, he thought. But maybe she did. She was a prophetess, wasn't she?

For a moment Kira had the uncomfortable sensation that she could see into his mind, that she could see what had made him stone and metal and water instead of flesh. For that instant he was back in the battlefield after the defeat of Lord Yoshimoto, and he was again wounded in the leg, and lying covered by the bodies of the dead.

Six days he had lain there, sucking dew from the ground, and moisture from the cold swords of the dead. He had tried to move, but his leg had been split open from hip to knee, and even if he had possessed the strength to cast aside the horse that lay over his lower half, he would not have been able to stand. So he had remained trapped there, and it was after two days that the bodies round him had started to fill with living things, and crawl with them. Rats had emerged from the stomach of the horse, chittering. Worms had crawled from men's eyes and nostrils, quivering in the air as if nosing the scent of death. Even frogs had made an appearance, and of course the flies, the endless flies.

By the time he was finally rescued, Kira had known that he could no longer be the same man, that he could no longer endure the insult of the organic. The men who had pressed against him in the mud of the battlefield had been fat and bloated with the gases of decomposition, roiling with the life of the low creatures that had infested their corpses.

That would never happen to Kira. From the day when he had been rescued, he had never again allowed flesh to pass his lips, or anything in fact but water, rice, and vegetables. He could not tolerate that the meat of another creature should be inside him, within the confines of his flesh, as those worms and flies had insinuated themselves into the dead.

The water of the stream, the roots of the earth, the rice of the field. These were the only things he would eat, and when he died, he would be burned as the samurai tradition demanded. Yes, he would leave nothing behind but grey ashes, clean and dry, just as the swords of Yoshimoto's men had remained unspoiled – uninvaded – in that cold mud, while the bodies of the men who had borne them rotted.

'Kira-*san*?' asked the samurai who stood behind the old woman.

Kira looked up. 'Ah... yes. I was thinking, that's all.' He leaned back from the table. 'Now, old woman. You had better tell us where the boy has gone.'

'I've seen the future,' said the woman. 'If you know anything about me, you know that I can do that. I've seen the future, and that means I know that I will never answer your questions, no matter what you do to me.'

'Perhaps not. But you'll have to endure the pain of the questioning, nevertheless.'

The woman smiled. 'Questioning is always painful. That's what people don't understand about fortune-telling. But, as much agony as I feel, I will tell you nothing.' She paused. 'No. Wait. I will tell you two things that you don't know.'

'Go on,' said Kira, his voice neutral.

'The boy is going to get the Buddha ball, and he's going to use it to kill Lord Oda.'

Kira sneered. 'The Buddha ball is a silly story.'

'You may think what you like. But Oda believes in it. Why do you think he wants the boy so badly?'

Kira's head was reeling, and again he wished that he had been able to find more to eat. Could it be true? But no, Lord Oda would have told him, wouldn't he? This was his mission... He had been... entrusted.

He caught the table edge just before he fell. He blinked. When he got back to Nagoya, he was going to have to ask Lord Oda some pointed questions. But then, what if he didn't go back to Nagoya? What if he found the ball for himself? He still only half-entertained the notion that it might be real, but... if it was! The possibilities. With that thing in his hand, he could rule the world. They said it was the very world model that the Compassionate One had held in his hands when he still lived in this realm of samsara, allowing him to see into and direct the hearts of every living thing, and the weather and the land and sea, too. It had been taken from the roots of the Bodhi tree in India, and after that had been lost.

Could it be here, in Japan? Could the boy be the key to finding it?

A rush of joyful, swooning anticipation went through him, and he almost fell again. With the ball he could tell his body never to rot, could command the worms of the earth and the flies of the air to leave it alone, to never take up habitation inside it.

'I really think you should take some fish,' said the woman. 'You do look very weak.'

'I don't eat fish!' he screamed.

'No, of course,' she murmured, and in that instant Kira was sure she could look into him, that she had been taunting him deliberately, and he was filled with a consuming fury. She was making it up, about the Buddha ball. She had seen into his being, and knew his fear of the low creatures that could invade his body – his fear of flesh and decay.

Yes, she had lured him with the ball. She knew his covetousness would make him take his attention from what was important – from the way that she was mocking him. The ball wasn't real. Only her cruelty and mockery were real.

If she imagined that he would not kill a woman, then she was sorely mistaken. He had killed women before – had, even, killed a ninja woman before. That whore of a girl who had claimed to be Lord Tokugawa's serving maid, but had in truth been sent to protect him by the ninja in Tokugawa's employ. When word had come from a traitor in the ninja ranks – Kawabata, his name had been – Lord Oda had sent Kira to eliminate the girl. It wouldn't do for Lord Tokugawa to benefit always from such protection.

It had been tricky, of course. The woman was a vampire, making her hard to kill, and not only that but she had fallen in love with Lord Endo, one of Lord Tokugawa's greatest samurai. Some even said she had made him a vampire too, biting him when he was on the verge of dying from a spear wound.

All of these things – the proximity to Lord Tokugawa, the protection of vampire strength, the alliance with the great swordsman Lord Endo – should have made the girl impossible to kill, even for a man who could stomach the murder of a beautiful young woman. But Kira had managed it nonetheless. It had been a simple matter, really. To anyone uninformed, the girl was just a servant, and so it had not been difficult for Kira to get close to her, as the men had been distracted by planning the next assault on the shogun's enemies.

He had taken her head off with a single sword blow.

The fortune-teller was staring at him with fear in her eyes, and then the fear left her and she smiled.

'What? Something amuses you?'

'I said I would tell you two things.'

Kira thought for a moment. 'You did. You said the boy would get the Buddha ball, and that he would kill Lord Oda.'

'That's one thing. I will tell you another, if you wish to hear it.'

Kira nodded. 'Very well.'

'It is this,' she said. She lowered her voice to a whisper. 'When you die, your body will languish for many moons, consumed slowly by the creatures of the night. Worms will eat your eyes. The eggs of flies will hatch among your sinews.' She paused, her smile growing wider. 'You cannot escape it.'

Kira's vision was awash with redness, like a sun was setting behind his eyelids, and he could feel his blood hammering in his forehead. He had never felt fury like this, not even when he had believed that his companions were never going to rescue him from that hell realm of liquefying corpses.

He looked at the white-haired prophetess through a film of red. 'You can see the future, yes?'

She nodded.

'Then you must have seen what I am about to do.' He looked at the samurai behind her and made a cutting gesture with his fingers. The man swung back his sword.

'Yes,' she said. 'Yes, I have.'

Shusaku led the way through ever steeper land, as they rose from the foothills into the mountains. Taro held his bow in his hand, the new string so taut it almost hummed as the air ran over it, as much an instrument as a weapon. It was good to feel its power once again. He was surprised to realize how much he had missed it, when the string had been softened and weakened by the sea. Yes, it had helped them when the ninja had attacked their palanquin, but it had been reduced to the status of a short-range weapon, like a sword.

Now Taro could strike from afar, sending an arrow almost a quarter of a *ri* with deadly accuracy. It was a comforting thought, given the danger the abbess believed was coming.

As they had gained higher ground, Taro had kept turning, to see the ever fainter light and smoke of the village where the abbess lived, but now they had left it far behind, and there was no sign of it in the dark landscape that fell away behind them.

'She'll be all right,' said Shusaku.

'No,' said Taro. 'She won't. She's a prophetess, isn't she? She saw her own death.'

Shusaku didn't answer.

'And it's our fault,' said Taro. 'There are people after us, people who want us dead. We led them to her door, most likely.'

Again, Shusaku didn't respond.

'What about the girls?' asked Hiro. 'Shouldn't we have taken them with us?'

'The abbess didn't want them to know we were leaving. We must comply with her wishes.'

Hiro sighed, and Taro thought he was missing Yukiko. The pair had bonded closely over their shared love of fighting. Taro himself was not happy to be leaving Heiko behind. There had been something admirable about her quiet strength and her intelligence – something that had reminded him, in fact, of his mother.

His mother. He had to focus on her. It was useless to think of what the abbess had said, to worry all the time about what his life might cost other people. If he could only save his mother, find her again, then perhaps he might repay some of his debt. He held her in his mind as he maintained a steady pace over the mossy rocks.

They were crossing a stream, skirting round a village whose light they could make out through the trees, when Hiro stepped on a corpse.

He squealed.

Shusaku moved like liquid night and clamped a hand over the wrestler's mouth.

In the darkness ahead was a group of men, moving slowly into the forest. They carried a sack.

Shusaku spread three fingers, then pointed at the trees – *follow*. He put a finger to his lips – *quietly*.

Taro moved off to the left as Hiro went right, and Shusaku jagged through the undergrowth between them. As they drew closer, Taro could see the figures more clearly.

Ronin.

They were dressed in samurai armour but bore no *mon* on their backs, their allegiance having gone with their honour, when they'd been defeated and refused seppuku, or when their lord had banished them. They looked vicious. One of them had some kind of dead animal impaled on the stag horns of his helmet.

Just then there was a *crack* as a dry twig was snapped by someone's foot. Taro turned and saw Hiro dropping onto his stomach. He hid behind some thick foliage as the *ronin* turned and scrutinized the forest.

Don't turn back, don't turn back.

They shrugged, and continued on their way.

Taro exhaled, and rose once more to a crouch, creeping through the trees.

Ahead, Shusaku suddenly ducked down behind a bush, stopping. Hiro moved forward as close as he dared. The ninja was watching a clearing, where the three *ronin* had gathered. In the darkness they were silhouettes, but starlight glimmered on the metal of their armour and weapons. Hiro moved slowly round the clearing, careful of the ground on which he stepped, so that he was almost as close as Shusaku, only on the other side of the circle. Taro circled in the other direction, until the three of them had the *ronin* surrounded.

As he watched, the man who was carrying the sack threw it down to the ground with a dull *thud*. Whatever was in that sack, it was heavy.

One of the *ronin* gathered firewood and began to make a fire. Now, for the first time, the men began talking. The words weren't completely clear from where Taro was crouching, but it seemed that they were arguing about how to share something out. One of the three – the one with the dead animal on his horns –

grabbed something from one of the others and ran to the other side of the clearing, gloating like a child who has stolen a friend's toy. The third man, still lighting his fire, grunted irritably and beckoned both men back. 'There's enough for all of us,' he said, his high voice carrying farther than the others'. 'Our man must have had a good day's trade at the castle,' he added.

'Yes,' said another. 'And he has another good day to live before he passes that jewel he swallowed.'

The other men laughed, and Taro thought, *Which man?*

And that was when the fire finally blazed into life and Taro saw that it wasn't a sack at all lying on the ground at the men's feet. It was a body.

It stirred, and groaned.

Lady Oda no Hana stepped out into the garden of the inn in which she was staying for the night. It was almost full dark, and the moon hung like a lantern over the bamboo fence, glowing blue-white. The garden was laid out very prettily to resemble the Kanto in miniature. A stream, flowing by the fence, served for the sea, while mounds of earth and rock echoed the mountains that surrounded the small property where Hana was staying.

It had rained all day but now was clear. Dew dripped from the chrysanthemums and orchids in the garden. On the ornamental hedges were tatters of spiderwebs, like gossamer fabric torn from a courtier's dress. Where the threads of web were broken, raindrops hung from them like strings of white pearls.

Hana breathed deeply of the cool night air, and the scent of flowers. She liked this time of night, when her ladies-in-waiting and guards had gone to sleep, leaving her alone to dream and to think. Her father even now was dining with a lord in his castle nearby, and had intimated to Hana that this man could one day be her husband.

The jokes and innuendos Hana had heard from the servants, however, gave her to understand that the lord in question was very fat, and that due to his old age and physical condition he would die of overexertion were he to rise from his place at the dining table, which he very rarely did. He was sixty-five, they said.

Lady Hana was sixteen.

Hana breathed the night air, the scent of blossoms. She was glad, despite all this husband unpleasantness, that she was far from the Oda castle for once, and its walls and its calligraphy tutors and its silences. Her father did not normally take her on these sorts of visits, but he seemed ... nervous lately – or, no, not nervous, exactly, for what did a sword saint have to be nervous of? – but restless, and wary.

He had insisted that Hana accompany him everywhere for the last few days.

So now she was here, in the garden, while he exacted whatever cruel payment he must require from the poor lord he had chosen for his daughter's wife.

Hana could almost feel sorry for the man, if the mere thought of him didn't fill her with disgust.

On this particular night Lady Hana wore a delicate jade necklace that drew attention to her perfect collarbones, as light and sweeping as a bird's, and deepened the dark pools of her eyes. Her porcelain skin shone in the moonlight, seeming more precious even than the gold she wore in her ears, and no observer would have argued with the common rumour that held her to be the most beautiful woman in all of Japan.

All in all, Hana was precisely the kind of woman preyed

upon by the unscrupulous ronin that lurked at that time on deserted country roads, the human flotsam left by the great wreck that was her father Oda's rout of Yoshimoto's army.

A light wind stirred in the garden, carrying with it a scent of jasmine. Hana considered herself a student of winds. For her it was the most endlessly fascinating of subjects.

There was the autumn wind at dawn, when she would lie in bed with the panelled doors wide open, the wind blowing in from outside, fragrant and stinging. There was the cold wind of winter, heavy with snow. The moist, gentle winds of spring evenings. And equally moving, the cool, rainy winds of late summer, which afforded Hana the delicious sight of fastidious people covering their stiff robes of unlined silk with padded summer coats. Hana herself would go out and dance in the rain, the strictures of her father's study schedule allowing.

And of course there was the wind that breathed under the wings of Kame, her hawk, speeding her towards her prey as surely as the sun draws plants to it.

But there was one kind of wind that was greater than all the others, and that was the wind that blew a promise – a promise of adventure and freedom. This was the wind that blew that night in the garden.

So Hana walked towards the back of the garden, which was meant to be next to the port of Gojo, going by the map embodied in the rock garden and stream and bonsai trees. Hana felt like a giant as she strode across it. Samurai guarded the gate that was set into the wall here, but Hana knew about more than just wind and flowers.

She flowed forward at the wall and leaped, as agile as a cat. Her fingers caught the top, and she levered herself sideways, the momentum of the jump carrying her legs up and onto the wall.

She crouched there for a moment, looking at the men standing by the gate, their *katana* drawn, ready to challenge any would-be assassins.

Fools.

She moved along the wall and dropped down into the alley, her feet in their cloth *tabi* completely silent as they hit the ground. Then she became a shadow against the wall and slunk out of the little village.

She turned onto one of the delightful country lanes that abounded in these parts, crossing a bridge over an irrigation stream. The moon hung now over the mountains to the south, illuminating stepped rice paddies. A few small buildings lay round the house that had been requisitioned for Hana and her party. Red lanterns hung over doorways shed a pink glow onto the ground.

Just outside the village was a copse of cedars, and it was towards these that Hana turned. She wished to hear the wind through the leaves, the crunch of leaves beneath her feet.

She had laid only one – ever so delicate – foot inside the woods when she was grabbed by rough hands and turned to look into a big, red face, topped off by a pair of long, wicked horns. She screamed. The face, she soon realized, was attached to a large armour-clad body, and the horns were merely part of a decorative helmet.

This didn't stop her screaming.

The man slapped her face, hard, and now she did stop screaming, if only to look round her with wide-eyed alarm. There were three men there in the woods, all dressed in samurai uniform and bearing swords. The one who had grabbed her was holding a sword to her throat. Yet no samurai would attack a woman – unless it were a female samurai, and the offence very great. There was only one possibility: *ronin*.

Hana trembled. She had heard terrible things about the *ronin*. They would do anything for money. Worse, they would do anything for sheer bloodlust. One of them grinned at her. On one of the horns of his helmet was impaled a pine marten, which Hana was horrified to see twitching, as if it had only just been put there. Most of the man's teeth were missing.

Then Hana looked down, and that was when she saw a large sack at her feet. It was moving gently up and down, as if something inside were breathing. *Oh, gods*, she thought. *That's because something inside is breathing...* She turned away from the sack, feeling sick.

'Well,' said the first man, who was still clutching Hana's arms. 'It looks like you lost your way. Perhaps we could help you find it again?'

'P-please let me go,' said Hana, feigning weakness. 'I am a lady at court. Lord Oda will pay a handsome ransom for my freedom.' She thought it best not to mention that he was her father – easier to kill her, if they knew that, than to let her live, and have to risk Oda's wrath.

Missing-teeth Man grinned. 'That would be very pleasing. However, the ransom of which you speak might be many days in coming. And yet your jewellery is here before us, as we speak! It seems so convenient that it would be remiss of us not to take advantage of it right now. They do say that a samurai should not hesitate, but act decisively in all things.' He bowed, parodying a noble's manners.

It was then that Hana let the thin blade concealed at all times in her sleeve drop into her hand, and moved her hand forward as fast as hawk flight.

Ii-aido: the discipline of the single strike, a test of pure speed over agility or technique.

Yes, Lady Oda no Hana was a girl who loved gardens, and the many types of wind. But she was also a samurai.

The blade was through the *ronin*'s chest and out again so quickly that an observer might have missed it. Even the *ronin* missed it. He looked down, saw no visible wound, smiled.

Then the blood began to well from the tiny wound, and he stumbled.

The man holding Hana tightened his grip, twisting her wrist until the blade fell. 'Little viper,' he spat, as his companion sank first to his knees and then to the ground, which from now on would hold him within it, and no longer bear his walking, living weight. He breathed a rattling death sigh, and Hana thought—

Gods. I've killed a man.

The big ronin held his sword to her throat and pressed gently. Hana felt blood spill from the wound. Then he grabbed the jade necklace round Hana's neck and brusquely broke it off.

Instantly Hana understood that she was going to die. It had been obvious before, of course – yet something in her had made her hope, had made her fight. But the way the thin filament of the necklace broke in that big, grubby hand, the way the jade pearls fell to the ground... It was a little thing – unimportant, really – but it spoke of worse; it seemed significant. A man who could break such a beautiful thing, reducing it to its parts... such a man as that was a man who could break anything.

Taro gasped when the *ronin* broke the lady's necklace, and the man whirled round, sword at the ready.

'That was a bird, idiot,' said the *ronin* who held the pretty young girl.

'Didn't sound like one,' said the other.

'And I suppose you're an expert on birds, are you? I thought you were only expert at cards, drinking, and fighting. Cards and drinking, anyway.'

The *ronin* who had been startled by Taro's gasp swore and turned back to the girl. But he seemed nervous still, and Taro saw him glance at the corpse of his companion, the one the seemingly harmless girl had killed, her hand moving so fast it had been a blur.

Taro had never seen anything like it, and the thought that such a girl – beautiful, fierce, unflinching – should be prey to such brutes as these was intolerable. She had jet-black hair – like crows' feathers – and her eyes were as softly curved as folded wings. Her eyelashes were long. As he watched her, Taro's stomach did a little flip.

He turned to look at Shusaku, who still crouched motionless behind his bush. Wasn't the ninja going to *do* anything? He felt another wave of revulsion. Once more he was impotent to prevent something terrible. Once more he was hamstrung, immobile, as the powerful picked on a weaker adversary. Who was Shusaku to criticize the honour of the samurai, when he possessed no honour himself?

But then Shusaku raised a hand. He held his palm up – *wait*. He formed a fan with his three fingers, jabbed it forward – *then we move*. He pointed at the *ronin*, then drew the flat of his hand across his throat – *and kill them*.

Lady Hana had been brought up in a samurai household – one of the oldest and most famous – where she had learned to face her death with cool reserve, including, if required, the ritual of seppuku.

She was certainly not prepared to let her demise be dictated by these brutes. If she was to die, it would be on her own terms.

She knew it would take only one movement: a jerk forward, a simultaneous grip on the big man's arms, and his sword would bury itself in her neck. She would die quickly.

She moved back a fraction, ready to bring her head forward with force and—

Shusaku leaped out from behind his bush. 'Let go of that woman,' he said, his voice full of a calm and deadly menace. Hiro roared, crashing through the undergrowth, and Taro launched himself forward, taking his bow from his shoulder...

Hana had only barely held her neck back from the tip of the sword. She watched as a peasant stepped into the clearing. His face was dark with some kind of growth – the ravages, Hana presumed, of a terrible illness.

Then a large boy came thundering into the clearing from the other side. Another boy, more slender, entered from the opposite side.

The *ronin* turned, their bodies tense. They had been taken by surprise – though Hana noticed that the man in front of her kept his sword still held to her throat.

The first boy was huge, with the build and bearing of a wrestler. The other was smaller, his features delicate, almost noble. Hana wondered if he was the son of a lord, or some such. In his hand he held a bow.

The peasant held up a hand. 'I must ask you to release the lady,' he said to the *ronin*.

The big man holding Hana laughed, his voice deep. 'Be on your way, peasant. If you're lucky, we won't chase you down and kill you when we've finished with the girl.'

'Please leave me,' said Hana to the peasants. 'I am samurai. I will face my death bravely.' She did not want this peasant or his boys to die on her behalf. Yet she was unconscious of the implication in her words: that only a samurai could die bravely, that valorous deaths were denied to the peasants of this world.

Yet the peasant took a step forward, to Hana's surprise. 'I said, release the lady.' There was something strange about the man's voice. It seemed altogether too calm, too measured for a man of his station – and situation.

The big man snarled now. 'And I said *be gone*.' He moved his sword away from Hana's throat and brandished it at the peasant.

'Ah, now that was a mistake,' said the man in rags. 'My only fear was that you might slit her throat by accident.'

'What the—' said the big *ronin*. Then a silver star blossomed in his eye. He fell backward, letting go of Hana. Blood gushed from his eye, even as an arrow tore through his throat. The boy had gone for his bow, somehow, and yet Hana had not seen it, though she had been watching him and his father carefully.

The other man turned, sword singing through the air, but he was too slow. The sword came down into empty space that had been occupied a heart's beat before by the peasant. That heartbeat turned out to be the man's last: as he pitched forward, unbalanced by the missed sword stroke, the peasant made a low, sweeping kick that knocked the *ronin* onto his back. Then the peasant somersaulted to his feet and brought his fist down onto the man's neck with a very final-sounding crunch.

The peasant walked over and offered Hana his hand. 'Perhaps we could escort you to your guest house, my lady,' he said. 'It would appear there are bandits about.'

Y OU DESERVE A reward,' said the lady. 'My father is... a very powerful man, and he would make you rich for saving me.' She swallowed, looking nervous. 'However, I was not supposed to be out tonight. If he knew, he would...'

'We quite understand,' said Shusaku. He bowed. 'We will leave you here.' They had escorted her to the edge of the village, wanting to make sure there were no *ronin* about, and now they stood between the darkness of the forest and the *obon* lamp glow of the nearest cottage.

'Please,' said the lady. 'Take my ring. It's not much, but—'

Shusaku held up his hands. 'My fingers are too large. And we don't need money.'

The lady turned to Taro, and he felt his heart hammer in his chest as her perfect face broke into a smile. She looked at his bow. 'Your skill with that thing saved my life.'

Taro felt his face flush hotly. 'It was nothing.'

'Nonsense. I have practised with the bow. It takes a steady eye to accomplish those kinds of shots.' She held out a hand. 'And it's a beautiful one. May I see it?'

Taro handed her the bow, and she lifted it with assurance, pulling back on the string with surprising strength. She let it go with a singing *twang*. 'Not the kind of craftsmanship I would expect to see carried by... people like you.'

Taro looked down, uncomfortable at being a peasant in the presence of a princess, and a beautiful one at that. 'It is my most prized possession,' he said. 'My father made it.'

She looked at Shusaku.

'No,' said Taro. 'He's not my father.'

'Ah. Your own father is...'

'Gone.'

'Ah.' Sympathy lit her features. 'But you love your father.' She said it as a statement, not a question.

Taro nodded.

'Then you are lucky indeed.' She handed him the bow. 'I wonder why he made the grip so thick,' she said, almost as an afterthought.

'I'm sorry?'

She touched the grip, and since he was holding it, her hand brushed his own, sending a tingling warmth down his arm. 'This part. It's not normally so thick. See?' She traced the wood, and Taro could see where the width of the grip gave way to the gentler curve of the bow itself – the grip standing proud of the single piece of wood that had been shaved into the shape of the bow. He had never noticed before. It was almost as if...

Shusaku cleared his throat. 'Sorry to interrupt, but we really should be going.'

Taro caught his eye and then looked away from the girl, blushing again, because he could see amusement in the ninja's expression – a wordless commentary on his obvious infatuation with the lady.

'Well,' she said. 'I shall let you go. Thank you again for saving me.' She turned to go, but then hesitated, looking at Taro.

'Your... protector would not accept my gift. But perhaps you will?' She proffered the ring. 'Consider it a gift. And a token of my regard.'

Taro glanced at Shusaku, who shook his head. 'Thank you,' said Taro, 'but you're too generous.'

'Please?' she said, and her beautiful forehead creased in a frown. 'My father will never notice. But I would not forgive myself if I did not do this one small thing.' She pressed the ring into Taro's hand, and he looked at Shusaku again, who shrugged.

Taro bowed. 'You do me honour.'

'No. You did me honour by coming to my rescue.'

With a little wave she hurried into the village. Taro looked down at the ring in his hand, a twisted band of gold and silver. It looked more valuable than anything he had seen before. He slipped it onto his little finger.

It fitted perfectly.

'Well,' said Shusaku. 'What a day. You're to be shogun, it seems, and you've already claimed the heart of a lady.'

Taro punched him on the arm. 'Very funny.'

But the heat on his face didn't come just from Shusaku's joke. It came from hoping that the ninja was right.

Shusaku cocked his head, gesturing for Taro and Hiro to follow him. 'We should cover our traces,' he said. 'See to that merchant.'

'You want to kill him?' said Taro, shocked.

Shusaku tutted. 'I don't kill *everyone* I meet,' he said in a hurt tone.

They returned to the clearing. The merchant who had swallowed the jewel was breathing regularly, though he still didn't wake. Shusaku and Hiro carried him to the edge of the village, and laid him down where the peasants would find him as soon as they went to their fields.

Then they returned to the woods and dug shallow graves in the undergrowth. They buried the corpses of the *ronin*, but not before Shusaku and Taro had drunk of their blood.

No one said the Amida Butsu prayer over the dead men. They assumed that these *ronin* would be sent straight to the realm of hungry ghosts, and the idea didn't bother any of them.

It was as Taro was patting down the earth with a branch that the sound of a twig cracking made him whirl round to face the darkness of the forest, and then a familiar figure stepped out into the clearing, followed by another that was equally known to Taro – shorter, more muscular, less elegant.

'Didn't take you long to get into trouble, did it?' said Yukiko.

CHAPTER 27

Lady Hana returned to her inn alone, where she told her retinue what had befallen her, only omitting to mention her rescuers – at their request. 'You must have been very brave to defeat those men,' said her chief guard. 'You should be proud. Only a true samurai could be so brave.'

Hana smiled. Once, she had believed it – that honour and bravery were the sole preserve of samurai, just as lines and nets were the preserve of fishermen.

But she believed it no longer.

CHAPTER 28

T HEY WEREN'T FAR from the mountain, according to Shusaku, but they hadn't left the abbess's house until far into the night, and now pale sunlight was beginning to filter through the leaves.

Shusaku led the way through the trees to a stream, then up the stream to a deep cave in a rock cliff face.

'We'll be safe from the sun here,' he said, moving through the clammy, cold entrance and into the darker, warmer recess behind. As he began to build a fire, he watched Heiko and Yuki-ko, who were looking round uneasily for somewhere to sit, wary of their expensive silk kimonos.

'So she just sent you away?' he asked.

'Yes,' said Yukiko. 'We were about to eat. Fish,' she added, irrelevantly. 'Her eyes went, and then when they came back again, she told us to leave right away. We didn't want to, but…'

'She can be very persuasive,' said Shusaku. Heiko nodded, then wiped at her eyes with her sleeve.

'Do you think anything's happened to her?' asked Yukiko.

Shusaku sighed. 'I don't know. But if it has, then she has kept you safe. You should be proud of that.'

Yukiko sniffed, nodding stiffly.

'How did you find us, anyway?' asked Shusaku.

'We followed *his* tracks,' said Yukiko, pointing at Hiro. 'He's like a buffalo on two legs.'

'Hey!' said Hiro.

'It's true,' said Heiko. 'You weren't very hard to track.'

'Hmmm,' said Shusaku. 'It's a good job we're close to the mountain.' He paused. 'But to be safe, I'm going to do a perimeter search. The sunlight is not yet bright enough to harm me.' He wrapped his scarves round his face and went to the cave entrance. 'I'll be back in a moment.'

Taro nodded, absently. He sat down on a rock and took his bow from his shoulder. He *twanged* the string experimentally, then ran his fingers down the belly of the bow. No warping. That was good. The first arrow he had shot at the *ronin* had veered marginally to the left, and he had been worried that the bow itself might have been damaged by the water. Putting the bow aside, he removed from his quiver the arrows that he had recovered from the men's bodies. He had already cleaned them on the grass, but now he checked the flights and the arrowheads, assuring himself that they would fly true. Picking up the bow again, he stringed one of the arrows and sighted down its length.

Good.

He put down the bow and began to slide the arrows into the quiver. From the corner of his eye he saw Heiko sit down beside him, absorbed in looking at his bow, no longer worried about the damp rock against her clothes. Yukiko and Hiro were wrestling at the mouth of the cave, each trying to throw the other into the stream.

'I wish they wouldn't do that,' said Heiko. 'Someone could get hurt.'

'Yes,' said Taro. 'It's not really fair to fight with someone so much weaker. You should really tell your sister to go easy on him.'

Heiko laughed. 'She wouldn't listen.'

'No. Nor would he. That's the problem.'

Heiko turned away from the two wrestlers. She was examining the bow, admiringly.

'This is beautiful craftsmanship,' she said.

'Thank you. My father made it.'

Satisfied that the arrows would fly true, Taro put the quiver aside. But when he turned to Heiko, she was looking at the inside of the bow's arc, frowning.

'What is it?' Taro asked.

'That symbol…'

She was looking at the little emblem carved into the bow's inside arc, the circle of hollyhock leaves.

'You know what it is?' said Taro, his eager voice betraying his own curiosity. 'I asked my mother, but she—'

Heiko put a hand on his arm and frowned, pensive. 'Taro. It is the *mon* of the Tokugawa lords.'

CHAPTER 29

T ARO SHOOK HIS head. 'It can't be. My father made that bow.' But something itched at the back of his mind. It felt like a mouse was turning restlessly inside his skull. For the first time Taro allowed himself to think a thought that he had always repressed: *What if he didn't make that bow at all?*

There was something else too – his bow was not the only thing that bore the symbol. Shusaku's sword, too, was marked with it.

Did Shusaku work for Lord Tokugawa? Or had he only stolen the sword?

'Perhaps your father *did* make it,' said Heiko, consolingly. She pursed her lips, looking unconvinced. 'Or perhaps… he stole it?'

'My father isn't a thief! I mean, he *wasn't* a thief.'

Heiko looked stricken. 'Oh, I'm sorry. I forgot he was— I didn't mean…' She looked down at the ground. Taro started to stammer an apology of his own, but she put her hands on his shoulders. 'I am truly sorry. I know what it is like to lose one's parents.'

Taro smiled. 'Don't worry. I wasn't offended, not really. It was a reasonable question.'

Heiko turned the bow over in her hands. 'This must have

belonged to one of the Tokugawa lords, or one of their samurai at least,' Heiko said, as she examined the bow. 'I wonder how your father got hold of it. Perhaps he served Lord Tokugawa?'

Taro thought of what he had heard behind the screen at the abbess's house, the story of Lord Tokugawa's assassination attempt on Lord Oda. He shook his head vigorously. 'No. We were vassals of Lord Oda's. It's not possible.'

'Your parents worked for Lord Oda?'

'Well, not directly. But they lived on his land. *We* lived on his land.'

'Your mother was an ama, right?' said Heiko. 'The abbess said the son of an ama would be shogun.'

'Yes. She dived for abalone, pearls, that kind of thing.'

'And your father?'

'Just a fisherman.'

Heiko frowned. 'It *is* peculiar. How would a fisherman living in the Kanto of Lord Oda end up with a bow belonging to Oda's worst enemy?'

Taro blinked. As far as anyone knew, Lord Oda and Lord Tokugawa were the greatest of *allies*, not enemies. As far as *he* had known too, until he'd heard the ninja's conversation with the old woman. What did Heiko know?

'You think Lord Oda and Lord Tokugawa are enemies?' asked Taro.

Heiko laughed. 'You don't?'

'No. I mean, yes, but only because I overheard something and...'

She put a hand on his shoulder. 'Ah, Taro. Such innocence.' Her eyes had taken on a mocking light.

Taro pulled away. 'What? Tell me!'

'I forget that you didn't grow up with a ninja for a foster

mother. The fact is, Oda and Tokugawa hate each other.'

Taro looked down at the bow in his hand, at the elegant *mon* of Tokugawa. All his life he had believed in the things symbolized by designs such as this – honour, respect, the friendship of samurai for samurai.

Now a curtain had been drawn, and he looked on a Noh theatre in which the actors had stripped off their masks, to show the corrupted human faces beneath. Shusaku – and now this girl – referred to daimyos dismissively by their names, not bothering to honour them with their title of lord. And they spoke of murder and intrigue as if it were commonplace.

'But they're *allies*,' he said. He knew even as he said it that he sounded like a child, petulant and foolish.

'Of course they're not. Before he died, Shogun Hideyoshi appointed six lords to watch over his son, the new shogun. Any one of them would love to kill the boy and take his place. That is the battle Oda and Tokugawa fight every day, even if no one sees it.'

'*Six* lords,' said Taro. 'So they should all be enemies. What makes Lord Oda and Lord Tokugawa so different?'

Heiko shook her head. 'No. Oda and Tokugawa were clever. They secured the allegiance of the more minor lords. They bribed, they murdered, they married off sisters and cousins, until four of the daimyos on the council of six were little more than vassals. And so now there are two poles of power in the country: Lord Oda and Lord Tokugawa. The other four lords are divided more or less equally between them. It's never possible to say for sure which side anyone is on, Oda's or Tokugawa's, from one day to the next. But what is certain is that either Oda or Tokugawa will be shogun one day. It remains only to be seen who will destroy the other.'

'Someone told Shusaku...' began Taro.

'Yes?'

'That Lord Tokugawa tried to have Lord Oda killed.' He placed a slight emphasis on the word *'lord'*.

'Doesn't surprise me. Either would love to wipe the other out. The problem is they're both so powerful. All-out war would practically annihilate their armies and leave them in a precarious position. So they pretend to be friends. It's like a game of Shogi.'

'Lord Tokugawa blamed it on his own son. And killed him for it.' Taro waited for the girl to burst out laughing, to say that this was ridiculous, that a samurai would never do such a thing.

She didn't.

'Clever,' she said.

'Clever? He cut his son's head off! It's... despicable, that's what it is. It's not Bushido. It's not samurai.'

Heiko rolled her eyes. 'Samurai commit seppuku, no? If called upon by their lord?'

'Well, yes, but that's if they fail or... something. Not when they are falsely accused!'

'Falsely accused, yes, but not without reason,' said Heiko. 'Tokugawa had to kill his son.'

'Why would he—'

'Think: now Oda and Tokugawa are at peace again, the murderer has been punished, everyone is happy. Tokugawa has sent his message. He is prepared to honour his alliance with Oda even so far as to kill his own beloved son in support of it.'

'But Lord Oda knows that it was really Lord Tokugawa.'

'Yes, well. Tokugawa has sent a private message also. That he is so ruthless in his pursuit of power that he is willing to sacrifice his family in order to preserve his position.'

Taro felt dizzy. This was not the honourable samurai life of which he had heard tell in stories. 'Why would Tokugawa's...' He corrected himself. 'Why would Lord Tokugawa's son die like that? Why not refuse?'

'He was samurai,' said Heiko simply. 'He knew his death would further his father's aims, bring him closer to one day being shogun. Total loyalty to one's lord and one's father is one of the basic precepts of samurai life. That is why samurai are idiots.'

Taro's mouth dropped open. He had never imagined that anyone – least of all a girl! – could so openly criticize the ruling classes.

'Sorry,' said Heiko sarcastically. 'I forget that samurai are sacred to you. I should have remembered. After all, you come from such a high-placed family. You must have come to know and respect many samurai when you lived in that little seaside village.'

'Oh, very funny,' said Taro distantly. But he was thinking about what she had said, even if she had meant it as a joke. Because that would be one reason why he would have such a bow, wouldn't it? And a good reason for ninja to want to kill him too. The old woman had said he would one day be shogun.

There was a natural conclusion, but it was so absurd that his mind could only grasp the edge of it, as if it were a structure so colossal the eye could not take in the entirety of its bulk.

What if he wasn't a peasant? What if he really *was* a samurai?

Heiko too had fallen silent, thinking. Now she turned to him. 'So a simple fisherman's son has a Tokugawa bow. One day ninja arrive, trying to kill him, and he is rescued by a ninja loyal to Lord Tokugawa—'

Taro cut her off. 'Shusaku works for Lord Tokugawa?'

'Didn't you know?'

Taro shook his head. 'No. But just then, when you said what the *mon* was… I remembered that Shusaku has the same emblem on his sword.'

'He must have kept it from when he was a samurai,' said Heiko.

'You mean… he was one of Lord Tokugawa's samurai? And now he's a ninja?'

Heiko nodded.

Taro was astonished. As a child the world had been so simple: there were samurai, who were principled and loyal; there were *ronin*, who were not; and there were ghosts and evil spirits, who were to be avoided. Now it seemed that there were samurai who could become evil spirits, and yet still retain their loyalty, their principles.

This thought, though, bumped against his own enormous and ludicrous suspicion, and Taro began to feel that it was not even an edge of the structure he was grasping – it was the merest corner of a window, a cornice, a stone lying by the building's wall.

Heiko frowned. 'What is it?'

'I was just thinking… I mean, it's ridiculous… but those ninja must have come for me for a reason. What if… I mean, what if I wasn't really a peasant? What if I was samurai? Why else would the ninja want to kill me?' He could see in her expression that she was coming to the same insane thought as him. 'What if,' he almost whispered, 'I was really someone important to Lord Tokugawa?'

So totally had he and the rest of the inhabitants of Shirahama been influenced by heroic tales of Lord Oda, that even to say this small thing seemed a betrayal.

Heiko stared. 'Gods. Yes. It would explain why you have the bow. And then there's the abbess's prophecy. She said the shogun would be the son of an ama mother. She didn't say anything about the *father*.'

Taro swallowed. She was thinking the same thing as him. She was groping at the same vast and improbable architecture. He could think of nothing to say.

Clearly interpreting his silence as confusion, rather than shocked wonderment, Heiko said, 'I wonder... What if the bow were given to you as a... a talisman, or an heirloom? Something like a seal, to prove your provenance? I mean, for the son of a fisherman to be shogun is one thing. But for the son of a daimyo—'

Just then Shusaku walked up to where they sat. He was followed a moment later by Yukiko and Hiro, who looked worn out. 'Getting to know each other?' he asked Taro and Heiko, his voice a little sharp.

How long was he listening? thought Taro.

'Yes,' said Taro. He watched in a sort of daze as Shusaku turned away from them and tended the fire.

Heiko looked at Taro, then at Shusaku. She sighed, then stood up, holding the bow.

'Shusaku,' she said. 'I think you'd better tell us what's going on. What does Taro have to do with Lord Tokugawa?'

Yukiko stared at Taro. 'What?'

The ninja straightened up, slowly. He folded his arms. 'What gave it away?'

Heiko held out the bow. 'Tokugawa's *mon*. Carved on the inside.'

Shusaku sucked air through his teeth. 'I should have paid more attention.' He drew his *wakizashi*, and for a crazy moment

Taro thought he was about to run Heiko through, kill her for working out the secret. But he just flipped the blade into his hand, then proffered the leather-bound grip to Heiko. She took the sword in her hand.

'I still have mine, too,' he said.

Taro moved closer to Heiko, looked down at the little stamp at the base of the blade, the one he had noticed in Shirahama and then forgotten about. The *mon* that marked the ninja out as a vassal of Lord Tokugawa Ieyasu.

Shusaku took his sword back. 'I stopped being a samurai when I died on a battlefield and was reborn a ninja. And I stopped caring about most things when the woman I loved was killed. But there is one thing about me that will never change. My life is dedicated to Lord Tokugawa, and I will protect him and his own from all injury and harm.'

He stepped closer to Taro.

'And that includes his family.'

A hush fell on all of them. Taro felt Heiko's hand tightening on his arm. Hiro was looking at him with wonder in his eyes.

'You see,' said Shusaku, 'Heiko was right when she said that the son of a daimyo might have a better chance of being shogun one day. The truth is, Taro, you are Lord Tokugawa's son.'

T ARO STARED AT the ninja who had saved his life, who had led him hundreds of *ri* from home, who had shown him the best and the worst of a warrior's life.

'I'm Lord Tokugawa's *son*?' he asked. 'So my parents...'

'Are not your parents. Yes.'

Taro felt the ground give way beneath his feet. His father, who had fished the shore of Shirahama all his life; his mother, who had dived its coral reefs... In his mind they were *safety* and *love* and *respect* and *home*.

But it seemed they were not *Mother*.

Not *Father*.

He sat down.

Shusaku bowed to him in the deep style reserved for the very upper ranks of samurai. 'Tokugawa-*san*,' he said, 'I am sorry for keeping this from you.'

No one had ever bowed to Taro like that before. It made him uncomfortable. 'Please,' he said, 'stand up.'

Shusaku rose slightly from his bow. 'Tokugawa-*san*,' he said, 'forgive me for keeping this from you. I did not know how to tell you.' He bowed again. 'Lord Endo Shusaku is at your service.'

'*Lord*?'

'Not any more. But once, yes. The days when I owned land and people are long gone, however. Now I own nothing but my sword.' Shusaku indicated his *wakizashi*.

Hiro looked at Taro, then at Shusaku. 'You're *both* lords?' he said. 'And me a peasant wrestler. My parents would be so proud.'

Yukiko was just opening and closing her mouth, and Taro almost wanted to laugh. She had been so jealous to see him already turned, and now he was a lord, too.

Taro left her gaping and smiled at Hiro. 'You had better start bowing to me,' he said to Hiro. 'Or I will have you beheaded.'

Hiro shook his head. 'I don't think so. I'll simply switch my allegiance to Shusaku – Lord Endo, I mean. He'll protect me from your violent excesses.'

Shusaku smiled too. 'I would gladly accept it, were you not already a true friend to Taro here, and the best of retainers.'

Despite himself, Hiro blushed with pride.

'My… My parents,' said Taro again, and was again unable to complete his question.

'Your parents are merely peasants. I believe your mother helped Lord Tokugawa once, when the ship he was aboard ran aground. Lord Tokugawa trusted her.'

'She's also an ama,' said Heiko. 'Like the abbess said.'

'Indeed,' said Shusaku. 'A shogun born of an ama… Perhaps it was no coincidence that Lord Tokugawa left you with your mother. Perhaps fate was at work when he left his son with a lowly fisherwoman—'

'My mother is not *lowly*,' spat Taro.

'No—no,' stammered Shusaku. 'I meant—'

'They are the people who raised me,' said Taro, still angry. 'My mother is my mother. And I will still find her when she writes to me; I will still go for her when that pigeon arrives.

Do you understand, Ninja? I love her. I will not see her come to harm on my account.'

Shusaku bowed deeply. 'Of course. And I will help you find her, as I promised. She is the woman who brought you up, who fed you, who embraced you, who healed your boyhood injuries. Those bonds cannot be cut.'

Taro nodded in return. 'Thank you.' And he *was* grateful, truly. He hadn't known whether to trust the ninja before, had even thought about abandoning him when he knew where to find his mother. But not since he had seen the ninja take on those *ronin*, for no personal gain.

Shusaku sat down by the fire and motioned for the others to sit too. But Yukiko stayed standing. She was staring at Shusaku, her eyes hard. 'You brought Lord Tokugawa's *son* to our house?'

'We needed shelter,' said Shusaku. 'Clothes, supplies… I didn't mean—'

Yukiko snorted. 'You didn't mean what? To kill the abbess?'

'We don't know—'

'Yes, we do. Probably they are torturing her as we speak.' She turned and fled out of the cave, sobbing. Taro felt awful. He hadn't wanted any of this to happen; he hadn't intended for the abbess to be hurt.

He stood. 'I—' he began, but Heiko stood and put her hands out.

'It's all right,' she said. 'She knows it's not your fault, not really. The abbess believed in the Tao, and so do I. If it was in the Tao for her to die, then it would have happened regardless. We are powerless against it.' She glanced at the cave entrance. 'I'll go after her. She'll calm down.'

Shusaku nodded. 'Go. But be back before sundown.'

'She was already angry that I was made a vampire before her,' said Taro. 'She'll hate me now.'

'No,' said Shusaku. 'She has a good heart, just a passionate one. She'll forgive you. As Heiko says, she knows herself that it's not your fault. She just needs someone to blame, for now.'

Taro knew the feeling. He could remember when he had transferred his anger over his father's death onto the ninja who sat before him, blaming him for his lack of honour, his ruthless attitude. And he liked Shusaku now, didn't he?

Yes, surely Yukiko would come to see that he was only a pawn in all of this, a single piece on the board, being moved by the great lords.

Shusaku spat into the fire. 'There are things we can blame ourselves for, but if we try to claim credit for everything bad that happens, we will drive ourselves mad. Is the abbess dead? We don't know. Might she have survived if we had not visited her? Perhaps. But we did not kill her.'

Taro nodded. It was true, but it didn't make the guilt any easier to bear.

There was an uncomfortable silence. Then Shusaku held his hand out for Taro's bow, and turned it over in his hands. 'Gods,' he said at last. 'Stupid of me not to notice. I did wonder how a village boy came to be armed with such a fine piece. But I assumed your father was a skilled craftsman.'

'But my father *didn't* make it, did he?'

Shusaku examined it, running his fingers over the belly of the bow, peering at the *mon*. 'No. My guess is that Lord Tokugawa made it himself. He is a fine craftsman. Unlike some nobles, he makes it his business to understand the work his vassals do. Only by knowing the daily life of your peasants and soldiers can you hope to rule them.' Shusaku spoke with admiration, and it was obvious that he still held Lord Tokugawa in high esteem. 'He must have wanted to give you a symbol of your heritage. Something that would mark you out as Tokugawa if – when – it became necessary to call on you.'

Taro tried to make sense of this. 'Why would he call on me? Why would he *hide* me in the first place?'

'Isn't it obvious? You're an heir. Lord Tokugawa chose to hide you for your protection. It's common for the lords who are currently contesting the shogunate to take one another's sons as hostages. Lord Tokugawa's younger son is at this moment a guest of Lord Oda's, at that man's castle. He is accompanied there by his mother, Lord Tokugawa's wife. This means that of Lord Tokugawa's two acknowledged sons, one is a hostage at the castle of his greatest enemy, and one is—'

'Dead.'

'Yes. How did you know?'

'I… I overheard the abbess telling you. I was in the garden when you were talking.'

Shusaku nodded. 'Good. You have a true ninja's instinct!' He laughed.

Taro drew in a gasp, as something occurred to him. 'Lord Tokugawa's wife. The one who is living with Lord Oda. Is she my mother?'

Shusaku made an evasive gesture. 'It seems likely. But a daimyo may name any heir he likes, and is free to father sons with any number of concubines.'

Taro grunted. The mother he had grown up with would always be his true mother, anyway. Let Lord Tokugawa and his concubines remain walled up in their castle. Taro would go with Shusaku to find his mother, and then he would have revenge on everyone who had stolen his life from him.

'So,' continued Shusaku. 'One of Tokugawa's son's is a hostage. The other is dead. But Lord Tokugawa took the sensible precaution of hiding *another* son with villagers he could trust. The middle one – the one no one knew about. You. A good idea, as it turned out.'

A thought so enormous entered Taro's head that it filled the confines of his mind, ungraspable, impossible to examine clearly.

'Someone tried to have me killed…' he began. 'And that man Kira was looking for us. We thought at the time it was because of the ambassador's palanquin. But maybe he was hunting me anyway…'

Shusaku nodded, leaning forward. 'Go on.'

'I am Tokugawa's son. So the person who would want me dead…'

Another nod.

'Is Lord Oda.'

The ninja spread his hands. 'And there you have it.'

T ARO'S EMOTIONS WERE in turmoil. He had grown up in Lord Oda's territory. He supposed that had been rather clever of Tokugawa – *of my father*, he corrected. But it also meant that he had been brought up to see Oda as a kind of minor deity, a just leader and a skilled fighter, a sword saint no less. Yet… it was clear that only Oda could have ordered the attack on his home, the murder of his father.

His own attempted murder.

In his mind's eye, an image flashed. His father's head, the pool of blood. He recoiled from it as from a snake, but the snake was inside him, and it was a lord who had murdered a fisherman for nothing but power.

Taro fought to reconcile what he had thought he knew with what he had only now learned.

Lord Oda is the murderer. He killed my father.

So Lord Tokugawa was right to hire those ronin *to try to kill him. He is noble and wise…*

But try as he might, the thoughts wouldn't stack up in his head, only kept falling down, like smooth pebbles laid on top of one another.

Because Lord Tokugawa ordered Lord Oda's assassination before *those ninja attacked.*

Taro looked up at Shusaku. 'Lord Oda learned about me. About where I was hidden. And he sent those ninja. There was no danger in assassinating me, because as far as anyone knows, I don't even exist. Right?'

Shusaku gave a sad smile and nodded. 'Yes.'

Taro thought some more. 'Lord Tokugawa wished to protect me, but he couldn't send his samurai because I was in Lord Oda's territory, and because he couldn't publicly admit that I was his son. So he sent you.' The words tumbled from his mouth in a rush, spiky and as hard as a landslide.

The ninja nodded.

'And why didn't my— I mean, Lord Tokugawa, send more men with you?'

'That, I truly don't know. He wished me to go alone. He was very clear on that.'

Shusaku looked at Taro, his head cocked slightly to the side. Taro took a breath. 'You weren't supposed to change me, were you?'

Shusaku shook his head. 'Of course not. I was forced to when you were injured. I was supposed to save you and take you back to the Tokugawa castle. Now I cannot. For a man like Lord Tokugawa, to have a vampire for a son would be worse than if I presented him with a corpse.'

A tear welled up, unbidden, in Taro's eye. 'If that's true,' he said, 'why did you save me? Why not just leave me to die?'

Shusaku coughed, embarrassed. 'Lord Tokugawa may prefer a dead boy to a vampire boy. But I do not.'

Taro looked away, touched. 'So my true father doesn't know I'm alive,' he said, changing the subject.

Shusaku shook his head again.

'But Lord Oda knows. The pigeon, remember?'

'Yes,' said Shusaku. 'But he won't tell Tokugawa. Even if he wanted to, he can't admit that he tried to kill his ally's son! They must both pretend the incident never happened. And anyway, even if he could tell Tokugawa you still lived, he wouldn't. It suits him for Tokugawa to believe his line to be finished.'

Taro thought again. 'My... father... thinks I'm dead. He'll be angry with Oda.'

'I think that's a safe assumption,' said Shusaku.

'And now he'll do something to hurt him.'

'Yes. I would not be surprised if he made another attempt to kill Oda himself, since Oda has no sons. As far as Tokugawa's concerned, he has no sons left. The one who is held hostage might as well be dead, for all the good he does. It is time for him to take decisive action.'

Taro made one more logical conclusion. 'When Lord Tokugawa decides to strike at Lord Oda again, he won't use *ronin*, will he? That method has already failed.'

Shusaku nodded, as if to say, *go on*.

'He'll use ninja.' He looked at Shusaku. 'He'll use you.'

'Not me personally. I imagine he assumes me to be dead too. But he'll use the community, yes. I expect a pigeon will arrive at the sacred mountain soon, if it has not arrived there already.'

'When it comes, will you be able to go?'

'Why would I not?'

'Lord Tokugawa thinks you're dead. Don't you have to hide in case he finds out you're still alive – and I'm still alive too?'

Shusaku smiled, his tattoos wrinkling. 'I knew Lord Tokugawa well, once. We... well, we were friends, at one point. My father fought on Lord Oda's side in the war against his enemies. I, however, did not agree with Lord Oda's ambitions.

When my father died, the lord dissolved his fiefdom and disinherited me. It was the greatest of dishonours. If your father had not taken me in, I would have become *ronin*.'

Taro leaned forward. 'So he is a good man, then? Lord Tokugawa? Tell me – what is he like?'

Shusaku smiled. 'This is how I would describe Lord Tokugawa: Everyone knows that Oda is a sword saint, that he defeated Musashi himself. Nobody knows anything about Lord Tokugawa's skill with a sword. But for all they know, he might be a sword saint too. Do you see?'

'He's sneaky,' said Hiro.

Shusaku laughed. 'That's one way of putting it.' He turned to Taro. 'Lord Tokugawa is samurai. I don't agree with his every action. But he is brave and clever and decisive. I see those qualities in you, too.'

Taro couldn't sort out his feelings – pride, that he shared blood and character with a lord; anger, that he shared nothing, it seemed, with the man he had always seen and admired as his father. 'My father – I mean, the one who is dead. He was brave too, and strong. When I was bitten by that *mako*, he carried me back to the village, over a cliff.' Taro pulled his robe to expose once again his shoulder, the arc of scar that curved round it.

Shusaku examined the old wound. 'You were lucky to live.'

'Not lucky. My mother and father sat with the healer for days. They didn't sleep, they didn't eat. And they paid him everything they had. Do *you* see?'

The ninja nodded, slowly. 'It is a long time since I knew Lord Tokugawa. But I think he would be pleased with the parents he chose for his middle son.'

Taro nodded, too moved to speak.

Shusaku shook his head, as if to dispel water from his ears.

'Besides, Lord Tokugawa thinks you're dead. And look at me. I'm a ninja, and my face is obscured by writing. Lord Tokugawa wouldn't know me from any other man in black clothes. It's been many years since he laid eyes on me, and I didn't have these tattoos then.'

'So when the order comes to assassinate Oda – *if* it comes – you'll go yourself?'

'Of course. I'm the best ninja there is.'

Taro nodded, picked up his bow. 'Good. When it comes, I'm going to join the mission. Oda killed my father. I want him for myself.'

Hiro stood up. 'And I'll be by your side.'

CHAPTER 32

WHEN HEIKO AND Yukiko finally returned, Yukiko stood awkwardly in front of Taro. She swallowed nervously. 'I know you didn't mean…' she began. She was looking down, and a tear glistened on her thick, dark eyelashes.

'I know,' he said. 'I understand why you were angry.'

She nodded. 'Thank you.' Then she turned and went to gather her things. The sun was dropping below the horizon, and Shusaku was keen for them to get to the mountain as soon as possible.

As they began walking up the valley towards the sacred mountain, Taro hung back. The forest they walked through seemed taken from the Pure Land. Elegantly twisted trees rose on all sides, luxuriant in soft green moss. Mounds of grass littered the ground, some of them revealing grinning carved faces of rock, especially near streams or unusually large trees – *kami*, placed here by local villagers to protect the forest.

Or found here by them.

As Taro walked, he attempted to conjure the face of his father, projecting it like a shadow puppet onto a screen in his mind that lay over the trees and moss, shimmering and transparent. But like a shadow puppet's, his father's features were dark, rough, impossible to make out. Taro grimaced, concentrating.

His eyes had been wide-set, had they not?

His mouth had been turned always in a smile.

No.

His eyes were narrow, catlike—

Taro cursed. Death had torn his father into pieces, like so much carrion – a hand he remembered clearly, the tendons and veins traced like rivers on a map; an ear, too, conch-shaped. But the whole was gone, torn limb from limb, and Taro could not piece it back together. It was impossible to picture his father in his entirety, the way that he had been when he lived.

Then, as Taro concentrated on the elusive image, which shook with the effort of his imagining, another image replaced it. A man in a rich robe, wearing the helmet of a samurai lord, his kimono adorned with a hollyhock *mon*.

Lord Tokugawa.

Taro had never even seen the man, yet his image dispelled that of his other father as effectively as a monk banishes a ghost. Taro spat, turned his eyes on the trees and their roots, which burst through the ground beneath his feet, and he quickened his pace.

The screen of his mind shivered, and went dull. But then another image floated up, completely unasked for – the girl they had saved, the one who had given him her ring. He cursed his own thoughts. She was just another impossible dream, come to taunt him, his admiration for her courage and beauty as useless as his curiosity about Tokugawa, or his grief over his father's death.

Because this was the real world, not the fairy-tale world of Heiko's stories. Nothing he felt for his father would bring him back from the Pure Land, just as nothing would bring Taro to one day stand in front of Lord Tokugawa and be acknowledged as a lost son and heir. He was a vampire, and, worse, he was a peasant. He might as well dream of walking the night sky to the moon as dream of that beautiful girl.

He twisted the ring on his finger, feeling its tightness against his skin as a form of mockery, yet equally unable to remove it, since it represented the only part of the girl he could see, and touch.

He didn't even know her name.

He could feel the bow on his shoulder, and its weight seemed unbearable. It too was a tangible symbol of the change that had come over him. Whereas before it had always been the bow his father had made him, decorated with a motif of leaves, now it was a Tokugawa bow, the magical item left with him to identify him as the son. It was as if the object itself had been taken away from him, and returned as something strange and changed.

His focus now was on the bow on his shoulder, not on the roots and stones at his feet, and so it was that he remembered what the girl had said, the lady they had rescued. Something about the grip being thicker than usual. Frowning, he took the bow from his shoulder, holding it up before him while hurrying to keep up with the others.

There had been something at the back of his mind...

Gods. He tapped the grip.

A thin, hollow sound reverberated down the length of the bow, and there was – he could swear it – a very slight rattle that accompanied it.

There's something inside, he thought. *Something hidden within the heart of the bow.*

His heart racing, he picked up the pace. He was remembering

what the abbess had said, about the Buddha ball. About how it had been returned by the ama's son to the woman who retrieved it from the deep. Couldn't another ama have recovered it from the sea? He glanced at the bow.

What if the Buddha ball is hidden inside? he thought. It was a ridiculous idea, but then so was the idea of being a daimyo's son. He felt slightly dizzy, as he thought that perhaps the bow might contain two legacies – one from Tokugawa, to identify him, but another one even more powerful and magical.

But no. The Buddha ball couldn't exist, could it? It was only a fairy tale. Even Shusaku didn't believe in it.

Still. When I get to the mountain, I will break the bow, even if it means destroying my only link to my real father. I must know what is hidden inside.

Then Taro was distracted by the sound of a sniff from ahead. He was surprised to see Heiko, walking alone, her eyes red. He hurried to draw level with her, when she turned and saw him.

'Are you all right?' he asked.

'Yes,' she replied. 'It's just... the abbess, you know. And Shusaku. I'm worried about him. I don't want anything to happen to him.'

'Shusaku?' said Taro, confused. Worrying about Shusaku seemed a little like worrying about an earthquake, or a tsunami. The man was a *ninja*.

Heiko sighed. 'You didn't hear what the prophetess said? And those tattoos. I can't believe he did that. It's like he's tempting fate!' She looked at him for confirmation but he could only shrug. 'Because of Hoichi!' she said, as if he were being very dense.

'I'm sorry,' said Taro. 'I don't know what you're talking about. Please, tell me what it is that's worrying you. If Shusaku's tattoos are putting him in some sort of danger, I want to know about it.'

'You haven't heard of Hoichi the Earless?'

Taro shook his head.

'He was a blind musician. He was tricked into playing his *biwa* for the Heike family, singing them the story of their defeat by the Minamoto, in the great sea battle.'

Taro shrugged. 'And?'

'The Heike family were all dead: every one of them killed in the battle, even the women and children. Hoichi was singing to their ghosts. And the palace he thought he was playing in was their graveyard. He didn't realize. It was only because a young priest in the seminary where Hoichi lived followed him to the graveyard that anyone knew what was happening. And of course he was becoming pale, and weak, from all that time with the ghosts.'

Taro shivered, imagining the blind man playing to people he didn't know were dead – playing to the *gaki* spirits of the lower realm, who were called hungry ghosts and who returned at night to the earth in order to feed on the force and vitality of the living, so constantly empty and needful had they become in their death.

'Anyway,' Heiko went on, 'the priest tried to help Hoichi…' She paused. 'This is a famous story. You've really never heard it?'

'No.'

'Honestly. What are they teaching peasant boys these days?'

Taro laughed. 'I'm very good at hunting rabbits.'

Heiko smiled. 'So… the priest, he wrote on Hoichi with his brush and ink – the Sanskrit text of the Heart Sutra, to protect the blind man from the ghosts, which he said would be unable to see him due to the power of the symbols. Does any of this sound familiar?'

'Gods,' said Taro. 'That's where Shusaku got the idea.'

'Presumably. But he is as arrogant and presumptuous as ever.' She said this, despite the harshness of the words, with a sort of sad admiration. 'He tempts the fates.'

'Why? I don't understand.'

'The priest forgot to paint Hoichi's ears. When the ghosts came for him, they ripped them off, and he died of blood loss. That is why the story is called Hoichi the Earless.'

Taro let out a long breath. 'I see,' he said.

But *your eyes will betray you* was what he thought. Like Hoichi, Shusaku had failed to cover one part of his body with the text. Was that what the abbess had seen? Would his eyes give him away to an evil spirit – to a ghost, or a ninja? Taro felt a chill run through him at the thought, but he smiled for Heiko's benefit.

'We're going to the mountain, though, aren't we?' he said. 'It's the ninja's lair. There couldn't be anywhere safer.'

'Let's hope so,' said Heiko, and then fell silent, and didn't speak again for a *ri* or more, as they crossed over increasingly steep terrain.

Soon they entered the final valley before the entrance to the sacred mountain. Shusaku cautioned them all to move with more care than ever before. It was here, near to the ninja's secret encampment, that it was most crucial to preserve secrecy.

Silently, they crept past a dark village. Smoke rose from one chimney. The others were still and cold. As they walked along the bottom of an irrigation ditch, a heron startled and took loudly to the air. Taro, panicked, dropped to the ground before he saw the silhouette of the bird crossing the waning moon.

It was only when they were climbing the terraced steps of rice paddies, the village houses below and behind them, as small as children's toys, that Taro realized he had dropped his bow in the ditch.

He gestured to Shusaku, who tutted when Taro told him what he had done. 'An ordinary bow? Bad enough. But a Tokugawa bow? There is no way to explain its presence if someone finds it.'

'I know,' said Taro. 'I'm sorry.' And of course it was not only that it was a Tokugawa bow that frightened him – it was the idea that it might, just might, contain the Buddha ball. For a peasant to come across it would be disastrous. He felt his pulse quickening, and reminded himself that a peasant might not notice the thickness of the grip. He hadn't, and neither had Shusaku. Only the noble girl had seen it.

And then, the Buddha ball didn't exist, anyway.

Probably.

He bit his lip. 'I'll go back and get it. You wait here with Hiro and the girls.'

Shusaku resisted for a moment, but Taro was insistent. Eventually the ninja relented. 'Go, but be quick.'

Taro headed back down the valley towards the village. He moved fast, keeping low to the ground, trying to minimize the part of him framed by the moon.

Then he saw it, a shadow moving between the trees. He could also hear singing; the toneless, tuneless song of a man who has consumed too much rice wine. Taro melted behind a tree, following the voice. As he drew closer, he could see that the man was carrying something.

A bow.

The man was singing a song of his own invention. 'Found a bow, gonna hide it; wouldn't want my wife to find it; found a bow, gonna sell it; wouldn't want my wife to... benefit. Ha, ha! Good one, Ito!'

Taro wondered for a moment who Ito was, then realized that the man was talking to himself. Taro considered his options. The peasant was drunk, clearly. He might not remember finding the bow, if Taro knocked him out and took it from him. And even if he told anyone, they probably wouldn't believe him. Taro knew from growing up in a village himself that a man who was drunk like this on his own one night was likely to be drunk on other nights too. Most likely, he was well known for it.

Taro searched the thicket floor as he insinuated himself between the trees. Soon he found what he was looking for, a heavy branch. He'd sneak up behind the man and give him one hard blow to the back of the head.

He hoped he could do it without killing him.

Ahead of him, the man was walking towards the end of the thicket, into moonlight. Taro quickened his pace. It would be better to ambush him in the trees.

But when he caught up, the drunkard was standing at the door of a small wooden building, standing on the other side of the thicket from the village. As Taro watched, he slid open a metal bolt and opened the door, then threw the bow inside. Taro just had time to see a mound of shimmering white inside, glowing in the moonlight.

A rice store.

The man shut the door again, muttering. 'Said I was lazy… I'll show them. Bow mus' be worth a fortune. "Look at Ito!" they said. "He fell in the ditch! What a fool!" I'll show 'em foolish. They only *think* I fell. Really a *kami* mus' have given me a push, so's I'd find the bow. Prob'ly it's magic – or it belongs to the shogun, or something. There'll be a reward, oh, yes!'

And with that, he put a key into the bolt and slammed it home, locking the door.

Taro cursed. This made things more difficult. But not impossible. He would overpower the peasant, take his key, and quickly recover his bow from—

A group of staggering men rounded the corner of the thicket and burst into derisive laughter when they saw the man Taro had been following. Taro ducked behind a bush.

'Ito!' one of the men shouted. 'Got out of the ditch, did you? What are you doing here? Surely you prefer dark, muddy places?'

Taro cursed. This wasn't the village drunkard – the whole *village* was drunk. It must have been some kind of festival for the end of the *obon* holiday.

'Hilarious,' said the man who had hidden the bow. 'Tha's really hilarious. Ackshually I was jus' enjoying a stroll in the moonlight.'

'Well,' said another of the men, clapping Taro's intended prey on the back, 'why don't you stroll with us back to the village. Your wife is asking after you. Said if you didn't come home you'd be living in the ditch on a more permanent basis.'

Grumbling, the man went with them, taking the path that skirted the thicket to return to the village.

And with that, the key, and Taro's bow, were gone.

CHAPTER 34

T ARO DIDN'T KNOW why he lied.

When he returned to the others, Shusaku asked him if he'd found the bow, and he said no – he had searched the ditch from top to bottom and seen no sign of it. Perhaps he was afraid of Shusaku's anger, if he ever discovered that the bow might be more than an heirloom, or perhaps he only wanted to solve his problems himself, for once.

For whatever reason, he didn't feel that he could tell Shusaku the bow was in a rice store, hidden by a drunken fool.

'You're sure you dropped it when the heron took flight?' asked Shusaku.

'No,' Taro replied. 'Now that I think about it, it seems possible that I left it in the cave.' He had been walking behind. He trusted that Shusaku might not have seen whether he was carrying the bow or not. At the same time, he listened to the words coming out of his mouth as if it were another speaking. Why lie to the ninja?

Yet this was something Taro knew he had to do alone. His bow, his birthright, his responsibility. He remembered something too from when Heiko and Yukiko were talking to Hiro of their training.

Heiko had mentioned lock-picking.

'Well,' said Shusaku, 'if it's at the cave, then we are safe. No one knows of its location besides the ninja. Let us hope that's where you left it.' He gave Taro a hard look and turned to carry on up the valley.

Soon the rice paddies gave way to rock, lonely pine trees, and moss. The air was thin and made for hard going. Even Taro and Shusaku, with their vampire blood, began to breathe heavily. They reached a meadow in which grew wild orchids, daisies, and poppies. Shusaku stopped.

'We've arrived,' he said. He pointed to a simple wooden hut that lay at the end of the meadow, abutting the bottom of a sheer-sided grey cliff. Aside from the hut, there was no other visible habitation.

Taro, Hiro, Heiko, and Yukiko looked round, confused. 'It's just a hut,' said Hiro.

The rock wall rose high above them, and seemed to continue round on either side, as if to bar the way to the summit. A thin covering of snow lay on the ground.

Shusaku smiled. He spread his hands, indicating the scene, turning as he did so. They were standing on high ground. Taro realized how high only now that he turned and looked back down the valley. Below them, hills stretched into the distance, as low and pale as sand dunes. The tops of the trees at the tree line were a long way down, and the trees themselves seemed tiny.

In fact, this was the highest point for miles, as far as Taro could see. Only the side where the cliff stood was cut off from view. On the other three sides they looked on the world from above, like crows.

In the midst of this high-land desolation, the hut stood alone, as if some mad hermit had taken it upon himself to live in this isolated place, high above everyone else.

'This is where our journey ends,' said Shusaku. He led them up the meadow to the hut.

'You're telling us this is the ninja base?' asked Hiro. 'I was hoping for something a bit grander.'

Shusaku smiled at him and opened the door.

Taro looked at Hiro. Hiro shrugged and followed Shusaku through the door. Taro went after him, the girls behind. The hut was dark inside, and smelled of damp earth. Taro looked round. The walls were bare. There was no furniture. The only feature in the room was a square rug on the floor. Of Shusaku, there was no sign at all.

'Where'd he go?' asked Hiro, bewildered.

'I don't know.' Taro lifted a corner of the rug.

Just then Shusaku's voice came up to them from below the floor. 'Under the rug,' he said. 'There's a trapdoor.'

Taro lifted the rug and, sure enough, underneath it was a small wooden door with a heavy metal ring set into it. He tugged upward, revealing an opening into darkness. Taro sat down, lowering his legs into the hole. His feet found stone steps, apparently cut into the very rock of the mountain.

'Spooky,' said Yukiko from behind him. 'We'll be like Hoichi down there – blind, and probably surrounded by ghosts.'

'Thanks,' said Taro. 'I feel much better now.'

He descended a few steps, holding the trapdoor up with one hand so that Hiro and the girls could squeeze under too. The door slammed shut behind them, plunging them into midnight darkness.

'Feel your way along the wall,' came Shusaku's disembodied voice. 'Soon you'll see me.'

Taro carried on down, plagued by the uncomfortable sensation of descending into one of samsara's hellish worlds: the realm of the demons, perhaps. The darkness was absolute, an almost tangible thing that lay heavily on his skin like silk.

Something brushed against him, and he bit off a scream when he realized that it was Hiro, holding on to his hand. The gesture – so simple, so childlike – filled him with a rush of fondness for his old friend.

'I never told you,' whispered Hiro. 'I'm afraid of the dark.'

Taro smiled. 'Me too. But it'll be over soon.'

'Did you just say you were afraid of the dark, Hiro?' asked Yukiko. 'And there I was hoping that the big strong wrestler would look after me. I guess I got it the wrong way round. The big strong wrestler needs a girl to look after *him*.'

Hiro grunted. 'It's a good job it's so dark in here, or you'd be in trouble.' Then he yelped and bashed into Taro. 'What hit me?' he demanded, in a voice that was unmistakably frightened.

'It's a good job I don't need light to see *you*,' said Yukiko. 'You take up the whole tunnel. If it doesn't widen up a little, you might get stuck down here *forever* …'

Hiro laughed, hollowly. 'The sooner we're out of this tunnel the better. For me, anyway. Not for Yukiko. She's dead meat.'

Taro didn't feel much better than Hiro. His fingers were trailing lightly along a cold, damp wall, whose rough striations of stone scraped against his fingertips. The surface was clammy to the touch, and Taro had an irrational fear that his hand might suddenly touch not wall but flesh – the face and teeth of a demon, lurking in a recess, or the gnarled hand of a monstrous old man waiting to pounce on him. He was reminded unpleasantly of a game he had played with his mother once. In the darkness, when the fire had gone out, she had proffered several open bags, asked him to put his hand in and guess the contents only from touch. There had been worms in one, a starfish, a squid. One of them had held a piece of whale blubber, smooth and gelatinous to the touch. Taro had squealed with boyish pleasure at this game, but it had scared him too, for in the second before he guessed, before his guess was confirmed or denied, the bag could contain anything his imagination supplied. A nest of baby snakes, a severed hand, an organ of some kind.

What hideous things could live on this wall, ready for his fingers to glide over, to stroke?

Taro forced himself to carry on, fighting the impulse to take his hand away from the wall. He could hear breathing ahead. He tried to still his pounding heart, bring his own breathing under control. It would be Shusaku, of course. Who else could it be? But there was no light, and whoever was up ahead didn't hail them.

Taro felt Hiro's hand tightening round his own. They had come close now to whoever was doing the breathing. Taro could *feel* a presence before them. He slowed, terrified, convinced that the walls were tightening in, that they had walked into a trap that they couldn't back out of.

Then a light flared, making spots dance in Taro's vision, and out of the white haze Shusaku's figure gradually resolved into focus. He held a torch in one hand. 'Come on,' he said. 'Let's get back into daylight.'

'You had a torch all that time?' asked Yukiko. 'That's cruel.'

'We don't light them till we're deep in the ground,' said Shusaku. 'Don't want light to seep out of the cracks in the hut. It might arouse suspicion.'

They followed him for a time. Taro could not have said how long, but he felt that they covered a fair distance, the length of the beach back home at least. Now that there was light, the tunnel had become only that: a simple passage through the rock, not frightening in the least.

CHAPTER 35

GRADUALLY THE TUNNEL began to lighten, shrinking the shadows cast by Shusaku's torch. It also widened until at last they stepped into a large cave, its walls carved with intricate figures – demons, bodhisattvas, animals, and graceful *apsaras* bearing musical instruments. The cave's roof was decorated with smooth flying arches that stood above the rock, as if to give the impression that the group was standing in the ribcage of a great creature. In thousands of small niches in the walls flickering candles stood, filling the cave with an unsteady yellow light and the smell of tallow.

Taro gazed round him in astonishment, his mouth open. The place was like a temple; it was magnificent. He had never seen anything like it.

Shusaku nudged his shoulder. 'Come on. You haven't seen the best of it yet.' He led the way through the cave towards a wide opening at the far end. Taro watched the walls as they passed – saw rock tigers leaping as if on the point of breaking their stony bonds, saw *apsara* angels smiting boar-tusked demons with delicate swords of hard granite.

'*Apsaras!*' said Heiko. 'This was a Buddhist cave temple once, wasn't it?'

'Yes,' said Shusaku. 'Only long forgotten by most. The rock carvings are masterpieces. But you will have plenty of time to study them later.' They passed a statue of a sitting Buddha, wedged into a large niche in the rock. It was as tall maybe as four men standing on end, and leafed all over in gold.

Heiko gasped. 'But this is extraordinary! Someone should be told—'

'For obvious reasons,' interrupted Shusaku, 'that would be a bad idea.'

They came to the cave mouth, and Taro, Hiro, Heiko, and Yukiko stepped out behind Shusaku into a large, round space – about thirty tatami mats across. Taro could just make out the rock wall at the other side. On all sides rose a single, continuous cliff face, its wall sheer and tall. This cliff was at least the height of three *torii* gates set one on top of the other. The effect was of standing at the bottom of an enormous well. The temperature here was appreciably lower than it had been on the mountain-side, outside the little hut that concealed the entrance.

Hiro pointed upward. 'Look,' he said. Above them was the night sky, bright with golden stars and a crescent moon – only, as Taro looked, he saw that the sky was not real, was instead some kind of illusion. The true moon was waning, yes, but it was far from being this thin. This narrow, curiously flat golden moon was not the real moon. Taro had seen the real one only an hour before, when they had stood outside the little hut, and he was not fooled. He strained his eyes. Yes, what covered the round space at the top of the bowl-like clearing was not the night sky but some kind of dark cloth painted with constellations. As Taro looked, he saw it ripple slightly, presumably with the outside wind. He couldn't help gasping.

'It keeps the sun off,' said Shusaku. 'And the rain, too, which is a shame for our small crops. We have an irrigation system that distributes springwater round our few paddies and vegetable plots, but they have never grown as well as those outside. The sunlight that filters through is dim at best. Still. It is a small price to pay.' He gestured at the artificial night sky. 'It always impresses visitors. Those few that we have, anyway.'

'Where are we?' asked Hiro.

'Haven't you guessed? We're standing in the cauldron of a dead volcano. Welcome to the home of my clan.'

T ARO LOOKED ROUND again at the smooth circle of rock that surrounded them. Of course. He could see now that they had followed the tunnel into a hidden valley; a crater that would only be visible to someone who managed the climb to the very top of the volcano.

Shusaku seemed to read his mind. 'It requires very few guards. We post a couple at the top of the mountain. We have one or two non-vampires, able to go up there by day. Very occasionally a peasant gets too close – looking for a goat, that kind of thing. Then we arrange a little fall for them. Nothing too bad, just a couple of broken bones. The kind of accident that discourages further exploration.'

As he spoke, a woman stepped into the clearing, apparently from nowhere. Taro squinted, and realized that the dark patch behind the woman must be a cave in the cliff wall. The newcomer smiled when she saw Shusaku, and walked over to them, her step springy and lithe – but she frowned when she saw Taro. She bowed to Shusaku. 'Shusaku. I am glad you have returned.'

'Kawabata-san,' said Shusaku. 'You look younger with every day. Your husband is a lucky man.'

The woman rolled her eyes, and Taro decided on the spot that he liked her. She had a grace and a humour that he had seen before, in some of the amas who'd dived with his mother, grace and humour that he associated with those who had decided not to let the vagaries of a dangerous life destroy their equilibrium.

It was the look of a person with inner strength.

Yes, he knew he was right, because even now, as she smiled, he could see that the laughter lines round her eyes echoed other, deeper lines – the signs of frequent worry creasing her forehead.

She turned to Yukiko and Heiko. 'The girls I know, of course.' She bowed to them. Then she directed that half smile, half frown at Shusaku. 'You decided it was time for them to complete their training?'

'Not quite. The abbess sent them away.'

The woman, whose hair was grey and whose face was lined with wrinkles, despite the agile grace of her movements, gave another little nod. 'They were troublesome?'

'No. She believed someone was coming to kill her. She wanted them to be safe.'

The woman looked concerned. 'What trouble are you bringing to our door this time?' she asked Shusaku. 'You know what my husband is—' She broke off, looking scared, and also ashamed. 'I mean…you know the precarious position we are in.'

'I'm not *bringing* anything.'

'And yet,' said the woman, turning to Taro, 'you brought *him*.' She closed her eyes for a moment. 'What were you thinking?'

'I had to. The situation was desperate. It was either that or let him die.'

'I see. Well, I'm sure your actions were determined by circumstance.'

'All actions are determined by circumstance,' said Shusaku, a smile on his lips.

'Indeed,' said a new voice. A fat man waddled out from the tunnel and stood beside the woman. He put a hand on her shoulder, and she flinched, then gave him a weak smile – and Taro saw from these two actions combined that he was her husband, and that she was afraid of him.

'For instance,' continued the man, in a wheedling, arrogant tone. 'Whoever the abbess was afraid of was no doubt looking for you, Shusaku, meaning that *you* got her killed. You were the *circumstance* that determined the *action* of her death.'

Shusaku's hand went to his sword handle, but then he composed himself. 'We don't know she's dead, Kawabata-*san*.' When he had addressed the man's wife, he had spoken her name with respect, but now he put an accent on the honourific *san* in the man's title that seemed to Taro sarcastic, almost as if he were implying, by making so much of it, that it had no business being appended to the fat man's name.

'*Lord* Endo,' replied the man, with the same contempt.

'Now, now, Husband,' said the woman nervously. 'We should listen to what Shusaku has to say.'

'Oh, yes,' said the man. 'I always listen to Shusaku. Even when he is telling lies.' He narrowed his piggy eyes at Heiko and Yukiko. 'Like these girls. You say the abbess sent them away? We both know she would not have parted from those girls in life.'

'Enough,' said Heiko, stepping forward. 'Shusaku didn't kill the abbess. Lord Oda did.'

'Nonsense,' said Kawabata. 'She is his fortune-teller. He wouldn't harm her.'

'He would if it led him to Taro,' said Shusaku, 'and a way to destroy Lord Tokugawa.'

'You maintain that Lord Oda entertains designs on Tokugawa?' said Kawabata to Shusaku with sceptical amusement.

'You know I do,' Shusaku replied.

Kawabata looked now at Taro. 'He is definitely the—'

'Yes. He is Tokugawa's son.'

'He knows?'

'Yes,' said Taro.

'Do you expect me to be pleased that you have brought him here? It could be dangerous for us.'

'We're ninja,' said Shusaku. 'Everything is dangerous for us.'

'Well, yes, but—'

Shusaku took a step forward, his manner suddenly stern. 'You are only the civil leader here, elected by the community. Your responsibilities extend to pastoral care and the growing of crops – no further. I am leader of this clan. You may be pleased or not pleased, that is your prerogative, but you have no authority over me. I was elected over you.'

Kawabata bared his teeth in a very nasty smile. 'As you say, *Lord* Endo.'

Taro was paying close attention to this exchange, so he didn't notice at first that many more people had appeared in the circular clearing. They were now surrounded by a crowd of smiling, jostling people of all ages. Here, a woman held a baby on her hip. There, a young man held a two-headed spear in his hands and looked at Taro, Hiro, and the girls gravely.

Taro felt suddenly very vulnerable. He didn't like all the attention. For days it had been only him, Hiro, and Shusaku. 'Who are all these people?' he asked Shusaku. 'They're all vampires?'

Shusaku smiled. 'No. Vampires are not born, only created. These are the wives of ninja, their children, their parents. Not everyone can go on missions. Some have to stay to look after the crops, the pigs, the weapons.'

Taro looked at the staring people. He felt the urge to be polite. He pointed at himself. 'My name is Taro.'

There was a murmur from the crowd at that, some sharp looks exchanged.

'And this is Hiro, my best friend. Thank you for... for welcoming us into your community.'

Then Kawabata stepped forward. 'Who said you were welcome?' he said. He turned to the crowd. 'Did anyone say he was welcome?'

The woman with the baby on her hip looked at the ground; the man with the spear continued to stare at Taro. Shusaku took a step forward. 'Kawabata-*san*,' he said, emphasizing the *san* again so that it became sardonic, rude. 'I told Taro that he and his friend would study here with us, just like Heiko and Yukiko here, who have been destined for the clan since I rescued them as babies. I told Taro that he would be welcome in my clan.' The word 'my', too, was lightly inflected. 'Would you contradict me?'

Kawabata stepped up to Taro and gave him a cold but appraising look, like a farmer inspecting a pig or a samurai inspecting a horse. 'Since you have told him so,' he said to Shusaku, 'I suppose there isn't much I can do about it. You're the leader after all, and a man who was once samurai.' He put the same emphasis on 'samurai' that Shusaku had put on the '*san*' in his name. 'What am I? Only the son of a ninja who was himself the son of a ninja. But I suppose you haven't thought about the jeopardy this could place us in, *Lord* Endo?'

Shusaku – Lord Endo – shook his head. 'Of course I've thought about it. But the boy is talented. The benefits far outweigh the risks.'

Kawabata waddled up to Shusaku. His stomach swung as he walked, his gravid belly reminding Taro of a pregnant woman's.

His legs, too, were effeminate – thin and delicate. Combined with his wispy beard, balding head, and bloodshot hooded eyes, the effect was grotesque – as if someone had put the head of a drunken merchant on the body of a young woman about to become a mother.

He jabbed a finger in Shusaku's chest. 'I'm still a ninja,' he whispered, though the words were loud enough for Taro to hear. 'Even if I haven't undertaken a mission in years. I think it would be better if you were to take the boy onto the mountain and dispose of him. His friend, too. No one would ever find them. Slit their throats and throw them into a deep ravine.' He jabbed his finger again. 'Imagine what would happen if he were to complete his training and join us. Imagine the results if he were to be turned! The effects would be disastrous! A son of a daimyo – possibly one day the shogun – turned into a vampire! We would be lucky not to start an outright war. We would be lucky if any ninja survived.'

Shusaku moved his hand very fast. It was little more than a blur as it shot out and then fell back to his side, as if it had never been anywhere else. Kawabata screamed, clutching his hand. 'Don't touch me again,' said Shusaku. 'And anyway,' he added casually, 'I've already turned him.'

Kawabata's jaw dropped, revealing a half set of black teeth. He was still cradling his injured hand. He flapped his jaw for a while, then managed to breathe out the word '*What?*'

'You heard me. The boy is already one of us. His friend is still human, for the moment, but he will join us if he proves himself, and I believe that he will.'

'Are you *m-mad*?' spluttered Kawabata. 'If Tokugawa were to hear of this…'

'He won't.'

Kawabata's eyes almost popped out of their sockets, making him look like a fat, angry toad. He was about to speak when a tall old man leaned in close to his ear and whispered something. Taro thought he heard the words 'negotiation' and 'advantage'.

Some of the colour began to return to Kawabata's cheeks.

'Yes, well,' he said. 'Perhaps we can accommodate young… Taro. But it is unfortunate that we must now hide you, Lord Endo. *All* of you.' Taro was reminded of squabbling children, and wondered whether Shusaku and Kawabata had grown up together. Such enmity between adults would be understandable, had they hated each other when they were much younger.

But they couldn't have, of course. Shusaku had been a samurai lord, and Kawabata had said that he was descended from ninja. They may as well have come from different worlds.

Kawabata took a step back. 'How will you conduct the grand initiation?' he asked. 'After all, the rules clearly state—'

'I know what the rules state. I and my fellow ninja will think of something.' A dozen or so men and women wearing the black hooded robes of the ninja stepped forward. Taro saw that they all wore masks over their faces. They bowed to Shusaku.

'Well…' said Kawabata, 'if all the ninja are in agreement…' He hesitated, as if hoping one of them would break ranks, but they simply nodded. He raised his hands. 'Fine. In that case…'

Taro felt a surge of hope.

'…we will test the boy's skill. You say he is talented, Lord Endo. Let him prove it. Then we will welcome him with open arms.'

Shusaku scowled, and Taro's stomach lurched, as if he were falling. Kawabata's request was clearly reasonable – the assenting murmur of the crowd confirmed it. 'Very well,' said Shusaku through gritted teeth. 'And the challenge?'

Kawabata looked at Taro appraisingly. Taro knew that he was trying to think of something that would be difficult for him, maybe impossible.

'The bow,' said the fat elder.

Taro smiled inside. A peasant boy, even one who was the secret son of a lord, would not be expected to master the bow. They were expensive weapons, and few apart from the samurai had access to them.

Shusaku only nodded, giving nothing away. Kawabata clicked his fingers and one of the villagers came forward holding out a long, elegant bow, and a quiver of arrows.

Shusaku turned to Taro. 'What do you think?' he whispered.

'It should be all right,' whispered Taro back. He nodded at the cliffs. 'The walls limit the distance he can ask of me. Even from one side to the other… Well, it would be a hard shot, but I can do it.'

Shusaku nodded. Taro liked his openness, his trust in Taro's opinion. 'Very well,' he said. 'The bow it is.'

Kawabata gestured to one of the boys in the crowd. 'You, fetch a small rider's shield.' The boy disappeared into a cave. There was a long, silent moment, while Taro looked round him at the expectant crowd and the cliff's blank, encircling face. Then the boy came running out again, breathing hard, and carrying a round wooden shield, about a forearm's length across. He handed it to Kawabata.

Kawabata put a hand on his wife's shoulder again, and again Taro saw her flinch. He put a chubby finger under her chin, lifting her face. She looked up at him with wide, nervous eyes. 'Since you feel so strongly that I should listen to Lord Endo,' he said, 'perhaps you should provide the test of his young charge's skill. You wouldn't mind, would you? I'm sure the boy's a good shot. After all, *Lord* Endo says so.'

The woman hesitated. 'As you wish, Husband-*san*,' she said finally.

At this, a fat boy of about Taro's age stepped forward from the crowd. Taro could see immediately from the shared facial features that this was Kawabata's son. 'Is this necessary, Father?' the boy asked. 'Why don't you just send them away?'

'I will do as I like with my wife,' said Kawabata. 'That is what love is for, is it not?' He turned to his son and smiled. 'You would not defend her if you had seen her flirting with Lord Endo earlier, as if he were a samurai on horseback, and she an impressionable peasant girl.'

The boy turned a hard, flat look on his mother, and stepped back. 'As you say, Father,' he said.

'Hold this, like so, just above your stomach,' said Kawabata, handing the shield to his wife, who accepted it with trembling hands. He showed her where he wanted it – below the neck, exposing both her throat and her lower belly. 'Over to the wall,' he said, pointing to the far side of the crater. Taro felt a sickening tightness take hold of his stomach, as if a ghostly hand were gripping his entrails. Kawabata pointed behind Taro. 'And you, over to the other side. Where you came in. You have one shot to strike the shield.'

Shusaku gave Taro another searching look, but Taro only nodded. It was too late to back out now. And even if he did, then what? He couldn't go back to the valleys, with men like Kira on his trail – the thin, cruel samurai who had killed that peasant only because the man had been taking some honey from a tree.

He simply had to make the shot.

He turned back and saw a crooked smile on Kawabata's face. If Taro missed the woman… Well, he wasn't skilled enough to join the ninja clan. But if he missed the shield and hit the woman… at this distance the shot would almost certainly not penetrate deep enough to kill her. But it would kill any chance Taro had of being accepted by this strange village.

Arriving at the entrance to the cave, Taro turned and took hold of the bow. He drew an arrow from the quiver and notched it carefully into the string. Once, twice, three times, he lined up the shot and drew back the arrow, feeling the muscles in his arms and chest tighten, feeling the string go taut and the wood bowing flexible and strong against his body. He took a deep breath – held it. A movement of the chest or diaphragm at the wrong moment, and the arrow could fly wrong. Better to be still, to be as dead.

As he watched, Heiko waved to him, then clasped her hands together, closing her eyes in a mime of peace and calm. He grinned.

He could do this.

Taro aimed straight at the woman's face – compensating for the distance, but it was a hard thing to do nevertheless, a *cold* thing. She had tears running down her cheeks and he could just make them out from here – and let go. The arrow streaked into the air, arcing with a flash of silver beneath the painted stars and moon, tracing a trajectory so beautiful in its curve and symmetry that for a moment every breath in the crater remained in its owner's lungs.

Then the arrow struck home, and the woman fell back against the rock, before sliding to the ground.

CHAPTER 37

LADY HANA GRIPPED the horse's reins with one hand and swung her sword with the other. The dummy – a straw man in samurai uniform – fell backward, a diagonal slash across its armour. Hana grinned, slowing the horse. She twirled the sword in her hand, enjoying its weight and the way that it reflected the afternoon sunlight.

'Very good, Lady Hana,' said Hayao. He was one of the samurai who had been assigned to watch over her during the day. They had to stay within the castle walls. Lord Oda had been quite particular about that. But Hayao understood Hana's need to get out, to improve her skills. He had lent her his own sword, and helped her to put together the dummy. Then he had set it up in the stable courtyard, at the rear of the castle. The yard was just wide enough so that Hana could get a horse up to a decent canter, before having to turn round.

The other samurai – a company of six had been detailed to Hana's protection, doubling her usual guard – stood silently at the sides of the courtyard, or kept watch on the walls above. They never spoke to Hana or seemed to take any interest in her training. She frequently sparred with Hayao, or practised her horseback sword skills, yet the other guards seemed indifferent to their exertions. This was unusual. Hana was used to having to sneak out to practise her sword moves, and fitting the time for training between her more refined pursuits.

There had not been any such lessons for quite some time. And of the four-year-old Tokugawa boy, there had been no sign.

It appeared, in fact, that Hayao had been ordered to help Hana train – though she had learned enough in her etiquette classes, and from her own painful experience, not to question her father directly as to his intentions. Certainly Lord Oda had taken little interest in his daughter's lessons in calligraphy or poetry of late, and his previous disapproval for her unladylike activities and martial inclinations – as well as anxiety that she might somehow mar her looks or injure herself – seemed to have been replaced by an indulgence that bordered on the cavalier. The other day he had walked past when Hana was throwing knives at a board, and he hadn't even blinked. At the same time he seemed nervous and distracted, and it was not hard for Hana to work out that some new threat weighed on her father's mind. A threat that had some bearing on her, perhaps? A threat so dangerous that the daimyo wished his own daughter to be able to defend herself against it.

Yes, it seemed to Hana that perhaps her father now wished her to train, and this was why he had assigned Hayao to watch over her. This gave her a little frisson of fear, even as she was pleased with the new freedom. Was she in danger? Her father had never looked very kindly on her fighting before, though he had tolerated the *bokken*. Now she was learning to use a real sword, with a wicked razor-sharp blade. And Hayao encouraged her to test her ability ever more with each passing day – wielding the sword on horseback, engaging in hand-to-hand combat, learning to use a bow.

'Turn the horse round,' said Hayao. 'For this next exercise I'm going to fire blunt arrows at you. See if you can avoid them while cutting down the dummy.'

Later that day Hana walked down one of the castle's many corridors towards a small courtyard where roses grew. Hayao had been teaching her some punches and kicks that she wanted to practise in private – where she didn't feel the unimpressed eyes of the samurai on her when she lost her balance and fell.

She was passing a servant's room when the sound of her father's voice made her pause. She crept over to the door, puzzled. What was her father doing in a servant's room? Lord Oda never noticed servants, unless to chastise them. And that usually ended with a beheading.

Hana saw that the door was open a crack. Inside, she saw her father facing a man dressed all in black.

'I thought Kira was looking for the Tokugawa boy,' said this man. Hana frowned. The Tokugawa boy? As far as she knew, he was playing in the courtyard of the castle, throwing rotten apples at passing traders and servants.

'He is. That is not what I called you here for.' Lord Oda paused. 'You will have noticed, I don't doubt, what happened to your… colleagues. The ones who failed to take the boy from his village. I expect better results from you.'

Village? What village? And was this Tokugawa boy the boy in the message that she had taken from the dead pigeon? The one who 'still lives'?

The ninja – for that was what he was, Hana realized with a shiver – nodded. 'I never fail.'

Lord Oda smiled. 'So I heard. I only wish you had been there for the attempt on the boy. Perhaps then it would have met with greater success. What was it you were doing at the time?'

'A pirate crew were preying on Portuguese ships trading with the shogunate in Kyoto. They had taken hold of a man-of-war, which meant they had cannons and guns at their disposal. Not only that, but the pirates were many, and desperate, while the Portuguese trading vessels they attacked had lost half their crew on the journey from China, to disease and storms, and those who were left had lost any will to fight. The pirates seemed unbeatable. So the shogun's advisers thought of me. They asked me to... remind the pirates of the shogun's trade interests. It took me some time to find them, and when I did, they were far from shore. I had to board the ship from the water, alone. It was one of my more interesting missions.'

'You delivered your message?'

'In a manner of speaking. One of them raised the alarm, which was unfortunate. I killed every man on board.'

Hana's father grinned a distasteful grin. 'Good. Because yours is the most important task of all. You must protect my daughter by night. By day, my own samurai will defend her. They will be there at night too, of course, but they will be vulnerable to... those of your persuasion. I need someone to make sure no ninja gets into this castle. And even if they penetrate the walls, they must not reach the fourth tower, which is where I will be moving my daughter.'

Hana's eyes widened. The fourth tower! That was where her father usually kept prisoners, men who had plotted against him or otherwise gravely offended him. It was the tallest part of the castle, and was protected by a circular staircase in the Portuguese style. In theory a single man could defend it. The staircase turned to the right as it ascended, meaning that a man stationed above could wield his sword in his stronger right hand, while an attacker would have to move his to his left. It had not escaped Hana's notice that her father had made the tower impregnable to all but himself – for who but a left-handed sword saint could hope to fight their way up? This was Lord Oda's way; he liked always to have insurance policies. The fourth tower would protect him and his family from attackers. But if for any reason he was outside and needed to get in, the tower was perfectly configured for his disability.

Hana turned her attention back to the room, where her father was still talking. 'Tokugawa will have heard by now what happened in Shirahama though he doesn't know his son is a vampire, and I imagine the traitor who saved him would like to keep it that way. So, of course, he'll think that his precious son Taro is dead, since that fool of a ninja who turned him will try to hide him.'

Precious son Taro? Hana had never heard of a Tokugawa son by that name. What was her father talking about?

'How do you know the boy is a vampire?' said her father's mysterious interlocutor. 'You're sure he'll come at night?'

'I'm sure,' said her father. 'My ninjas saw him turned, on the hillside in Shirahama. They said he recovered from a dose of steel two hand-spans wide, right through the stomach.'

'And you're sure the ninja will hide the boy's transformation?'

'Yes. He'll be terrified that Lord Tokugawa will never forgive him for making his secret son a vampire, instead of merely rescuing him as he was ordered.'

'He's probably right.'

'Of course. But that isn't the point. The point is that Tokugawa now believes his son to be dead. He has already killed one of his sons, and sent the other to me. To lose the last is unacceptable. If I know Tokugawa, he will not rest until our situations are rendered equal.'

'Meaning?'

'He will kill Hana.'

Behind the door, Hana stifled a gasp.

CHAPTER 38

Taro's breath came out in a rush that he didn't know was a scream, and he was running across the crater floor, as Shusaku ran too…

He got there moments after Shusaku, moments before Kawabata, who puffed heavily behind him. He dropped to his knees as he ran, letting his momentum carry him in a painful skid up to the wife's body. She sat against the rock face, smiling, holding the shield in her hands. She passed the round target to Shusaku. Her face sagged with relief, and her mouth rose at the edges in a grin. Tears continued to fall.

Shusaku held the shield above his head. Right in the middle was the shaft of the arrow, standing perpendicular to the wood. There was a collective sigh from the crowd.

'Gods!' exclaimed Yukiko, her voice carrying as usual. 'He's brilliant! Why didn't you *say*?' she demanded as she bounded up to Taro. 'Here I've been wasting my time wrestling with *that* lump' – she pointed to Hiro – 'when I could have been learning the bow with you.'

Hiro waved a dismissive hand. 'The bow takes delicacy and grace,' he said to Yukiko. 'You'd be hopeless at it.'

She gave him a playful punch on the arm, and Taro felt a

warm spreading gladness in his chest to have people on his side
– more than one – and a place in the world. He smiled at Yukiko.
'Are we… friends?'

She nodded. 'I'm sorry about before. I was upset.'

Heiko squeezed her sister's arm and smiled. Then she gave
Taro a little bow. 'That was magnificent,' she said softly.
'Certainly worthy of a daimyo's son.'

Taro blushed.

Kawabata stood in the middle of the crater, glowering. He
put an arm round his wife, who did not look at him. Then he
pointed at Taro and Hiro, followed by the two girls. 'Let us all
welcome our new apprentices,' he said, with bad grace.

There were a few nervous hellos from the assembled people.
The ninja bowed. The young man with the spear nodded at Taro,
an unsmiling but not unfriendly gesture. Taro raised a hand
awkwardly to greet the silent people. Then his eye caught on a
boy standing a little apart from the others. The boy was chubby,
his red face set in a scowl of scorn and anger. His mouth, firmly
closed in an expression of exaggerated disgust, put Taro in mind
of a clam's closed shell – pink flesh squeezed white in places by
pressure.

Kawabata's son stared at Taro with undisguised hatred, and
Taro shivered – not just from the cold. His arrival at the clan's
stronghold could not have gone much worse.

Shusaku turned to Taro, Hiro, Heiko, and Yukiko. 'Come on.
I'll take you to your sleeping places.'

But Taro was thinking of his mother – or, at least, the woman
he had always known as his mother. Heiko and Yukiko may
have been destined from a young age, as the ninja had said, to
become ninja. But he was here for one reason and one reason
only – to discover where she had gone, and to find her. 'The

pigeon,' he said to Shusaku. 'Has it arrived?'

Shusaku went over to Kawabata and spoke to him for a moment. Taro saw Kawabata shake his head, and he felt his body ringing like a struck bell.

'No sign of it,' said Shusaku when he returned to their side. Seeing Taro's expression, he added, 'But don't worry. If she has travelled far, the pigeon may take some time to get here.'

Taro nodded. But how far could his mother have gone? He may have been an illiterate peasant, but he was smart enough to realize that a pigeon could cover ground faster than a person on foot, and hadn't he and Shusaku and Hiro covered many *ri* in their walk to the mountain?

The pigeon should have been here before them.

'It was my best bird,' said Shusaku. 'It will come. And if not, then I will help you look for her myself. I swear it.'

Taro smiled at the man. He believed him. 'All right, then,' he said. He was suddenly overwhelmingly tired. 'Show us where we sleep.'

Shusaku led them into a cave that gave off the crater. Again Taro had to hold back a gasp. They followed a corridor that opened onto another corridor, and leading off to either side were passageways lit by candles, doorways from which people peered in open curiosity, and even pens from which pigs gazed with their friendly, mindless eyes. Taro recognized a stable as they passed by it at Shusaku's customary fast pace. The horses followed him with their eyes, their long noses tracking him, their nostrils flaring. Even the horses could spot a new arrival.

Taro was sure that he would never be able to retrace his steps. This was no cave – this was a network of roads, of alleyways. It was a village inside the rock. Every so often they passed an opening that didn't give onto another tributary passageway. Instead he would get a glimpse of a dining room, the floor laid with tatami mats, small lacquered wood tables set with bowls and chopsticks, or a simple room furnished with cushions and decorated with painted screens. In some of these rooms people looked up as they passed and watched them with hard eyes.

Finally, they turned into a passageway deeper than the ones before, and then they came into another cave. This one was carved with wild animals, gods, and demons. And again, candlelight glowed in myriad sconces. This cave was filled with equipment: wooden horses, sword racks, tables on which had been laid a number of bows and crossbows. Armour lay strewn on the floor, and in some cases had been placed on straw-and-leather mannequins, which as a result looked like the headless ghosts left behind by some terrible military campaign. The whole scene made Taro think of an army encampment, transported by mischievous *kami* from the field of battle to this eldritch cave.

Shusaku laughed. 'Quite impressive, isn't it? This is the weapons room. You'll sleep here, along with the other children – including Little Kawabata, the son of the charming man you met out there. We like to accustom our young people to the presence of weapons.'

'We sleep *here*?' asked Hiro. He poked at a leather chest guard with his foot.

'Not right here, no.' Shusaku crossed the room and showed them where holes had been carved into the rock. These were the length of a man, and their mouths were shaped in a semicircle, flat side down. Each niche was lined with piles of blankets, and illuminated by a large candle set into the wall. They were snug little sleeping caves.

'*This*,' Shusaku said, 'is where you'll sleep.'

'Only if you're lucky,' said Heiko. 'Little Kawabata snores like a pig. You can wrap a scarf round your ears, but it does no good. Sometimes I think the little brat does it on purpose.' She looked at Taro. 'Little Kawabata was the fat boy who glared at you out there.'

'You know him already?' said Taro.

'Yes. We have trained with him a couple of times, when his father came to consult with the abbess. He's a nasty child.'

'You shouldn't speak ill of such a senior ninja's son,' said Shusaku. But the amusement in his voice undermined his reprimand. 'And anyway, to show personal dislike is unbecoming of a ninja. Remember, you should be always as passive and yielding as the river in its banks, which is soft and without desire or hatred but can cut through solid rock.'

Heiko smiled, and bowed. 'Of course, Lord Endo. I don't dislike Little Kawabata. It's merely that I'm jealous of him, because he is the son of an important man and has been better provisioned than I with intelligence, good looks, and skill.' She winked at Taro, then turned and walked with exaggerated elegance and bearing towards the beds.

Taro had been hoping to get Heiko on her own, so that he could ask if she would accompany him down to the rice store when the others were asleep. He wanted the bow back, and he was going to do it without Shusaku's help, even if that meant asking Yukiko instead. She knew how to pick locks, and she could fight. But Yukiko and Hiro were engrossed in the weapons, and Taro could not see how he would manage to get her alone. He would have to put off the expedition to the next night, and hope that the bow wasn't moved between.

Just then, Little Kawabata entered the room. The similarity

with his father was astonishing – the same fat belly, the same waddling walk. He glared at Taro. 'So, another samurai who has turned traitor and become a ninja. I don't know if it's better or worse that you thought you were just a peasant.'

'He didn't ask for any of this,' said Shusaku.

'Of course not,' said Little Kawabata. 'Nor did you, when you took my father's rightful place as leader. That ninja girl turned you for *love*, isn't that your story?'

Shusaku sighed. 'I was dying. She bit me to save me.' His voice sounded weary, as if he had gone over this many times.

'Yes, yes, so you say. And then she just *happened* to die, on a day when there wasn't even any fighting! How convenient.'

Shusaku took a step towards the boy, his fists clenched, and Taro thought for a moment that he was going to strike him. But he just rubbed his mask with his hand and stretched his neck, cracking the bones. 'Run along now,' he said. 'Your father cast these aspersions before you, and you're the only person to whom they ever stuck.'

'I don't know why he wasted his time with accusations,' said Little Kawabata as he turned on his heel. 'He should have just had you executed as a murderer.'

THAT SAME NIGHT Junichiro the tanner's son walked down the mountain stream towards the tanneries, which were down-river so as not to pollute the village's drinking water. He was on the lower slopes of the sacred mountain, far below the small hut by the cliff that they said was haunted and should never be approached. But even here it was steep enough that walking demanded concentration, and often levied a fine in the form of a twisted ankle if that tribute were forgotten.

He kicked at a pebble, sending it skittering into the water. Once again the other children had not wanted to play with him, something that had been abundantly clear to Junichiro when they had begun to pelt him with mud and stones, sending him running back towards his house. This was the last time he would try.

Junichiro was *eta* – untouchable. His family made the leather that adorned the bodies and horses of samurai. But because the preparation of leather involved rubbing skins with brain mash and urine, the very same samurai scorned the *eta*, and their children, as well as the children of peasants, were taught from an early age to hold them in contempt. The Buddha forbade the killing of animals, and so no right-thinking person would involve themselves in the preparing of a material that depended on such death.

Of course, the Buddha didn't forbid wearing leather. He merely required that other people – untouchables – be the ones to make it.

As Junichiro descended the hill, he could smell the sour-sweet stench of macerating animal skin.

Junichiro had never considered himself to be unclean. He bathed daily like anyone else, and growing up he had not realized he was different. So stubbornly, with childlike hope, he had tried to join in with the village children's games. But his hope had been beaten out with sticks and stones, his stubbornness weakened by flying mud. He would not try again.

Food was another thing. The harvest had been bad this year, so Junichiro's father had said, and the share of the rice that was normally given to the *eta* in payment for their work had been halved. Everyone was hungry. Junichiro had seen elderly tanners, distant members of his own family, sucking leather to draw some strength from it. Guards had been posted on the grain store, to protect the village's food reserves from marauding bandits, or the hungry populace of other villages.

So when Junichiro saw a fat pigeon approaching from down the hill, flying with smooth powerful strokes, he reached automatically for his sling. He bent down and picked a round pebble from the ground, then set it snugly into the leather pouch. His mother would be pleased if he brought something home for dinner – real meat! The *eta* were already outcast and beyond the love of Buddha, so he had no fear of the terrors that were supposed to await those Buddhists who killed other living beings. This was why the samurai relied on them, to provide them with leather. And while the peasants ate only rice and the occasional fish, the *eta* survived on whatever they could scavenge.

Junichiro wrapped the thongs round his fingers just so, whirled the sling round his head, and let the pebble fly. It struck the pigeon, which was now just overhead, with a dull crunch, and the bird plummeted to the ground, landing on a stone by the stream. Junichiro ran to it and snapped its neck before it could suffer too much or, more important, flap and struggle its way into the stream, to be borne down and away.

He was tucking the pigeon into his robe when he noticed something white that had been wrapped round its leg. He untied it and found that it was a small note, written in very neat, delicate characters. If he could have read, he would have realized that the writing was feminine in its strokes. If he could have read, he would have understood the short message it conveyed:

My dear Taro, I am hidden at the Hokugawa monastery, near Fuji mountain. Ask for the lady hermit when you come.

From your loving mother.

But he couldn't read, so he merely shrugged, screwed up the note, and dropped it to the ground. For those as hungry as he, the concept of a messenger pigeon was utterly unknown. There was only the concept of food.

CHAPTER 40

THOUGH TARO REMAINED worried about his bow, he wasn't able to sneak out the next night either; nor the night after that.

He was too exhausted.

There was Little Kawabata's snoring, of course, which was just as bad as Taro had been warned, and kept him awake much of the night. Then there was the training.

The first morning after they arrived, it seemed as though Taro had hardly slept when he was awoken by a rough hand shaking his shoulder. He peered up to see Shusaku looking down on him. 'Come on,' the ninja said. 'It's time you learned to handle yourself with weapons. Now that we are in the crater, we can train before nightfall, thanks to the caves and the covering over the main hall.'

Hiro, Yukiko, Heiko, and Little Kawabata joined them, though Little Kawabata wouldn't speak to Taro, or even meet his eye. In that first lesson Shusaku showed them the basic principles of *taijutsu* – unarmed combat.

Hiro challenged Yukiko to a fight straight after their lesson.

He lost.

Soon they progressed to the sword, which all of them took to naturally, as if they had spent their early childhoods wielding *katana*, and had simply forgotten about it. Initially they were given wooden *bokken* to fight with, unable to cut flesh, but hard and heavy enough to break bones if the attacker – and the defender – were not careful. However, Taro progressed so quickly with the main forms of *kenjutsu* that Shusaku soon entrusted him with a *katana*. Taro loved the elegant blade, despite the nicks and scratches in its body. He slept with it next to him, encased in a silver-chased sheath.

Little Kawabata, too, was rapidly fighting with a real sword.

When Shusaku wasn't instructing them, Yukiko and Hiro would go off together, wrestling or sparring. They were both excellent sword fighters, and often as Heiko and Taro played, there was the ringing sound of metal on metal, for they had all been allowed to practise with real swords, so quickly had they progressed.

Though none of them were as good as Taro.

He had never felt anything like the joy – the *rightness* – that he felt when wielding the sword. It was one with him; it was meditation in movement. There were the stars of the crater, and the tedium of lessons; there were the games of Shogi with Heiko, who had taught him to play, and the conversations with his new friends; but always in his mind's eye there was the flash of steel.

And always there was the joy of swift movement, the cutting of the air.

But on this occasion Shusaku did not want to spar. He wanted to show Taro one of his own kata, a formal sequence of movements that a swordsman practised over and over again, until its execution flowed from a particular mistake of the opponent's as quickly and unstoppably as ripples from a stone dropped in water.

'Can't we just spar?' asked Taro. 'Learning sequences by heart is not going to help me in the real world.'

Shusaku sucked his teeth. 'Most sword fights in the *real world*,' he said, 'are over before your heart can beat twice. If you practise these katas every day, so that you can perform them without thinking, you will have an advantage over your opponent.'

Taro nodded, unconvinced. He liked the random spontaneity of sword fighting, the sense that the fight itself was alive, evolving all the time out of the movements and snap decisions of its violent actors. Katas seemed to him boring and rigid, like the rules that governed a geisha's life. They didn't seem suited to ninja, who should be cunning and unpredictable, rather than restricting their motions to rote patterns.

Shusaku gave a little bow, which Taro returned. Then the ninja raised his sword. 'Get ready,' said Shusaku. 'Hold your sword as you normally would, ready to block me if necessary.'

Taro warily drew near, his eyes fixed on the ninja, his sword trembling slightly in his hand. 'Good,' said Shusaku. 'Now imagine we are deadly enemies. Try to destroy me quickly. React as you normally would.' As he said this, he moved forward, tipping his sword a fraction to his right, but keeping his eyes low, on Taro's face.

Taro glanced down at the ninja's feet, looking for the telltale muscle contractions the older man had taught him about, the ones that revealed a person was about to spring forward, lowering his sword.

Shusaku's feet were perfectly flat on the ground.

Taro grinned inside. He recognized the ninja's intention. Shusaku wanted him to believe that he was about to lunge, but in fact he was going to slash across Taro's body. Taro had seen the slight movement of the sword's tip, and knew that the ninja planned a strike from the right – and that, by readying himself for it, he was leaving an opening. Seizing his chance, Taro snapped his sword up and then round in a tight curve, through the channel of empty air that led to the ninja's neck.

But Shusaku's sword was suddenly raised in a vertical block that stopped Taro's blade, and then in a continuation of that blocking motion the ninja flipped his wrist over, bringing his sword under Taro's.

Taro looked down.

Shusaku's blade was pressed against his stomach.

'That,' said Shusaku, 'is a kata. I call it the high block and gut-slash. And if we were fighting for real, you would be dead.'

Taro swallowed. The whole thing had been so fast. He'd moved to exploit the man's opening, and a heartbeat later he had been dead. In theory, anyway.

'Show me again,' he said.

Shusaku's eyes sparkled. 'Of course. But remember, this one only works if your opponent underestimates you.'

Taro blushed. He *had* underestimated the ninja. He had thought he'd learned so quickly, had grown so strong. But of course he'd only been there a few days, and it was arrogant to think that he would have advanced so far in such a short time.

Taro lifted his sword.

'This time,' said Shusaku, 'you try it. Come a little closer to me, then let your sword tip waver a little to your right, as if you're planning a high slash. Not too much. Yes, that's it. Now I think I can strike at your neck…'

Shusaku went for the same attack that Taro had adopted, and Taro raised his sword to block it. Then he tried the wrist flip to turn the block into a low belly strike, but he wasn't quick enough, and Shusaku blocked him in return, before bringing his sword to shivering rest against the skin of Taro's neck.

It felt cold.

'Not fast enough,' said Shusaku. 'That's why you practise over and over.'

Taro nodded, a little ashamed. 'Yes. I see. Sorry for—'

But Shusaku waved the apology away. 'Until you see how quickly it is possible to lose a sword fight, you don't know how important it is to be quick, and to move without thinking. The kata should become unthinking reactions, just the way that your body responds to certain attacks. In a way, they're spontaneous. It just takes a lot of boring practice to make them so.' He laughed.

Taro laughed too, although the muscles of his forearms ached already. 'So,' he said. 'This wrist flick...'

Shusaku stepped closer and put one hand on either side of Taro's wrist. 'You turn it like this,' he said, pressing down with his top hand. 'As it goes over, push your forefinger forward. That will help the sword to bite forward in a low arc, and you only have to give a little push with your arm to finish the slash.'

Taro tried it, and again he wasn't quick enough, and again Shusaku put his hands on his wrist to show how it was done. Taro was reminded of when his father had taught him spear-fishing, patiently repeating the wrist flick time after time as they shivered in the cold water of the bay.

At that thought, he fumbled the movement, and more than just being slow this time, he twisted his hand too hard and caused the sword to drop from his fingers. He cursed.

'Something wrong?' asked Shusaku, concern in his eyes, and again Taro was reminded of his father's solicitude, the way that he had so patiently showed Taro time after time how to make the spear leap forward from his hand.

And now his father was dead, and he was standing in a crater many *ri* from home, practising katas with an assassin who had not only extracted Taro from his old life, but had imposed on it too a new and terrible addition – a real father, a samurai, a stranger.

But for Taro there would only ever be one real father.

Ignoring the sword at his feet, he stepped back from Shusaku's well-meaning touch as from a snake.

Shusaku bent to pick up the sword. 'It takes time,' he said. 'You'll get it eventually.'

Taro walked away, not bothering to tell the ninja that it wasn't the kata he was worried about.

He knew that he would get it in the end. After all, it was a matter of coordination and speed, and those things were in his power. What was not in his power was to bring his father back to life, to speed that cursed pigeon towards the mountain, with its news of his mother.

Taro walked over to where Yukiko and Hiro sparred with swords. Yukiko parried a strike from Hiro and, pirouetting lithely, executed a perfect movement that would have taken off Hiro's head if she hadn't stopped the blade just in time. He held his hands up in surrender.

Hiro stomped over to Taro.

'Commiserations,' said Taro.

Hiro grimaced. 'She cheats.'

'What, by being more skilled than you?'

'Exactly. I'm bigger and stronger than her and she knows it, so she should lose. But she doesn't. Therefore, she is a cheat.'

Taro laughed. 'One of these days you'll best her, my friend.'

'One of these years, maybe,' said Yukiko, walking past. Hiro gave her a push, and soon they were fighting again.

But Hiro had not been the wrestling champion of Shirahama

for nothing. The next day, Hiro came swaggering up to Taro, Yukiko rolling her eyes behind him. 'I beat Yukiko at sword fighting *and* wrestling just now,' he said. 'She is like a child before my superior skill.'

Yukiko jabbed him with her elbow. 'One victory, and he thinks he's Yamato Takeru.' This was a famous prince who had defeated many enemies, and who had fought in later life with the legendary sword Ame-no-Murakumo-no-Tsurugi – the Gathering Clouds of Heaven – which Susanoo, the *kami* of storms, had taken from the belly of the sea serpent.

'Two victories!' said Hiro.

'Two in one day only counts as one. Think of the number of days on which I have beaten you.'

Hiro sighed good-naturedly.

Taro was glad for Hiro that he had found a new friend, while a small, jealous part of him wished that he could keep the big wrestler to himself. But so much had changed for Hiro. It was good that he had found a measure of happiness in his new life.

All in all, life at the crater *was* good, though something always seemed unreal about it to Taro – as if the death of his father and the unknown fate of his mother existed in some other world, some other realm of samsara, far from this hidden place.

It was a sort of magical realm in which they lived, learning to fight and to move in harmony, no longer bound by the twin worlds of day and night, but living in a constant semi-darkness, illuminated by torches. Taro felt that he would like to remain there forever, though the thought of his mother was always at the back of his mind, and once he had dreamed a terrible dream that his father, the one who had brought him up, still lived – that his death was a colossal mistake – and he had come to Taro with open arms, saying 'I am here. Don't cry any more.'

Then Taro had woken, and his father was still dead, and he had cried till he thought the moisture would be wrung from his body, and he would be wrinkled and dry, like a piece of fruit left too long in the sun.

He would have liked to stay in that dream forever, by the sea, with his father fishing its depths and his mother always by the fire in the evening. But he had been rudely awakened.

And unfortunately, it was about to happen again.

CHAPTER 41

THERE WAS A rough hand on his shoulder. Shusaku leaned over him.

'*Taijutsu*. Get up.'

Taro followed, bleary-eyed, as Shusaku woke the others and began clearing a space in the middle of the weapons hall.

First, Shusaku explained that no ninja ever fought *entirely* unarmed. This, in fact, was one of their great secrets.

Each of them was given a wooden ring to wear on their right hands. The ring – called a *shobo* – was rough and unevenly textured, designed to stand out from the hand. It could be used to strike pressure points on an opponent's body, immobilizing or even killing him.

Shusaku stood, his shadow shivering under the candlelight. 'First I'm going to show you some grips and throws. These are moves that send an assailant's body – or part of it – in an unexpected direction. Now… I'll need two volunteers.' His gaze travelled round the room, until it came to light on Little Kawabata. 'Come on,' he said. 'Let us see if you're as good as your father. He was a talented fighter before he got so fat.'

Little Kawabata, scowling, came forward.

Shusaku once again scoured the room. Then he called Taro

forward. Heiko gave Taro a little smile as he passed her. 'Make sure you beat him,' she said.

Little Kawabata turned and gave her a nasty smile. 'The only one doing any beating will be me.'

The two boys stood in the middle of the cave and stared at each other. Taro saw malice and amusement in the other boy's piggy eyes. He knew that Little Kawabata had hated him almost on first sight – for making the arrow shot that had secured his entry to the school, for being a vampire already, for showing up his father by so easily passing the test he'd set him.

Shusaku stepped up to Little Kawabata. 'Strike out with your arm flat, as if to hit me with a direct punch, then keep your arm outstretched.' The chubby boy did so, and Taro saw that the layer of fat was deceptive. Little Kawabata was fast. And strong.

Shusaku put his two hands out, placing one under Little Kawabata's wrist, palm up, and one above it, palm down. He rolled his hands in opposite directions, and Little Kawabata's legs gave away as he screamed a high-pitched scream. Shusaku helped him up, then showed him how to place his hands in order to do the same thing. The teacher put his own arm out, and Little Kawabata demonstrated the move, forcing the older man to the ground. Shusaku nodded. 'Well done.'

Taro walked over to them, anxious to learn the trick himself, but Shusaku waved him back. 'Patience,' he said. 'You will learn it soon enough. For the moment I want you to keep trying to strike Little Kawabata. Let us see how well he can do it when it really matters.'

Shusaku positioned Taro right in front of Little Kawabata. 'All right. Start punching.'

Taro let out a right-hand strike to the head, which was too

fast for the clan leader's son. Little Kawabata yelped and clutched his ear. But Taro's next shot, a left to the solar plexus, was caught in a vicelike grip, and suddenly Taro's upper body was twisting despite itself and he fell to the ground. He got up again and lashed out instantly, his vampire's speed allowing the uppercut to find Little Kawabata's chin. Little Kawabata staggered backwards, and Taro moved in to press the advantage, but the other boy wasn't only fast, he was a quick learner, and Taro's next few strikes were all easily caught, depositing him onto the floor. The pain was not as bad as it might have been if he were human, but bad enough – with the humiliation – to sting.

Taro struck out viciously, again and again, and each time he was parried or caught, and his muscles sang out with the strain of the torsion. Involuntarily, he began to sob. Why wasn't Shusaku putting a stop to it?

He fixed his eyes on Little Kawabata's, gathering his strength. His blood thundered in his ears, and his arms throbbed. Surely with the speed and agility that came with his vampire nature, he should be able to defeat this fat, spoiled child? He grimaced, spat out a mouthful of blood. The last fall had been a hard one.

Collecting all his *chi*, Taro let fly with a feint to the left, followed by a devastating blow to the right, which would have connected with Little Kawabata's neck and probably knocked him out, if not killed him by snapping his spine – but the leader's son twisted out of the way and caught Taro's arm as it passed him, putting all his body weight into twisting it.

Taro crashed to the ground, his arm flapping as he tried to push himself upright again.

Little Kawabata laughed. 'You're not fishing now, boy. I'm harder to catch than the sprats in your little bay.'

Taro grunted.

'Get up,' said Little Kawabata. 'Your feigned injury insults me.'

Taro turned his head. His arm was hanging at an unpleasant angle from his shoulder. Dislocated. He got up painfully, shaking his head. Surely Shusaku had to stop it now? He was hopeless. He was already a vampire, and he couldn't even beat this stupid, pudgy brute.

He staggered to his feet, then stumbled forward. He pawed at Little Kawabata, looking for purchase, staining the fat boy's robes with blood.

Little Kawabata sneered. 'Peasant, your manners are a disgrace. No doubt you tricked my father, too – put the idea in his head of testing you with the bow somehow. You will pay for your insolence.'

Taro caught his breath. Yet, as much as he hated the boy, he couldn't help feeling jealous. *At least you have a father*, he felt like saying. All he said, though, was 'Ugh.'

'Stop,' said Shusaku. Taro gave a little whimper of relief.

Thank the gods.

He looked up through a film of sweat and blood, not all of it his own, and saw Shusaku staring grimly at him. Then the sensei threw a heavy *bokken* to Little Kawabata. At the same time, he held out his other hand to Taro. 'Hand me your *shobo*. You will fight now with no weapons.'

'What?' said Taro. 'Why? Why are you doing this to me?'

'Be quiet. Hand me the ring.'

Taro pulled the wooden ring off his finger and handed it to the man who had rescued him, the man who had escorted him halfway across the country, the man he had *trusted*. He was incredulous. Was Shusaku trying to get him killed? To make a martyr of him in front of the class and so prove some kind of point? Or was he hoping to exhaust Little Kawabata's supply of hatred, by making Taro his punching bag for the afternoon? If so, Taro thought the teacher was badly mistaken. No amount of one-sided combat could satisfy Kawabata's bloodlust. He would not be content until Taro was dead.

And if he died, he would never find his mother again.

Someone had stepped up from the ring of students – Hiro. 'What are you doing to him?' he asked. 'He has no weapon. This is unfair.'

Shusaku whirled on Hiro. 'Sit. Down. Now.' His voice was deadly cold. 'A ninja always has a weapon.' He turned to Taro. 'Remember that. You always have a weapon.' Then he put a restraining hand on Hiro's chest and snapped his fingers in Little Kawabata's direction. 'You are free to attack as you wish,' he said to the grinning boy. Little Kawabata advanced on Taro, brandishing the stick and grinning.

CHAPTER 42

B LOWS RAINED DOWN on Taro, and he covered his head with his hands. He thought he felt bones splintering in his fingers. He barely even cared. His world had shrunk to this cave – its hard rock floor, its dusty crevices, its leering carvings.

He crawled towards where he thought Shusaku was, his broken hands scraping clawlike at the rock. He could dimly hear Hiro, Yukiko, and Heiko shouting at the master, calling on him to stop the rout. Taro couldn't make them out. His eyes were half-closed by bruises, his cheeks and nose swollen from numerous blows. Blood trickled into his right eye.

What had Shusaku meant by that? *You always have a weapon.* Was he supposed to meditate, make a *mudra* of protection with his shaking hands? Tentatively, he formed the *mudra* for banishing evil – hand outstretched, palm out. He was on his knees with his hand stuck out towards Little Kawabata; the boy simply smashed it down with his stick, sending a jarring pain right down Taro's arm and pinning it to the ground.

Little Kawabata turned, his stick still trapping Taro's hand, readying a spinning kick that would catch Taro in the jaw. A drip from the rock ceiling landed on Taro's forehead, cold and slick, like an intimation of mortality.

Taro thought about that little drop.

You always have a weapon.

Moving so quickly he felt his arm reach out before he was conscious of the desire to move it, Taro scrabbled at the floor and came up with a handful of dust, in which nestled a couple of sharp stones. He could feel them pricking at his hand. He could also feel the bones knitting already, a warm spreading sensation as the fingers healed. He grinned, tasting blood that dripped into his mouth. In an instant his warmth, his compassion, his pity, all fell from him like vain ornaments.

He was not himself; in the space his body normally occupied was a spectre that thought only of blood and violence.

He moved.

Little Kawabata's head turned towards Taro before the rest of his body as he unleashed a textbook spinning kick, lining up the target before bringing his foot round. His eyes just had time to widen in surprise as Taro surged upwards and towards him, knocking the fat boy's stick aside and throwing a handful of glittering wicked rock dust into his eyes.

Little Kawabata screamed and fell blindly backwards. He had kept only one leg to the ground as he'd turned into his kick, and now he toppled like a tree, hitting his back hard against the stone floor. Immediately Taro was on him, grinning like a lunatic through a mask of blood and tears. The vampire held the *bokken* in his right hand, and as Little Kawabata watched, powerless, Taro swung it in a hard, low arc. Little Kawabata felt his head snap to the side, then darkness descended like a sheet of heavy rain.

Just before he sank into dark water, Little Kawabata had one thought, which echoed like a mantra.

I'll kill him.

Taro stood shakily. He dropped the stick, then knelt by Little Kawabata. He felt the boy's pulse. Weak, but present. He staggered over to Shusaku. The ninja smiled at him and put a hand under his arm to support him.

'When I say that you always have a weapon, I really mean it,' he said. 'You always have your mind with you, your greatest weapon. And it's amazing what your mind can find to fight with, even in an empty room. Or a cave. Very rarely are you ever *completely* unarmed, even if you lose your *shobo*.'

Shusaku summoned Hiro and handed Taro to him. Taro felt a little better as soon as he felt his friend's hands under his armpits. He walked past the other students, Hiro taking most of the weight off his feet. He passed Yukiko, who looked ashen, and Heiko, whose eyes were lit by a kind of pained triumph. He smiled weakly at them.

'Take him to the sick room,' said Shusaku. 'He will need patching up. Even vampires can be hurt.'

Little Kawabata lay on the cold, hard floor, listening to Shusaku's hateful voice. How this man had taken over the clan was beyond him. His father had told him the whole story – how the clan had sent a ninja girl named Mara to protect Lord Tokugawa, and how Lord Endo Shusaku had learned her secret and forced her to turn him, before murdering her in cold blood.

The devious brilliance of it was that no one could accuse him, because everyone had to pretend she was only a serving girl. And for the same reason, Little Kawabata's father had never been able to prove what Lord Endo had done. Lord Endo claimed that the girl had been killed by some mysterious agent working for Lord Oda, and how could anyone contradict him? No one had seen her die.

But for Lord Endo to become such a strong vampire that he ended up leading the clan, at the expense of the man whose envoy he had tortured and killed?

That was unbearable. Worse was that where before the clan had done work for all sides, hiring their services to the top bidder, Shusaku had insisted that they work only for Lord Tokugawa, for whom he had been a spear-carrying samurai, one of the top ranked.

And now, to add insult to injury, Shusaku had brought another samurai vampire to the mountain. Tokugawa's son, of all people. This would destroy the clan, Little Kawabata was sure of it. How could Lord Oda allow such a boy to live? How could Lord Tokugawa allow it? He was willing to use the ninja, but to have one as a son? It was grotesque.

Little Kawabata's head was aching terribly, and his mouth felt filled with broken glass. But he felt strong, he felt good. His father had never succeeded in ridding himself of Shusaku, but his father had always relied on words. Little Kawabata thought words were perhaps not the best way to deal with one's enemies.

He spat something white out onto the floor – a tooth. In his mind he still heard Shusaku saying *Even vampires can be hurt*. He was relying on it.

CHAPTER 44

IT TOOK SEVERAL days for Taro to recover from his injuries, and he passed them in a fog of boredom and frustration. The only thing he looked forward to was the occasional visit from Shusaku, who was teaching him where to apply pressure with his *shobo* ring if he wanted to incapacitate an enemy – permanently or otherwise.

Every time Taro looked down at the simple wooden ring, he couldn't help comparing it to the one the noble girl had given him, which he wore on his other hand. It was almost as if the two rings symbolized the two halves of himself, his dual nature as both vampire and daimyo's son. The one ring rough-hewn and possibly deadly; the other elegant, though ultimately – like Taro himself, who could never reveal his existence to his true father – useless.

Finally, enough time had passed that Taro moved more easily, and was able to think again about going to recover his bow, which he felt sure now held the answer to everything, the power that would enable him to resolve the two sides of himself into one complete being.

That night he waited until everyone had gone to sleep, then sneaked over to the niche in which Heiko slept. He touched her arm and was surprised when she woke immediately. 'Shh,' he said. 'Will you come with me? I need your help.'

She followed him out of the weapons room, and they followed the tunnel towards the crater. When they had gone far enough, Taro stopped and explained to the girl about his bow, and how he wanted to get it back from the rice store. He didn't say anything about his crazy suspicion, that there might be something hidden inside the grip.

But if it *was* the Buddha ball, then he would be the most powerful man in the country, wouldn't he? He could avenge his father's death, avenge the abbess's death, if indeed she *was* dead. In short, he could do anything, and conquer anyone, and he would certainly be able to improve the lives not only of Heiko, but also of everyone he loved.

And if it *wasn't* in there, and he told Heiko it might be, then he would look an idiot. All in all, a small lie seemed better. 'You can pick locks, can't you?' he asked. He looked at her hopefully.

She nodded slowly. 'Yes… if I have the right tools. But they're with my things, back in there.' She pointed back to the weapons room.

Taro blanched. 'If Little Kawabata were to wake up and find us gone…'

Heiko smiled. 'That would be bad,' she said. 'But I can be very quiet.'

She turned and crept back to the weapons room. Taro waited for several anxious moments. At one point he heard something fall to the ground. It made a striking sound like metal on stone.

He froze.

Time seemed to hang suspended in the air, like droplets of water on a spider's web.

270

But no one stirred or spoke, at least as far as Taro could hear, and gradually he relaxed again. A moment later Heiko returned, holding a small leather bag. 'That was close,' whispered Heiko. 'I knocked into something, and I was scared for a moment that someone might wake up.'

Taro had hidden black cloaks and *hakama* trousers behind a statue in one of the stone corridors, and now he and Heiko changed into these clothes that would camouflage them against the night. Taro also slid a short-sword into a scabbard concealed at his waist.

It was as well to be careful.

He and Heiko tied on their heads the three scarves – the *sanjaku tenugui* – that made up the ninja mask, leaving only the eyes uncovered. Then they followed the tunnel to the hut on the mountainside. Taro found it far less frightening this time, though it did take longer than he had hoped to negotiate the complicated system of tunnels. They came out of the hut into a clear, crisp night. The moon was dark, and the only light came from the myriad stars sparkling in the sky.

Heiko suggested descending through the rice paddies, instead of following the walkways that crisscrossed them. It was a good choice, as the deep water kept their profiles low, and anyone on the lookout would have expected them to arrive on the path. Soon their feet and legs were soaked from wading through the terraced plots. Each time they came to a step in the terrace, they lowered themselves down silently, crouching instantly to keep their silhouettes invisible. Once, Taro thought he heard a light rustling noise from behind them, but when he turned, all he could see was the ascending plateaux of the rice paddies, and the moon's blue light on the water.

Winter was coming on, and they could see snow glittering on

the mountaintops. Their breath misted in the air as they walked, making ghosts that hung in their wake.

In the space of three or four incense sticks, they had reached the village. Its roofs were visible through the trees ahead, and smoke spiralled into the night sky above the treetops. Taro pointed out a dark shape in the paddy below – someone keeping watch. He signalled to Heiko, who took out a blowpipe. The arrows were anointed with a drug that would cause the recipient to sleep but not to die. She aimed at the man and fired. His body fell down face first in the paddy.

The water! The man would drown!

Taro leaped lightly down into the paddy and crouched by the body. Sure enough, the face was immersed in the water. He turned the body over, checked the breathing. Shallow but regular. He breathed a sigh of relief. Then he saw what the man had been holding: a bow and arrow. Nor had he seemed to be hunting. Taro thought he was a guard.

'They're keeping watch on the village,' he whispered to Heiko.

She looked at the bow, then at the man, who was also wearing dark clothes in order to blend into his surroundings. 'It would seem so. There was a drought this year. Perhaps their food stocks are low. They wouldn't want anyone stealing their rice.'

Taro cursed. 'In that case, getting into the rice store might be tricky. We can turn back if you like.' Annoyed, he contemplated the idea of never again seeing his bow – his one link to his true father, Lord Tokugawa, and perhaps the object in which was hidden his destiny.

No. They had to go on.

Heiko laughed softly. 'This just makes it more interesting,' she said.

They continued, crossing a little stream and then entering a wood that surrounded the village.

At this point Taro passed within a body's length of his mother's message.

But he didn't see it.

Instead he spotted another guard, standing just behind a tree. He made a series of hand gestures to Heiko. She nodded. He shinned up the nearest tree, a tall pine, and used its regular branches to climb easily to its upper reaches. Then he tensed his muscles and leaped onto the neighbouring tree, landing as lightly as a monkey, his small body coming in useful for once. He passed from tree to tree this way, until he was above the guard. Then he shimmied down until he was just above the man's head. Clinging on with his legs, he allowed his upper body to flop downward, bringing his head to the same level as the guard's, only upside down. For a second their eyes met and he saw the man's mouth open to scream, but Taro's *shobo* ring had already found a pressure point in the man's neck, and the guard slumped to the ground.

There were a couple more guards, but Heiko dealt with them easily, knocking one out with a deft flick of her *shobo*, and taking down the other with the blowpipe.

The stone-built rice store was accessible only through one door, and so this was where the two final guards stood. Taro and Heiko climbed up onto the roof, shimmied along, and then dropped silently next to the guards. The men had barely time to turn in alarm before a pair of *shobo* rings to the neck had knocked them unconscious.

Heiko knelt by the door and examined the lock. 'Traditional Japanese,' she said. 'Not Portuguese. That's good.'

She explained that a hollow metal bolt slid through two

staples, and was held in place by pins that fell down inside one of the staples to fill corresponding holes in the bolt. To spring the lock, a key was inserted down the length of the bolt. Prongs that matched the shape and number of the pins would push these back up into the staple, allowing the bolt to be slid out.

She took a long key from the bag at her waist, with two prongs at the end like the remaining teeth of an old man. 'Most locks in this canton are made by the same blacksmith, and he is too lazy to change the key mould very often,' she whispered.

She slid the key in, then raised it up. There was a click. Heiko pulled on the bolt and it slid easily out of the staples that held it to the door. She lowered the bolt to the ground. 'It's a good idea to always remove the bolt. The key is not required to lock it. The pins will fall into place as soon as the bolt is returned to its positions, so it can be unwise to leave it in place, in case someone locks you in.'

They went inside. Piles of rice, like drifts of white snow in the dimness, rose almost to the ceiling. Taro peered round for his bow. *There it is!* He picked it up and clasped it to his chest. Then he held it out in front of him, gripped either end, and bent it back on itself, against the grain of the wood. It resisted for a moment. Then there was a loud snap and the bow broke in half, the hilt falling to the ground. The broken ends whipped up into the air as the pent energy in the bow was released, and one of them passed fractionally in front of his eye.

'What—' began Heiko, but Taro put his finger to his lips. He bent down and picked up the hilt. When the body of the bow had broken, it had cracked open the cylindrical piece of wood that had formed the main of the grip, and only the tape wrapped round it held it together, like a bandaged broken leg. He shook the tube.

Something fell out.

He caught the object, and even as he felt its weight hit his fingers, he knew that it could not be what he had hoped. He sighed, lifting it to see what it was.

A note, rolled up tight and secured with thread.

He held it out to Heiko. 'What does it say?' he whispered, his voice betraying his disappointment.

She broke the thread and unrolled the little piece of paper. 'It says, "The boy who bears this bow is Lord Tokugawa's son." We know that already, though.'

He nodded, miserably.

She handed the note back. 'You expected something else?'

'I thought… It was stupid, but…'

Understanding lit her features. 'Of course. The Buddha ball.'

He shrugged. 'A silly idea. But it would have helped so much. I could have destroyed Kira, and Oda. Made them pay for… well, for everything they have done. My father. The abbess. I should have liked to do something for you and Yukiko.'

She smiled at him. 'I am sure you will do all that, one day. But for now I'd prefer you stayed alive. Revenge has a way of consuming people.'

Just then there was a sharp bang and Taro whirled round on the spot. Behind him the door had been shut. He pushed against it, but it didn't yield.

From the other side of the door came Little Kawabata's voice, unmistakably reedy and nasal. 'I wonder what that upstart Taro could be doing in this rice store,' he said to himself in a stage whisper, 'when he's supposed to be sleeping! I should probably notify my father that Taro and Heiko have crept out of the crater at night.'

Taro banged on the door. 'Little Kawabata, let us out!'

'*Little* Kawabata?' said the boy in a silky, dangerous voice. 'Are you mocking my weight? Since you insult me, perhaps I'll wait until daytime before I inform my father of where you are.' His voice moved round to the side of the hut, and then Taro saw fingers appear through a crack in the wood and wiggle up and down. 'There'll be lots of light in there when the sun come up. I hope that doesn't *hurt* or anything. But then, being turned early has to have some disadvantages.'

Taro gazed round the stone storeroom. Moonlight, filtering through the thin gaps between planks, pierced the air above the rice mounds in shafts that crossed over one another, filling the room with a latticework of dim blue light that shimmered with motes of rice dust.

Soon that light would not be moonlight.

It would be bright autumn sunlight.

'Gods…' he whispered – not because he was afraid that someone might hear, but because the awfulness of his realization had robbed his speech. 'He means to kill me.'

Heiko's eyes widened. 'Of course… the light. It'll burn your skin.'

She too began to bang on the door and shouted to Kawabata to let them out. But to no avail. The boy simply laughed, low and slow, then walked away. 'I'll be back for you when daylight comes, Heiko. If you know what's good for you, you'll think about your version of events, in case anyone thinks to question me. I wouldn't want you having any *accidents* during your time at the crater.'

They heard the sound of his footsteps softening and finally disappearing as he walked back up the hill towards the crater.

Eventually, they turned to each other. 'The bolt,' said Heiko. 'He picked it up and slid it back in. We're locked in.'

Taro groaned. 'The men we incapacitated will wake up soon. Then they'll rouse the village. And we have no more than one incense stick of time before dawn.'

Heiko looked aghast. 'But… how can he do this? He'll kill you!'

Taro closed his eyes and took a deep breath.

Gods, he thought. *This is it. This is how you die.*

But when he opened his eyes again, Heiko was looking at him, eyes wide with anxiety, and he knew that he could not simply dissolve into purposeless terror. He didn't want to die, and his heart was pounding with the fear of the coming daylight, but he would fight to stay alive.

'We have no time to lose,' he said to Heiko. Tensing, he aimed a hard kick at the door. It barely shivered. He kicked again, then again. Heiko joined in, but the door would not budge. The stone walls, too, were unmovable. Taro even climbed up into the rafters, looking for gaps in the roof that might permit him to climb out. But there was nothing.

By the time they gave up, slumped against each other, lying against a pile of rice, the light that streamed through the roof was already brightening. One of the shafts moved across the floor towards Taro's foot. Heiko winced, as Taro yanked his foot away from the light. 'We need to get you out of here.'

Taro nodded. Then a branch cracked outside, and Taro whipped round. He could hear voices approaching, laughing and joking. 'It's a shame to start on the dried rice already,' said one of the villagers.

'It's always a shame when harvests are bad,' said another.

'And when lords raise their taxes at the same time,' grumbled a younger, deeper voice.

'Shush!' said another, as if it were dangerous even in the middle of nowhere to speak of such things.

Taro and Heiko glanced at each other nervously. They were about to be discovered!

Taro knew there was no time to lose. The light might hurt him, though it was not yet full daylight, but at least he would draw attention away from Heiko.

There came a shout from just outside the door. 'The guards! They've been overpowered! Hideo, get the key! We have thieves!'

Taro pointed at the mounds of rice. 'Burrow under there,' he said to Heiko. 'I'll be safe. I promise.' He wished he felt as confident as he sounded.

There was a metallic click, and then the door began to creak open.

Tensing against the pain he was sure would come with the light, Taro launched himself at the doorway.

In a flash he saw that one of the men framed there – a village elder, Taro supposed, from the extra body weight the man carried round his soft belly – had a drawstring money pouch on his belt, and that gave Taro an idea. If he took their money, they'd have to follow him.

And that would leave Heiko safe in the storeroom.

He ran straight at the men. They stepped back in surprise, giving Taro the space he needed to duck, grab the money bag, and snap it off the man's belt. One of the men snatched at Taro as he ran past them, catching at his cloak, but Taro twisted and managed to throw him off. Then he was running down the path and away. He glanced fearfully at the sky. Light was creeping over the treetops, and when he looked down, he saw a glow spreading on the fallen leaves.

He rubbed at his skin. No pain yet, but he knew it would come.

If he didn't get into the shade soon, he was going to die.

The men turned, shouting, and ran after him. Taro found

himself having to slow down in order to let them keep up. He was so much stronger now, so much faster, that it was easy to get carried away. He paused, looking behind him. The men came thundering along, panting heavily. One of them pointed at him. 'Ninja!'

Taro turned and ran, coming off the path and into the woods. He was heading uphill now, and the going was steep. The ground was littered with rocks and roots. Taro hoped to tire the men out; perhaps, if possible, twist an ankle or two. He leaped lightly over the ground, his coordination and reflexes getting better by the day. He felt exhilarated, untouchable – and then there was a glare that he recognized as the sun rising above the trees, and the scene was flooded with light.

It felt as though everything inside him had turned to rushing water, and he wondered distantly whether the roaring sound he could hear was out in the world – a storm, maybe – or only in his ears. *No*, he thought. *I can't die before I see my mother again*.

He closed his eyes.

A moment later he opened them again.

He frowned down at himself as he realized that there was no pain at all.

Strange.

The light flooded the world now, so bright after days and days of night that he had to blink to clear the shapes that flashed and flared in his vision. He stopped and turned his hands in the sunshine. They were completely exposed, and yet nothing was happening. He flexed his fingers.

Still nothing.

Had Shusaku lied to him about the light? But why would he do that? And then, Little Kawabata too had thought the light would harm him. He had counted on it, in fact.

Taro closed his eyes, and the light of the sun was red against his eyelids. *Do I always* have to be different? he thought.

But then there was a crunch of a foot on leaves behind him, and he turned to run once again, leaping over rocks and ducking under overhanging trees. He glanced back. The men were catching up. A branch was suddenly in front of his face, and then he was lying on his back, all the breath knocked out of his body. Pain flared from what felt like a broken nose – not as intense as when he'd been human, but bad nonetheless. He tried to move but found that his arms and legs would not obey.

There was a shout, a footfall that snapped a twig.

'Ah, here you are,' said a voice, somewhat out of breath. A face swam into Taro's field of vision – one of the men, the youngest in fact. The man grinned in triumph and reached down to grab Taro by the throat. With his other hand he reached for the money bag still gripped in Taro's fist.

Taro listened carefully. His hearing too had improved vastly. The other men were far behind, clearly less used than this one to such exertion.

He made a snap decision, hoping that he could move again. He intercepted the man's arm, clasping his wrist. He pulled, hard, yanking the man off balance and towards him. At the same time he rolled, letting the man fall face first onto the ground where a second ago he had lain winded.

Twisting the man's arm behind his back, Taro reversed his roll, kicking with his feet so that his body spun in the air to land, knees down, on the man's back. 'I'm sorry,' said Taro. Then he leaned forward and sank his teeth into the back of the man's neck. He hoped he could stop before he killed him.

With the fresh blood pumping in his veins, Taro ran easily through the woods, taking a long detour back to the rice store.

He heard dim cries from behind him, in the woods, where the pursuers had found their companion. Taro was almost certain the man would live; he hadn't drunk for long. But he hoped that the men would now keep away from the rice store. As far as they were concerned, the thief had got out and was on the run.

Soon he reached the hut and skidded inside, closing the door behind him. He didn't want anyone else seeing the open door and deciding to investigate.

CHAPTER 45

S O YOU CAN go outside in the light, even though you're a vampire?'

Taro nodded. 'So it would seem.'

'And that means that when Little Kawabata comes back, you'll be waiting for him.'

Now Taro grinned. 'Oh, yes. I have an idea about that.'

Obeying Taro's instructions, Heiko stood by the door inside the hut, while Taro slipped outside. He had explained to her what he wanted her to do.

Taro locked the bolt from the outside, then slipped the key under the door so that it was only partly exposed to anyone coming from outside. He was making an assumption: Little Kawabata did not have a skeleton key, and would be expecting to have to pick or force the lock. If he saw Heiko's key sitting there under the door, chances were he would try to pick it up, to make his task easier.

Taro hoped that Heiko would remain alert. Her job was to keep an eye on the key, most of which was on her side of the door. There was a gap between the door and the ground just high enough for Little Kawabata to get his hand under it. As soon as his hand appeared, she was to grab it. The rest should be easy after that.

Taro sat, waiting, on the roof of the rice store. Despite the fullness of the daylight, he was invisible from the ground. So he hoped, anyway. The sun hung high up in the sky now, illuminating the slopes of the valley with hard, flat light. Yet it didn't hurt him, and he was at a loss to understand why. He had seen Shusaku's pain on the beach in Minata, when the rays of the sunlight had reached him. He ran his tongue over his long, sharp canines. Yes, he was definitely a vampire.

One, it seemed, who could go abroad in daylight.

Even as one part of Taro's mind fussed over the strangeness of this, there was another part that thought something else. That thought, *This could be useful*. Idly he spun his sword in his hand. Little Kawabata was taking his time. As he waited, Taro's mind wandered. He thought of the story of Susanoo, *kami* of storms, and the eight-headed serpent – for this was what had inspired his idea.

Susanoo, who was a powerful god of the sea, was roaming the northern mountains one day when he came across a grieving family of *kunitsukami*, gods of the land, led by Ashi-na-Zuchi. When Susanoo asked the leader what was wrong, the *kami* of the land told him that his family was being ravaged by the fearsome Yamata-no-Orochi, the eight-headed serpent. This monster had carried away and killed seven of Ashi-na-Zuchi's daughters, and now it was coming for his eighth and final daughter, Kushi-inada-hine.

Susanoo looked on the eighth daughter, and saw that she was beautiful. (In fact, he had seen this before he'd stopped to speak to Ashi-na-Zuchi. He wouldn't have taken an interest in the tedious problems of land gods, had there not been a beautiful girl involved.) He asked Ashi-na-Zuchi for his daughter's hand in marriage, in return for defeating the serpent, and the old land god readily agreed.

Immediately, Susanoo prepared eight bowls of sake, since it was known that all monsters were great lovers of rice wine. These he placed on eight platforms, which he had the men of the village build. These platforms in turn were placed behind a new fence, with eight square gates just large enough to allow the passage of a serpent's head.

Sure enough, the serpent took the bait and put each of its heads through each gate, slurping up the sake with each green and monstrous tongue. Thus distracted, the monster did not see Susanoo as he calmly walked along the fence, chopping off each head in turn. The later heads attempted to extricate themselves, of course, but as anyone who has ever been a child knows, it is much easier to push your head through a fence than it is to pull it back out again. Soon all eight heads were sliced off, and Susanoo chopped off the tails, too. In the fourth tail he found Ame-no-Murakumo-no-Tsurugi, the greatest sword ever to cut flesh, which he presented as a gift of appeasement to Amaterasu, his half sister and the goddess of harvests and plenty, with whom he had an enduring rivalry…

There was a noise from below. Taro looked down and saw Little Kawabata kneeling by the door.

A wave of hot anger ran through Taro as he looked on the podgy boy who had tried to kill him. Then Little Kawabata yelped, as if something had happened to his hand.

This was Taro's cue. He leaped down from the roof, landing next to Little Kawabata. The boy's right hand was under the door, and his face was pressed painfully against the wood. He had gone down on his knees. Taro supposed that Heiko must be putting a nasty little hold on that hand, to make Little Kawabata squirm so.

Taro put his hand on Little Kawabata's chin and turned his face so that the fat boy could see him. Then, very deliberately, so Little Kawabata could see, he drew his sword and held the blade over the fat boy's wrist.

Little Kawabata gasped, and his face blanched, as if he had seen a ghost. Perhaps that was really what he thought After all, how else could Taro still be alive, and standing in the morning sunlight?

'Listen carefully,' Taro said. 'Heiko has your wrist held tight. At a single movement from you I will cut off your hand. Do you believe me?' To underline his point, he drew the blade lightly along Little Kawabata's skin, leaving a shallow cut.

Little Kawabata nodded, whimpering.

'But I don't want you to die, even if you tried to kill me. Do you believe *that*?'

Little Kawabata nodded again, eyes wide.

'Good. Then we will return to the crater, and you will never seek to hurt me again. Understood?'

Little Kawabata nodded. 'Y-yes,' he stuttered.

CHAPTER 46

Lᴏᴛᴛʟᴇ Kᴀᴡᴀʙᴀᴛᴀ sᴛᴀʀᴇᴅ up at the vampire boy, his skin shimmering in the sun. He was used to being beaten by his father whenever he was caught doing something bad – and yet here was Taro, forgiving him for attempting to kill him!

At that moment Little Kawabata felt something he had never felt before: a flicker of admiration.

If anything it made him angrier, stoked his jealousy just as soft, clear air stokes the flames of a vicious fire.

CHAPTER 47

TARO LED THE way to the crater, keeping always to the shadows of the trees, not to preserve himself from the sunlight but to keep them from the view of any passing villagers. Little Kawabata followed behind, breathing heavily. Taro was setting a quick pace. He was worried about getting back before their absence was noted, but he also couldn't help feeling slight pleasure at Little Kawabata's discomfort.

Soon they reached the little hut at the top of the meadow that opened into the cave system.

Taro opened the door and went in. It was as he stepped into the cool twilight of the interior that a hand closed over his shoulder, and a familiar voice spoke.

'Got you,' it said.

CHAPTER 48

T ARO TWISTED TO see Shusaku standing over him. Next to him was Kawabata the elder, looking furious.

Then Shusaku surprised Taro by throwing his arms round him. 'I thought you might have died,' he said.

Taro found that he was more glad than he had expected to see the ninja again, even if he *was* in trouble for sneaking out. He hugged Shusaku tightly. But then Shusaku broke away and stared at him, incredulous.

'You just walked up the mountain in the daylight?'

'Yes,' said Taro. 'It didn't hurt.'

Kawabata frowned. 'You definitely turned him?'

'I know how to make a vampire,' said Shusaku. 'Look at his teeth.'

'Vampires don't walk round in the sunshine,' said Kawabata.

'No.' Shusaku was thoughtful now. 'They don't. Once again, young Taro, it seems there is more to you than meets the eyes.' He looked down at the broken bow in Taro's hands. 'But we will talk about that later. For now you have some explaining to do. Well?'

Taro looked down. 'I... that is...'

Shusaku grunted. 'Really? Well, that explains everything.

How foolish of me to worry about you. I thought perhaps Kira had found you and taken you to Lord Oda. I thought you might be in *danger*. Do you understand that, Taro?'

Taro could think of nothing to say. He had caused Shusaku distress, and he hadn't meant to, but that didn't make it any less horrible.

Kawabata glared at him. 'And why did you drag my son into it? He's a good boy. Yet ever since you arrived he has become uncontrollable!' The leader turned to Shusaku, his face purple with anger. 'Perhaps you should be more careful about the brats you bring here, in future. I will not have my charges – and my son – corrupted by outside influence.'

Shusaku raised a hand to cut off Kawabata's flow of outrage. But when he turned to Taro, the disappointment was evident in every movement of his body, and Taro felt a pang of guilt.

'Your explanation, please, Taro,' said the ninja.

'I'm sorry, Shusaku,' Taro said. 'I went to get my bow. I took Heiko with me.'

'I thought you left the bow in the cave.'

'No. I dropped it, in the ditch at the village down the mountain. A man took it... and I wanted to get it back, without your help.'

'It's broken,' said Shusaku dully.

Taro shot a glance at Heiko, a glance that said, *Keep quiet*. 'Er... yes. The man who took it, he must have snapped it. I don't know why.'

Shusaku narrowed his eyes. 'I see. And why did you go looking for it on your own?'

'You're always saving me and... Anyway, I asked Heiko to go with me. The bow was in a locked hut, you see, and I knew that she could pick locks.'

'You show resourcefulness. There is that to be grateful for.'

'He shows insubordination,' said Kawabata. 'He is a liar and a sneak. He probably kidnapped my son. As it is, I will have to punish Little Kawabata severely. He is a disgrace to me. He has thrown the safety of our community into jeopardy, as have you all.'

'No...' said Little Kawabata, voice trembling.

'Little Kawabata was only helping me because I asked him to,' Taro said.

The elder Kawabata turned on his son and gripped him by the upper arms. It was then that he saw the thin cut on the boy's wrist.

'What's this?'

Little Kawabata trembled. 'It's nothing.'

'No. It's a sword wound. Who did it?'

Shusaku looked down at the arm and turned a questioning glance on Taro.

Little Kawabata pulled away from his father. 'No one.'

Kawabata slapped him, hard. 'Who. Did. It?'

The boy hung his head. 'Taro.'

'What did you do, boy?' demanded Kawabata, stepping forward threateningly.

'He said he would cut my hand off!' said Little Kawabata, warming now to his role.

'That's rubbish!' said Heiko. 'I mean, he *did*, but only because Little Kawabata tried to kill him!'

Shusaku stared. '*What?*'

Kawabata spluttered, unable even to find voice for his shock and anger. His face had now turned a deep purple that was close to black.

'It's true,' said Heiko. 'Taro would never tell you – he's too honourable for that. But I don't have time for honour, especially when it comes to boys like Little Kawabata.' She almost spat these words out, her eyes narrowed at the leader's son.

Taro slumped against the wall of the hut. This was not what he had wanted.

'Tell me everything,' said Shusaku to Heiko.

And she did. Soon Shusaku was shaking his head in disbelief as she recounted how Little Kawabata had taunted them through the door, telling them about the light that would soon filter through the walls. Little Kawabata looked down, shaking slightly, a tear running down his cheek.

Shusaku put a hand on the boy's chin and tilted his face up. 'Is it true? Did you lock them in?'

Little Kawabata nodded miserably.

'Then you will die,' said Shusaku simply. Taro gasped. 'Even your father cannot prevent it,' continued the ninja.

Kawabata looked like a pig's bladder from which the air had escaped. He seemed diminished, in physical height and in presence. 'I would not even try to prevent it,' he said with revulsion, as if the words tasted rotten and he wanted them out of his mouth. 'He is no longer my son.'

The fat man turned away.

'But…' said Heiko. 'I… Gods… this isn't what I wanted to happen.' She looked stricken. 'I only knew that Taro wouldn't tell you the truth.'

Shusaku touched her arm. 'You did the right thing.'

Taro was horrified. He could not have another boy die because of him, even if the boy was a nasty little grub. 'But I got his word that he would never try to hurt me again,' he said to Shusaku. 'And the light *didn't* hurt me. And anyway, I *forgave* him.'

Shusaku looked at him with kind eyes. 'Perhaps you have,' he said wearily. 'But the ninjas do not forgive so easily. Little Kawabata attempted to kill you. He believed that the light would be fatal to you. The fact that it wasn't is irrelevant. There has never before now been a vampire who could stand the sunlight, so he could never have anticipated the eventuality. Our rules are very clear, when it comes to one ninja murdering another of his clan, or trying to. Little Kawabata must be punished, in the only meaningful way. He must lose his life.'

Taro looked imploringly at his rescuer, the man who had saved his life, and then led him halfway across the country, surprising him all the time. 'Please, Shusaku,' he said. He swallowed. 'I would not ask if it was not important to me. Please. Spare him.' He glanced at Little Kawabata, who was looking at him with a sort of wretched hope. Kawabata senior still faced the wall, only the heaving of his shoulders betraying his emotion. Heiko watched the exchange, eyes wide.

Shusaku put his hands on Taro's shoulders. 'You plead for the life of this boy, who tried to kill you? This boy who has done nothing but seek to harm you since you arrived here?'

'Yes.'

Shusaku sighed. 'It's impossible. The code is strict.' But the scarf wrapped round his face creased as he spoke, as if his eyebrows and mouth were moving with thought.

'No,' said Taro. 'There is another way. I see it in your face.'

'You can't see my face,' said Shusaku.

'Nevertheless.'

Once again the ninja master sighed. 'Very well. There is another way of settling a dispute, if Kawabata-*san* is in agreement.'

The leader turned, frowning. Shusaku leaned forward and whispered something into his ear.

Kawabata nodded, his face ashen.

'Then it is decided,' said Shusaku. 'You and Little Kawabata will fight to the death, with weapons of your choosing.'

Heiko's eyes sprang wide open. 'But Taro's a vampire! He's practically unbeatable, by a mortal opponent!'

Shusaku nodded. 'Yes,' he said. 'That's rather the point.'

Little Kawabata fainted.

CHAPTER 49

T ARO SAT IN a corner of the cave system with Hiro, Yukiko, and Heiko. Little Kawabata had gone off on his own, refusing to speak to anyone.

'I'm so sorry,' said Heiko. 'I had no idea this would happen.'

Hiro put a hand on Taro's shoulder. 'He deserves it, you know,' he said. 'He tried to kill you.'

'It doesn't mean he deserves to die,' said Heiko.

Taro said nothing.

'Have you chosen your weapons?' asked Yukiko.

'Yes,' said Taro. 'We will fight with the sword.'

'But… you're like a demon with a sword,' said Yukiko. 'He won't stand a chance.'

'No,' said Taro, wishing he didn't have to conceal his purpose, wishing he could share his plan with his friends. 'He won't.'

The look Heiko gave him, her eyes wide with horror, filled him with shame.

Shusaku sat on the wood-and-leather horse that had been set up in the storeroom to simulate fighting on horseback. 'No,' he said. 'I've never seen any vampire who could withstand the sunlight.'

Taro pursed his lips, toying absently with some nunchakus.

'I'd have thought you'd be pleased,' said Shusaku. 'This is a great gift. And it will give you a huge advantage.'

'You think?'

'Of course. None of us can move about in the day, and so no one expects ninja outside the hours of night. You have surprise on your side.'

'I suppose,' said Taro. 'I just... don't like always being different.'

Shusaku patted the false horse's back thoughtfully. 'Yes. I can understand that.'

'You've really never seen it before?' said Taro. 'Not once?'

'Never.'

'Then why? Why would I be different?'

Shusaku shrugged. 'Your guess is as good as mine. My only thought is... Well, I don't know if it is not just a stupidity.'

'What?' said Taro, curious.

The ninja spoke as if thinking aloud. 'I told you that some claim we are descended from the *kami* of night-time, that some of the attributes of those old god-spirits are passed through the blood when we are turned.'

'Yes. You said you didn't believe it.'

'I didn't. Only... I simply wondered whether... Let us say, that is, for argument's sake, that it is true. Do you remember the story the abbess told? About the ama who recovered the Buddha ball, and how her son honoured her after death?'

'Yes.'

'In the story she became almost a god herself. She reached a higher state of grace, of enlightenment. That was what enabled her to curse the prince's line and ordain that her descendant would become leader of the country. Well, it strikes me that... if that descendant is you... then perhaps the blessing of that ama, a woman who had become not the dead spirit of a person but a bodhisattva, could protect you from the light. Sunlight after all is the gift of Amaterasu, the *kami* goddess of the sun. A bodhisattva could solicit her favour, ask her not to burn her distant descendant.'

Taro stared at him, unbelieving. All this talk of *kamis* and bodhisattvas, as if they were real. He knew that the peasants made offerings to Inani, wishing for bountiful crops, and that the fishermen worshipped Susanoo, the god of storms – or feared him, more precisely – but they existed in some parallel realm, surely, far from here.

Didn't they?

'As I say,' said Shusaku, 'I am far from believing that the *kamis* exist. I think perhaps we are no more than a slightly different species, like wolves are to dogs. Or, less glamorous perhaps, vampirism may be a mere disease. This business of the ama woman… it's just an idea.'

Taro shrugged. At any rate, it didn't seem likely that anyone was going to explain his resistance to the sun. He would do better to be grateful for it. But there was something else he wanted from Shusaku, something he needed if he was going to make his plan work in the fight against Little Kawabata tomorrow.

'When you were made a vampire…' he began, watching Shusaku's body language carefully. He'd never asked the ninja about his past before, and he was worried about offending him. 'Heiko said you were… badly injured.'

Shusaku stiffened a little, but he nodded slowly. 'A spear to the neck. It was during the war against Lord Yoshimoto, when the Lords Oda and Tokugawa joined forces to defeat the old shogun's enemy.'

'You were dying?'

'Actually,' said Shusaku, 'I think I may have been dead. There was a girl… She *appeared* to be a serving maid to Lord Tokugawa. She and I… had become close. But that evening, as I bled into the ground of the battlefield, she bit me, then cut her own palm and let her blood run into my mouth. When I awoke, I learned that she was a vampire – a ninja – sent by the people of this very mountain to watch over Lord Tokugawa. She saved my life.'

'Like you did with me, when the sword pierced my stomach.'

'Yes. Rather like that.'

'So the vampire blood, it heals?'

Shusaku leaned his head to the side as if thinking. 'In a manner, yes. But at the price of making the… patient… a vampire.'

'Of course. But that is better than being dead.'

Shusaku laughed. 'Not everyone would agree, I'm sure. But I certainly think so.'

Taro looked at the paintings on the cave walls, the angels and demons and gold-robed Buddhas, and thought about what he would have to do the next day. But now that Shusaku was speaking to him about his own life, he found himself wanting to know more. 'Heiko said she… the ninja girl, I mean. Heiko said she—'

'Died, yes. Someone in that camp learned what she was. I found her by the water pumps early one morning, her head cut off.' Shusaku leaped down from the horse and began pacing.

'You loved her.' It wasn't a question.

'Yes. I still do.'

The ninja began to walk away, signalling an end to the conversation. Taro understood, it was still too painful for him to discuss. Taro wondered if he too would be like this one day. If he didn't ever find his mother, would he be pacing this room when he was Shusaku's age, unable to talk about her loss? He knew that his father's death would always live inside him, that a small part of him would always be watching his body lying in a pool of blood, the shadow of the ninja who had killed him detaching itself from the darkness. But he felt that if he could just find his mother, see her again, then some part of that wound might heal over, and he could carry on with his life.

Also, of course, he would go with Shusaku to Lord Oda's castle, and he would have his vengeance on the man who had sent those ninja to Shirahama, who had as good as killed Taro's father with his own hand.

Shusaku gave a low bow, taking his leave. Before he left the cave, though, he turned round. 'Good luck tomorrow. I'm sorry you chose this path. It might have been easier to let Little Kawabata be executed.'

'No,' said Taro. 'It wouldn't.'

Shusaku nodded. 'I think I see.'

He disappeared into the darkness of the tunnel system. Taro spun the nunchakus in his hand. Only some of his questions had been answered, but he had confirmed the most important thing. Shusaku had given him the information he needed to face the fight tomorrow – to step boldly into the circle, sword held tightly in his hand—

And to kill Little Kawabata.

CHAPTER 50

TARO DID NOT sleep much, and it seemed he had only just
closed his eyes, at last, when Shusaku came to his sleeping cave
and woke him.

'You're ready?' asked the ninja.

'No.'

'Good,' Shusaku said. 'You would be a fool if you believed you
were.'

He led Taro – and Little Kawabata, who joined them in the
corridor – to a bare cave near the crater itself. Little Kawabata
was given a simple meal of rice. Taro, as usual, had pig blood.

Hiro, Yukiko, and Taro spoke among themselves while Little
Kawabata sat hunched in the corner. Heiko held her knees close
to her chest and remained silent. Taro was nervous. He could
feel a whooshing sickness in his stomach, like the feeling
between when you trip and when you hit the ground. Yukiko,
too, looked anxious. She bit her lip often, and broke off in the
middle of sentences.

Little Kawabata said nothing – only stared at the rock wall,
grinding his teeth. Taro didn't really know why Little Kawabata
hated him. He suspected that in part it was because his father
hated Shusaku, and so Little Kawabata had simply taken this

hatred of his father's as if it were an heirloom. It had been Shusaku who had decided to turn Taro, to bring him here, even though he was the son of Lord Tokugawa – and so in a way Taro symbolized Shusaku, was an emblem of his divided loyalty, half ninja, half samurai.

In a way, Taro *was* Shusaku, only younger.

But Taro thought, too, that Little Kawabata was jealous. Like Yukiko, who had borne it better, he was hurt that Taro had been turned before him, had been made a vampire without training or ceremony. Taro wished he could undo his turning, wished he could be an ordinary boy, and not someone different to be hated. At the same time, he felt angry with Little Kawabata for being envious. Did the fat little weasel imagine that it was easy to see your father die, to lose your mother, to be taken from everything you knew and loved?

And Taro wondered how jealous a person would have to be, how easily wounded, to want to try to kill someone only because they felt threatened by them. If Little Kawabata had been prepared to see him die in that rice store, then perhaps the boy was truly dangerous, perhaps there was little he wouldn't do in the service of his own twisted ego.

Taro hoped he was not about to make a big mistake.

Shusaku came for Taro and Little Kawabata early. He led them down the stone corridor and into the crater.

Taro gasped. Great bonfires had been lit at the four corners of the compass, casting a shimmering glow all round. Wooden benches had been erected round the circular wall of the great round space, and on these benches sat hundreds of people. Some were eating; some were laughing and joking among themselves; all fell silent when the three children entered the arena. In the centre stood Kawabata, who gazed contemptuously at his son before indicating a wooden scaffold next to him. On it were displayed two swords, their blades gleaming in the firelight. These were full-length *katana* – not the usual short-swords used by ninja.

The three walked behind Shusaku to the middle of the crater. The ninja turned to Taro then and made the mudra for dispelling fear, holding his right hand out, palm outward. Taro felt a rush of affection for this complicated man – killer, teacher, friend – and bowed, hands together, in the gesture of *gassho*, the mudra of respect.

Shusaku smiled.

Little Kawabata seemed very pale. He turned to his father. 'You're not really going to make me do this, are you?' he asked. His eyes were glistening. 'I'm your *son*.'

Kawabata senior turned away. 'You have broken our oldest law,' he said. 'I would execute you myself, if the duty fell on me.'

Little Kawabata stared at his father with horror. Then, seeing that Taro was looking at him, he wiped at his eyes with his sleeve and turned away.

Taro closed his eyes for a moment, focusing on clearing his desires and attachments, washing his mind of his pity for Little Kawabata, who would never be good enough to impress his father, and who would therefore always be angry, always wanting to bring low those who were stronger and happier than he.

Taro felt his compassion for the fat boy blossoming painfully in his chest, and he crushed it tight within himself, pushing it down, making his inner canvas as blank as possible. Only with perfect clarity would he be able to go through with his plan.

They reached the scaffold on which were arrayed the swords. 'The choice of swords must be fair,' said Kawabata, 'so that there are no possible recriminations. You will each choose one of these chopsticks.' He held out two wooden sticks to the contestants. 'Each is numbered, and each number has a pair that is written near one of the swords. Whichever stick you choose decides your sword. Taro, as the aggrieved party, you may choose first.'

Taro shook his head. 'I chose the type of weapon. Let Little Kawabata choose the weapon itself.'

Little Kawabata grunted something that might have been an acknowledgement. He reached out and took one of the chopsticks. He looked at it, then went over to the scaffold and removed his sword. Taro followed, receiving a wickedly sharp *katana* sword. He waved it round and turned it in his hand, admiring its shallow curve, its thinness, and its beautiful construction. A pale blue wave ran down the steel face of the blade. This was a far finer weapon than the one with which he had been practising.

Shusaku and Kawabata removed the scaffold between them, then returned to the centre of the crater. 'Taro and Little Kawabata, please proceed to the centre of the crater,' said Shusaku. 'There is only one rule of the fight. One of you must die. And if neither of you is capable of killing the other, the boy who is adjudged by the leaders of the clan – that is, me and Kawabata – to have fought the least valiantly will be put to death. Do you understand? One of you will die here today.'

Taro's stomach flipped like a fish.

Kawabata gave his son a sharp slap on the back. 'Die with honour, even if you could not live with it.'

Little Kawabata let out a small sob, and Kawabata the elder glared at him. 'On *hai*, you fight,' he said. Then he and Shusaku led Hiro, Yukiko, and Heiko over to the benches.

Taro looked at Little Kawabata. The chubby boy regarded him with a calculatedly blank expression. Taro gave a shallow bow. Little Kawabata bowed back. Form had now been observed. Neither boy's sword was sheathed. This was not *ii-aido* but pure sword fighting. The speed of the draw did not count here. Only skill with the blade.

Taro, like Little Kawabata, stood in the basic stance, his left foot forward to brace his weight, the sword extended before him, sharp side up. Shusaku had told them that the ultimate stance in sword fighting was *ku*, or emptiness. A swordsman had truly attained greatness when he was able to stand casually, with no stance at all, and move from that emptiness into any form of attack or defence.

But Taro and Little Kawabata were a long way from that kind of skill, and so they stood in the stance they had been taught. Taro felt a drop of sweat run down his cheek, and he started to turn towards Shusaku because surely they couldn't go through with this. It was insane to—

'*HAI!*'

Little Kawabata leaped forward, swinging his sword in one of the canonical opening moves. Taro parried easily, his movement flowing thanks to hours of practice, his arm moving practically of its own accord. He lunged forward, scraping his blade along the underside of Little Kawabata's, hoping to flick the other boy's sword out of his hand and into the air. But Little Kawabata saw the danger and snapped his sword to the left, twisting Taro's, and Taro had to grip tightly to avoid losing his own weapon. He danced backwards, getting his equilibrium again. He could hear the roaring of the crowd, yet only dully, the voices combining into a distant rushing noise like waves on sand.

Little Kawabata struck at Taro's shoulder, forcing him to raise his blade to block the blow, then turned his feint into a sweeping stroke that only just missed Taro's stomach. He jump-ed backwards just in time. Taro was faster than Little Kawabata, but the leader's son, despite his bulk, was very skilful.

Their swords clashed several times in succession as they read each other's moves successfully. Then Little Kawabata found a gap and slashed Taro's thigh, opening up a thin, shallow wound. The crowd gasped.

Taro gritted his teeth. He moved forward, bringing his sword down in a wide sweep. Just as it neared Little Kawabata – and the pudgy boy almost disdainfully raised his sword to parry the obvious strike – Taro reversed his grip on the sword's pommel, so that the blade was moving sideways, not downward, its arc changing in a flash. It wasn't a move Shusaku had taught him – just pure instinct.

Little Kawabata's block would have stopped the original strike, but now Taro's sword came in with a far flatter angle, and it bit home under Little Kawabata's arm. Taro had to pull hard to recover his sword, which must have cut into a rib.

Little Kawabata staggered backwards, a red stain spreading on his side. The crowd fell silent. Taro made a quick feint to Little Kawabata's injured side and noted the slowness of the other boy's reactions as he turned and batted away his sword. Moving with complete focus now, Taro made a few more strikes, some more clever than others, designed to wear Little Kawabata out.

A low murmur came from the crowd as the spectators saw the trouble Little Kawabata was in. Taro thought he heard the clan leader shout out, scared for his son.

Little Kawabata's movements were pained and sluggish, his eyes half-closed. The blood had soaked as far down as his baggy *hakama* trousers. He waved his sword ineffectually at Taro, as if it was very heavy.

Taro felt that the time had come to end the fight. He sent up a final plea to the Compassionate One.

Lord Buddha, make this work – for him if not for me.

He countered a weak strike from the other boy, then struck with force and determination. His sword flew out in a deadly, straight motion – like an arrow – and buried itself in Little Kawabata's stomach. The leader's son blinked once, opened his mouth wide as if to say something, and then toppled forward.

He lay motionless on the hard ground, in a spreading pool of blood.

CHAPTER 51

I N A VOICE that was only slightly shaky, Shusaku called out, 'Taro is the winner!'

Taro looked up. Kawabata senior was running over from the benches, his face drained of colour. Heiko looked at Taro, aghast. On her face were written excitement, horror, and disappointment, all together. She looked at him as if he were a stranger, as if she had never believed that he would go through with it.

Taro ignored both of them. He had no time to lose.

As Kawabata ran up, Taro bent over the man's son, who lay lifeless before him. He remembered what had happened at his home, how Shusaku had turned him after he'd been mortally injured. And he remembered what Shusaku had told him about the girl who'd saved him when he was dying – or dead.

He hoped it would work the same for Little Kawabata.

Leaning in close, he bit Little Kawabata's neck. The boy's heart was no longer pumping, so Taro had to suck to drink of the blood. It was warm and sickly, with a metallic, rusty taste. He felt a spreading heat in his body, a sensation of growing strength. He wasn't sure precisely what to do, but he reached for his sword and drew its blade across his palm. Blood welled up from the wound. Then he turned his hand over Little Kawabata's mouth.

'What are you doing?' shouted Kawabata, who had arrived at the centre of the circle and grabbed Taro's shoulder. Taro shook him off, pressing his hand over Little Kawabata's mouth, using his fingers to pry it open. He tensed, feeling the blood dripping, repeating like a mantra in his head the two words *just work, just work, just work* …

Kawabata pulled him roughly out of the way, and Taro fell to his back. He looked up at the artificial stars, still hoping. He rolled until he could look at the boy, with his father kneeling beside him, weeping. Kawabata picked up his son and cradled him in his arms. There was something embarrassing, something personal, about the leader's uncharacteristic tenderness.

Taro stared. It hadn't worked.

Then Little Kawabata coughed and shook in his father's arms. He drew in a deep, rattling breath. Kawabata, shocked, dropped him, and the boy fell once more to the ground. But he twitched and then, his movements jerky, pulled himself into a sitting position. He turned to Taro and bared his teeth.

His canines glinted in the firelight.

CHAPTER 52

TARO AND LITTLE Kawabata were helped over to the benches, where Heiko threw herself round Taro's neck, weeping.

'When you – you killed him…' Heiko stammered, 'I had no idea what you were planning. I thought… And I saw in your eyes how much my lack of faith must have hurt you. I'm sorry. I should have trusted you.'

Taro put his finger to his lips. 'I couldn't tell you. I'm sorry.'

Kawabata hovered, fulminating. His red face was streaked with tears and his voice quavered. 'This is a disgrace!' he said. 'In all the years of the volcano this has never happened before! Taro should be punished. This was meant to be a fight to the death. The rule clearly states—'

'According to the rule, your son would be dead,' said Shusaku. 'In fact, Taro clearly bested him. According to our rules, Little Kawabata should still be put to death.'

Kawabata's mouth flapped, silently. The other spectators had all turned to watch the drama unfolding on the benches. The leader was about to protest, but Taro cut him off. 'Actually,' he said, 'I believe that Little Kawabata has acquitted himself of his crime. The rules state that one of us must die. Little Kawabata did. When I turned him, he was not breathing.'

Kawabata stared at Taro. 'He tried to kill you. Why would you spare him?'

Taro wasn't even sure himself. The answer seemed as large as his own nature; as much as anything, he had had a conviction, as integral to him as his bones and muscle and sinew, that he couldn't cause the other boy's death. He had not consciously thought about it. 'I just… didn't think he deserved to die. What he did to me was bad, but…'

'But what?' said Kawabata.

'But it wasn't really him, I don't think.'

'What do you mean?' said Shusaku.

'His father hates you. So you could say that his anger was not really his own. He inherited it. And that means he was not deliberately cruel. He deserved mercy.'

Little Kawabata was staring at him all this while, and Taro didn't know what the boy was thinking. Did he hate him even more, now that he had saved him? It would not be beyond him to think of it as a humiliation, to prefer to have died.

But Taro couldn't worry about such things. He had done what seemed right, to him, and that was all that mattered. If Little Kawabata chose to make it a point of enmity between them, to seek revenge, then that was unavoidable.

Shusaku was staring at him too. 'You are a constant surprise to me, boy.'

Kawabata turned away from Taro, and from his son, with disgust. 'Mercy is for peasants,' he said. 'A ninja does not need it.'

'Nevertheless,' said Shusaku, 'you can't deny that the rules have been upheld.'

Kawabata glared at him, grimacing, and it seemed to Taro that he was trying to think of an argument against the fight's outcome, but apparently he failed, because finally he nodded.

'The matter is settled, it would seem,' he said. Then he turned and walked away, without a backward glance at his newly turned son.

'Father!' said Little Kawabata, hurrying after him. But his father did not turn round.

As Little Kawabata headed for the cave entrance, he paused for a moment and looked back at Taro. 'I—' he began, then closed his mouth again. He scowled, unable to complete his sentence, and a moment later he was gone.

'Ah,' said Shusaku. 'Well, mercy must be its own reward, I suppose.'

CHAPTER 53

T HAT NIGHT, AS Taro and his friends were discussing and reliving every moment of the fight, Shusaku came into the weapons room. He held up a pigeon in one hand. He released it, and it flew to the roof of the cave, where it found a stone ledge and sat down, preening. He unrolled a small scroll. 'I've just received this message.'

Taro sprang to his feet. 'From my mother?' Even as he asked, though, he was looking at the white breast of the pigeon on the ledge that fussily arranged its feathers, and he could not remember the pigeon Shusaku had given his mother having that patch of whiteness. It had been grey, that one, and flecked with black.

But perhaps I didn't see clearly in the gloom of the hut, he thought desperately.

Shusaku looked at him. 'No. I'm truly sorry.'

Taro felt as though he had swallowed a lump of ice.

'You'll find her,' said Yukiko. 'I know it.'

Taro smiled wanly. 'Yes. I hope so.' He turned to Shusaku. 'So what is the message, if it's not from her?'

Shusaku held it up. 'This is from my – *our* employer.'

'Lord Tokugawa?'

'Yes. He requires the… *execution* of a delicate task. Taro, I would ask that you come with me. The mission calls for someone of… shall we say, unique talents. A truly talented ninja guards the premises by night, meaning that whoever carries out the… task… must be capable of moving by day. There is also a certain poetry to your involvement.'

'Oda?' asked Taro.

Shusaku nodded.

Taro looked at the master. 'When do we leave?'

Shusaku smiled. 'I have informed Kawabata and the other ninja that we leave tonight.'

Little Kawabata was about to enter the cave where his father and mother slept, when he heard them talking. He paused at the entrance, leaning against the rough rock wall. His father's voice was raised. Even so, Little Kawabata was not sure he would have been able to hear it through the rock had the peasant boy not turned him.

'…will not tell me how to proceed, woman.'

His mother sounded placatory, wheedling, and Little Kawabata felt disgusted by her weakness. No doubt his father had decided on some hard course of action – one that would intimidate a lesser man – and his mother was trying to persuade him out of it, to keep him safe.

But Little Kawabata's father was brave. He would not listen to such blandishments, and he would not turn from difficult duty.

'You would betray Shusaku?' asked his mother. 'And our own employer, Lord Tokugawa?'

'A thousand times over,' said his father, his voice almost a growl.

Little Kawabata frowned. This didn't sound like the plan of a valiant man.

'Kawabata-san,' said his mother gently. 'Don't you think it's time to let Mara go? Why are you still so angry about the past?'

'He stole her from me. She was mine.'

'But...I thought it was me you loved...'

'Then you're a fool.'

Little Kawabata's thoughts bumped and turned in his head, like fish in a barrel. His father had been in love with Mara? This wasn't something he had heard before.

'But she didn't love you!' said Little Kawabata's mother, her voice shaky with shock. 'How can you say he stole her?'

'She belonged to me.'

'Nonsense. She belonged to no one – until she met Shusaku. She never promised herself to you.'

'Be quiet,' said his father. 'Or I'll make you quiet.' His voice was laced with deadly threat, and Little Kawabata's mother started to cry. Despite himself, Little Kawabata felt an urge to go to her, to protect her.

No, she is insulting your father, he told himself. But he wasn't sure he believed it.

'She didn't need to promise herself,' said his father, on the other side of the rock wall. 'She was a young ninja. I was the leader-in-waiting of the clan. It was a formality that I would be elected!'

His mother was sobbing. She did not reply.

'I will be obeyed and respected,' said his father, and it sounded like he was talking to himself as much as to his wife. 'I will be treated as befits my status.'

'Yes, Kawabata-*san*,' said his mother, her voice cracking.

'It's too late, anyway,' said his father, his voice shiny with menace. 'I have already sent a messenger to Lord Oda. He is the fastest of the men loyal to me. He'll arrive at Nagoya Castle well ahead of Shusaku.'

'But…Shusaku will be killed. Have you gone mad?'

'Shusaku deserves to die.'

'You don't still think he killed Mara?'

Kawabata laughed dismissively. 'No, you blundering ox. I know who killed Mara. Do you imagine this is the first time I have sent Lord Oda a secret message?'

A sharp intake of breath. 'Have you lost your senses? You killed the woman you say you loved! And now you betray Lord Toku—'

There was a flat report that Little Kawabata recognized as a slap. Abruptly, his mother stopped crying. *'Only I have been betrayed!'* his father screamed.

Little Kawabata let his weight fall against the wall. Shusaku hadn't killed the girl called Mara, had never killed her. Everything he had thought was a lie. Mara had died because of his own father, and her only crime had been to choose Shusaku instead of him.

His father was a *murderer*.

From the other side of the rock, the sobbing started again.

'Silence,' said Little Kawabata's father to his mother. 'Or I'll kill you, too.'

CHAPTER 55

Heiko, Yukiko, and Hiro insisted on going too, of course. Shusaku tried to resist it, but he knew that a bond had been formed among the young people, and that the trip would offer many opportunities for training.

They wasted no time in gathering supplies for the three-day walk to Lord Oda's castle. They dressed in the simple unornamented garb of peasants, stowing black ninja clothes and scarves in shoulder bags. Shusaku chose for each of them a sharp *wakizashi*, short enough to be easily hidden in the folds of their clothes, and he also packed blowpipes, darts, and miniature bombs.

I'm a ninja now, thought Taro. At one time the thought might have filled him with horror, or with a frisson of illicit excitement. Now, as he watched Shusaku select weapons to be concealed about their persons, he felt only a dull hope that the preparations would be enough to guarantee the death of the treacherous Lord Oda.

Finally, everything was ready. It was as they were about to enter the tunnel to the hut that Kawabata came waddling towards them, an angry expression on his face.

'What is it?' asked Shusaku, impatient.

'My son has gone.' Kawabata ran his eyes over them. 'Do you have him?'

'*Have* him? No. You think I would take him from you?'

Kawabata sneered. 'You have taken things from me before.' He sounded truculent, like a child denied a favourite food.

'I don't know what you're talking about,' said Shusaku. 'But I can tell you that I have not kidnapped your son.'

Kawabata's anger did not diminish, but he did lower his shoulders wearily. 'No. I see that.' Then he turned on Taro. 'This is *your* fault,' he spat.

'Taro hasn't kidnapped him either,' said Shusaku, in a voice that was half a sigh.

'No. But he beat him, and then he turned him. He has corrupted the boy, made him weak. How do you think it must have affected him, to lose the fight, and then to be denied the death that should have followed?'

Taro stared at the man. 'Are you saying… you would rather he had died?'

'Of course. Better death than dishonour. He is a loser, and you have forced him to live with that knowledge.'

Taro blinked. There was nothing he could say to this. When he had been young, he had loved to hear stories of adventure and honour. Now it seemed to him that honour was often just an excuse for cruelty, a way for the strong to bully the weak. He turned away from Kawabata. 'Let's go,' he said.

Shusaku nodded, stepping into the tunnel.

'If you should come across him…' said Kawabata.

Taro paused. Could it be that Kawabata was really concerned about the boy?

'…tell him not to come back,' the fat man finished.

Taro turned his back on the man, sickened.

CHAPTER 56

Starlight washed the dark mountain air as they picked their way over the mountain pass leading back to the wide plain, and beyond it to Lord Oda's castle in the town of Nagoya.

'Our target is in the fourth tower,' said Shusaku as he crossed a small stream. 'It's the hardest part of the castle to access. There is a spiral staircase in the European style, so that it can be easily defended from above.'

'Guards?' asked Hiro.

'Many. Also, Lord Oda has hired the services of a ninja called Namae to protect the tower. I've encountered him before. The man is a ghost – he appears and disappears like mist. Where he goes, he leaves corpses strewn behind him. He's dangerous.'

Coming from Shusaku, that meant something.

'Can we get past him?' asked Yukiko.

'*We* can't. But Taro can.'

Yukiko stared. 'He isn't fully trained!'

Shusaku smiled. 'He doesn't have to be. You see, Namae can guard the tower only at *night*. He's meant to be a protection against ninja.'

Yukiko gasped. 'Taro can sneak in during the day!'

'But what if Oda isn't there in the daytime?' asked Taro. 'What if I get in and he's out somewhere?'

'My employer informs me that the target will be there,' said Shusaku. 'Oda is afraid to leave the castle. He feels that the fourth tower offers the best insurance against attack.'

Taro felt a sort of nauseous excitement bubbling inside him. He couldn't wait to face the man who had ordered his assassination, whose pawns had killed Taro's father. And there was something else, too. Something he would never dare to put into words, or even think too clearly, for fear that just by articulating it he could somehow lose the woman who he still thought of as mother.

But the thought was there, even if it was quiet and as shadowy as a fox in the night of his mind. *Lady Tokugawa is staying at Lord Oda's castle. What if she is my real mother, the one who gave birth to me, and what if I get to meet her?*

For a moment Taro allowed an image to rise up in his mind – an image of himself standing before a woman who resembled him, who had the same fine features and grey eyes. Perhaps, for the first time, he would belong.

But he chased away the corrupting dream. He *did* belong, wherever his own mother was, wherever she had hidden herself after the attack on the village. Shusaku's pigeon had still not come, bringing news of her, but he had not given up hope.

Kill Lord Oda, he told himself, *then go and find her, whether the pigeon has arrived or not.*

His thoughts revolved in this way for many burned incense sticks, never allowing him a moment's peace. Daylight found them in a hunters' hut high up in the mountains. When night fell, they descended from the hills into lower ground, crossing arable land that felt dreadfully exposed to Taro, until they entered the wide open plain leading to Nagoya Castle, which they had crossed in the opposite direction what seemed a lifetime ago.

With all that he knew about Lord Oda now, Taro felt that the empty huts had taken on a new, sinister meaning. What before he had taken for the effects of war seemed instead a warning, communicating to any visitors the depth of Lord Oda's contempt for those in his care.

However, whatever else the empty huts may have meant, they also meant shelter, and as the sky to the east was already paling with the first signs of dawn, Shusaku led them through various fields and small hamlets. As the first rays of dawn suffused the landscape, they came upon a young deer. Taro shot it down with a dart, and he and Shusaku shared its blood before handing the carcass to Hiro to carry and cook later on a fire for the others. Not long afterwards they found an abandoned place in which they could sleep for the day.

As they settled down on the hard ground, and Shusaku pinned black silk *hakama* to the windows with daggers, in order to keep out the light, Taro looked about him and felt almost content. Hiro was building a fire in the corner, ready to prepare the deer's meat. As he worked, he looked up at Taro and smiled.

Taro smiled back. He had not realized how much, in the mountaintop lair, he had felt trapped and confined, a feeling that had reached its apogee in the rice store, when Little Kawabata had locked him in. Here, he was a part of the landscape, grass for his pillow, the moon for a lamp. And he was with four people he knew, and trusted, and liked.

It was the next evening as they set out that he began to feel uneasy. Coming after the solitude of the high places, the great flattened bowl of the plain before Nagoya Castle, with its fields and croaking frogs and plumes of smoke rising here and there into the too-wide air, seemed an expanse in which it was possible to be trapped in another way – spotted by enemies, and then encircled, with nowhere to hide.

'It feels like the land itself is against us,' said Yukiko.

Taro nodded. They were standing on the road to Nagoya, and it was clear that the others shared his trepidation. 'It's Oda's land, that's why,' he said. 'It doesn't want us here.' As he spoke, a crow cawed loudly, wheeling above their heads.

Shusaku shook his head. 'The land will love us for freeing it from Oda's rule. It is on our side.'

Taro was grateful to the ninja for saying it, but he was not convinced. The wind was soughing in the bamboo and the leaves, and he could almost have believed that it was the wasted land itself uttering this terrible noise. The entire landscape seemed possessed of a sort of ancient, idiot sentience. The trees took on the shapes of creatures, and the whistling of the wind seemed to issue from the very throat of the fields, a low keening, meaningless and malignant.

Above it all rose the hill of Nagoya, overlooking the cruelly abandoned valley like a baleful eye. The quickest way forward was the straight road that led to the town, and, disguised as they were as simple peasants, Shusaku led the way onto it. Taro looked round nervously at the fields surrounding them, at the broad and empty road before them, its straightness affording anyone coming from either direction a good view of the group, and from some distance away.

He felt too exposed. In the light of the stars and moon the waterlogged rice fields seemed a shimmering sea, and on it the five of them seemed small and vulnerable, too visible to predators, even if some of them were predators themselves. Taro felt as they entered the inland sea of light that they were so small and insignificant that a net might at any time close about them, seizing them all together, and a rough hand throw them on the black sand of some terrible shore.

'Well,' said Heiko, 'we can turn round now. Or we can go through with this, and you can avenge your father, Taro.'

'I'm not turning back,' said Hiro. Taro felt his heart swell with pride in his friend, and already the landscape before him seemed less formidable. 'If anyone sees us,' Hiro continued, 'we will look like peasants. And anyway, they won't be expecting us to have two girls with us.' He looked at Yukiko. 'Having you here is a good disguise. I knew you couldn't be *completely* useless.'

Yukiko rolled her eyes. 'Don't think I'll hesitate to say that you kidnapped me as a hostage.'

Taro and Heiko exchanged a smile. If they did come across Kenji Kira, or any of Lord Oda's ninja, then Taro knew at least he didn't need to worry about Hiro and Yukiko.

Actually, he was more worried about anyone who felt it wise to fight them.

The matter of turning round or not turning round settled, they set out along the road. It was after they had been walking for perhaps four incense sticks that they passed a peasant couple, pulling a small cart on which had been piled what looked like their possessions. Shusaku turned to look at them but said nothing.

Half an incense stick later, they came upon another family, fleeing towards the mountains.

As they passed, Shusaku bowed to them in greeting. 'Trouble ahead?' he asked.

The peasants seemed fearful, their heads turning this way and that in quick, sharp, saccadic movements, like the heads of crows. 'A *kyuuketsuki*,' the man whispered.

Shusaku started, and the man took this as alarm. 'You could always turn back,' he said.

'No,' said Shusaku. 'We need to reach Nagoya.'

The man shrugged. 'As you wish.'

He began to walk again, but Shusaku stopped him. 'What makes you think there's a *kyuuketsuki*?' he asked.

'Up ahead. A man was bitten. His body was left on the roadside. In plain view!'

Shusaku looked at Taro, and Taro could guess what he was thinking. Subterfuge was to ninja what heat was to a sword smith – they could not work without it. To leave a body by the roadside did not sound like the mark of a ninja. 'This person who was killed,' said Shusaku. 'He had two puncture wounds?'

'Yes. On the neck.'

Shusaku thanked the man and returned to the group as the peasants left. 'I don't like this,' he said.

But they continued nevertheless, and it was soon afterwards – and after passing several more people fleeing the other way – that they came upon a small village, little more than a couple of houses by the road, really, and saw a group of people gathered by the roadside. It was immediately obvious to Taro that these people were gathered round the dead man. They communicated with one another by means of expansive, frightened-looking gestures, seeming engaged in a sort of mummery designed to leave no passerby in doubt as to the violence to which they bore witness.

Taro and the others approached the group and, by jostling, were able to see what they were looking at. A man lay in the ditch right by the road, his head lolling to one side, a pair of circular wounds in his neck where the teeth had gone in.

Shusaku suddenly stiffened, then pushed through to kneel by the man.

'Are you a doctor?' said a woman.

Shusaku looked up, distracted. He was pulling aside the dead man's lips to look at his mouth. 'Ah… yes,' he said. 'And I can tell you that this man is *definitely* dead. There's nothing to be done.'

The woman stared at him, as if he were insane. Shusaku ignored her, stepping away from the body and then pulling Taro and Heiko by their arms, leading them from the scene. Hiro and Yukiko followed. When they were out of earshot of the group, still walking towards Nagoya, Taro turned to the ninja.

'What was it?' he asked. 'What did you see?'

'That man was killed by a vampire,' he said. 'But he was a vampire himself.'

Taro frowned. 'You mean… he was a ninja?'

'Yes. Long, sharp teeth. Pale skin. And anyway, I recognize him from the mountain. He was called Yoshi, a good friend of Kawabata's.'

'Why would a ninja kill another ninja?' asked Hiro.

'I don't know,' said Shusaku. 'The strange thing, though, is that the other ninja *bit* him. Vampires feed on human blood. The blood of another vampire gives no nourishment. In fact, it is quite unpleasant to drink.'

'So… perhaps someone only wants us to think he was killed by a vampire?'

'I don't think so. I'm sure a vampire did it. The bite wound was unmistakable. But the man's neck had been broken – I felt the separated vertebrae. The bite was done after he died.'

'Why?' asked Taro.

'I think…' said Shusaku, 'it must have been a message of

some kind. Whoever killed that man wanted it to be known that a vampire did it. And then, leaving the corpse by the road like that. It's almost as if the killer wanted people to find it. Or wanted us to find it, even.'

Taro shivered. He didn't like this plain anyway. The thought that someone might be ahead of them, waiting for them – someone who wished them ill, and was a murderer – made him feel even more vulnerable and exposed than before.

Shusaku must have been feeling the same thing, because he was scanning the road before and behind them. 'We need to find a cart, or the like,' he said. 'We shouldn't stay out on this road.'

CHAPTER 57

I T WASN'T LONG before they managed to find a peasant with a fabric-covered cart who was willing, in return for some of Shusaku's seemingly endless gold coins, to hide them in the back of his vehicle. The cart, when they found it, contained rice. Shusaku's gold was enough that, some time later, rice sat by the side of the road in small shining heaps.

A keen eye would also have noticed pieces of cut-off wood and sawdust that indicated someone had been working with planks.

So it was that, rocking on the axles of the simple cart, listening to the lowing of the water buffalo that pulled them, they covered a night's walk in the space of a handful of incense sticks. There was no need to stop for the sun either. The taut apron of canvas that covered the semicircular frame of the carriage kept the sun off them, as well as the light rain that began in late morning.

It was as they were passing through a small village that they came upon Kenji Kira and his men, and one of their number was lost forever – cast, twitching, on that darker shore.

CHAPTER 58

TARO FELT THE cart come to a stop. The peasant, who sat up front holding the reins, talking non-stop to his buffalo, suddenly fell silent.

'Halt. What's your cargo?'

Taro recognized the haughty tones of Kenji Kira, the so-called samurai who had killed the old man in the mountains, and who had been looking for *him*. An icicle of dread settled against his spine. Now he heard the grumbling neighs and shuffling hoof percussion of a group of horses forming themselves into a circle round the cart.

This was bad.

'N-n-nothing,' said the peasant.

'Nothing?' asked Kira very softly. 'That is a very large cart for carrying nothing. What use could a man such as you have for so much nothing?'

'Er...'

There was the sound of a *katana* sliding from its scabbard. Taro would have recognized it anywhere. It resembled the sound of blood hissing from a man's neck, instants after being cut by that same *katana*. Taro hoped he would not hear the second sound.

'Now, sirs—' began the peasant.

'Enough,' said Kira. 'You are sweating. You seem incapable of simple articulation. You are transporting, so you claim, empty air in a cart large enough to hold a year's supply of rice. Either you tell me now what you are up to, or I kill you. Whether or not you open your mouth to speak and tell me what I want to know, I *will* see inside that cart. I am seeking… an item of valuable contraband. We have it on good authority from a local hunter that what we search for is close by. Perhaps it is behind you as we speak.'

Taro felt Shusaku's hand on his arm as he knelt, holding his breath, to look out through a low crack between the boards of the cart, which he kept stuffed at most times with a scarf in order to block out the light. 'Stay,' the ninja whispered. 'Don't do anything hasty. There are a lot of them.'

Taro nodded, though he itched to get outside and protect the old peasant. And part of him burned with the old anger against Shusaku, and the ninja's lack of honour. Taro refused to watch Kira kill another innocent man, even if he had learned some of the older ninja's pragmatism. For the moment he would stay still. But if it came time to act, he would act.

He put his eye to the crack, moving the scarf just so much that he could see, without allowing light in to hurt Shusaku.

Taro concentrated. Outside, Kira was sitting on his horse just in front of the buffalo, separated by it from the peasant who sat on his raised platform, holding the reins in trembling hands. *That's good*, thought Taro. *It will take Kira a moment to ride forward and strike, if he decides to kill the man.*

But Kira's sword was drawn, as were those of the men who sat on either side of him on their horses. There were at least a dozen of them, all wearing the horned helmets of Oda's samurai, and armoured so heavily that arrows would be useless against them. Taro cursed.

Nevertheless, the blood pounded in his ears. *Honour*, he thought. *When I was young, I dreamed of honour. I wanted to be a hero. Perhaps it was not so stupid to dream of such things.*

He turned to Shusaku. 'I'm sorry,' he whispered, and moved quickly towards the rear of the cart, and the outside world—

And fell, hard, to the wooden floor. He felt and heard his nose break, warm blood splashing into his eyes. The pain was excruciating. 'What the—' he said, feeling the rope that bound his ankles together.

He heard Kira, outside, say, 'What was that?'

The man's voice was sharp and as hard as steel. Again the peasant stammered an incoherent response.

Taro twisted, his vision strobing with the pain of the impact, and saw that Shusaku looked as confused as he was. The ninja raised his hands in a gesture that did not say *I'm sorry*. It said, *Not me*. Then a dart appeared in Shusaku's neck, feathers fluttering. His eyes crossed and he collapsed against the cart wall, unconscious.

That was when Heiko swam into Taro's vision, leaning over him. She had wrapped her black scarves round her face, concealing everything but her eyes. She cast aside a blowpipe and took Shusaku's short-sword. She pulled Taro up and dragged him back to his place beside Shusaku. Taro was surprised by her strength. He saw that Hiro and Yukiko were also lying on the floor, darts visible in their flesh. They didn't stir.

'What are you *doing*?' he asked.

'I'm sorry,' Heiko whispered. 'But you would have gone. Do you see? You would have gone, and you would have died, and so would my sister. But you are Lord Tokugawa no Taro. One day maybe you'll kill Lord Oda, and avenge yourself for your parents and mine. And so I have planned for this moment, when I would save you. You too have a task, however. You will remember me as I wish to be remembered – dying by steel, with honour, so that the true shogun may overthrow our enemies. That is why I left you conscious, so that you would witness my sacrifice. Tell my sister of it.' She kissed him, once, on the cheek, and he felt her hands dig into his back as she hugged him. 'And watch out for Shusaku. Remember Hoichi, and what the prophetess said.'

Then she *moved*.

In an instant she disappeared through the hole in the floor that they had cut for that purpose, leaving behind her a flash of daylight that framed her leaping silhouette for a moment, as if to fix it forever in his memory. Then the trapdoor fell closed again and the cart was once again thrown into gloomy twilight.

Taro bent over and struggled against the tight, yet carelessly tied knot. He would have it undone in a moment, and then—

But his fingers fumbled clumsily and the carriage appeared to rock. The motion of it left trails on his vision, like slow ghosts of the objects he saw.

A dart. She had drugged him.

He fell to his knees, as if in prayer, unable to stand.

Head spinning, vision blurred by blood and tears, his face was now pressed – as surely Heiko had intended – to the crack. He remembered looking out from another wooden carriage, on another ambush. He remembered Shusaku fighting those two ninja and defeating them.

This would not end so well.

Heiko walked very calmly up to Kenji Kira, unseen by him or his samurai. Taro's vision was watery and blurred, whether by the drugs or the tears, he was not sure. He could no longer move, but he watched the events unfold as if underwater.

The samurai, noticing her later than they should have, for she walked as quietly as a fox, soothed their horses as they shied away from the figure all in black.

She was magnificent. In her black cloak and *hakama*, her scarves covering her face, she looked like a ninja from a story, all grace and controlled violence.

She stepped up to Kenji Kira, who looked down at her from his horse, his face revealing a struggle between various emotions: surprise, happiness at facing his enemy, but also – Taro was sure – fear.

'I am he whom you seek,' said Heiko in a deeper voice than she normally used.

Taro breathed in hard.

Kenji Kira only smiled. 'Taro. Perhaps you think I will fight you honourably. If so, you are *gravely* mistaken.' He turned to the samurai that surrounded him. 'Kill the boy. Then kill the peasant. His lies are an affront to me.'

Heiko raised a hand as the samurai moved forward. 'Wait.' They stopped, waiting to hear what she had to say.

'Please, leave the peasant alone,' she said as the samurai held their hands, wavering, over their sword pommels. 'He knows nothing.'

Kira laughed. 'He knows nothing, and he transports nothing. Truly, it seems his whole life amounts to nothing.' He paused. 'Which is fitting, really.'

It all happened so fast.

Kira lunged forward, his horse responding instantly to the cue and leaping towards the peasant. The man flung his hands up, as if that could stop the sword that was even now descending towards his neck—

Heiko leaped, sword extended, and with a ringing clash her sword blocked Kira's strike.

But one of the samurai was there, his sword swinging with a perfection of form that seemed to Taro in that moment unutterably grotesque.

The blade bit into Heiko's side, almost severing her in half.

She fell to the dust.

Taro let out a strangled sob.

Kenji Kira calmed his horse, then swung easily out of the saddle and landed beside Heiko. He bent down and tore off her scarf.

'It's a *girl*!' he exclaimed.

'Fooled... you...' murmured Heiko.

Kira straightened up, his expression furious. 'Find the boy!' he screamed.

'Too late,' said Heiko. 'He's gone. Wasted your time... killing me.'

Kira spat. His face was livid with anger. 'You're not dead yet, vampire,' he said, and with a single stroke cut off her head.

Kenji Kira turned to his men. 'The girl was a distraction. Taro is probably far from here by now. Let's go.' He jumped neatly onto his horse. 'But first check the cart quickly. You never know.'

THE SAMURAI WALKED towards the canvas slit at the back of the cart. His companions were mounted already, waiting to set off in pursuit of the boy, who had fooled them again – this time convincing a girl to die for him.

The samurai wondered if it maybe wasn't so stupid after all to think that one day this boy Taro could threaten Lord Oda. It seemed that he naturally inspired those round him – even peasant girls – to protect and serve him as a samurai would, even dying for him when required.

The canvas was light in his hand, and moved aside easily. A smell of rice greeted his nostrils. He cast his gaze round the confines of the wooden walls. Rice was piled up high in soft mounds that extended all the way back to the far wall. He had put a foot up on the board to get inside, when one of his companions called.

'Anything?'

He turned, putting his foot back down to the ground. 'Only rice.'

'You hear that?' said Kenji Kira, speaking to the man whose cart it was. 'It seems your life is not forfeit. This time, at least. But in future, learn to speak when spoken to. It is a valuable gift

333

that makes conversation so much easier.'

The peasant stammered. 'Y-y-yes, samurai-san... S-s-sor—'

'Oh, shut up,' said Kira. He raised his voice. 'Let's go!' he ordered. 'Fusaku, leave that rice alone and get on your mount. You are tolerably well fed, are you not?'

The samurai sighed and hurried back to the others.

He did not notice that the far wall of the cart was a little closer than the true length of the vehicle.

CHAPTER 60

Yukiko bent over the body of her sister, wailing. Tears streamed down her cheeks. Her agony was painful to watch. It shocked Taro that in the usually pleasing melody of her voice these notes of dissonant, high-pitched grief had been hiding all along.

A moment earlier they had dropped through the hatch, everyone else having risen groggily to wakefulness when Taro had splashed cold water in their faces. Taro estimated that a single incense stick might have burned in the time since Kira and his men had left. As the others began to stir, he heard peasants whispering outside, clearly afraid to approach the cart, or the body before it.

Finally, the potion had worn off, and he had been able to stand. Then he had taken water from a skin and doused the faces of his companions.

He had led Yukiko out first, holding her shoulder as they approached the body of her sister.

Now the younger girl crouched over the corpse, something animal in her pose and the choking sounds that escaped from her, as if the human soul in her had been drowned out by grief.

By the side of the road huddled groups of peasants, their heads held low.

Shusaku knelt by Yukiko and touched her hair. 'We need to move her,' he said gently. 'We had better not stay here with the cart. They will be back.'

Yukiko looked up, and Taro took a step back. Her face when it turned to him was twisted by anger, her eyes narrowed to predatory slits. He barely recognized her.

'You killed my sister,' she said, her voice devoid of any apparent emotion – something that was worse than if she had spoken through tears, or a throat choked with wracking grief.

Taro stared at her. 'I d-d-didn't.'

Shusaku stroked the girl's hair. 'Taro didn't kill her. Kenji Kira did.'

'Kenji Kira works for Lord Oda. Lord Oda wants Taro dead. Therefore it is Taro's fault that Heiko died.' She glared at Taro. 'I wish you had never come to our house! You have destroyed everything. The abbess. My sister. What else would you take from me?'

Taro felt his knees weakening. 'I didn't mean… She… Your sister surprised me. I couldn't stop her from leaving the cart.'

'*Then why didn't you save her?*' she hissed.

'I was… I told you, I couldn't move.'

'You moved for Little Kawabata. You saved *him*. Afterwards – after she was dead – you could have turned her.' It was as if she were tearing the words from her throat. Taro half-expected them to come out covered in blood, and drip down her cloak.

'I tried,' said Taro. 'I wanted to, but she'd drugged me. She drugged you. She knew what she was doing. I wish…'

He began to cry.

Shusaku stroked Yukiko's hair. 'Even if he had been able to

get out of the cart, they'd cut off her head. He could not have done for her what he did for Little Kawabata. And this is assuming that the samurai had not killed him, which they would have, for sure. There were too many of them.'

'So you say,' said Yukiko. Her face was as white as the snow that gave her her name. 'Perhaps Taro merely felt that Heiko was less important than becoming shogun.'

'She did it for honour!' said Taro. 'She said I had to kill Oda and become shogun! That I had to tell you she had died in steel and in honour!'

Only then did Yukiko's features soften. A tear traced the contour of her cheek. 'Perhaps. That sounds like her.'

She turned back to her sister, touched her head, where it lay separated from the body. Then she looked up, a troubled squall of emotions raging on her face – sympathy, anger, shock.

'That man,' she said to Shusaku. 'Who killed my sister. He works for Lord Oda?'

Shusaku nodded.

'Then I will accompany Taro on the mission. I'm not a vampire. I can go abroad in daylight. I will help him to kill Oda, and if I see this man who laid low my sister, I will kill him, too. Do you understand?'

Shusaku placed his hands together in the *gassho* mudra, as if to underline the seriousness of his words. 'Yes. You shall go with him.'

CHAPTER 61

A<small>S THEY CONTINUED</small> towards Lord Oda's castle, Yukiko remained quiet, withdrawn – her features seeming drained of blood and life. They had abandoned the cart, of course, and now they made slow progress, skirting the road to walk through the limited cover of the rice fields, and the occasional tree. Yukiko walked among them like a pale ghost.

On the road, which they kept always in sight, few travellers passed. The land seemed benighted, exhausted, and even the frogs and birds called with weak voices. Aside from the odd peasant hurrying home, they passed only one larger group, a sorry collection of *eta*, the tattered rags they wore almost indistinguishable from their sore-ridden skin, carrying what Taro presumed to be bundles of leather, to sell to the samurai of Nagoya.

It was only when they drew close to the castle that Taro saw the bridge over the river and remembered the checkpoint. He pointed it out to Shusaku, and the ninja grimaced.

'I had hoped to think of something by now,' he said.

Hiro was looking at the ninja suspiciously. 'I'm not pretending to be a leper again,' he said.

Yukiko stared blankly at the guards. 'We could just kill

them,' she said, her voice flat. Looking at her, Taro felt guilty and ashamed. Heiko had died for him, though he hadn't asked it of her. She believed that he would be shogun, that he would bring low those men who had wreaked so much devastation on the land – Lord Oda, Kenji Kira.

But what if he couldn't? Then she would have died in vain.

Taro looked away from her, his face burning. He had left Heiko and Yukiko once, crept away in the night so that they would be safe. And what had he achieved? Only the death of their foster mother, and the destruction now of Heiko, who had believed of all the stupid things that she'd been sacrificing herself for him.

Whatever I do, he thought, *I will always bring pain and death to those round me. Even when I try to avoid it.*

A tear spilled onto his cheek.

When he looked up again, Shusaku was indicating the guards at the bridge with his hand.

'There are too many of them,' said Shusaku. 'We'd be killed.'

Yukiko shrugged, as if that was a matter of little consequence.

If anything, the samurai presence on either side of the bridge had been increased, and Taro could see the fires of other encampments at regular intervals along the river, so as to stop clandestine crossings by boat, or by swimming. He cursed. They could see Lord Oda's castle now, its four towers rising sharply into the night sky, as if to bite the heavens. Yet this checkpoint stood in their way.

But what Hiro had said was tickling at the back of his mind.

'That thing, with the finger,' he said, thinking out loud. 'It was clever, because no one wants to touch a leper. But also because no one would be fool enough to dishonour themselves by *disguising* themselves as a leper. So the samurai didn't expect it.'

'I was tricked into it!' said Hiro, wounded at being called a fool. 'I didn't mean to.'

'I know,' said Taro. 'What I mean is that the disguise was powerful because to impersonate a leper is literally unthinkable. We know how much the samurai cling to their honour, even if their lords exploit it. It would never have even entered their minds that a person might pretend to have leprosy, might deliberately throw away their honour like that.'

Shusaku was nodding. 'Yes. You're right. Did you notice, when we saw Kenji Kira kill that peasant in the mountains? He asked if the man had seen two boys and a man, and he said that one of the boys was a leper. Even he, with all his experience of lies and interrogation, was influenced by his samurai preconceptions. It didn't occur to him that the leprosy might be faked.'

Yukiko turned her dull eyes on the pair of them. 'So?'

Taro took a deep breath, hardly able to believe he was about to say this. But he'd learned a lot about honour, hadn't he? He'd learned that an idea – such as loyalty – is only an idea. It is the behaviour of the individual that counts. A person could talk grandly about loyalty without possessing as much of it, even in his most self-indulgent daydreams, as Hiro.

Shame, too, was only an idea. If humiliation had to be endured in order to achieve something great, then wasn't the humiliation only a step in the journey, an obstacle to be over-come? If shaming himself was the price he had to pay to avenge his father, then so be it.

'Back there,' he said, watching his companions' eyes anxiously to gauge their reactions, 'we passed a group of *eta*.'

Taro ADJUSTED THE rope belt round his ragged cloak, and picked up a bundle of leather. At the bottom of the bundle, hidden beneath the skins, were his short-sword, ninja clothes, and other sundry weapons. The boy before him wore Taro's clothes, and such was the closeness in age between them that Taro had the uncomfortable sensation of looking into a glass.

'Thank you,' said Taro. 'It fits well.'

Shusaku had spent his remaining gold coins buying not only the leather the *eta* carried, but also the clothes from their backs. Four of them, including the boy of Taro's age, were now outfitted in clothes that, despite being peasant garb, were still elegant in comparison to the *etas'* patchwork rags. Yukiko, Hiro, and Shusaku wore cloaks as stained and torn as Taro's.

Taro had expected that Yukiko might object to the plan, but she had only nodded silently, and now she stood unflinching in the rough raiment of an untouchable, her eyes on the road before them, thinking, no doubt, of her sister. Taro could almost admire her single-minded focus on revenge, though he wished that she would not stand and stare like that, without saying anything. It made him think of a statue.

Now the boy in front of Taro gave a little bow. 'We will return to the mountains, then,' he said.

'And forget you ever saw us,' said Shusaku.

One of the older *eta* grinned, revealing a handful of black teeth. 'For this gold, we'd forget our names,' he said. He gestured to the boy whose clothes Taro wore. 'Come, Junichiro. Let's go.'

The boy smiled nervously at Taro, then turned and began to walk away. 'Goodbye,' he called behind him.

The idea of bowing to an *eta* was unthinkable, but then so was the idea of outfitting oneself in their clothes. Taro bowed slightly, and was rewarded by a surprised grin from the boy, who also bobbed his head in a bow as he ran to join the other *eta*. Taro felt something like a tugging as the boy departed, almost as if the two of them were joined by some invisible filament, and he pursed his lips. The boy was *eta*, and unknown to him, and thus by rights should mean nothing.

But Taro had the inexplicable sense that their fates were in some way intertwined.

Shusaku called for him to hurry, and he shook his head. He must have been imagining things.

As Taro had expected, the disguise worked perfectly. So blasphemous and repugnant to the ideals of the samurai was the race of the *eta*, let alone the notion that anyone might seek to be seen as one, that the guards gave no more than a cursory glance at the four companions crossing the bridge, bags of leather slung on their backs, before they returned to searching the rice sacks of emaciated peasants, as if assassins might be found contorted within them.

Shusaku had rubbed dark river mud all over his face, and though in fact the *eta* from whom they had bought the clothes had been clean-skinned, the dirt that obscured his tattoos accorded so well with the samurai's opinion of what an *eta should* look like, that it drew no attention or remark.

Taro was learning something new about ninja. He had thought of them as peerless men of action, achieving their ends through skill and grace of movement, roaming the land in their distinctive black clothes. Now he realized that the true effectiveness of a ninja lay often in not appearing to be one.

That, and they weren't all men.

Yes. Openly walking across a heavily guarded bridge at night, their weapons slung casually over their backs in bags that, had they been searched, would have immediately betrayed their bearers – *that* was what it meant to be a ninja.

Taro's heart was pounding in his chest as they stepped off the bridge and onto the road that led between Nagoya's houses, and he knew that his pulse sped not only in fear of being caught, but also in excitement. He saw Hiro's glittering eyes and knew that his friend was feeling a similar mixture of emotions.

That night they followed directions given by the town's lowlifes – it was impossible, dressed as an *eta*, to engage with anyone of any stature – to a squalid inn in the poor part of town, and there they formulated a plan of action. The next morning, Shusaku would lie low inside – the sun would kill him if he ventured out. Taro and Yukiko would make their move at dawn, when enough of the grey of night remained to conceal them from casual view but the sun's light was bright enough to deter any other ninja from action.

They would head for the back wall of the castle, which, according to the map Shusaku drew in the dust of the room's grimy floor, led to a courtyard and from there to the tower where their target was to be found.

But it wasn't going to be easy.

From a quick reconnaissance it had become clear that there were guards posted all round the castle walls in such a way as to cover, among them, the entire approach to the castle. Behind them, forming a second cordon, was a moat that reached right up to the castle walls.

This was where Hiro came in. Working with Taro, he would create a diversion that would draw one of these guards away from his position – hopefully permanently, but at the least for long enough to allow Taro and Yukiko to swim the moat and scale the wall to drop down into the courtyard. From there they could easily cross to the fourth tower and ascend to the room at the top.

Shusaku guessed that Oda feared a ninja attack most of all. As a result, he would be relying on the services of Namae to keep him safe. The tower itself would not be heavily guarded by day – in theory, anyway. Taro and Yukiko would climb up the wall to the top room. There, Taro would kill Lord Oda before fighting his way down to the courtyard with Yukiko's help, using the advantage of height over their opponents. Anyone coming up the spiral staircase would be hampered by its clockwise twist, unable to properly wield their weapon in their right hand.

And if they encountered Kenji Kira, Yukiko would take his life, in exchange for Heiko's.

Parts of the plan even worked.

CHAPTER 63

Taro, Yukiko, and Hiro were glad when they were able to leave the filthy inn as the first grey light of dawn showed on the horizon – though looking at his companions' faces, Taro guessed that they were as nervous as he was.

Taro was dressed in black *hakama* trousers. He wore hard shoes with sharp spikes at their tips – perfect for finding purchase between the bricks of a tower wall. In a soft linen bag on his back were another pair of hard shoes, these ones equipped with a stamp on the bottom that would turn Taro's shoe prints – as he left the area after swimming back across the moat – into the webbed footprints of geese.

Also in his bag: a short *wakizashi* sword, a dagger, and a blowpipe, along with the black mask scarves that he would don as soon as he and Yukiko began their assault on the wall. The masks were not just for disguise. In the half-light, they would conceal their wearer against the darkness of the castle wall.

Walking quickly, they drew closer to the castle. They did not speak unless they had to. Yukiko remained cold and distant, hiding within the cool ivory carapace of her grief. Hiro was uncharacteristically silent, whirling suspiciously at every little noise.

Finally they reached the circular street that abutted practically onto the castle walls, running round the edge of the moat. Thatched-roof houses clustered here by the dark, cold moat, many of them using it as both a water source and a latrine – two somewhat incompatible uses that explained the poor health of many of the town's inhabitants.

The early morning was cold, and Taro's breath misted before him as he skirted the backs of the houses, following the moat. A couple of times he heard noises behind them – soft noises that could have been made by shoes on mud. Hiro and Yukiko, too, occasionally glanced behind suddenly.

'What was that?' Hiro whispered, as a splash caught their attention.

They stopped dead.

Then a duck appeared, floating serenely on the moat. Taro let out a breath. 'Let's go.'

Yet still that feeling remained.

Taro saw nothing, but he felt the urgent prickle on the back of his neck, the raising of the little hairs there, that warned of someone watching. But who could be following them? He forced his heart rate and breathing to slow. He was nervous, yes, but also excited. The time had finally come to wreak revenge on his adopted father's killer, on the man who had tried to have him destroyed, purely in the name of power.

Eventually, they came to the place where he could see a drawbridge raised against the castle wall. Shusaku had told him that this could be lowered when someone wanted to take one of the horses out from the stable, though no one had done so in some time, due to the heightened security in the castle. On the bank opposite the castle stood a guard – from here just a dark figure in the embracing darkness, though the reddening light of dawn caught the metal of his sword, making it shine like a beacon, or a talisman against evil spirits.

But right now Taro was the spirit. And a sword wasn't going to stop him.

This was the section of the wall they would climb. Looking up at its height now, Taro had to fight a wave of nauseous terror as his confidence of only a moment earlier dissipated. It was too high. There was no way they were going to get up there, and then to get past any guards and fight his way to Lord Oda, it was just—

But Hiro put a hand on his shoulder, and smiled at him, and Taro looked again at the wall and it seemed to have diminished in size. He was glad his friend was with him. Perhaps all of this was meant. Perhaps it had been not only coincidence that Taro had been on the beach when Hiro and his parents were attacked by the *mako*; perhaps all of this had been fated from the beginning, as the abbess had claimed, and now everything was coming together in the same way that the first few hesitant notes strummed on a *biwa* slowly rose to form chords, melody, and soaring structure.

I hope I can climb that thing, thought Taro. The wall seemed once again impossibly tall, and slick from moat water, and lacking in such things as conveniently jutting bricks with which to hold on and pull oneself up.

But they were drawing near to the guard now, who stood in full samurai armour before the moat, and there was no more time for thinking. Hiro fell back, stepping into the overhang of a shop's roof, and so as the guard turned to see Taro and Yukiko approach, he saw only a young couple out for an early morning stroll. Yukiko's hair was pinned up in the manner of a wealthy geisha, and Shusaku had procured for Taro an embroidered jacket that made him appear a dissolute young dandy.

As expected, the guard barely acknowledged them. They were the kind of wastrels that flourished in a town overseen by an amoral lord, and they were of no consequence.

But then rapid movement from behind the couple caught the guard's eyes, and he whipped his head round as Hiro came running up to Taro. Hiro bashed Taro on the head with a stick, grabbed his bag, and continued running, turning onto one of the narrow side streets. 'Thief!' screamed Yukiko.

'Hey! Stop!' shouted the guard, abandoning his post to chase after Hiro as he disappeared into the alley. Taro sat in what he hoped was an awkward-looking position on the ground, rubbing his head.

As soon as the guard entered the alleyway, there was a dull thud. Moments later Hiro emerged, wearing his helmet, armour, and sword. Swaggering a little, he walked over to where the guard had stood, and assumed a bored but arrogant stance, imitating perfectly the way the guard had cast his contemptuous gaze up and down the length of the moat.

'Quickly,' he said. 'I hid the body as best as I could, but someone is bound to find it. And anyway, I only knocked him out. That drug of Shusaku's doesn't last for long.'

The moat was broad, and slit windows in the castle walls permitted those inside to watch over it carefully. Taro and Yukiko ducked down among the reeds on the bank. Taro took something from his bag – his blowpipe. Lowering himself into the cold, sucking mud, he squirmed forward on his belly until he flopped into the water of the moat. A moment later Yukiko lowered herself into the water beside him, slippery and as graceful as an otter.

They kept their heads underwater, breathing through the thin tubes of their blowpipes.

Ninja liked things that accomplished more than one purpose. It saved weight.

Tendrils of waterweed snagged on Taro's ankles and pulled at his arms. They were slimy and cold, and Taro imagined that the water was full of nameless dread creatures. He swam quickly, scared by the dark, cold water. Soon his right hand struck the opposite bank and he hauled himself up out of the water. He moved quickly against the castle wall, keeping himself flat against the stone to avoid the view of any guards posted at windows. Yukiko pulled herself out of the water and joined him, her breathing rapid. They were two shadows on a castle wall, about to break into the stronghold of Lord Oda.

Taro had never felt so vulnerable, so simple to break.

He turned to face the wall, then took special gloves from his bag. These had been customized by the ninjas of the mountain with sharp spikes that had been sewn into the ends of the fingers, allowing him to grip the wall more securely. He handed a pair to Yukiko, then began to pull on his own. But his cold hands were curled like fern sprouts, and he had to breathe on his fingers before they were pliable enough to insert into the gloves. Then he reached up and grabbed hold of a jutting brick.

The wall next to the drawbridge was not high, the height of two men standing one atop the other, perhaps. Within the space of half an incense stick, Taro and Yukiko were sitting on top, looking down on the courtyard below. Taro could smell horses, and the flagstones below were strewn with hay and manure.

He turned back to look out over the town. Hiro gave a little wave from below, where he still stood before the moat, keeping their return route safe. If anyone looked out from one of those arrow-slit windows, they would see the guard with his feathered helmet, bearing his sword and wearing his armour with the Oda *mon* upon it. As far as they would know, this section of the wall was unbreached.

But of course the deception would not last for long, and so the return journey would have to be made quickly.

And before that, Taro and Yukiko had to get to the top of the tower, kill Lord Oda, and then get out again alive.

Taro let his eyes linger on the mostly sleeping town, on its thatched roofs and storks' nests, and then allowed himself one more look at his friend in his borrowed armour.

After all, it might be the last time he'd see him.

CHAPTER 64

THEY DROPPED TO the courtyard floor.

Taro was moving towards the tower door, Yukiko behind him, when a shape detached itself from the wall and moved forward. Taro reached for his sword, still in its bag, but his fingers were cold and slow. The figure resolved into a cloaked man wearing a black mask and black clothes that covered every inch of his skin. Over his face was a veil of grey silk.

Namae.

Early morning light suffused the stable courtyard, but the ninja was well protected by his dark clothes. He would have to go inside soon, but for now he could move freely.

They had misjudged the time.

Taro scrabbled at the drawstring of the bag. His heart had been replaced by a small bird that fluttered inside his chest, trying to escape the confines of his ribs. He heard Yukiko gasp behind him.

The ninja – Taro could just make out his eyes through the veil, and they seemed as black as his mask – flicked his wrist, and Taro felt a sharp pain, like a pinprick, in his chest. He looked down to see a small dart protruding from his body.

Finally he got the bag open and pulled out the *wakizashi*,

swinging it forward. But the sword seemed heavier than ever before; he could barely lift it. It clattered to the stone flagstones as he fell to his knees. A fire was in his veins. *The dart*. It was poisoned.

He twisted his head.

Yukiko.

He was only in time to see her fall, clutching at her neck.

The ninja stepped forward, drawing his own short-sword. His eyes narrowed as he looked down at Taro. 'They send mere children? I don't know whether to be pleased or insulted.' He raised his sword.

Taro didn't have the strength to move. He closed his eyes. *I'm sorry, Father*, he thought. *I have failed you*.

He didn't know which of his fathers he was referring to.

CHAPTER 65

T HERE WAS A low hum as the sword arced down towards Taro's neck. He felt its breath as it stirred the air it cut through.

Then there was a hiss that did not sound like a sword.

Taro looked up. The *wakizashi* had stopped a finger's width from his head. The ninja wielding it was looking down at his arm with wide eyes. A *shuriken*, its many-pointed blades gleaming, stuck out from the flesh.

Namae cursed, reaching for the *shuriken* with the fingers of his sword hand.

Who threw that? thought Taro.

Namae was looking round, trying to answer the same question. Taro tried to get to his feet, taking advantage of the distraction, but his legs would not obey him. By the looks of her, Yukiko was having the same problem. She glared at him as if it were his fault they had been surprised, his fault that they would die. Tears were in her eyes.

'Step away from the boy,' said an oh-so-familiar voice.

Namae and Taro turned at the same time to see another ninja drop to the ground from the wall behind them. His face too was covered, but Taro recognized those eyes immediately.

Shusaku.

The master reached over his shoulder and drew his *katana*, the one bearing the Tokugawa *mon*. Namae took a step back from Taro, obviously judging the boy to be a lesser threat than the man. He shifted his sword from hand to hand.

'I know only one ninja who fights with a samurai's sword,' he said, his voice surprisingly light and refined. '*Lord* Endo.'

'Namae,' said Shusaku, beginning to move in a large circle.

Namae made a sudden, fluid movement, and Taro just glimpsed a *shuriken* as it flew towards Shusaku. But the ninja master flicked his sword and the *shuriken* was deflected with a bell-like *ding*, embedding itself in the stable wall. Shusaku spun, lowering his free hand to his waist, and when he came out of the turn to face Namae again, his arm extended abruptly, sending a little round ball flying towards the other ninja.

Namae twisted out of the way as the miniature bomb exploded harmlessly in the air. The two continued to circle, moving ever closer together.

Taro could feel strength returning to his muscles. Namae's poison must have been temporary, a trick to disable someone for a moment – since a moment is more than long enough to slit a throat. He pulled at his bag once again and removed the blowpipe. On wavering legs he stood.

He armed the blowpipe, raised it to his lips, and aimed at Namae.

He blew.

The ninja didn't even turn towards the dart – he simply whipped his sword out, backhand, and shattered it in the air. Then he turned the motion of the sword into forward momentum, and closed in, sword whirling, on Shusaku. The two ninjas' swords met in a clash of metal on metal. They danced across the stable yard floor, their swords blurring. Taro was astonished by how quickly they both moved. He raised the blowpipe again, but it was impossible to aim with any accuracy. He could just as easily hit Shusaku.

'Taro! Get into the tower!' shouted Shusaku. 'I'll hold him off.'

He parried a blow from the other ninja, keeping his blade against his opponent's, and rammed his shoulder forward, trying to unbalance Namae. But the notorious ninja snapped his sword downward, dragging Shusaku's blade from his hands. He raked the sword upward again, tracing a line up Shusaku's torso that turned the black silk almost immediately red with blood, as if by some dark magic.

Shusaku stumbled back. Taro cried out, 'No!'

Namae turned from the injured master and ran towards Taro, his sword spinning in his hand.

But Taro had the sword in his blood – Shusaku himself had said it.

His blade skipped up into the air and forward, as if it had itself acquired the means of locomotion and Taro was merely an appendage to it.

Namae feinted, but Taro saw it clearly and ignored it, bringing his sword up to block the true strike. The blades rang together.

The ninja let loose a flurry of strikes, but Taro was ready for them all and his sword flicked and slashed, restless for blood. Namae was breathing hard. He redoubled his effort, pressing forward, looking for a gap in Taro's defence. But Taro was younger, and quicker. He pretended to falter, stumbling on his back foot, then cut under Namae's attack and opened up a wound on the man's shin.

'Gah!' said Namae. But the blood was already stopping, the man's vampire healing working quickly.

Taro was a *mako* now, though, and the blade his teeth. He scented blood, and he wanted more. He lunged forward, sword whirling.

And Namae was somehow not where he was meant to be but was beside him, slashing his blade across Taro's chest.

Taro looked down, shocked, as his robe and then his skin fell open like a scroll, his scraped ribs the writing underneath.

He fell, and Namae raised his sword once more to end him. Then there was a grunt, and the ninja turned back to Shusaku. Taro saw that a *shuriken* was sticking out of Namae's back. 'Leave the boy alone,' said Shusaku. 'Your fight is with me.'

'My fight is with anyone who tries to enter that tower,' said Namae, looking back and forth, from master to pupil. It was clear that he didn't know which to eliminate first. If he concentrated on Shusaku, the boy might be able to gain entry to the tower, and Namae had been hired to kill anyone who tried. But if he killed the boy, he'd be vulnerable to attack from Shusaku.

A boatload of pirates was one thing. Lord Shusaku Endo was another.

Taro could feel his flesh knitting, his skin beginning to heal over. He was stumbling to his feet when he saw what Shusaku was doing. He screamed.

'NO!'

But the ninja master ignored him. 'Go,' he said as he removed his mask. Immediately his face was invisible to Taro. A smell of burning filled the air.

Taro felt hot tears running down his cheeks. *No, master*, he thought, *don't do this, don't do this for me*.

In his heart Shusaku's name rang with the heavy tone of a funeral bell, echoing against the name that already resonated there, the name of his father. Taro did not think he could bear to see another man die in his defence. He staggered towards Shu-saku to stop him, but the distance was too great, and his ribs still ached.

Namae looked at Shusaku as he undressed. 'What the—' he managed.

'The Heart Sutra,' said Shusaku.

'Oh... you fool,' said Namae. 'Have you not heard tell of Hoichi?'

In Taro's mind echoed the warning of a dead girl.

Yukiko sprang at Namae, drawing her sword in the same motion. 'Shusaku, don't!' she shouted. But Namae was ready and his sword clashed with hers.

'Stop,' he said. 'I won't harm a girl.'

Yukiko ignored him, her *wakizashi* darting. 'Then a girl will harm you.'

Namae sighed. 'Very well.'

The ninja knocked Yukiko's sword aside and planted a hand in the centre of her chest as he made a long powerful stride forward with his right leg. His palm collided with her torso with a loud *slap*.

And she was thrown back against the wall, her head hitting the stone, and then slumping onto her chest.

She lay motionless.

Taro turned to her, and in that moment Shusaku stepped out of his *hakama* and was naked. Taro saw it in the corner of his eye and screamed.

For a moment Shusaku's eyes were visible, and then they went out like lanterns as the older man closed his eyelids, draw-ing down blinds of ink, and disappeared from Taro's view. His sword clattered to the ground. Namae cast about, holding his sword out before him like a talisman against the darkness.

'Show yourself, Endo!' he shouted. 'Have you no honour at all?'

'No,' said Shusaku. 'Honour is for samurai.'

Taro moved towards the voice, but a force he couldn't see planted itself in his chest and pushed him back.

'Go, Taro,' whispered the ninja. 'Please. It's too late for me anyway.' His voice sounded weak.

And Taro smelled burning.

'I can't just—'

'Yes, Oda must pay. Or Heiko will have died for nothing. Namae is too strong for you.'

Namae saw Taro talking to the air. He turned, letting fly with a *shuriken* that Taro sidestepped. 'Show yourself, demon!' he snarled.

'No,' said Shusaku, and he was already gone from that spot when the next *shuriken* flew. Namae turned this way and that, slashing at nothing with his sword.

A voice came from behind Taro – Shusaku's.

'You told me there was no honour in this. In fighting invisibly. You said it was unfair. Do you believe it still?'

Namae spun and advanced on Taro, who began to step backward.

Shusaku had made his decision. There was nothing Taro could do without stealing the meaning from Heiko's sacrifice. He turned and glanced at the door to the tower, at Yukiko, who lay unconscious on the ground. He backed away from Namae, until there was a hazy movement off to the left, as if it were the air itself moving, and the ninja cried out, stumbling from some invisible blow.

Taro's eyes welled with tears. Had he ever thought that Shusaku had no honour? It seemed impossible now. He was watching the man sacrifice himself for another. Truly, he was a samurai lord still. Namae whirled round, throwing *shuriken* in a fanning pattern.

One of them found its target and stopped, bloody, in mid-air, as if it were the accusatory evidence in a Noh play involving murder and ghosts.

Above it, two eyes appeared, open wide in surprise.

Namae moved faster than Taro had ever believed possible, faster than Shusaku at his best. His sword raked across Shusaku's eyes, cutting them out, then darted forward, as quick as a cat, and buried itself in his stomach. Namae let go of the sword hilt with a flourish of contempt.

'NOOOOOOOOO!' screamed Taro for his mentor, his friend, and his saviour.

For a moment the invisible body remained rooted to the spot, as if fixed to the air by the blade, then Shusaku collapsed to the ground, like a puppet. Blood gushed from his eye sockets, tracing his face out of nothingness as it flowed down his cheeks. A stain spread on his stomach, round the blade of Namae's short-sword.

Namae stepped forward, towards the mask of blood.

He did not see – and nor did Taro – the hand, unstained by blood, that crept on the floor, searching for the handle of a sword.

Nor did Namae see the blade as it whipped up and round, meeting his throat as he stepped forward, half-cutting his head from his shoulders, leaving his face to hang by a thread of gristle over his shoulder.

Namae hit the ground, a question that would never be spoken dying on his lips.

'I'm sorry,' said Shusaku, his voice fading. 'You deserved a better death. But I am protecting the son of my lord.'

As the sun burned him, his body began to appear out of nothingness, a shadow that grows darker as the light brightens.

Shusaku fell to his knees then, his entire body smoking. Taro ran to him, crying out a nonsense stream of 'No, no, no, no…'

But though he stopped the ninja's body from falling, he was too late to stop the life that fled from the man's body.

Shusaku's blind eye sockets seemed to look up and into Taro's very mind as Taro put his hand on the slippery, bloody hilt of the sword and tried to pull it out. Even as he did it he knew it was hopeless – the sword wouldn't kill the ninja, but the sunlight would.

'Leave it,' said the ninja. 'It's too late for me. Find Musashi, the sword saint. Tell him I sent you. He will give you the skill you need.'

He paused. '*Shogun*,' he breathed, his eyes on Taro.

And he died.

CHAPTER 66

F LASHES OF LIGHT and darkness played on Yukiko's vision, as if she had stared at the midday sun. Her skull was agony; her body wouldn't work.

She saw Namae, his head cleaved nearly from his body, and she was glad.

Then she saw Shusaku. The man she had thought of as an uncle lay on the ground, eyes a mess of gore, stomach bleeding. Taro knelt beside him, his hands gripping the sword that had run him through. As Yukiko watched, Taro let go of the sword and stumbled to his feet.

Yukiko's eyes went wide. Had Taro killed Shusaku? And if so, why?

A horrible thought crossed her mind. *He knows that his destiny is more important.* To be shogun was all that mattered to the boy. She thought of her sister. Apparently, Taro had forgotten her already, just as he had forgotten his master, who even now burned on the flagstones as the sun scorched his flesh, the acrid smell of his immolation stinging Yukiko's nostrils.

Everywhere Taro went, he took death with him. To the abbess, to Heiko, and now to Shusaku, too. For all she knew, Hiro was also dead. Taro was like a poison on the world – like a plague, as if his very existence infected those round him with the taint of death.

And really, what had Lord Oda done? Only tried to clean this stain from the earth, remove the source of the infection. His man, Kenji Kira, had killed her foster mother and sister, it was true, but he had done it in the name of seeking Taro.

If Taro didn't exist, then Kenji Kira would not have had to do those things, and no one would have had to die.

Yukiko watched Shusaku burn, as Taro staggered towards her, the blood of his master staining his clothes.

Yes, Taro had forgotten him, as he had forgotten Heiko. But Yukiko remembered. She remembered the way that Taro had fought Little Kawabata, the skill he had shown. He said that he had been helpless to save Heiko, that he had watched paralysed as she'd died. But Yukiko had been drugged too, and she had not been paralysed.

She had been unconscious.

And Taro would say anything, wouldn't he? His ambition was limitless. There he was, the peasant son of an ama, dreaming of being shogun, leaving his friends to die.

When Yukiko looked at him, she saw not a peasant, not a shogun, not even a vampire.

She saw a traitor.

CHAPTER 67

Taro turned in a daze and walked to the wall of the tower.

Yukiko had risen unsteadily to her feet. He put a hand under her arm and helped her towards the door. For one moment she turned a strange look on him, her eyes as hard as pebbles, then she grunted.

'You cry for him,' she said.

Taro wiped away a tear. 'Yes.'

'Hmm. But Oda must die, yes? We carry on.'

'Yes,' said Taro. Yes. They would carry on.

He missed the fire in Yukiko's eyes, the way she bit and bloodied her lip.

Taro opened the door, half-expecting samurai to spring on him. But there was no one.

Namae had not raised the alarm. Perhaps, in his arrogance, the ninja had believed that no reinforcements were necessary.

Still, Taro had enough presence of mind left to assume that guards would be posted on the stairs, protecting the room at the top of the tower. 'No,' he said to Yukiko. 'We shouldn't use the stairs. They will be defended.'

Again he pulled on his spiked gloves, and led Yukiko to the stone wall of the tower. 'We climb,' he said.

They sought handholds and began.

The tower was considerably taller than the wall they had just scaled, and soon Taro's arms were burning with the effort of pulling himself up. Twice they had to stop to rest, but Taro was conscious that – clinging onto the wall of the tower like this – they were very conspicuous. Finally, he reached the uppermost window, a wide slit that gave onto a large, dark circular room. The window was big enough to fit through – this high up, who would be able to enter it?

Taro tumbled through the gap in the stone wall, head first. He flipped in the air, like a cat, and landed on his feet. His feet made no sound when they landed on the ground.

A moment later Yukiko landed beside him.

Taro glanced round furtively. They were standing in a luxuriously furnished bedroom that was nevertheless carpeted with a thick layer of sawdust. Taro guessed that the room must have been used for some other purpose, before Oda retreated to his tower-top eyrie.

(He was right. Had he brushed the sawdust aside, he would have seen the blood that stained the stone beneath it.)

One corner of the round room was divided off by paper screens decorated with cranes and flowers. Taro could just see that behind it was a bed, covered with silk sheets that pooled expensively on the floor at its foot, soft and as white as the foam on the waves of the Kanto.

Taro padded round the circle of the wall, examining the rest of the room. Yukiko followed, her hand on the hilt of her short-sword. There was a desk, on which sat pieces of cream paper and an ink quill. There was also a chest, carved with monstrous reliefs – dragons, demons, devils. And there was a slender stand on which perched a magnificent chicken hawk, its head hooded.

As Taro and Yukiko crept about the room, the hawk turned its head to follow their near-silent tread.

A noise from the bed startled him, and Taro whirled round to see a torch flare into life on the wall behind the bed, projecting the clearly defined silhouette of a standing figure onto the paper screen.

Then the figure stepped out from behind the screen.

Golden light from the torch filled the room. Taro moved forward. He drifted in a dazzle of sawdust, the motes spangling the air round him as if he walked through diamonds.

Through that constellation of air, he saw his victim's face.

It was not Lord Oda.

It was a girl.

The same girl they had rescued in the woods, from the *ronin*.

Hana got out of bed. She had heard a noise in the room, and had risen to investigate. It did not occur to her for a moment that there might be intruders, interlopers in her bedroom. That ninja, Namae, was outside, after all. The one she'd overheard with her father. She wasn't supposed to know that he was there. She wasn't really supposed to know that she was in any danger, in fact – and the truth was that while she knew it, she didn't really understand it. Moving to the tower felt like an imprisonment, not a necessary precaution for her safety. For days she had banged on the door, trying to rouse a response from the guard outside, trying to get an answer from her father. But all that came was her twice-daily meal, pushed under the door.

She was furious.

She wanted too an explanation of what had happened to the Tokugawa boy and his mother. She had watched them being dragged to the tower, and suspected that they had been sequestered in the room below this one. But while she had heard dim cries at first, on her arrival here – had caught the odd plaintive echo through the stone – she lived now in a solitary silence unpenetrated by human voice or form.

Until she stepped round the paper screen and saw, on the other side of her room, two ninja. One of them was holding a short-sword already. The other held a surprisingly small and delicate hand to the pommel of his.

Hana opened her mouth to scream. But with a speed that seemed impossible, the larger ninja had dropped the sword and was upon her, holding his hand over her mouth.

'What are you doing here?' he whispered urgently.

Surprised, she tried to answer, but all that came out was a grunt. His fingers crushed her lips, while his thumb pressed against the bottom of her jaw, holding her mouth closed to stop her biting. The ninja leaned in close, and she was struck to see that his eyes were clear, kind, and, most of all – young. She felt she recognized them from somewhere.

He mimed a question. *If I move my hand, will you scream?*

Hana found herself more curious than afraid. She shook her head. Rousing the guards would be pointless, anyway – from the speed with which the ninja had leaped across the room, she guessed he could gut her before the scream had fully exited her lips.

The ninja considered for a moment, then withdrew his hand.

'I should ask you, what are you doing here?' whispered Hana. 'This is my bedroom.'

'No...' said the ninja, apparently in some shock. 'You should be Oda.'

'Yes,' said the smaller ninja, stepping forward, and Hana was startled to realize that it was a girl. 'You should be Oda, and you should die.'

'I am Oda. My name is Lady Oda no Hana. I am Lord Oda Nobunaga's only daughter.'

The boy ninja gasped. 'But Shusaku said...' he whispered, seemingly to himself. An expression of confusion, then anger, flitted across his face.

He fell back, confusion written in his movements, as the lines of a calligraphy character can betray the turmoil of its author.

Hana felt suddenly sorry for this clear-eyed ninja. He did not appear very threatening. She put a hand on his arm. 'Tell me,' she said. 'What are you doing here?'

Taro looked into the girl's sea-grey eyes. She was asking him what he was doing there, but he found it hard to concentrate on anything other than the cool roundness of those irises, the graceful splay of those long dark lashes. The pain of losing Shusaku was still there, but as he looked at the girl before him, the pain seemed to fade, to melt into the background, like words written in ink that has dried in the sun.

'I won't kill you, if that's what you mean,' he said. 'I'm supposed to, I think... but I won't do it.'

'You... expected my father?' asked the girl.

'Yes. And I didn't expect *you*.'

'What do you mean?'

Taro took his mask off, and Hana gasped. 'You! From the woods!'

Taro held out his hand, showing her the ring he still wore on his little finger, the one she had given him after they'd saved her. It seemed right that they should meet again like this, as if fate, once more, were at work. He remembered that she had been

367

reluctant to tell them who she was, that she had spoken of rewards but had said that she couldn't tell her father she was out alone.

No wonder, if she was Lord Oda's daughter.

Taro's head spun. They had been so close to Oda, all those weeks ago, when they had killed those *ronin* in the woods! They had saved his own daughter! He felt as though he were taking part in a vast and complicated play, in which nothing was mere coincidence. For a brief instant, he entertained the shameful notion that if they had known who the girl was, that night in the woods, they could have taken her hostage.

But no. He would not become like Lord Oda in the service of killing the man. He would not view people as mere playing pieces, helpful to the execution of his aims.

And besides, he suspected with a more cynical and lizard-like part of his mind that Lord Oda would have seen the girl die, rather than have her be used as a bargaining chip. Taking her hostage would have achieved nothing.

All this went through his mind in a fraction of a moment, and then he made his decision, and bowed. 'Taro, at your service.'

Yukiko stared at Taro and Lord Oda's daughter. She didn't understand at all what was happening. It seemed like Taro and the girl knew each other, but at the same time it appeared that they were strangers. Which was the truth and which was the pretence?

It was impossible for her to tell.

One thing she knew. Since her sister had died in Taro's defence, she had felt as a samurai in armour – girded in cold metal, no signs of the human life inside.

That was until Taro had left Shusaku to die. Then she had felt anger take hold.

Now it burned fast, feeding on the aridity inside.

Heiko had died for Taro, and now here he was facing the daughter of their greatest enemy, and stammering, as if he were in a love story, rather than a story of revenge and violence.

She poked Taro with the end of her sword, and he turned to her, frowning. 'What was that, about the woods?' she asked. 'And what is that on your finger?'

He held his hand out to her. 'It's her ring,' he said. 'She gave it to me.'

Yukiko felt as though the ground were giving way beneath

her. 'Lord Oda's *daughter* gave you a ring?'

'Yes. I mean, I didn't realize it then, but—' He paused in his babbling. Yukiko didn't know what was happening, but she could see one thing. Taro was a liar and a traitor, and was certainly not the peasant he had appeared to everyone – including Shusaku!—to be. Here he was gazing into the eyes of Lord Oda's daughter, and wearing her ring. She was sure of only one thing, and that was that nothing had been what it appeared. 'We saved her life,' he said now. 'In the mountains. Well, Shusaku did, mostly.'

'You're too modest,' said Lord Oda's daughter. 'Your work with the bow was extraordinary.'

Yukiko stared at him. 'You saved her life?' she asked, incredulous. 'She's the daughter of your enemy.'

Heiko gave her life for him because she thought he deserved to be

shogun. She is dead not two days and now he stands before Lord Oda's

daughter, the spawn of his worst enemy, like a love-struck fool!

Then the most horrible thought of all struck Yukiko with the force of a heavy *bokken* blow to the head, worse than before, when it had passingly crossed her mind.

He could have saved Heiko. He was not paralysed, and I was a fool

to believe it.

He lied.

Yukiko backed away from them, disgust turning in her stomach like a trapped fish.

CHAPTER 69

L ADY HANA STARED at the boy. She had heard the name Taro only the other day – and in extraordinary circumstances.

It was when her father and the ninja guard were speaking.

She looked into the boy's startling grey eyes. 'I heard that Lord Tokugawa has a son named Taro,' she said. 'A secret son.'

As she had half-expected, the boy blinked. 'I... I mean, yes, that's me.'

She'd wondered, but the confirmation shocked her nevertheless. 'You're really *Tokugawa*?' Lady Hana asked the boy ninja, incredulous. The enmity between her father and Ieyasu Tokugawa had been her favoured topic of gossip with her serving girl, Sono, but it had seemed less distant and abstract after Lord Tokugawa's wife and son had been hauled off to the tower. Now she found herself experiencing a confusing mixture of emotions. Anger with her father, for his violent temper and harsh treatment of others, vied with a deep-seated mistrust of the Tokugawa clan that had been instilled in her almost since birth.

'Yes. My father hid me in a fishing village. Lord Oda tried to have me killed.' He looked pained then. 'Sorry. But it's true.'

Lady Hana waved away his apology. It did not surprise her

that her father would attempt to kill a mere boy. She knew his character better than anyone else.

Anyway, she was not overly given to tradition, in any of its forms, even if tradition did demand that she should defend her father's honour. Looking at this boy, she felt a strange feeling in the pit of her stomach – a swooping, dropping feeling, as if the core of her had been stolen by a seagull, and it was flying about with it. She felt something for this boy, some powerful connection that went beyond the bonds she felt to family or teachers.

'Can you climb back down the tower?' she asked.

The boy ninja – Tokugawa no Taro – shook his head. 'The surface is too smooth. Climbing up was hard enough – the plan was always to go down the stairs.'

Hana stared. 'There's sure to be a guard. Maybe more than one. You could be killed.'

Taro gave her a wan smile. 'My mother always used to say, *Ame futte ji—*'

'*Katamaru*,' completed Hana. Her own mother had said it too. A samurai girl can expect a lot of rain in her life, and has a lot to harden herself against, so the expression had been frequently apt. She smiled at the boy ninja. 'Your mother was a wise woman.'

A troubled expression crossed his face, and Hana had the sense that something had happened to his mother, or had happened between them. 'As was yours, it would seem.' He bowed, then frowned, looking round him. 'The other... ninja. Where did she go?'

Hana cast her eyes round the room. 'I don't know.'

Taro swore. 'Is Kenji Kira nearby? She has... business to conclude with him. She may have gone to find him.'

Hana shook her head. 'Kira is abroad in the country, looking for something. I think…it might be you.'

Taro grunted. 'Well, she won't find him then. Let's hope she can find her own way to safety.'

A moment later Taro was at the door that led to the spiral staircase. He felt Hana's hand on his arm. 'I'm coming with you,' she said. She began to pull on a heavy cloak over her sleeping garments.

'What about your father?' asked Taro, shocked. Already he feared that he might not leave the castle alive. To be weighed down by this girl, even if she was a samurai's daughter, would be suicide. 'Shouldn't you stay here with him?'

'What for? To be married for my father's convenience? I would rather die.' She looked at him sharply. 'You're worried I'll slow you down, aren't you?'

Taro stared at her. That was *exactly* what he was worried about.

Sighing, she reached behind her back. A *katana* appeared in her hand. She brought it round in a flat swipe to end up a hair's breadth from Taro's neck. He gulped, looking down dumbly at the blade. He hadn't even known she was carrying it – and if she'd wanted to cut his throat, he wouldn't have been able to move before blood was spilling from the wound.

Taro moved the blade aside, gently, with his finger. 'I saw you kill that *ronin*, remember?' he said. 'No need to convince me you know how to handle a blade.'

Hana spun the *katana* in a couple of graceful moves, and Taro saw that her skills of *kenjutsu* were superior even to his own. 'Good,' she said. 'Just don't forget it.'

'All right,' he replied. 'Let's go.'

The girl held up a hand to stay him for a moment. She went to her bed and picked up a few items, which she placed in a silk bag. Then she lashed a leather guard to her left forearm. She went to the stand and coaxed the hawk onto her wrist.

Taro looked pointedly at the bird.

'She goes with me,' said Hana.

Taro shrugged, resignedly. He opened the door to see a sword swinging towards his face, held two-handed by a burly samurai wearing a tusked face mask designed to resemble a wild boar.

Instinctively Taro ducked. He felt stirred air on the nape of his neck as the blade passed overhead. He struck at the man's legs with his own short-sword, opening a wound on one meaty thigh. The samurai cursed. Coming out of his duck, Taro met the man's next blow, deflecting it with the side of his blade. Then, feeling a tap on his right shoulder, he sidestepped to the left, striking backhand at the right side of his opponent's face, bending his elbow to create a wide space between his arm and his body. He hoped that he had interpreted Hana's signal correctly.

The samurai raised his sword to parry the stroke – a mistake. At that moment Hana thrust her sword through the triangular gap created by Taro's arm, plunging it into the samurai's abdomen. The man gurgled and fell backwards against the far wall of the narrow corridor. His head slumped.

Hana nodded. 'We make a good team.'

Taro looked at the lord's bright-eyed daughter, with her bloody sword, and thought he had never seen anything so beautiful.

They started down the stairs. Another samurai was on his way up, no doubt investigating the noise of his companion's death. But his sword arm was obstructed by the turn of the stairs, and Taro dispatched him with a single judicious stroke. He moved quickly now, taking the stairs two at a time.

'Wait,' said Hana as they passed a wooden door.

Taro stopped.

'You are Lord Tokugawa's son, are you not?'

Taro nodded.

'And your mother?'

'I don't know. Shusaku – that's the ninja who saved me from Lord Od— I mean, from the ninja who tried to kill me – he said that it might be Lady Tokugawa, or it might be a concubine. There's no way of knowing.'

Hana shook her head. 'There is one way of knowing.' She gestured to the door. 'Lord Tokugawa's wife and son are in there. That is, if they're still alive. I saw them being dragged to the tower before I was moved to that room.'

Taro's stomach believed suddenly that he was falling from a great height, and rushed accordingly upward into his mouth. He felt his pulse hammering in his veins. Lady Tokugawa. *Would it be a betrayal of my other mother to see her?* He felt almost as if to see her would kill his old mother, would cause the pigeon she had been given to drop dead from the sky.

But that couldn't be true, could it? It was only superstition, not clear thinking.

'Come on,' said Hana. 'We must be quick. I see you're afraid to face her, but you deserve answers, don't you?'

That decided him. Yes, he did deserve answers. And to ask them did not betray the memory of his father and mother, and the love they had shown him. This was about his heritage. It wasn't about love.

He turned to the door. It was heavy, and locked with a tumble-pin mechanism. He shrugged his bag from his shoulder, rummaging inside it. Did he still have it? Yes! The key Heiko had used in the storeroom lock. He kissed it once, for luck. What were the chances that a locksmith all the way over here, in Lord Oda's territory, would use the same key as one who worked near the crater?

Hana watched, eyes wide, as Taro slid the key into the bolt. Distractedly, she stroked the hawk that sat on her wrist.

Taro pushed the key upward.

There was a click, and the bolt slid free.

CHAPTER 70

Yukiko walked up the steps of Lord Oda's private audience chamber. A samurai ushered her before him, his sword tip pressing into the base of her spine.

She entered the room. Cool, sharp shadows crossed on its smooth wooden floor like swords.

A scent of *o-cha* – green tea – rose from a lacquerware vessel set on a silver platter. Lord Oda Nobunaga finished pouring, not even raising his eyes, then lifted the cup – it was adorned with black-ink cranes and moons – and breathed deeply. Yukiko guessed that, for the lord to be relaxed enough not even to look at her, there had to be more steel aimed at her than the sword tickling her back. Most likely there were arrows trained on her heart – niches in the walls where archers awaited a single motion from the daimyo.

She tried not to look up.

She noticed, though, that Oda poured the tea, then lifted the cup, with his left hand. His right hung in the shadow, the arm attached to it looking thin and wasted.

'I was in the middle of the tea ceremony, as you see,' he said. He was a muscular man, sitting not on a throne, as Yukiko would have supposed, but on a simple cushion on the floor. 'So your reason for disturbing me had better be pressing.'

Yukiko smiled. That at least she was sure of.

'Taro is here.'

Lord Oda sprang to his feet, the tea spilling on his robe. He didn't appear to notice. He moved across the long floor.

'Where?'

Yukiko raised a single elegant finger. 'No. First you do something for me.'

Lord Oda paused, unsheathing a *katana* from behind his back. He wielded it left-handed, something Yukiko had never before seen.

This was a formidable man. She would have to be careful.

'You give me Kira, and I give you Taro,' she said. 'Kira killed my sister. I would kill him in return.'

Lord Oda walked towards her, the sword tracing lazy spirals in the air. 'You're very confident,' he said. 'What if I torture Taro's whereabouts from you, then kill you?'

Yukiko took a deep breath. 'Well,' she said, 'then I would be *very* angry.'

Lord Oda laughed out loud, surprised.

'And,' continued Yukiko, 'my anger is a terrible thing. Look what I am doing to Taro, for betraying me. If you killed me, maybe I'd come back as a ghost and make you sorry.'

Lord Oda's eyes were bright with amusement. 'I like you,' he said. Then he turned to the samurai who had led her in. 'Leave. Take the other guards with you. Taro is mine.' He turned back to Yukiko. 'Kira's life is yours, to do with as you choose. And yours is mine. Do you understand? You will live, but you will suffer. Otherwise how can I be sure of your loyalty?'

Yukiko bowed. 'I expect to suffer. It is in the nature of revenge.'

Taro RECOILED, HORRIFIED. The stench of the room was awful. There was decay in it, but also blood and sweat. The circular space was dark, unlit by windows. Huddled on the stone floor was a figure – barely discernible as human – under a ragged blanket. As Taro stepped inside the room, holding his breath, the figure stirred and he saw that it was a woman holding a doll, its porcelain skin covered in dirt, its hair a filthy thatch.

Taro peered closer, and a shudder ran through him.

It wasn't a doll. It was a dead child.

The woman lifted her head with visible difficulty and looked up at Taro, eyes wary but resigned, as if merely curious as to what fresh torture he wished to visit on her. Her shoulder bones protruded from her skin. She was dressed in sacking cloth.

Taro, speechless, gazed at his mother's face. She had been attractive once. The heart shape of the face could be seen beneath the scars and lesions; the eyes were as black as night. But she had been starved, clearly, and subjected to the worst kind of treatment. He knelt beside her, touched her hair. The child, to which she clung tightly, had apparently been dead for some time. Sores festered round its mouth, and in the corners of its eyes small flies crawled. Most of the stench seemed to come from this tiny corpse, but Taro's true mother clung to it nevertheless, as if her embrace had the power to restore it to life.

The child was no more than four years old.

Taro knelt. 'My name is Taro,' he said to the trembling woman who was his mother. 'I don't have much time. I…'

He broke off, gulping.

'Taro is your son, Lady Tokugawa,' said Hana. She too knelt in the bloodstained sawdust, her silk gown trailing in the dirt.

The woman stared. 'My son?' Her words rattled in her throat like pebbles carried by a stream, and Taro saw that it was an effort for her to speak. 'I have only two sons. One died by his own hand… seppuku… an honourable samurai's death. The other is here, in my arms.' She looked down at the dead boy and kissed his cheek, then held him tight to her. 'You cannot take him from me. I won't have another of my sons die.'

She thinks he's alive, thought Taro. *Gods, she's lost her mind.* He wondered how long she had been confined here, alone in the dark.

But he would not have this chance again. He looked into her eyes, and told her what Shusaku had explained to him, about Lord Tokugawa's decision to keep him secret, wanting to spare him from Oda's clutches, about the ninja who had saved him from death. And most of all, about what he suspected, that she was his real mother, this broken woman before him.

Lady Tokugawa smiled, a sad sight on a face so ravaged. 'Come closer, that I might look on your face.'

Taro leaned closer, trying not to overcome his revulsion at the woman's smell.

'Ah. No. I do not know you. I'm sorry.'

'But—but—' stammered Taro.

Lady Tokugawa was still smiling. 'I said…you are not my son.'

Taro couldn't believe it. 'Then what… Why…'

Hana put her hand on Taro's arm. 'Let her finish.' Sure enough, Lady Tokugawa's mouth was still open to speak.

'You are not my son. But you *are* my husband's. I see it in your face.'

'But…' Taro started. 'What does that mean?'

'You… have… a mother?' asked Lady Tokugawa. 'One who raised you?'

'Yes.'

'Then… I presume… she is your mother. My husband… is not… faithful.'

Taro could think of nothing to say. *My mother is my real mother after all!* he thought with joy.

And a moment later, with sadness, he thought, *My father was not.*

Yet he raised me with her, knowing as he must have done that the boy he looked after was Tokugawa's son.

Taro felt a wave of love for his adoptive father crash over him, and he remembered again the frail body on the bed, the severed head – and the anger filled his veins like molten steel.

Lady Tokugawa raised her hand, shaking, and placed it on his. 'You… kill… Oda. Support your father. Understand? *Lord Tokugawa must be shogun*. My son died for it, and so will this one. As I too must soon.'

'No!' said Taro. 'We'll carry you. Come—'

She shook her head, letting herself slump to the ground. 'Too late for me. You must run. Take your brother. If my husband dies, he and you will take up the fight.'

Taro looked down at the dead boy. Lady Tokugawa was

proffering the corpse, as if it were a living thing that could still be saved. He began to back away, revolted, but Hana nudged him and made a little hissing sound under her breath, and he reached out his hands, every nerve in his body trembling.

She handed over the body, and he was surprised by its lightness. He could feel the bones through the flesh. He felt not revulsion, as he had expected, but a terrible sadness. He looked at Lady Tokugawa. 'I will look after him,' he said gently.

'Thank you,' she breathed.

He was backing away through the door when Lady Tokugawa raised a clawed hand, shaking with the effort.

'Oda Nobunaga... must... die,' she said.

And then she closed her eyes.

CHAPTER 72

OUTSIDE, HIRO HEARD nothing – no footfall or splash of water or crunch of leaf that would warn him of an approaching danger – before he felt the cold steel edge of a blade against his neck.

Keeping the blade there, the person holding it stepped round into Hiro's field of vision. The figure wore a black three-piece mask that covered the face apart from the eyes.

A ninja.

CHAPTER 73

T ARO BACKED OUT of the room, holding the body of his young brother in his arms.

'What do we do with him?' he asked Hana.

'Get him out of this place, and give him a proper funeral,' she answered.

He began to walk down the stairs, carefully, so as not to drop the child. His heart pounded in his chest, fear of capture coursing through him. He hadn't heard an alarm, but he and Shusaku had killed the ninja Namae, and he and Hana had killed two samurai, too.

Their absence might well have been noted.

The staircase continued to turn to the left, growing steadily brighter as they descended. Taro could feel the coolness of outside air now, stirring his hair and his dreams of escape. He began to move more quickly. If they could just get to the moat—

Shhht. Shuffle. Shhht. Shuffle.

Taro stopped, and Hana barrelled into his back, cursing. Taro almost dropped his brother. 'What—'

He held his hand up for silence.

There was no sound now, but his highly attuned vampire

ears had caught something, a quiet susurrus as of expensive silk clothes whispering together, as of a person trying very hard not to be heard. Taro drew his sword and motioned for Hana to do the same. Then he began to descend again, more slowly this time. He spoke loudly. 'Hayao, Shigeru – when we get to the courtyard, you two head for the lord's residence. Understood?'

Hana raised her eyebrows at him, then slowly nodded, understanding. He was trying to make it appear that there were more of them.

Taro gently laid his brother on the steps, then continued downward, Hana behind him. He and the man coming up the stairs saw each other at precisely the same time. They both struck out with their swords, acting from pure instinct, and the blades rang loud against each other in the narrow stone stairwell. In the grip of his vampire's urge to fight, and the unthinking, deeply ingrained pattern of a sword fighter's movements, Taro was only dimly aware that something here was wrong.

Taro's blade was forced aside, the movement smacking the weapon into the wall with a *ding* and banging his knuckles painfully against the stone. His opponent was strong. Taro pulled back the sword and used it to parry another strike, and that was when he realized what the problem was.

The samurai coming up the stairs was attacking with his left hand. And he was enormously powerful with it, despite his movements being hampered by the turn of the stairs. He wore no armour but his sword was magnificent. His right arm was withered and thin. It reminded Taro of a tree branch, half-broken off by a storm and now hanging desiccated and fragile from the stout trunk.

All this Taro registered in a fraction of a second. But his

385

distraction was sufficient for the samurai to punch him in the gut with his pommel, then turn his sword over and into a thrust at the chest.

'Father!' said Hana.

Now it was the samurai who averted his eyes for a moment.

Lord Oda, thought Taro.

'*Nobunaga!*' Taro shouted, deliberately insulting the daimyo by using his personal name. He cut up and under the older man's strike, slashing his forearm. Oda grunted with pain and surprise, stepping backwards down the stairs.

'Filthy peasant,' he said as he raised his sword. 'You will address me as Lord Oda before you die.'

Taro grinned. 'Then you will address me as Lord Tokugawa.'

He pressed the advantage of height, his sword moving faster than it ever had before as he forced his father's killer ever downward. He grinned, lost to himself, his eyes locked on Oda's. The Lord's small, hard eyes nestled in deep wrinkles, pebbles on rumpled silk. His skin was sallow, patchy with red in places. He wore a mustache that reached his chin on either side in greasy points.

'You killed Namae,' said Lord Oda. 'You must have been lucky, for I find you weak.' Sparks flew as his sword struck Taro's clean in the centre, knocking aside a blow that was meant to sever his left arm.

Taro held the man's eyes as he had been taught. *Never watch the sword. It will lie to you about where it is going. But the eyes never lie.*

Sure enough, he saw Oda's eyes twitch to the left, and a moment later his sword followed – but Taro had already moved his own blade to block the strike and rake the lord's knuckles, cutting them open.

Oda spat, slicing at Taro's legs and opening a long, shallow cut on his thigh. 'Little brat. You should have died long ago. But if you want a job done…' The lord attacked.

Taro's sword hand danced. He was barely aware of it. It was as if this part of his anatomy moved of its own accord, a white spider that liked to slash and cut.

Somewhere behind him was Hana, screaming.

In his joy he forgot her.

But gradually his grin began to fade. His strikes were still as fast as ever, but Oda always seemed to know where his sword would be next. The lord began to smile now, as if stealing even this from Taro – his father, his simple future, and now his smile.

Sword flashing, Oda hissed at Taro. 'Give me the ball. I know you have it.'

Taro parried a strike. 'The ball?'

'The Buddha ball, boy. I must have it.'

Taro's eyes opened wide. He was breathing hard from the exertion, his sword arm weakening. He remembered the story the old woman had told, the ama who had dived for the Buddha ball, who had said that the son of an ama would be shogun…

He had presumed that Lord Oda wanted him dead because of the prophecy.

But it seemed it was the *ball* he wanted.

'It's not… It's not real,' said Taro. 'It's a story! It's—'

Oda brought the hilt of his sword down hard on Taro's hand, and flicked the tip of its blade up, cutting Taro's chin. Taro gasped.

'It is not a *story*,' said Oda in an inhuman shriek. 'It is everything. It is power over this world, and all others. Why do you think the emperor wanted it?' His sword found Taro again, cut a gash down his arm. 'Anyway, Kira said it exists. He had the information from the abbess, before he killed her.'

Taro looked at the man, sickened. 'I don't know what you're talking about.'

'Oh, yes, you do,' said Oda. 'And you will tell me where the ball is or you will die here.'

'I don't know where it is. I didn't... even know... it... was... real.' Taro's strength was fading fast. But even as he said it, he was thinking of something, something that had bothered him when they'd been with the abbess.

It was his mother.

That day, when his father had been killed, hadn't she been diving by the old wreck? And hadn't the abbess said the ball, when it was first lost, had been drowned with the wreck of a royal ship? An ama had recovered it, for the prince.

What if an ama had put it back? What if his mother had been keeping it, and on the day when she'd heard the merchant speaking of ninja, she'd decided to make it safe?

Taro thought he had a good idea, actually, of where the ball might be. His mother had returned it to the wreck near the Shirahama shore. Perhaps the abbess had been right, perhaps Fusazaki *had* stolen the ball. Perhaps Tankai's heir had been foolish to think that simply because he didn't choose to exploit its power, he hadn't removed it from the clutches of those who had, or might.

An image formed in Taro's mind. He had no way of proving if it were true or not, but it felt right, it felt possible.

It was an image of Fusazaki giving the ball to the ama girls in Shirahama, the ones who reminded him so much of his dead mother, and asking them to hold it in their safekeeping, to guard it for the one whose coming his mother had predicted, the ama's son who would rule the country.

For him.

All the while he was thinking this, he was parrying Oda's strikes almost without paying attention to him. The man was skilled, it was true, but he didn't have the strength and reflexes of a vampire. Now Oda hissed. 'Hana! Stab him in the back!' he said. 'Get him!'

Hana sobbed. 'No!'

'Do it! I order you!'

'NO!' screamed Hana. 'Don't kill him, Father!'

'What?' asked the daimyo. His voice was smoothly, dangerously calm.

'I said don't kill him!'

Taro tried to ignore them, concentrating on the fight, the gleam of steel that streaked and pirouetted in front of him.

Lord Oda redoubled the intensity of his strikes. 'You will commit seppuku,' he hissed at Hana. 'You are no longer the daughter of a samurai. You are without honour.'

Hana gasped.

Anger burned in Taro's throat, like bile. He struck out, slashing Oda's face. Blood sprayed. He knew that in the narrow confines of the spiral staircase Hana was trapped behind him, unable to help, only capable of standing by as her father and her new acquaintance – too early even for friends – fought to the death.

'You tell her to stab me in the back,' said Taro, 'and you accuse her of being without honour. You are a stain on the samurai class.'

Oda growled, his eyes dark with anger. 'And you ninja are so honourable? It was your friend who betrayed you. The girl, Yukiko.'

Taro gasped. Yukiko had given him away? He cast his mind back to when he had last seen her, in the tower.

Oh, no.

He had been insensitive, talking to Hana like that, admiring her beauty. To Yukiko, it must have been the greatest of betrayals. This was the daughter of the man who was responsible, indirectly, for all the deaths that had befallen her – her foster mother's, her sister's. And far from killing her, Taro had spoken softly with her, shown Yukiko a ring she had given him.

My gods, he thought. *Perhaps she thinks I knew Hana all along; perhaps she thinks I planned all this. The ring… And she doesn't know about the time in the woods, when we saved her from the* ronin.

She may think that I have been lying, all this time, about being a simple peasant.

All this time he continued to fight. It was impossible that the swords should continue forever to twist, turn, and clatter together, without one of them finding its mark. It took only one mistake, one flat wrist that sent the arc of the blade too high, and the fatal opening formed itself out of nothingness, out of the absence of a defending blade.

Oda's sword sprang forward like a viper, impaling the palm of Taro's bare left hand, which had shot out in a final, unconscious gesture of self-preservation. The blade carried on through his stomach. Taro felt the cold metal grating against the bones of his spine as the tip of the sword burst through his back. Then Oda pulled out the sword again.

Taro fell to his knees, his bones jarring against the edge of a step.

Behind him, a girl from far away and long ago called out his name. Something warm was running down his—

He stared up at Lord Oda, who grinned wide now through the snake's tongue of his mustache—

The scene before Taro began to flicker and darken. Oda

raised his bloody sword—

Hana screamed. 'Stop!'

The blade shivered in the air, a finger's breadth from Taro's face, seeming almost to hum with its stopped energy.

Hana stepped forward to face her father, trembling but defiant. 'Don't, Father. He saved my life. He was sent to kill me, but he spared me. He has honour.'

'Is this true?' Oda asked Taro.

Weakly, Taro nodded.

Oda turned from him and approached his daughter, cupping her face in his hands, his eyes gentle and sad. 'Ah, my blossom-girl. You know I love you, don't you?'

Hana cast her gaze down. 'Yes,' she whispered.

'You share your mother's beauty. You always have. But you also share her compassion.'

He tilted her face upward. 'And that is why you must die.'

CHAPTER 74

Hana gasped, struggling against her father's hands, which now held her face tightly. Taro tried to rise, to help her, but his legs would not support him.

'The boy is Tokugawa's son,' continued her father. 'He will not give me what I want. For both reasons he must die.' His voice was sad. 'Hana, Hana. Your compassion blinds you. It has no place in the Oda dynasty, in the Oda shogunate that soon will rule this land. And it will corrupt the blood of my grandsons if I allow you to live.'

'But—'

'You are no longer samurai.' He paused to wipe a tear from her cheek with his thumb. 'Don't cry, blossom-girl. Believe me, your death will hurt me more than it will hurt you. But I did not lead my clan to victory over Yoshimoto by being kind, or compassionate.'

Hana screamed, struggling against her father's grip. She swung out with her sword, but he knocked it casually aside with his knee, connecting so hard with Hana's wrist that the sword went clattering up the steps. He threw her against the wall, hard. There was a harsh *ki, ki* from Hana's hawk, which clung to her wrist and flailed violently with its wings.

Hana herself made a noise like a whale blowing steam, and slid to the ground. Lord Oda brandished his sword, ready to eviscerate his only daughter as punishment for her insolence.

Taro tried to stand, but his thighs trembled. His *hakama* were soaked now in his own blood.

Lord Oda thrust the sword at Hana's stomach.

And then two things happened, almost at once.

Hana must have let go of the hawk's bindings, because it flew suddenly into the air, crying an angry stream of almost human invective –

Ki, ki, ki, ki, ki, ki.

Blinded by its hood, it nevertheless could hear, and it slammed into Lord Oda's face, claws scraping at his skin, still screaming and beating its wings.

Oda dropped his sword, seized the bird, and dashed it against the wall, where it moved no more.

But then there came, from below, the sound of running footsteps. 'Ah,' said Oda. 'My guards. Perhaps I will leave them to kill you both.'

But the figure that appeared from below was clad all in black, and wore a mask. Oda whirled to face it, then turned back again to Taro and Hana, his sword wavering.

Even in the gloom of the stairwell, Taro recognized the ninja's eyes. Then he saw Hiro come puffing up the stairs behind the ninja.

'He took me by surprise,' he said. 'I'm sorry.'

Little Kawabata shrugged. 'The boy is fat and slow.'

'Look who's talking,' said Hiro.

Oda's eyes were jerking back and forth between Taro and the new ninja on the stairs below him. 'Who are you?' he almost squealed.

'My name is Kawabata,' said the boy. 'And Taro nearly killed me once. I've come to make things even.'

Lord Oda smiled.

CHAPTER 75

Y OU SHOULDN'T SMILE,' said Little Kawabata. 'I said he almost killed me. The point is he saved my life. Now I'm going to do the same for him, if I can.'

Oda spun, his sword whipping from Taro to Little Kawabata, but in the cramped stairwell his movement was obstructed, and Little Kawabata was already moving into him, his shoulder striking the lord in the chest and throwing him against the wall next to his daughter.

The lord of the castle slumped, head down, unmoving. Little Kawabata jabbed him with his foot, but his head only lolled like a doll's. The ninja nodded, pleased. 'Out cold,' he said.

Hiro ran up the stairs and threw his arms round Taro. 'You're alive!' Then his smile faded as he stared at Taro's wound, saw the way his friend was kneeling on the steps, clutching his bleeding stomach. 'Oh… that's bad…'

As if on cue, Oda peeled himself away from the wall, swinging out with his sword at Hiro's neck.

Those would have been Hiro's last words, but seeing the bigger boy had given Taro the energy – and the distraction – he needed to pull himself to his feet. Stretching out with his sword, he blocked Oda's strike, then held his blade trembling before him.

His mind went back to a day in the mountains, when he had withdrawn from Shusaku as from a snake, and he wished that he could go back to that day and put his arms round the ninja instead.

He couldn't.

But he could do *this*.

Compensating for Oda's left-handedness, Taro let his sword waver a little to the left, simultaneously letting some of his weight settle visibly on his left foot, as if he were about to make a slash from left to right. Oda grinned, bringing his sword flashing up and round in a strike at Taro's exposed neck. But Taro never made the slash he had signalled. Instead, as Shusaku had taught him, he kept his sword vertical, pushing it forward into a block.

Then, even as Oda's eyebrows were quirking down in a half frown, Taro flipped his wrist, pushed forward with his forefinger, and brought his blade round in a low sweep, under Oda's sword and across his belly.

With a sound like a wave hitting a sand beach, Oda collapsed. But Taro didn't want him to die, just yet.

First he needed the lord's blood.

Drawing on his final reserves of strength, Taro let gravity carry him down the stairwell. His knees struck the stone floor and he vaguely registered the pain, then his hands hit Oda's shoulders and clung to them.

He opened his mouth.

He felt his teeth extend, little weapons hidden in his gums.

And, clutching the lord close, as if in an embrace, he sank his fangs into the man's thick neck.

He drank deep, feeling the lord's lifeblood enter him, feeling the great strength of the man. Already he felt that he would recover from his terrible wound.

That which was killing Oda was giving Taro life.

It was perfect.

From her position on the stone floor, Hana gasped. 'No!' she shouted. 'Father!'

Oda swayed for a moment, like a man on a ship in hard weather. Taro let go, tearing his mouth from the already dwindling supply of blood.

He got one glimpse of Oda's face, drained of blood, as white and accusatory as a wronged ghost's, then the massive body with its shrivelled arm went tumbling down the stairs, the clangs and bangs of metal on stone accompanied by organic slaps and crunches that made even Hiro wince at the cruel lord's fate.

Taro felt Hiro's hands under his armpits. He started to say *No, help the girl first*, but he saw from the corner of his eye that Hana was already standing, cheeks wet with tears.

He couldn't look at her. He'd killed her father, and that was unforgivable, even if her father was a murderer and a—

I'm a murderer, too, he thought, the realization stealing his breath. *I'm as bad as the ninja who killed my father, and on whom I vowed my revenge.*

He pushed Hiro away from him, using up the last of his strength, then stumbled to kneel before the girl he had orphaned. He handed Hana his sword and bent his head. 'I am samurai,' he said. 'I choose this death freely, of my own will, in recompense for my dishonourable action.'

Hana wiped tears from her cheek. She pressed the sword back into his hand. 'I don't cry for *him*.' She inclined her head to indicate the body, lying on the steps below. 'I cry for the father I believed in, who I today learned was no more than a child's story.'

'I'm sorry,' said Taro simply. He could think of nothing else to say. He almost wished that she had taken him up on his offer, had let the blade slice through his neck and condemn him to nothingness.

'Yes,' she said. 'I know you're sorry. I won't ever forgive you for killing my father, not really. But I won't ever forget that you saved me from him either.'

She sobbed, then seemed to impose her own will on herself like straightening armour, and stood firm. 'Enough,' she said, seemingly to herself. 'Let's go.' She turned to Taro, concern in her eyes. 'Can you walk?'

He nodded.

'Oda's blood has revived you?' asked Hiro.

Taro narrowed his eyes at his friend, who looked at Hana and then shut up. She knew nothing about vampires, this girl, and he wanted to be able to explain it properly later.

He took a step back, and fell once more to the ground.

'Not enough, it would seem,' said Hiro. With casual strength, he picked Taro up. 'Let's go before others come.'

'What did you do with—' began Hana. Her eyes were on Taro's teeth.

'I'll explain later,' said Taro. He turned to Little Kawabata, who had held back as Taro and Hana spoke. 'What are you doing here?' he asked. 'I thought you hated me.'

Little Kawabata's eyes narrowed, not with anger but with what looked like shame. 'I discovered that my father had betrayed you. He sent a messenger to Lord Oda, meaning to warn him of your mission. I left the mountain to stop him.'

Taro's mind was making a connection. 'The ninja by the road, on the plain.'

Little Kawabata nodded. 'My father's man. He was bound for here, to tell Lord Oda you were coming. I got to him first. But

I left him there, as a warning to my father, in case the news reached him.'

Taro remembered that Shusaku had said it seemed like a message, and it seemed the older ninja had been right. But now he looked at Little Kawabata's smooth, undamaged hands, the skin clear and unburned by the sun. 'How did you get up here?' he asked. 'It's full daylight outside.'

'It was you who turned me,' said Little Kawabata. 'I think you must have passed your ability to me. I noticed when I was on the road.'

Taro couldn't believe it. It seemed that by saving Little Kawabata he had made him a stronger vampire than he'd intended, one who, like him, could withstand the sunlight.

It was good, therefore, that the boy seemed to have decided he was an ally, not an enemy.

'Your father...' he began. 'I would have thought that you would support his agenda, not fight to prevent it.'

Little Kawabata looked pained. 'I found that... my father was not the man I thought he was.'

Hana touched his hand. 'I know how that feels.'

'We should really be going,' said Hiro, who despite holding up Taro was breathing normally, as if his friend's weight were nothing more than a slight inconvenience. 'We'll have time later to discuss all this, if we even get out alive.'

'You're right,' said Taro. 'Hana, are you coming with us?'

'I think,' she said, 'I had better, don't you?'

Hiro began to walk down the stairs, stepping carefully so as not to trip and drop Taro. 'Shusaku's dead,' said Hiro. His arms were trembling very slightly with the effort.

'I know,' said Taro. The wound from the sword caused him less agony than the wound this memory gave him, and the wound was healing, the process sped by Oda's blood. He thought perhaps the wound caused by Shusaku's death would never heal.

He had avenged his father's death by killing Lord Oda, and yet he felt nothing. And now he had done nothing but cause the death of another man who had taken care of him, another man who had become in the last weeks almost a kind of father himself.

'I'm sorry,' said Hiro. 'He was a good man.' He paused. 'And Yukiko? Also dead?'

Taro shook his head. 'She... changed her allegiance, told Lord Oda where we were. I didn't explain properly how I had met Hana before. I believe she thinks I'm a traitor.'

Hiro's eyes were wide open. 'But... Yukiko... she and I...' He frowned. 'We were *friends*.'

'I know,' said Taro. 'I'm sorry.'

Hiro's face settled into a hard expression. 'Well, if anyone knows how she likes to fight, it's me,' he said. 'If she comes after you, she'll have to get through me.' But it clearly pained him to say it, and Taro felt a wave of pride in his friend.

Hiro obviously hadn't looked at Hana properly, and now he turned his head in the stairwell and examined her. 'You're the girl from the woods!' he exclaimed. 'The one who gave Taro a ring. You're Lord Oda's daughter?'

'Yes,' said Hana. 'Pleased to meet you again.'

Hiro thought for a moment. 'I can see why that would look bad to Yukiko.'

'Me too,' said Taro wearily.

'Well,' said Hiro, 'we should go. Before Yukiko sees that Oda is taking too long, and comes after us herself.'

Taro touched Hiro's arm. 'Wait.' He turned to look at Hana. 'My brother. We can't leave without him.'

Hana looked at him silently a long moment, and he knew what she was thinking. *He's dead anyway; he'll weigh us down; he may get us killed.*

But she nodded. 'I will get him.'

She turned and ascended, and a moment later came down carrying the boy over her shoulder. His body was so wasted by his starvation that she supported him easily.

Then Hiro shifted his friend's weight, feeling Taro's blood warm on his hands, praying to the Compassionate One that Taro would not be taken by death, not yet. He passed the corpse of Lord Oda, his limbs now contorted in unnatural configurations.

Taro forced himself to look at Oda. The man was unmistakably dead.

Hana looked at her father's broken body, and a fresh blade of grief eased between the muscles of her stomach, cutting her open; she was surprised to look down and see that she didn't bleed, surprised her body could contain such pain.

She felt the delicate bones of a Tokugawa heir through the boy's parchment skin, and felt the coldness of his dead body. She saw a living Tokugawa before her, many times over the better of her cruel, honourless father. She hardened herself. From now on, this was her care, this her responsibility.

Taro felt Hiro's muscles and tendons straining.

Taro looked to his side. Hana's tears were drying on her cheeks. Little Kawabata walked beside her, helping her to support the weight of the younger brother Taro would never know. It seemed to him amazing that this boy who had tried to kill him in the rice store on the mountain was now walking down the steps of Lord Oda's tower with him, having helped him to get his revenge, and to survive.

He looked down. His blood dried on his friend's robe.

Together they walked down the stairs as hard as stone, as hard as the path they still had to travel, and into the light.

None of them saw the drops of blood that fell from Taro's terrible wound and laid a vivid trail on the stone.

None of them saw the drop that fell, as if ordained to do so by some cruel god, whispering on the air to distort its flow, into Oda's open mouth.

And certainly none of them saw when, a moment later, the eyelids of that broken man opened wide, and he took in a rush of breath, the air whistling as it passed through shattered bones. The onyx eyes fixed on his enemies' departing backs with a gimlet stare, as if to sear their semblances onto his mind, where they would burn in the lord's hateful memory until he could exact his payment.

Lord Oda's fury was like the waters of a dam following heavy rain. He felt it pressing against his eyes, his hands, seeking to burst forth. He felt it in the coils of his entrails, which protruded slick and glistening from his slit stomach, though already the wound was beginning, painfully, to close itself up.

His own daughter had betrayed him, had proven to be weak.

Yet the monks teach that Zen brings balance to those who are patient. A girl he didn't know, a relative only in spirit and not in blood – Yukiko, she had called herself – had warned him of the Tokugawa boy's presence in his tower. For that he would reward her.

Yes. He had lost a daughter, but an opportunity to redress his injury had arisen. It was perfect. He would make Yukiko his own, replacing that other who even as she walked into the sunlight was dead to him.

It would be beautiful: a child to kill a child. *She* would destroy

Taro. He would train her. He would make her his tame sword saint, broken into doing his every bidding.

But first he had to live.

Fortunately, Oda knew much of the vampires, and that presented a way to mend his broken form, to staunch the life that even now was flowing out of him. There was risk, too. He weighed it in his mind.

You will be a monster.

On the other side of the scales, a shorter thought, more simple—

Otherwise you will die.

He decided.

He rolled himself over, gasping at the astonishing pain from his broken limbs, and began to lick up the drops of Taro's blood. A thought crossed his mind.

Yukiko. I will make her vampire, too. A vampire girl to kill a vampire boy.

As he worked, and his bones began slowly to knit, a person standing in that small, twisting space might have observed that his canines began to lengthen, and gleam.

But no one did.

CHAPTER 76

$\mathbf{K}$ENJI KIRA STRETCHED his back. These hills were ruining his poise, his balance, his inner calm. The ground was too steep for the horses, which he and his men had consequently abandoned in the care of villagers in the valley below. As a result the muscles in Kira's back ached constantly, as did those in his calves and thighs. He cursed this hilly country, in which there was nothing to be found but pine trees, peasants, and rice paddies.

The men, too, were beginning to question his judgement, he was sure of it. Ever since he had killed the girl, that upstart of a ninja who had insulted him, they had grown quieter, more downcast of gaze. This was a matter of degree, of course, for the men always looked down at the ground when Kira was near, in the deferential stance that he preferred – not that he had ever been required to imagine any other stance, since the lower-ranking members of his coterie had always stood thus while in his company. Indeed, he was of such rank that no one apart from Lord Oda had looked at him directly since he was a child, and those who had known him then were all dead, either by time's slow sword or by Kira's own *katana*, which was sharper and had sent almost as many to their deaths.

He knew the men were asking themselves if he had lost his eye, were questioning the long search in the mountains that had led so far to nothing.

Yet he had been so sure. Several nights before, while his men had been carousing at an inn, Kira had made the company of a seasoned old soldier, now turned private guard, who had recently left the employ of Lord Oda. Or, more precisely, had been asked to leave, his drinking having grown to be an embarrassment. This man told an extraordinary story, of Lord Oda's daughter, whom he had been paid to defend, and how one night in the country she had run away.

Kira had had a certain experience in the matter of runaway women. He usually caught them in the end.

Yet Oda no Hana had come back, to everyone's surprise. It had been assumed, with some sympathy for her plight, that she had been escaping the marriage her father had arranged for her. And more surprising still, she'd come back with an amazing story – of how she had encountered four *ronin*, and killed them all with their own weapons.

To his surprise, Kira had found himself leaning forward intently as the old man laid out his tale, which Kira had never heard from his employer, Lord Oda, and he suspected the story had been covered up by the girl's entourage.

Extraordinary – that the clue, the greatest clue, should come from Lord Oda's daughter herself. Imagine if the story had never come out!

According to the guard, the tale showed that Lady Hana was a true samurai – brave, unhesitating, skilled.

Kira disagreed. He thought it showed she was a liar.

However, it was impossible to prove the question one way or another, since when the guards had gone to the place indicated by Lady Hana, the very next day, there had been no sign of the bodies.

'What could it mean?' asked the guard. 'What happened to them?'

Kira smiled, for he knew what it meant. Hana had met the ninja.

The next day, the old guard – remembered by everyone as a friendly individual, garrulous when in his cups, but who wasn't? – was found in the irrigation canal, his throat slit and his blood nourishing the village's rice crops. Kira was already on the move. A couple of days later, he heard a strange report about a man who had confronted a rice thief – a day's ride away, no more – and had been bitten on the neck by this same thief. The people of the villages saw the malign influences of the spirits. Again, Kira saw the ninja.

And then had come the incident at the village of Suto. The ninja girl who had slowed them down by pretending to be Taro. It had taken place so close to where the man was bitten – only a single valley away!

But since then the trail had gone cold.

Now, days later, Kira stretched his back as he pissed into a mountain stream. As usual, the activity was unpleasant. The Portuguese doctor sent by his merchant masters as a gift to Lord Oda had said that there were stones in Kira's bladder, and Kira was greatly pleased by it. So long had he lived on water and the things that grew in the land, avoiding all flesh, that his very body was *becoming* stone. It was almost beautiful.

Unfortunately, it was also very painful.

The urine, which had always flowed easily at his command, now trickled out in excruciating drips – sometimes even containing blood. That was when he was able to make it flow out of him at all. It was ironic, since in his professional life Kira had experienced something like the opposite of this phenomenon. He had found, as he got older, as his skills of persuasion increased, that information flowed more easily towards him than ever.

Sometimes it contained blood.

Kira decided that he had probably got as much out as he ever would, and turned to go back to the men. He cursed them. They were younger than he, and more suited to roaming round on mountainsides, chasing after the *gakkyo* imaginings of some foolish peasant, who had probably only been bitten by a snake or something equally boring.

As he turned – that was when he saw the crumpled-up piece of paper, wedged between two stones by the side of the stream. Kira stooped, picked it up, unfolded it. It began *My dear Taro*.

Kira grinned, all thoughts of pain and aging suddenly gone. He turned to his men. 'Turn round. We're going to Fuji mountain. The boy's mother is there.'

CHAPTER 77

Near Lord Oda's Castle, Nagoya

Yukiko walked through the tradesmen's district. It was not a good place to be out at night, all alone.

And that was why she wanted to draw her assassin here. Deliberately she wore a fine silk gown, *tabi* unsuited to fighting, knuckle-dusters that looked like jewels.

She knew that Tokugawa had sent a ninja after her. She knew because Lord Oda knew, and the things Lord Oda knew were true because they were sealed in blood.

Lord Oda knew also that Kenji Kira was on his way to Fuji mountain, there to seek Taro's mother. The fool had put this in a pigeon message to the lord, not knowing he was signing his own death warrant.

In a moment – the time it takes to ink the strokes of a name character on a piece of paper – a man's fate can be sealed. As they had agreed, Lord Oda would give Kira to Yukiko to kill, and she would give him Taro in return.

Once this ninja was dispatched, she would mount horse with a couple of samurai and go meet Kira there. Perhaps she would arrive before he killed Taro's mother, and that would give her the gift of finding the Buddha ball first, and the greater gift of presenting it to Lord Oda.

Look, how I repay your trust.

Of course, she wouldn't give it to him. He was still the spider at the centre of the web that had trapped the abbess and Heiko.

No, she would hold it out to him, taunt him with it, then use it to kill him. But first, she would kill Kira.

Slowly.

The ninja dropped from the roof on the left side of the street, where Yukiko had until now been listening to his progress. A moment before, he had killed a cat, thinking to preserve what he thought was the silence of his operation. Yukiko thought that was a little cruel.

The ninja crouched, absorbing the impact of the ground, and leaped straight into a kick to Yukiko's face. She staggered back, though her apparently fearful movement disguised the way she leaned with, and diluted, the force of the kick.

The ninja reached for his short-sword, lowering his eyes for a fraction of a second.

In a moment a man's fate can be sealed.

A moment later Yukiko looked down on the corpse of the first man she had ever killed. A single tear rolled down her cheek.

But she expected to suffer. It was in the nature of revenge.